Favoured BY Fortune

To Jian —
All the best!
Colleen Kelly-Eiding

Coming Soon

by
Colleen Kelly-Eiding
Face of Fortune

Also from Phase Publishing

by
Emily Daniels
A Song for a Soldier

by
Laura Beers
Saving Shadow

by
Rebecca Connolly
The Lady and the Gent

by
Grace Donovan
Saint's Ride

Favoured BY Fortune

THE SHADOWS OF ROSTHWAITE
BOOK ONE

COLLEEN KELLY-EIDING

Phase Publishing, LLC
Seattle

Text copyright © 2019 by Colleen Kelly-Eiding
Cover art copyright © 2019 by Colleen Kelly-Eiding

Cover art by Tugboat Design
http://www.tugboatdesign.net

Phase Publishing, LLC first paperback edition
August 2019

ISBN 978-1-943048-86-1
Library of Congress Control Number 2019908787
Cataloging-in-Publication Data on file.

Acknowledgements

To Clive, Connie, Sandy, Allison, Amani, and Steven.
Thank you for all your help in this journey.

To my daughters, two incredible women of whom I am so
proud. Thank you for your love, humour, and
encouragement.

And to the love of my life, Paul. Thank you for your
support, patience, and love.

PROLOGUE

Had she known as she raced up the mountain path what was to come, perhaps Charlotte would have been better prepared, but then, she was only ten years old. Her brother, Thomas, chased after her, gaining fast. Now neck and neck, they ran breathlessly upward until they fell, laughing, onto a soft patch of grass at the base of the sheer rock face of Raven Crag below the summit of Glaramara. Sitting up, they viewed the vast panorama that stretched for miles to the north from Borrowdale, past the blue of Derwentwater, all the way to Skiddaw's Peak. Charlotte was sure that this was the most beautiful place in the world.

Thunder rumbled overhead. She took note of the storm clouds gathering over Great Gable to the south. "We should go back, Tommy. Remember the bogles," Charlotte warned. "Mrs. Mungris told us to be careful."

Thomas ignored her plea and looked irked.

Charlotte realized she'd made a mistake in calling him Tommy again after he had told her he would only answer to Thomas. He'd told her many times that he was thirteen after all and almost a man. He would do as he wished.

He pointed to the dark, jagged entrance of a cave a short distance off. "I am going to explore." He began to pick his way over sharp rocks and soggy earth. Charlotte almost wished her brother had been a little scared of the housekeeper's stories of evil spirits inhabiting the fells.

Still, she watched him, admiring his agility and his bravery. She desperately wanted to follow him, but their mother's warning about the cave's dangers and Charlotte's own fear of bogles froze her to the spot. She adored her brother but, at the same time, he drove her to distraction. He always laughed at Mrs. Mungris's stories of spirits, enraging his sister because she believed every word.

And what about the white stag, Charlotte thought. Her brother had seen it, too. It had appeared the day that Charlotte, her mother, and her brother had arrived from Coventry, certain from Mrs. Mungris's letter that their grandfather was dying. They had ridden pack horses from Keswick all the way to the tiny village of Rosthwaite, then up the hillside to their grandfather's house, Whitestone.

Charlotte's grandfather, always a strong and healthy man, had lain in bed looking like a skeleton. Mrs. Mungris had shooed the children outside, advising them to stay out of the stinker plant unless they wanted to smell like dead rabbits. As they climbed to the ridge above the house and looked at Rosthwaite to the west and Watendlath to the northeast, Charlotte suddenly saw the white stag. A more beautiful creature could not exist, of that she was sure. Its antlers looked as if they were made of pearl that glistened in the sun. Thomas moved, and the stag bolted across the fellside. The children gave pursuit, but it disappeared as if by magic.

When Charlotte and Thomas returned to their grandfather's house, they found a miracle had occurred. Their grandfather had opened his eyes and smiled. As the rejoicing died down, Charlotte told the adults of the stag's appearance.

Mrs. Mungris clapped her hands, saying, " 'Twas a sign, child, yer white stag, d'ye see? A change in fortune, 'twas tellin' ye."

And now only a fortnight later they were on an outing with their mother and grandfather. It would have been sooner, but rain had fallen in sheets for two weeks. Being confined to the house was difficult for the high-spirited children, and Charlotte's mother, Dorothy Byrd, had on more than one occasion chastised her daughter for being an Amazon. As Charlotte attempted to tiptoe by her mother while preparations were being made for the day's outing, she overheard Mrs. Mungris warn Dorothy of a new sign.

"Such a howlin' there was last night. Ya musta heard it, Mistress Dorothy."

"It was only the wind. What is troubling you, dear Mrs. Mungris?"

"I dinna think it was the wind, Mistress Dorothy."

"What else could it have been?"

"I hate to say the name."

"Please, tell me."

"The barghest," Mrs. Mungris whispered.

"Mrs. Mungris, I will not entertain such an idea. No one is in harm's way. Papa is recovering. The children are healthy. Please, you are alarming yourself unnecessarily."

"There 'twas the stag and now this. They are signs. Ya canna deny that your father is back to us after t'white hart appeared. I know what I heard, and 'twas not t'wind."

Charlotte's grandfather, being impatient to get underway, hollered for his daughter to come outside and join them in the farm cart. Dorothy patted Mrs. Mungris's hand, called for Charlotte to follow and they left for their picnic on the fells.

A flash of white to the right of her brother jolted Charlotte's thoughts into the present. It was the white stag.

"Tommy!" she called out. Her brother glared at her over his shoulder. She pointed, jumping up and down. He looked where she indicated, but the stag, startled by her movements, dashed up the path. Thomas scrambled over the rocks, pursuing the deer. Charlotte, forgetting her fears, followed on her brother's heels.

Below, the children's mother and grandfather were just finishing their meal and heard Charlotte's shouts. Hurrying up the path, they saw the children running after the stag. Dorothy Byrd attempted to call them back, her voice filled with fear for their safety.

But they could not hear her over the thunder rumbling loudly above the peaks. The clouds that had gathered over the mountains now burst open, spilling torrents of water down with such speed that the stone kettles at Glaramara's summit overflowed in a matter of minutes. A wave surged forward, channelled between the high banks of the two narrow becks that fed Hind Gill. The white stag, attempting to jump the spot where the two becks joined, missed its mark in the rain and slid down the steep, muddy bank. There was no time to avoid the wall of water surging toward it. Engulfed, its thin legs flailing, lungs filling with water, the stag struggled to right itself.

Thomas ran to a fallen tree that crossed Hind Gill. Perhaps he thought to stop the animal's progress, but he obviously had figured on neither the weight of the stag nor the force of the water. When the flood hit the place where he knelt, the tree snapped in two and Thomas went under.

He came up entangled with the stag, whose thrashing hooves sliced his face.

Charlotte screamed for her brother as she rushed along the bank next to him. Raindrops hit her face with such stinging force she felt they must be needles. Horrified, she watched as the stag and Thomas were swept over the edge of the cliff as the water hurtled down to Seathwaite below. By some miracle, the stag's antlers caught in a tangle of roots and stones at the top of the cataract, and there, Charlotte saw her brother desperately clinging to the deer's body.

She crawled out onto a narrow rock ledge, telling herself all the while not to look down. There, she lay flat and stretched out her hands until she touched her brother's arms.

"Can you grasp hold?" she cried out to him over the water's roar.

He turned his face slightly toward the sound of her voice. Blood ran freely from the corner of his eye down to his throat.

She saw him nod. This made her bold, and she inched out a little further while wrapping her feet around the edges of the rock.

He grabbed for her hands, and moving as quickly as his cold limbs would allow, he found a toe-hold. Then fortune turned its face, and the stag's body broke free.

Charlotte fought with all her strength to hold onto Thomas, but the stag's antlers caught hold of his sodden clothes and tore him away. A terrible scream escaped Charlotte's lips as she watched him fall. The deer hit the rocks a split second before Thomas. The pearl antlers caught him, piercing his neck and shoulders. The torrent of water carried them downstream as one body.

Charlotte lay sobbing on the little spit of rock. She felt a hand touch her back and looked up to see her grandfather's ashen face.

"I tried to save him, Grandpa." She looked to her mother, who stood staring at the rapids below. "Mama… Mama…" she implored, her voice barely audible in the storm that raged around them.

CHAPTER ONE

Hotwells, Bristol
18 July, 1760

My dearest Emma,

Why did I not insist that you accompany me on this journey? I desperately long to share with you, at this very moment, what has transpired.

I have been transformed. Shall I call it my epiphany? I can describe it as no less of an experience. Whatever shall I do, Emma?

But forgive me, for you must wonder why I carry on so. Today, as Mama and I walked abroad along the Avon for our health, she decided we should stop to take the waters in the Pump Room. We were seated but a few minutes when, gazing out the window, I beheld a young man, a soldier of some considerable rank, in fact, who chanced to pass by, deep in thought. His grace of motion as he approached entranced me. I gawked at his face, I blush to say, which in the brief moment that I saw it appeared to hold such a good-natured spirit that I wished to cry out for him to halt that I might speak with him. My modesty for once held me back, and he passed us, unmindful of the prisoner he took with him.

What longing overtook me when he was gone! Oh, to hear his voice, for the tones that would fall from his lips must be of such melodious nature that they would play like a sweet song upon my ears. He must be the most favoured by fortune of any gentleman I have yet beheld. Would that I might see him just once more, I should be happy to live alone, a hermit, with that memory for the rest of my life.

But who is he? I could not mention him to my mother. She thinks me so wilful and forward that she has threatened to forbid my taking part in another Season in London if I do not act as a modest young lady should.

He was tall and fair of complexion. His hair was his own and an exquisite colour of golden barley! He wore no wig nor any powder.

Dear, dear friend, what shall I do? Adieu, my dear Emma.

Yours with sincere affection,
Charlotte

Four long days would pass until Charlotte was at last in Bath, walking with her friend, Lady Emma Bosworth, in Emma's family's garden. Charlotte stood a head taller than Emma, and where Emma was round and soft, Charlotte was tall and angular. They loved each other dearly and shared their secrets with relish. Charlotte took hold of her friend's hand and stopped.

"Did you receive my letter?" she asked as they approached a secluded marble bench beside the garden path.

"I did, Charlotte," Emma responded, barely able to contain her eagerness.

"Do you think me quite mad?"

"Never! I am envious beyond description. To have had such an experience, Charlotte! I long for it."

"But who could he be? I am cast into a melancholy humour to think that I will never see him again." Charlotte sat on the bench dejectedly. Her dark, auburn curls fell over her cheeks as she looked down at her hands resting in her lap.

Emma sat beside her, taking her hands. "You must not despair. There are so many young men lately returned from the Indian wars in Canada and the Colonies. Bath is the most likely place for any man of fashion to take respite. Dear Charlotte, there is a private ball this evening given by Lord Sumner. You must go with Mama and me."

Charlotte happily agreed, pending her mother's approval, which was quickly forthcoming, since her mother, Dorothy Byrd, though new to London, understood the importance of cultivating aristocratic friends who could open up the higher social circles to her family. Charlotte knew her mother suspected that her father's business partner, Audley Pruitt, might profess his interest in her in the future. Dorothy had mentioned that she'd noticed him watching her tall, graceful daughter as she moved about their parlour. He was discreet as a man in mourning must be, but Dorothy insisted that he was definitely interested.

She had often praised Charlotte's beautiful, pale complexion, rosy cheeks, and striking green eyes. Then, she would add a reminder that Charlotte's fortune was not small, making her even more attractive. There would be many suitors, and some might even have a title, she'd said. Charlotte had to admit, when it came to business, her mother was as astute as her very successful father.

As she rested that afternoon, spending her quiet time

reading and doing her needlework, Charlotte's mind wandered to the evening ahead. She thought of her potential dance partners and wondered whom she might enjoy dancing with.

A horrible thought interrupted her pleasant reverie. What if that Lieutenant Harvey Shelbourne was in attendance? She prayed he wouldn't be there. The man danced as if he were attempting to break a horse. Unfortunately, he was a great admirer of Charlotte's. If need arises, I shall refuse him, she thought to herself. I would rather sit out the entire ball than be trampled once again by his big feet. The idea of him nearly made her change her mind about accompanying Emma.

Then, a much more pleasant thought banished Harvey Shelbourne completely from her mind. What if her young man was there? With that, the rest of the afternoon passed sweetly, with all her thoughts centred around the stranger.

When the Bosworth's coach arrived, Charlotte was handed up into it. Emma was full of news of a family friend by the name of James Clarke, of the Clarkes in Devon, who had arrived in Bath that very afternoon. Emma's mother told Charlotte that he was a war hero in the campaigns against the French. He had just been decorated for his bravery in the battle of the Plains of Abraham. He would only be in England briefly, since he had been transferred to fight against France on the Continent. Charlotte smiled politely, trying to appear interested.

Arriving at the ball, Charlotte despaired when Lieutenant Shelbourne came noisily across the room to greet her. She agreed to dance with him in an attempt to be polite and in hopes that someone else might ask her as well. After being pushed around the dance floor, her arms ached, and she longed to be home working at her embroidery or taking a nap. Though Shelbourne begged for another dance, Charlotte successfully sent him off to get her some punch.

Her moment of peace was disturbed by Emma, who announced, "He is here, Charlotte. You must come and meet him."

"Who?"

"James Clarke, the young man my mother spoke of in the coach."

Guiltily, Charlotte left her seat, knowing that Lieutenant Shelbourne would return to find her gone. That, she thought, would be the height of bad manners and would pay him back for stepping on her feet. With Emma leading the way through the crowd, Charlotte fought the panic that threatened to overwhelm her from being in such a crush. She would not flee, she told herself, as she had done from Lady B's rout in London last Season. That would be too much of an embarrassment. Relief flooded over her as Emma finally pulled her to the side.

"There he is," she whispered, pointing to a young man surrounded by admirers. "He appears to be escorting Lady Samantha Toland, though why, I cannot imagine. She is pretty, but so haughty and ill-mannered."

Charlotte felt herself grow exceedingly warm. She caught hold of Emma's sleeve. "That's him!"

"Yes," Emma responded, perplexed by her friend's inflection.

"That's him, Emma!" Charlotte said emphatically.

"Yes, James Clarke."

"He is the man from Bristol," Charlotte spluttered.

"No dear, he is from Devon."

"Emma! He is the one I saw at Hotwells. The one whom I wrote about."

"No!" Emma said, dumbfounded. "Jemmy?"

"Jemmy! Oh, my dear lord, you call him Jemmy?" Charlotte asked.

"Well, you must be introduced," Emma announced.

"Oh, no! I cannot." Charlotte turned quite pale as she took a step back.

"Fie, come this instant," Emma insisted as she pulled Charlotte forward.

Just as she and Emma reached James Clarke, Harvey Shelbourne appeared, punch in hand. "Ah, there you are, Miss Byrd. I thought you had flown. Ha, ha." Shelbourne laughed at his own wit.

Lady Samantha Toland turned slowly and elegantly. Looking contemptuously down her nose at Charlotte, she hissed, "Charlotte Byrd, the ribbon merchant's daughter, here?"

At exactly the instant that Lady Samantha, in an attempt to snub Charlotte, pushed brusquely past her, Harvey Shelbourne thrust out his big hand holding the punch and attempted to place it in Charlotte's palm. Lady Samantha's ample bosom made abrupt contact with Harvey's hand, causing the drink to fly into the air. It exploded onto the front of Lady Samantha's person from head to toe.

Charlotte wished herself dead. As the initial shock wore off, Lady Samantha's face turned scarlet, and she let out a howl. She lifted her arm to strike Charlotte but was halted by James Clarke.

"Dear lady, I am sure this assault was unintended. Allow me to see to your needs while you calm your nerves." He swept Samantha off before she had a chance to protest.

As he walked away, he turned his head and looked at Charlotte. His eyes were sea grey. She was entranced. He smiled at her. His eyes drew her in, she was perplexed and charmed.

The rest of the evening passed in a blur, as Charlotte's thoughts kept wandering to the handsome James Clark. Each time she caught sight of him, her breath would quicken, and her heart would flutter. She was sure her cheeks were flaming, as well.

She was quiet on the way home, and Emma asked several times if she felt well. Each time, she'd reassure her friend that she was, indeed, well. Just fatigued from the dancing.

The next day, Charlotte learned that James Clarke had gone to the Continent. She begged Emma to tell her all she knew about him. Emma gladly agreed. Their families were well acquainted. Emma had spent several summers at Kirkmoor, the Clarke's house in Devon. James's sister, Elizabeth, was a dear friend of Emma's.

James had always been of a sensitive nature, crying over the slightest injustices he felt one fellow did to another. He treated his hunting hounds and horses as if they were human. His father was most unhappy seeing his son so inclined, which only grew worse after James's and Elizabeth's older brother was killed in riding accident.

Since James was now to inherit the title of baronet, his father had vowed to make a man of him and sent him to Eton. Elizabeth confided to Emma that she thought he must have suffered terrible persecution there, though he would not admit it. At last, upon finishing at Eton and Oxford, he had purchased his commission in the army, and he appeared to finally become the man his father wanted.

Elizabeth hadn't had much time to speak with her brother before he was sent to the Colonies.

During the next two years, Charlotte received occasional news of James Clarke through Emma, which always excited her. He had lately been transferred to Portugal to fight under Generals Burgoyne and Campbell. However, as the girls' lives filled up with activities of the most recent Season in London, they spoke less and less of him.

One day, as Charlotte and her mother were working on their needlework, they received a visit from Carolina Chamier, a family friend. Carolina told them news from the wars in Europe, as it related to people of their acquaintance. There was one particularly horrific account of a battle between the English and Spanish in Portugal.

"Portugal!" Charlotte cried involuntarily, reminded suddenly of James Clarke. Dorothy looked questioningly at her daughter. Charlotte focused intently on her needlework, avoiding her mother's gaze. At last, Dorothy bade Carolina to continue.

"There is a young man, James Clarke, perhaps you know of him. The Clarke family are close friends of Lord and Lady Bosworth."

"I do seem to recall hearing the name," Dorothy answered politely.

"This young man, a major by rank, was in the very centre of the battle. He survived, but his nerves are quite shattered. He is in seclusion on the Isle of Man."

"The Isle of Man! Why, we are to embark on a voyage there just next week. My husband has business with the weavers in Douglas."

Carolina blushed. "Forgive me, my dear. I was aware of

your plans from an innocent informant, Emma Bosworth. Lady Bosworth sent me today to ask if you would carry a letter for her to Major Clarke. I confess I know little of the contents except that she hopes it might cause a reconciliation between father and son. I believe, because of the personal nature of the letter, she wishes it to be carried by a friend rather than by post."

"Why did Lady Bosworth not come to me herself?" Dorothy asked.

"She did not want to trouble you, but I assured her that since I was planning to call anyway, I would undertake to ask you, and that knowing your kind nature, you would not refuse."

"Very well, since you ask it, I shall do it," Dorothy responded, her tone indicating that she felt both flattered and perplexed.

Throughout this interchange, Charlotte held her breath. Would she see James Clarke again? Would he remember her? Was he so much changed? She tried to hide her blush. If Dorothy ever discovered her daughter's infatuation, she would never allow her anywhere near James Clarke. Of that, Charlotte was quite sure.

The rough seas on the voyage to the Isle of Man left Charlotte and her mother feeling ill for the first three days they were on the island. On the fourth day, Dorothy announced that she would call on Mr. Clarke and fulfil her promise to Carolina. Charlotte had been thinking of nothing else since they left London but had dared not utter a word about it. She suppressed her joy when her mother requested that she accompany her on the visit. Dorothy sent her card to James Clarke's house, planning that they would visit the following day.

After rising early and changing her clothes several times, Charlotte attempted to stay calm as the coach drove slowly up the wooded path toward the Clarke home. Like her grandfather's house in Rosthwaite, it was made of fieldstone, though of a browner hue. When the coach stopped, they were handed down into deep puddles.

As they attempted to shake the water from their shoes, the front door opened abruptly, and there stood James Clarke, looking dishevelled and red-eyed, a hound on either side of him. His hair was hastily pulled back. One stocking drooped around his ankle. He stared at the two women, smiled weakly, and slammed the door.

"Never have I received such rude treatment!" Dorothy exclaimed. "We shall leave at once. Come, Charlotte. I have half a mind to throw Lady Bosworth's correspondence in the mud."

Befuddled, Charlotte tried to think clearly, but found it impossible with her mother carrying on. If only she could talk to James, she thought, to understand what had caused such a change in him. Charlotte found herself drawn to his vulnerability.

Her mother was nearly back in the coach when the door opened again, and a well-dressed servant of advanced years addressed them apologetically.

"Please pardon the master's behaviour. He was expecting you at a later time, and your arrival took him by surprise. He humbly asks you to enter his house and partake of some refreshment."

Charlotte wondered how often this poor man had had to present this speech.

Mother and daughter entered the main hallway of the house, Dorothy still muttering angrily under her breath.

The walls were dark green and hung with the portraits of stern-looking people posed with their dogs and horses. James Clarke made his entrance down the intricately carved oak staircase that was the centrepiece of the hall. There were no dogs this time and he appeared a different man from the one they had seen a few minutes before. Now in control of himself, he walked with grace and confidence.

He bowed to both women, who returned his greeting with curtsies. His eyes hesitated just an instant too long on Charlotte's face. She flushed and averted her eyes, chagrined to see her mother watching the interchange intently.

He addressed Dorothy. "Please excuse my impudent behaviour, Mrs. Byrd. I am overcome at points and act in a most inappropriate manner." He paused and stared at something unseen by the ladies. He closed his eyes and drew a long breath.

Charlotte felt herself breathing with him. She wished desperately to touch his shoulder and bring him back. His attention returned again to the present and, without further comment, he invited them into the drawing room for tea.

Dorothy presented the letter from Lady Bosworth. James thanked her for bringing it to him. They spoke of mutual acquaintances and life in London. Charlotte fought against resting her gaze too long on his face, but finally gave up, so overcome was she by the sweetness of it. Then, the letter presented, and the tea consumed, it was time to depart.

Mr. Clarke escorted them to the waiting coach. He handed Dorothy into it first. Seemingly an afterthought, he said, "Miss Byrd, forgive me, I had wished to present you with a small token from the island. Please, accompany me

11

back into the house." Dorothy attempted to protest and exit the coach, but he raised his hand to stop her progress. "Mrs. Byrd, I assure you I left it just inside the door."

Charlotte, not daring to look at her mother, followed him quickly inside the house. He motioned her into the drawing room. She obeyed. Gently grasping her hand, he held it to his lips, then rested it on his cheek. "What peace I experience when I look at your fair face. I am forever in your debt, Miss Byrd." He let go and slipped a small, white, fan-shaped shell into her hand. She held it tightly.

"Thank you, sir," she whispered and looked full into his eyes. Walking quietly out to the coach, he handed her in. Now under her mother's watchful guard, Charlotte formally thanked him for his gift, being sure to politely avert her eyes.

She saw him once more on the island. The gloomy morning that Charlotte and her parents were leaving for the ship, she happened to glance out the window of the coach to see Mr. Clarke some distance off, walking his dogs. His head was down. She attempted to will him to see her, but he did not turn his face in her direction.

Charlotte did not soon forget James Clarke, but once again the whirl of London life made his memory come less and less frequently into her thoughts. When the Season was in full sway, she found there were many young men eager for her company. There was one gentleman who paid her increasing attention, namely her father's business partner, Audley Pruitt.

Pruitt was the man who had insisted that Charlotte's father, William Byrd, would do well to move to London. He was correct in his reasoning, for though William Byrd employed more than two thousand ribbon weavers in

Coventry and enjoyed an honoured place in that town, it was, after all, the provinces. A move to London put William in a capital equal to none for business and fashion. By merging with Pruitt, he found himself a wealthy international silk merchant in three short years.

When William agreed to move to London, Audley suggested that the Byrds buy the house next to his own in Spitalfields, a thriving area of East London. The house was well built with a spacious garden. There were stables and a carriage house behind on the mews. Charlotte's father liked its proximity to the weavers' houses and to the offices of Pruitt and Byrd Limited.

Audley Pruitt inherited his home from his father. Soon after it passed from father to son, Audley renamed it Bellagio House. He explained to William that much of his fortune came from his business dealings with an Italian aristocrat, Count Francesco Cesi. This gentleman lived in an impressive villa in the town of Bellagio situated on the shores of Lake Como in the Italian Alps.

"The hunting in the mountains is without equal. Every sort of prize you could want, right there," Audley told William time and time again.

The two partners of Pruitt and Byrd Limited began to travel to the Continent with great frequency. On one of their visits, Audley purchased a beautiful Italian linen fichu with exquisite jasmine blossoms in whitework embroidery, which he presented to Charlotte at a dinner party given by her family upon their return. Charlotte was delighted with the triangular shawl but had the uneasy feeling that it was the prelude to a proposal from Audley. It was not that she disliked him. On the contrary, at times she found him charming. He was witty in his way, and his business acumen was not to be disputed. Yet, she hoped he would not ask for her hand. He was close in age to her father and not nearly as lively or handsome as many of her other suitors.

Besides the house, Audley had inherited the business from his father, who had the good fortune to inherit it from his father. This gentleman, George Pruitt, had the foresight to befriend a number of gifted Huguenot silk weavers when they fled France in 1686. These people, being God-fearing Calvinists with a strong work ethic, settled into their new life in East London's Spitalfields, producing enviable works of fabric art, thus making George Pruitt, who sold the cloth to aristocratic buyers, a very rich man.

Audley Pruitt was a man of medium height, standing an inch or two above Charlotte, with his pumps on. He was not a particularly pretty person, but when dressed elegantly, which was to be expected since much of fashionable London wore his silks, his appearance was pleasing. His manners were impeccable, and he spoke French, Italian, and German fluently. At any assembly, he could always be found at the centre of some important discussion on business or politics. He had little time for art and poetry, and the theatre generally bored him. He was a no-nonsense man. The one diversion he did enjoy was hunting, especially fox hunting. If he had his eye on a trophy, he would possess it in the end. Perhaps this was what Charlotte sensed as he began to be an avid suitor.

William and Dorothy Byrd were in favour of the match. Since they had lost their only son, this would ensure that the business would stay in the family. When the idea of marriage was first broached, Charlotte objected because Audley was twenty years older than she.

"Oh, fie, Charlotte," Dorothy responded to her

objections. "He is a strapping man, in good health, and his age and wisdom may give him some advantage in dealing with your headstrong nature. I have told you, on more than one occasion, that I will not tolerate an Amazon in the family. You know your Aunt Mildred was that way, and she died an unhappy spinster, though I suppose for all her trouble, she did have the last word. This is an excellent match for all concerned, so you will accommodate yourself to it."

At their next discussion of the match, Charlotte played the only card she could that allowed her some personal power.

"Mama," she said, "I will agree to the marriage on the condition that in my marriage settlement the solicitors set up my own separate estate that will include whatever monies and property Grandpapa and Papa may decide to settle on me." This news sent Dorothy skittering out of the parlour and into her husband's library. Charlotte's parents were locked in conference for some time until at last, her mother returned.

"Your father has accepted your terms. It will be a considerable amount that shall be settled upon you. I know for a fact that my father has a fair fortune, though he chooses to live modestly. Your father with his business interests has done well for all of us. I do not know how Mr. Pruitt will look upon your request, but that is for your father and his solicitors to negotiate with the gentleman. He may say that you have a right of dower and nothing else. Charlotte, why must you make your life and my life so complicated? I simply do not understand why you act this way." Exasperated, her mother left the parlour to go lie down, a practice she resorted to more and more of late.

15

Audley Pruitt agreed to Charlotte's requests, finding them, he told her father, a charming aspect of his intended wife's character. He wanted a partner in his spouse, one who would aid him in his business as well as bring him domestic bliss. A date was set for the wedding and a license obtained from Doctor's Commons. In *Gentlemen's Magazine* for May of 1764, the announcement read: "Audley Pruitt of Spitalfields, Esq. to Miss Charlotte Byrd of the same place."

On the morning of the wedding, Charlotte was filled with apprehension. She told herself that she would make the best of it, but her mind wandered to the fells of Cumberland, and she wished she could be at the crest of the hill above her grandfather's house, looking down at the little village of Rosthwaite. Audley had already told her that he would not travel north to "that gloomy, barren, frightful country," not for their wedding trip or any other time. She tried to convince him otherwise, but he would not be moved.

The wedding trip, he decided, would be to Italy in the warm, golden south. Coincidentally, he did have some business matters there to attend to. Everyone Charlotte told about the plan commented enthusiastically on his good taste. Emma was the exception. She sensed her friend's distress.

Now, as they waited to go to the church, Emma asked, "Are you happy, Charlotte?"

"No, I do not believe I am, Emma. My mother, as always, attributes my melancholy humour to my wilful nature. After all, I have every reason to be merry, do I not?" She bit her lip, attempting to stop her tears.

"Perhaps you are simply overwrought with all the

preparations," Emma suggested.

"Yes, let us say that is what it is. Is the coach here yet? If it does not come this instant, I may flee."

Emma looked out the window. "It has just arrived. Charlotte, it is time to go. Will you come?"

Charlotte hesitated, the image of James Clarke pressing the shell into her hand passed so quickly through her thoughts, she hardly had time to notice it. "I am coming, Emma. Wish me good fortune, will you not?"

The first night of her marriage Charlotte quickly learned one of her wifely duties. Anxiously, she lay in bed awaiting her husband's arrival. She had been told nothing directly about what was to come next. Her mother refused to talk about it when asked. Charlotte's lady's maid had given her some information, but Charlotte refused to believe what Betsy whispered. It was too barbaric, she thought, to be possible. Audley entered wearing his nightshirt and cap, a broad smile on his face.

"Dear, dear wife," he said softly in her ear as he moved next to her under the blankets. He threw up her skirts, rolled on top of her and entered her without another word or a caress.

So shocked was Charlotte that she had no time to resist. The horrible searing pain she experienced caused her to cry out. Audley appeared to take this as a cry of pleasure and pushed all the harder. Tears ran down Charlotte's cheeks as her husband finished his business, and with a shudder and a sigh, he rolled off, content.

"Thank you," he said and fell asleep.

Charlotte lay staring at the frame of the bed that loomed up over her head. The second she heard Audley snore, she ran to her dressing room and vomited. She straightened up queasily, spittle dripping from her mouth, and Audley's seed running down her legs. Regaining her senses, she began to wash herself. To her horror, she found blood on the cloth she ran between her legs. She vowed to never again be caught unawares. She would endure this because it was her duty, but she would never be a part of it.

CHAPTER TWO

The first three years of their marriage passed quickly. However, no children were produced from Audley's many visits to Charlotte's bed.

Audley rose every day at four in the morning. He spent at least an hour writing in his journal and his account books. He kept careful records of all his dealings with the weavers, as well as all the orders for specific kinds of silks.

Charlotte oversaw the house and supervised the work of the servants. There were frequent dinner parties, which she planned after Audley gave her the guest list. Charlotte became an excellent card player, though she gambled very little.

Her favourite pastimes were going to Vauxhall Pleasure Gardens and the Theatre Royal Drury Lane, when she could convince Audley to accompany her. Hunting parties in the Cotswolds were a diversion as well. Audley had inherited a home from his first wife that lay just outside Broadway. His aged spinster aunt, Polly Pruitt, happily lived there, tending her garden and watching over Audley's hounds.

There was sadness during this time as well, for a few months after the wedding, Charlotte's parents received the news that Dorothy Byrd's father was dead. Heartsick,

Charlotte accompanied her mother north for the funeral. Mr. Byrd was unable to attend because of pressing business in London, he told them.

The funeral over, the women returned home to find Mr. Byrd sick in bed. The doctor came but was at a loss to explain what was wrong with his patient. He left after administering some powders, but a few hours later, Mr. Byrd died.

Distraught, Charlotte and her mother visited Whitestone for two and a half months with Audley's blessing. Coming back to London, Mrs. Byrd complained of chills. She took to her bed, racked by coughs and a high fever. She died three days later.

Charlotte watched as Audley sold her parents' house and most of their belongings. Whitestone, however, was hers, since the lease now passed to her. She also had a large sum of money coming from both her grandfather's and her father's estates that had been agreed upon in the marriage settlement.

In March of 1767, as Audley was making ready for his annual continental tour scheduled in April, he received a letter from one of his most valued clients, Countess Lucretia Cittidini, urging him to bring Charlotte with him to Venice. The two women had met briefly during Charlotte's wedding trip, when Audley had found it convenient to conduct some business on their way back from Naples.

The countess informed Audley in her letter that she would be giving a masquerade ball, and assured him that the elite of Venice would be in attendance. It was a perfect business opportunity for him. His young wife would surely charm his potential clientele, the countess suggested.

Audley, seeing the possibility of expanding his business, immediately agreed to include Charlotte in his plans. He informed her of his decision after he had sent his response to the countess.

The couple arrived in Venice just after Easter. Charlotte felt as if she were a child let loose on a giant game board as she walked through the winding streets, delighting in their twists and turns and marvelling at the omnipresent water.

Countess Cittidini, a most gracious hostess, insisted that they stay with her in her beautiful home overlooking the Grand Canal. She set her dressmaker to fashioning a dress for Charlotte for the masquerade. It was of exquisite Italian silk, royal blue, with small white and gold flowers and the finest lace for the sleeves and stomacher. The robe was designed to fall off of Charlotte's shoulders, which was the Venetian style.

"I cannot wear it, dear countess," Charlotte protested. "You are most generous, but I simply would feel myself undressed."

The countess laughed, not unkindly, at Charlotte's modesty. "My dear Mrs. Pruitt, your skin is so white. You are most pretty. Let the men admire you. You are young. You are a woman. Why do you want to hide your charms?"

"But I am married. I would find it unseemly to attract attention to myself in such a manner."

"You are not dead, my dear. A woman may still enjoy the attentions of men when she has a husband."

"Yes, that is true, but for what purpose?" Charlotte replied, finding herself growing sad.

The countess, noting her change in humour, pressed on in her inquiry, "You are not happy?"

"I have a melancholic humour that often overcomes

me, I'm afraid. I am young. I am healthy. My time is taken up with my home and helping Mr. Pruitt in whatever way he will allow, but I do find that I must at times fight a terrible sinking feeling which overtakes me." Charlotte smiled, attempting to hide her embarrassment at having confessed such a secret. "But perhaps it is simply our English weather." She looked out the window. "I cannot imagine ever suffering from such feelings in Venice. The sun seems to always be shining here."

The countess smiled. "Perhaps you should take a lover. That has always helped me."

Charlotte was dumbfounded. Then she burst out laughing. "Yes, perhaps I should, though one man in my life is quite enough of a nuisance. Whatever should I do with two?"

"I am sure you would manage. So, shall we make the dress to fit the English taste, or will you dare to be Venetian?"

"I shall bow to your wisdom and let my shoulders be exposed."

"Excellent. A bit of daring should help to lift your spirits."

As the day of the masquerade grew closer, Charlotte's excitement mounted. She watched in awe as the food was brought from all over Europe. Plates and linens that had been ordered months before began to arrive. Candelabras and chandeliers were polished, and candles put in place. Charlotte watched the countess directing all the proceedings with perfect poise, her admiration for the great lady growing by the minute.

A few days before the masquerade, she breakfasted with the countess on the balcony overlooking the Grand

Canal. The morning was balmy, and a more perfect temperature could not have been wished for. The countess was regaling Charlotte with all the latest gossip about everyone on the guest list. It was necessary, the countess told Charlotte, that she should know who everyone was when they began to arrive. After all, it made the whole affair so much more amusing. Charlotte had never laughed so much or heard so many intrigues. Truly, she thought, the Venetians are a wonder.

Audley stepped onto the balcony looking crestfallen. Charlotte's heart went out to him, he appeared so sad. He greeted Countess Cittidini and then placed himself directly in front of Charlotte, looking down on her.

"Charlotte, I will come straight to the point. I must travel to Bellagio immediately. Count Cesi has sent a letter expressing his disappointment in my latest shipment to him. I stand in jeopardy of losing his business. I must go, and he insists that you accompany me, due to your knowledge of the language and the silks." Audley stopped to catch his breath.

Charlotte did not hesitate. "If you feel it necessary, husband, we should go directly." She turned to the countess and expressed her sincere apologies.

Countess Cittidini clucked her tongue and said several words in Italian that Charlotte had not learned in her study of the language, but by their explosive nature, she understood the displeasure they expressed.

The countess calmed herself. "I shall miss *you*, dear Charlotte. My cousin, Count Cesi, is extremely thoughtless to call *you* away in such a manner. He shall hear of my disapproval. When you return to Venice, rest assured, I shall tell you all about the ball."

23

Count Cesi sent a coach as well as messenger to summon the Pruitts. The road to Milan was fast, but it was still several days until they began to climb into the mountains. The journey became rough and tiresome as they neared Bellagio. Charlotte nursed her anger at Audley for tearing her away. She brought the ball dress along, convinced that she would wear it to breakfast, dinner, and supper to make her disappointment known. She would never express her opinion aloud, but there were other ways to show what her humour was in the matter.

They reached the pass that brought them their first sight of Lake Como. Charlotte was so struck by the view that she took an involuntary breath. The sun was setting, and the lake was coloured in bright rose and creamy yellow. Small lights were shining around its shores, and the first stars of the night appeared in the sky. Charlotte found herself moved to tears at the beauty of this place. By the time they arrived at the count's lakeshore villa, the moon was just beginning to rise.

Count Cesi himself came out to greet them. He was a small, thin man, elegantly dressed. He kissed Charlotte's hand, saying, "Why has your husband kept you all to himself? I shall have to speak to him about it." He laughed and welcomed Audley, then ushered them inside, saying, "Refresh yourselves, and we shall partake of a little supper."

Charlotte and Audley were shown to their room. They changed clothes and returned to join Count Cesi for a sumptuous seven-course meal that lasted over two hours. No mention was made of business.

After they bade the count goodnight, they fell into bed exhausted and full of food. Charlotte was soon awakened by Audley's moaning and tossing.

Anger and disappointment that had abated with the new company and surroundings now welled up in her as she realized the masquerade must be in full sway. The groaning next to her drove her from the bed. She crossed to the double doors that looked out onto the veranda and the moonlit lake beyond.

Opening the doors quietly, she felt the rush of cool air on her body. Her skin tingled, being at last loosed from the confines of her traveling clothes. The slight breeze lifted her nightdress and robe as she stepped outside. They gently floated down onto her legs and arms as the wind passed. The moonlight illuminated a grove of trees by the shore in dreamlike blues and purples.

The lake was near, perhaps seventy-five feet from her as she came down the steps from the veranda to the sand. The water shimmered and seemed to be alive and breathing. No one was about, so she walked barefoot to the shore. The mountains across the lake looked like sleeping giants. She shook her head and ran her fingers through her hair. Stretching her arms to the sky, she put a toe in the shallow water.

Just as she began to lift the hem of her nightdress to keep it from getting wet, a hand touched her shoulder. She jumped and whirled around, almost losing her footing. The hand caught her elbow and helped her to shore. She stared, terrified, at the bemused face that greeted her. It seemed familiar, yet quite out of place.

"I have given you a fright. Please, accept my apologies, dear lady."

That voice! Charlotte felt like a total fool as she realized who stood before her. James Clarke! But how in heaven's name was that possible? She staggered to a marble bench near at hand and sat down heavily. Looking up, she saw him gazing innocently at her, his head tilted to one side. "I pray I have not given you too much of a shock."

She could not speak. No words would form. She was sure she had been struck mute. There he stood with his shirt untied at the neck. The moonlight turned his fair hair white, and with his loose-fitting shirt and white stockings, he had the appearance of a ghost.

At last, Charlotte managed an utterance. "I am... surprised, sir."

"I have been visiting the count for several weeks. Very soon, I shall be off to Constantinople. I learned from him that you were in Venice, and I asked him to invent some pretence that I might see you." He smiled boyishly. "Would you care to take a walk?"

"Yes," Charlotte found herself saying, not allowing herself to think about the consequences of accepting such an invitation.

James led her to a grove of trees a short distance away. In the grove, hidden among the trees, was a domed structure that looked out onto the lake. They stood gazing at the water. Charlotte's mind was full of thoughts that ran and collided into one another. One thought shouted loudest of all: Whether this be a dream, or reality, do not turn away; choose to live.

James kept a steady eye on the lake and began to speak softly. "Forgive my boldness, but I must speak of my love for you. It may be my only opportunity. Since I last saw you, I have regretted every day not pursuing a proposal of marriage. I do not know whether you would have had me, but I was a coward. I do not have much to offer, what little fortune I have is tied up in Devon. My father has no love for me. I am a fool. But you fill my thoughts. I have longed to caress your hair, to touch your face, to hear your voice." He turned and looked at Charlotte, his eyes filled with sadness.

"I, too, have wished to be near you." Charlotte knew she was overstepping any polite restraints. "It is an impossible situation. Kiss me, will you? Only once." He looked at her, and she returned his gaze. Charlotte's inner voice cried out, "Kiss me before my knees buckle, or I flee in panic!"

He put his hand on the small of her back. She moved into him. Her lips touched his neck where his shirt was untied. Her knees gave way, and he caught her. Holding her gently, he kissed her on the forehead. She found the strength to put her arms around his neck and, drawing him close, kissed him on the mouth. Charlotte would have been hard-pressed to say if they embraced for a long time or a short moment. Their bodies touched, and like smoke from two fires, their spirits blended together, and they could not be parted.

"Charlotte! Charlotte! Are you out here?" It was Audley! Charlotte panicked and turned to run. James grabbed her around the waist with one arm, turned her back toward him, and put his hand over her mouth. She was captive. Crouching down in the shadows of the trees, he pulled her close.

Audley passed very near them, and Charlotte felt sick with fear. What, she wondered, was she doing? What could she have been thinking, to put herself in such jeopardy? She had to get back to their room. She must think, but she could not. She closed her eyes tightly and pushed closer to James. Please help me, God, she prayed fervently. I am a sinner, and I am in great need of Your guidance. She heard her husband's footsteps retreating back toward the villa. She dared open her eyes a little. Peeking up, she saw James looking at her.

"I am sorry that I have compromised you so. Pretend that you fell asleep here. Wait a few minutes before you go back. When you enter your room, do so as if you have no reason to be in haste." Charlotte had no time to respond. He was gone. She heard no sound of his footfall. Perhaps, she mused, he *is* a ghost. Yet she knew from the kiss he was not.

She did as he instructed. She attempted to brush some of the debris from her clothes and hair. Her heart pounded. She rested against the pillars. The stone felt cold against her hot face. She watched the moonlight on the lake and imagined herself floating far out in the middle. She sat on the marble bench and lay down, intending to wait only a few more minutes before going back.

"My God, Charlotte, what are you doing out here?" came a shrill voice that startled her from her slumber. It was Audley. He had found her. She could not say how much time had passed, but the sky now looked pale and only a few stars were visible.

"Audley, is that you? Where am I…?" she managed to splutter as she sat up.

"What on earth are you doing outside?" he asked crossly.

"I could not sleep. You were groaning. I came outside to take the air. I must have fallen asleep. Dear Audley, I am so sorry for upsetting you. Please, do forgive me," she said, smiling up at him.

He ruffled her hair. "I worry about you, that's all.

Come, you must get out of this chilly air."

Later that morning when Charlotte and Audley came to breakfast, they were greeted by Count Cesi, who inquired if they had slept well.

Audley glanced at Charlotte and apparently decided not to mention her midnight walk. He turned back to the count and answered, "Never better, Count Cesi. The mountain air is most healthful. A salubrious climate, I must say. Your invitation could not have been more welcomed by Mrs. Pruitt and me."

Breakfast, like supper, was served in several courses, after which the count encouraged them to walk through the flower garden that stretched between the villa and the lake's edge. "Your Robert Adams, the fine English architect, has visited me and most highly approved of the garden's aesthetic. I hope you find it as enchanting as he did."

With that endorsement, the Pruitts rose from the table with the intention of venturing outside. Their forward progress was stopped, however, when James Clarke appeared. Charlotte observed Audley as he took in the stranger. James's hair was neatly pulled back into a queue. Audley would find this out of fashion, Charlotte was sure. Otherwise his white silk shirt with its handsome ruffle at the neck, his sky-blue waistcoat and breeches and his silver jacket would undoubtedly meet with approval.

Count Cesi took delight in doing the introductions in English. Then after some discussion, the count insisted that he and Audley must work on the contracts for more "exquisite Spital silk".

He entreated James to put aside whatever plans he had and instead accompany Signora Pruitt on a tour of the gardens. James declined at first, but when Audley asked him also, he acquiesced graciously.

Charlotte alternately felt guilt and delight as she watched the two men play out what she assumed was their scheme to whisk Audley away, leaving her and James unchaperoned. When the task was accomplished, James bid her follow him outside and into the gardens, which she did willingly. To break the silence, she teased him.

"Sir, I must inform you that your plan has cost me the opportunity to attend Countess Cittidini's masquerade in Venice. She had the most beautiful dress made for me, and now I shall never have occasion to wear it, being much too bold for English routs."

James did not respond immediately, instead he stared across the lake. Charlotte was unsure that he had heard her and felt embarrassed for prattling on. Her curiosity piqued at the object of his attention, she asked, "What do you gaze at so intently?"

"Do you observe the small island, there, with the villa?"

"Yes, it is a beautiful setting."

"That, dear lady, is where you will wear your elegant gown!" His tone changed abruptly. "It is indeed a beautiful setting, signora."

A voice from behind Charlotte rang out. "Egads, Sir James, but you sound Venetian with your accent." Audley laughed as he came to Charlotte's side. "Are you finding your tour informative, wife?"

"Yes, I am, husband. You are finished so quickly with the count. Is all in order as you would have wished?"

"It is indeed. However, I fear the count is urging me to accompany him to Rome. He needs my expert advice, so he says, to help him choose damask for his villa there. Egads, how many houses does the man have, I wonder?"

He laughed and lowered his voice. "I find no joy in gallivanting all over the country, but he assures me that I shall find new customers in Rome. M'dear, the contracts he just signed will buy us a home in Portland Square, I venture."

Charlotte smiled dutifully. "This is an opportunity not to be missed. I shall see that we are packed at once."

Before she could step away, Audley raised a hand to stop her. "No, dearest, Count Cesi wishes that you stay and enjoy his villa. We shall be gone only ten days, a fortnight at most. The Count suggested, Sir James, that I might impose upon you to see to my wife's pleasure. Not that a bachelor like yourself has much time for women, but Charlotte is better than most."

"I am at your wife's service, Mr. Pruitt, if she is desirous of my company."

Charlotte prayed silently, dear God, help me. I am a sinner, and my flesh is weak. At that moment, her knees were weak indeed. Audley's smile vanished. "Charlotte, you have gone white as a sheet. Do you need to sit down? I shall get you a drink of water… or wine. Sir James, will you attend to my wife?" He ran off with great urgency in the direction of the villa, leaving Charlotte on James's arm.

Charlotte found herself unable to look at him. She grew dizzier, her face going from white to scarlet. He began to hum a minuet then stopped. Lips close to her ear, his voice soft as a caress, he whispered, "The masquerade commences, m'dear."

The rest of the day found Count Cesi and Audley making preparations to depart. Charlotte oversaw the packing of her husband's belongings with trembling hands and a head filled with arguing voices. That night in bed,

Audley was an ardent and speedy lover. His thirst for her soon quenched, he rolled off her and began to snore.

Sleep evaded Charlotte, but she forced herself to stay in bed. Over and over, she imagined herself throwing open the doors to the outside and finding James waiting for her. She attempted to suppress fits of nervous laughter followed by the deepest sighs but was unsuccessful. Thankfully, Audley slept despite the noise. At last, the sky began to lighten, and she could rise without explanation if Audley woke.

Her morning toilette was finished when Audley rose. He was quick about his dressing. Soon he and the count were ready to be off. Charlotte kissed her husband gently on the cheek, and he returned her affection with a tremendous hug.

"None of your melancholy vapours, m'dear. Entertain yourself as best you can, and I shall return in no time."

Charlotte smiled weakly, promising to do her best.

The Count kissed her hand. "Please, signora, my house and villa on the island are at your disposal. You will take pleasure in them, I hope."

The two men boarded the coach and the driver urged the horses on their way.

Charlotte waved until the coach was out of sight. Walking back into the house, Charlotte noted that the servants seemed to have disappeared for the moment. All was silent. The drawing room was flooded with morning light. She sat down, relieved that Audley was gone. In the next instant, an argument began to rage in her head between the voices that urged her to remember her wifely duties and those that would have her explore her feelings for James Clarke. She closed her eyes and rested her head in one hand.

32

"What shall I do?" she asked aloud.

"Pray, accept my invitation to the island this evening," came the answer.

Charlotte started, looking up to find James standing in a shadow in the corner of the room. He put his finger to his lips and advanced toward her, stopping only to close the door to the hallway. Charlotte shuddered with delight, watching him approach. She noted how he walked with assurance and grace. His height and slender form pleased her immeasurably. He stood in front of her, then suddenly sat upon the floor like a small boy, gazing at her with affection. "You are the most beautiful of women."

Charlotte blushed and averted her eyes.

"I spied on you all day yesterday as you moved about and all this morning as you said your good-byes. I can think of no more pleasurable pastime." He hesitated, smiling mischievously. "No, I am in error. There is one."

He raised himself to his knees, taking her hands in his and kissed them. Charlotte grew light-headed. He crept closer until his face was very near hers, his lips brushed her cheek. She breathed in his scent and felt his breath on her neck. His mouth found hers. Charlotte nearly swooned as his tongue explored her lips and found its way inside her mouth. After a long kiss, he sat back on the floor and rested his head in her lap. Charlotte stroked his hair and tried to slow her racing heart.

Looking up at her, he spoke softly. "Charlotte, I would be most pleased if you would wear your Venetian gown tonight."

"I shall, sir."

James stood and smiled. "A boatman will call for you at sunset. He will carry you to the island and to me." He took her hand as if to give it a kiss but licked it instead.

"James!"

His smile broadened at her surprise. "Madam, until this evening." He bowed slightly and was gone from the room.

Charlotte fell back in her chair and closed her eyes. Opening them, she looked heavenward and called out quietly, "Dear God, I am a sinner. Forgive my lust. I am a daughter of Eve, I know, but I am in love."

Charlotte spent the rest of the morning walking along the shore of the lake. Wading into the cold water, she recalled childhood days at her grandfather's house where she took long walks on the soft days. A fine mist would cover her face, and her hair would become a mass of tight, dark red ringlets. Once, she found a stray black dog that adopted her and the two of them ran up the slope in front of the house and slid down in the mud. She'd always loved the squish of the wet earth. Now, she pushed her toes into the mud of Lake Como and watched it slide up between them. She rinsed her feet and did it over and over. There was an immediacy and an abandon in the act that brought back the joy of childhood. She was determined that she would hold on to this elation for the next however many days she had with James, whatever the consequences might be.

Returning to the house, she took great care in bathing and dressing. The maids who attended her marvelled at the beauty of her gown. She told them about the preparations that had been made for the masquerade in Venice. They all looked heartbroken when she revealed that Audley and she had been called to Bellagio at the last minute. She knew as she spoke that each of them probably suspected why she now dressed with such care. Again, the voices in her head cried out for her to be careful, and again she silenced them.

Betsy, Charlotte's lady's maid, was much quieter than usual as she helped Charlotte ready herself for the evening. Granted, she did not speak Italian, and so perhaps she felt left out of the conversation between Charlotte and the Bellagio maids. However, Charlotte feared Betsy might have guessed why her cheeks were flushed and why she wished to look her best. When the maids of the house had been excused, Betsy began to brush Charlotte's freshly washed hair in preparation for dressing it.

"For tonight, Betsy, I desire no pomatum, nor cushions, nor frosting of powder."

"Whatever shall I do with it, mum?" she asked.

"Pin it up, just very simply," Charlotte instructed her.

"As you wish, mum," Betsy answered.

"My husband has asked Sir James to keep me company while he is in Rome."

"And the gentleman is agreeable to Mr. Pruitt's request, mum?"

"Yes, he has planned some entertainment on the island for this evening. Doubtless there will be other guests as well. I would rather have spent the evening reading or at my needlepoint, but I shall attempt to be an agreeable guest."

"I am sure the gentleman will find pleasure in your company, mum."

Charlotte took a step she hoped would ease Betsy's trepidation about keeping any important information from Audley. "Betsy, do you remember that rose silk gown that you admired so? The one I wore to Ranelagh last spring?"

"Oh, aye, mum."

"Well, I have grown tired of it, though I think it's one of the prettiest I own. Would you care for it, dear Betsy?"

"Thank you, mum. I would be proud to have such a lovely dress. I have always told everyone that I am the luckiest of ladies' maids to have you as my mistress." So, the unspoken agreement between the two women was sealed. Betsy's silence about the goings on during the next ten days was assured.

Charlotte finished her preparations for the evening. She sat before the mirror, amusing herself by trying on her mask. Its silver form adorned with peacock feathers hid the upper half of her face, letting only her eyes shine through. She imagined a new identity for herself, a wicked lady of the Venetian court, like one Countess Cittidini had described. But when the mask came off, she sighed at the innocent face that greeted her.

Deliberately ending her fantasy, she was ready when the boatman called for her just after the sun set. As the two oarsmen rowed towards the island, Charlotte watched the villa she had just left growing smaller and smaller. Her old life seemed to be falling away as if it were just a dream. If that is the dream, she wondered, what will "real life" on the island be like?

CHAPTER THREE

The island was small and rocky, just big enough for the villa and a flower garden. The vine-covered walls of the villa by the dock were sheltered by trees and flowering bushes. To Charlotte it seemed a sanctuary far from the world. Once docked, the boatman helped Charlotte disembark. She carried her mask and her cape, for the evening was warm. She was met by a manservant in handsome livery who led her to the villa's entrance by way of a path lit with torches. He presented Charlotte to yet another servant who ushered her into the ballroom.

She was charmed by what she beheld. The floor was composed of large, black and white marble tiles which glowed in the light of hundreds of candles placed about the room in candelabras. Shadows on the pale-yellow walls danced in the flickering light. The far wall consisted entirely of windowed doors that led onto a veranda overlooking the far side of the lake and mountains beyond. There was little furniture, only a few marble benches along the walls. To Charlotte's left, there was an ensemble of musicians playing a minuet.

A servant approached her, bowed low, and said, "Sir James Clarke requests your presence on the veranda for dinner. Please, follow me, signora."

He led her across the ballroom and through one of the many doors to the outside. There, she found a beautifully set table with a centrepiece of flowers. Their sweet scents filled the air. However, James was not there.

Perplexed, Charlotte turned to the footman, who responded, "I believe, signora, that the gentleman is to be found down the path." He pointed to a stairway that led down into the garden.

Charlotte descended the steps slowly. She was beginning to be overcome with shame for her impetuous nature. Perhaps, she thought, I should not even see him. I should return to the boat and demand to be taken back to the house. She hesitated and almost began her retreat, but a sound caught her attention. It was the music of a wooden Irish whistle, a little flageolet, with high piping notes. It was a familiar tune from her childhood, though at this moment she could not name it. She set off at a quick pace in the direction of the song, her heart racing.

She found James sitting atop a large rock by the edge of the lake. Several torches surrounded the rock, their flames dancing in the light breeze. He saw her but continued to play, so she sat on a nearby marble bench to listen. As the tune played on, she felt herself transported to Bristol and Dublin and other seaports she had visited as a child. She was delighted.

Upon finishing, he looked down at her and smiled. His face grew serious. "You could have turned around and gone back. I have instructed the boatman to stay for an hour. It is not yet too late to reconsider."

She looked up at him. "I have chosen, sir, to accept your invitation for the evening."

Somewhere in the back of her mind she heard a great

shout of "NO!" uttered by all the cautious and honourable voices in her head. She refused to acknowledge them. Feeling free and exhilarated, she cocked her head and raised an eyebrow. "And what about you? You are not withdrawing your invitation, are you?"

"Never!" he cried out in mock astonishment. "Let us dine! I am famished." He jumped down from his perch, landing next to her. "And you must promise me to wear your mask at least for the first dance. Will you, dear lady?" He begged.

"I shall, if you will don yours as well!" Charlotte replied with a laugh.

He looked at her with affection but grew serious again as he took a step back from her. "Dear lady, forgive me."

"Whatever for?" Charlotte responded anxiously

"I am remiss, for I have forgotten to compliment you on your gown. Please, allow me to view it properly from front to back."

She stood still as he walked around her, sighing with delight.

When he arrived back in front of her, he spoke. "The gown and the form that it graces are both exquisite. Oh, but wait…" and he turned her around. He moved in very close. Placing his hands on her bared shoulders, he began to kiss her neck and breathe in the scent of her hair. "Thank you, dear Charlotte, for accepting my invitation. May I escort you to our table?"

The meal was delicious. The servants appeared and disappeared as if by magic. Charlotte drank her wine slowly, wanting to be able to walk and dance when she rose from the table. She caught herself staring at James's face, wishing to hold his image forever, but knowing she could not.

Sadness overtook her, and she looked away into the darkness.

"Charlotte, you look melancholy," James said. "Have I offended you in some way?"

"Forgive me. All of this seems such a fantastical dream. My sadness springs from the knowledge that I must wake."

"We both shall wake, but at present we have the opportunity to fulfil the promise of this dream." He held out his hand. "Dream with me?"

She placed her hand in his as the musicians began to play.

James kissed her fingers, declaring, "To the masquerade!" He put on his white half-mask.

Charlotte raised hers, thinking briefly of the Venetian lady she had imagined in her mirror. A shiver ran down her spine. She stood and took James's arm. They entered the ballroom as two mysterious strangers to begin their minuet.

James was a graceful dancer. Watching him, Charlotte was filled with a desire she had never before experienced. They danced several minuets and a cotillion, improvising as they went along, since it was just the two of them.

Then, he instructed the musicians to rest. Guiding Charlotte back to the veranda, he placed her cape around her shoulders. Taking her hand, he led her down another path consisting of tiers of steps that descended into the garden. At the top of the last tier he dropped his mask and took her into his arms. They kissed. When they stopped Charlotte shed her mask. Embracing a second time, they held onto each other, neither wishing to speak.

Suddenly, James cried out, "The tarantella!"

"James!?"

"You should learn the tarantella! Come to the ballroom

with me. Come, come."

With great haste, they returned to the ballroom. Charlotte was breathless from running and laughing. James introduced her to the conductor, Signor Gallini. He was a well-known Italian dancing master, James informed her. He had recently spent three years in London and knew all the latest dances. "His book on deportment and manners is renowned throughout the Continent."

"Sir James, your introduction does me great honour," Signor Gallini said. When James asked if he would possibly teach them the tarantella, the dancing master agreed, saying, "It is, as you know, quite a lively dance."

"We should have other dancers, as well," James declared, and he enlisted several footmen and maids to join them for the instruction.

After everyone appeared to understand the dance, James insisted that wine be poured for all assembled. He proclaimed a toast to the evening's festivities, then the dancing began in earnest.

When they finally rested, Charlotte inquired of Signor Gallini if he knew English country dances. He named several, the last of which Charlotte had learned as a girl in Rosthwaite. "Oh, Signor Gallini, would you teach that one to our dancers?"

Signor Gallini inclined his head in a slight bow. "Pray, allow me to speak with the musicians to learn if they may know the necessary music, madam." He returned with an affirmative answer. "They are a most accomplished ensemble, madam, and would be pleased to honour your request."

Charlotte clapped her hands with delight and thanked him.

By the end of the evening, everyone in the villa was dancing, eating, drinking, and laughing. At last, James invited Charlotte to follow him to her room. Once inside, he lifted her up into his arms and kissed her. She put her arms around his neck, allowing herself to be held like a child. He walked to the bed and laid her gently down upon it.

"Goodnight, my sweet Lottie. I shall see you when you wake." He kissed her on the forehead and was gone.

She fell immediately to sleep and woke the next morning still in her Venetian gown. Sitting up groggily, she was bewildered and didn't know quite what to do. She had brought no other clothes or necessities, not even a brush or tongue scraper. She rose rather unsteadily from the effects of too much wine. As she surveyed the room, she found a wash basin with a pitcher of water and a towel. Next to the basin was a note.

Dearest Charlotte,

I pray your dreams were pleasant ones. I have taken the liberty of placing clothing for you in the wardrobe, as well as other items you might find necessary for your use this morning. I would be most pleased if you would join me for breakfast on the veranda.

Your humble servant,
Jem

In the wardrobe, Charlotte discovered all the articles she needed for her toilette. She was most delighted to find a saffron yellow gown with dainty white flowers that could not have fit her better had her dressmaker sewn it for her.

She did not tarry, dressing quickly, even without the aid of Betsy or any other maid servant. She retraced her steps from the previous evening and with only two wrong turns found the ballroom, now deserted, and the veranda beyond.

James was there, his face lighting up when he beheld her. He stood immediately, and crossing to her, presented Charlotte with a white rose.

"Please sit down," he invited, offering her a seat.

She accepted and thanked him for the gown, commending him for his thoroughness in all he had provided.

He smiled. "I am so pleased that I have been able to delight you. Would you care for tea?"

"Yes, thank you." She reached for the pot, but he stopped her.

"Allow me."

He poured, and Charlotte took the cup and saucer from him.

"After breakfast, I wish to present you with another surprise, but you must eat first."

Charlotte ate and drank heartily even though she had consumed great quantities of food and drink the night before.

James laughed with pleasure at her appetite. "A good north-country girl, eh?"

As soon as she finished, he jumped up. "Come now and see what is in the garden."

He led her down the path to the top of the steps where they had kissed the night before. Now in the morning light, they looked out over the sculpted garden. Its centrepiece was a domed marble rotunda in the style of Palladio, surrounded by brilliant red flowers.

"Advance and look," he urged as he guided her towards it.

It was like a temple, its marble floor encircled by columns. Charlotte took a step back, for in the centre was a gracefully carved wooden bed.

"Sir, tell me…" her words stopped, as she saw the smile that played on his lips.

"All the servants are gone, save the cook and one footman, both of whom I have instructed to stay inside or on the other side of the island. The musicians have left at my behest, though their music would have been welcomed. I thought privacy, however, to be more important. No one is here in the garden but you and me. If this isolation is not to your liking, we could go back to the mainland, though I would have to be both boatman and oarsman."

Charlotte could suppress neither blush, nor smile. To make love outside, in the daylight, felt deliciously wicked and distinctly un-English. Both appealed to her.

"You, sir, must be my teacher. I am your willing pupil."

"We must start with the dance." They walked hand in hand into the temple. He stepped over to a large, wooden music box that sat on the floor and wound it. It began to play a slow, sad song. He held Charlotte close and their bodies moved as one to the tune. His hands glided down her back and onto her buttocks and hips. She had only a shift on underneath her gown and when his hands cupped her breast she inhaled audibly.

"Is it all to your liking, dear student?" he asked in a whisper.

She looked at his face. His lips were parted, his eyes closed. "Yes, teacher," she replied with a shudder as his fingers played with her nipples.

Slowly, he untied the ribbons on her gown and let it slip to the floor. Charlotte took a step back. James lifted off her shift. She stood naked before him. His eyes took in her body, and he smiled. He guided her to the bed, and she reclined while he stripped of his shirt, breeches, and stockings. Lying down beside her, his body was warm and his skin soft to her touch. They held each other, breathing deeply, and began their long, slow explorations.

Charlotte had never before felt a man's gentle touch or been asked through word or gesture what she desired. She was unsure at first what to do, but James was a patient teacher, and each moment she fell more deeply in love with him. There was no shame in this act, only a growing ecstasy. When he entered her body, she welcomed him, there was no need to bite her lip as she did when Audley forced his way into her. The tears that fell now were of pleasure, not of pain.

He dried the tears and looked at her face, tilting his head to one side to see if he had hurt her. Her face broke into a wide smile at his concern. He sat up, bringing her with him. She wrapped her legs around him and he carried her to a nearly shallow pool. He waded in and sat down. They were up to their waists in warm water. Charlotte giggled as James tipped over into the water, bringing her with him. They came up laughing and shaking the water from their hair. Then they rested, sitting in the water, their two bodies, one, as the sun dried their backs.

Suddenly, James snapped his fingers. "I have forgotten the wine." He slid Charlotte off his lap and took her hand, leading her back to the bed. He poured two glasses of wine and offered a toast. "To you, dear lady, and our island."

"And to you, sir, and our island." The wine made

Charlotte giddy.

When she finished her glass, James asked her to lie down on her stomach. He brought out scented oil and proceeded to massage her neck, arms, back, and the rest of her body. When he turned her over, she was as limp as a rag doll. He began to work down her front.

When he was done, she asked him quietly, "Please, will you enter me again?"

He was prepared to fulfil her desire, for the massage had excited him as well. Charlotte felt as if her entire being was opening to him. She took his body in and enclosed herself around him. Neither could control what happened next. The moment of their climax came fast. It burst upon Charlotte with a flash of white light. Her body contracted several times, and James moved in her with a rapid rhythm. He moaned and sighed. She began to cry from joy and release. He kissed her tears. She wanted him again.

The lovers spent their days and nights in intimate embrace, strolling in the garden, swimming in the lake, and learning all they could about each other. Each hour was unique, filled with discoveries and new delights.

The Count kept up a frequent correspondence with James. It evolved that he and Audley would return in twelve days. He lamented that he could occupy his English friend no longer than that. "Would that I might give you the gift of a month, dear friend," he wrote in one of his first letters, which James shared with Charlotte.

On the third day, Charlotte sent the footman with a note to Betsy requesting clothes, a few books and her needlework. She instructed Betsy to mend a pair of Audley's breeches and see to the washing that needed to be done.

"I shall use my time in contemplation and reading. The quiet of the island has already done much to settle my nerves and repair my felicity." Betsy, Charlotte knew, would not believe a word, but at least she could not spy on her.

The days passed all too swiftly, and on the ninth day Charlotte began to dread her separation from James. She could not stop herself from asking, "What shall we do?"

James put his finger to her lips and drawing it away, kissed her. He would give her no answer. When he slept, she lay awake next to him. She imagined running away together or facing Audley with the truth. Either scenario was filled with complications and ended unsatisfactorily.

On the morning of the tenth day, Charlotte woke to find James gone. She spent the morning perched on top of a rock, watching the ever-changing sky and water. James found her on his return and sat beside her.

"Charlotte, I promised Francesco that I would assist him with some pressing business matters in Constantinople. He is one of my few true friends, and I am forever in his debt for bringing you to me. I sail within the week."

Desperate at the thought of being separated, Charlotte spoke. "Take me with you, James."

"That is impossible. When I have finished, I will return to London."

"I cannot bear to be parted from you."

"We have no choice," he responded heatedly. "I have thought about this matter at great length. I shall absent myself before your husband's return. I think it best he does not see us together. I fear one if not both of us would betray our feelings. There is nothing else to be done. Would you excuse me?" He jumped down from the rock and strode up the path.

His angry tone and sudden withdrawal shocked Charlotte. The image of him standing dishevelled and distracted in the doorway of his house on the Isle of Man danced before her. She determined to be silent on the subject of their separation. She retreated to her room and lay down. My God, she thought, what have I done? I am in love with a madman. She was dizzy and unable to concentrate. Her head felt as if it might explode. She wept until she had no more tears, but still the wrenching sobs would not abate. Her head was buried in her pillow, and she did not look up when she heard footsteps enter the room.

James sat of the edge of the bed and slipped off his shoes. He lay down at her back. "Lottie, I shall come to you in London. We will find a way to be together. My dearest, I have never before felt such a passion. You have become part of my soul. I am, if you will have me, yours forever."

Charlotte turned over and pressed her face into his chest.

"I will not abandon you," he continued. "I am not a bad man, not a seducer. But there is a weakness in my spirit. I wish I had proposed to you before Pruitt, but I was afraid. All my life I have attempted to rid myself of my melancholy. My family despairs at my behaviour. My father has always thought me a lunatic. He nearly had me drowned once.

"I was twelve years old. It was after my brother's death, and I was distraught. My father had read Wesley's *Primitive Physick*. He had four of the servants hold my head under a cataract until I could breathe no longer. The fear of him flaying their backs held them in their place. Finally, afraid they had drowned me, he relented and allowed them to pull me out."

"And did it affect a cure?" Charlotte asked, aghast.

"No, but it taught me self-discipline. I was never again quick to allow my choleric or melancholic vapours to overtake me, at least not in my father's presence." A fleeting smile played on his lips, then he was serious again. "Perhaps, my dearest, I should never have pursued you. Then we would not find ourselves in this position. Yet my desire for you overcame any honourable or rational sentiments that I possessed. And far from quenching my desire, our hours together have made me a man more obsessed. Forgive me." He pressed his lips to her forehead.

Charlotte looked up at him. His eyes were red and brimming with tears. "James, you fill my heart with joy. I, too, am weak. I allowed myself to be bound to Audley when I care little for him. And now when I should honour my commitment as a wife, I have no strength for it. I have prayed to God to help me, but His voice is silent, or perhaps the desire of my body sings so loudly I do not hear Him. You have awakened my heart, and I wish it never to slumber again. You must get word to me somehow of your health and your travels. Please, promise me that you will." She bit her lip, anxiously hoping he'd agree.

"I promise I shall, my beloved." He took her hand in his and kissed it. They rose and went to dinner.

In the late afternoon, a fog began to settle upon the lake and a light mist fell. James became concerned. "Lottie, I had wished us to spend this last night on the island, but if a storm should descend, we might be trapped here when your husband returns."

"Then we must sail back with haste. James, there is a part of me that wishes he would know the truth."

"You would be unprotected, Charlotte. I have too little

income to support you. My father has threatened to disinherit me if I do not return and help him with our estate. I must settle my quarrel with him before we think of you separating from Pruitt. If I do well with my affairs in Constantinople, I may make a goodly amount. If that comes to pass, perhaps we might settle in France." James looked out the windows and saw the wind was growing strong. "We must depart, or the storm will be upon us."

Charlotte assembled her few belongings and met James at the boat. He rowed them back across the choppy waters. Charlotte kept her eyes on him all the way. He met her gaze only briefly. On seeing the sadness in his eyes, Charlotte's throat tightened. It was nearly dark when they reached the shore, where they parted without a word.

Charlotte found Betsy and set her to work seeing to her clothes. "I shall take a walk. The rain seems to have passed us by. Please, see that my night clothes are laid out and my bed turned down."

Finding James's room, she slipped in without the servants observing her. He was reading. He put down his book and extinguished the candles. Charlotte reached over, touching his face, running her fingers along his eyebrows, and noting the soft skin on his eyelids. She closed her eyes and attempted to see every detail in her mind's eye. Yet the more she tried, the more frustrated she became at the impossibility of the task.

James took her hands in his. "Charlotte, I love you. I know what you are doing, but please, be here with me now."

She nodded her agreement, and they made love slowly and quietly. Afterwards, they rested in each other's arms.

At last, James broke the silence. "I shall join you for

supper. Return to your room first, as if from your walk, so your maid servant will have less cause for suspicion.

When the meal was finished, and the hour was late, they walked by the lake to the marble bench where he had first surprised her. "Lottie, it is no longer safe for me here. I shall ride tonight to an inn in Milan, and from there, I shall leave for Constantinople."

"Write to me, James. Send the letters to Emma Bosworth. I trust her to keep our secret."

"I shall, Lottie. I promise."

They embraced, and James left for the stable where his horse was already saddled.

Charlotte felt as if she were falling into a dark abyss as she watched his retreating figure. Going inside, her heart aching, she readied herself for bed. Hot tears came to her eyes, but she knew she must school herself. Audley must never have cause to suspect her secret. She attempted to fall asleep, alone in the darkness. All joy and tenderness were gone. The light of dawn had just shown itself, when exhausted, she fell asleep.

CHAPTER FOUR

The morning was fogbound and grey. Charlotte had no appetite, but she knew she must rise and prepare for Audley's arrival. Dressing in his favourite gown, she had Betsy prepare her hair with pomatum and powder. She was determined to go on, if only to see James again.

A little after noon, Audley and the count arrived in the coach. Charlotte came out to greet them. Audley jumped out and rushed to her. He grabbed her, giving her a tremendous hug. She looked at him with tears welling up in her eyes. They did not go unnoticed. Audley stepped back.

"Tears! Did you miss me that much? Come wife, into the house. I have presents for you from Roma!" He laughed and rushed in ahead of her.

Count Cesi stopped, and taking her aside, whispered, "Your sorrow tells me that your days were well spent. Be brave, signora. Passionate love brings us both life and death. You have lived and now you die a little. But know that resurrection awaits." He kissed her hand softly, took her arm, and led her into the villa.

Audley regaled Charlotte with his adventures in Rome. His enthusiastic stories and his sentiment when presenting Charlotte with his gifts made her sadness ease momentarily. He smiled and announced that they would be the count's guests for a fortnight longer. Charlotte panicked. She could not stay there to be daily reminded of her assignation with James.

"Dearest," she said, attempting to hide her distress, "what about your business? Should we not be returning home? We do not wish to impose on the count's hospitality too long."

Audley smiled. "Was there ever such a wife, beautiful and shrewd, Count Cesi? She is forever concerned about my business. She gets it from her father, and I have taught her as well. Mrs. Pruitt, it is at the count's request that we stay. He has planned a hunting trip in the mountains for him and me. What do you think of that?"

A voice screamed in her head. What do I think about it?! Why did the count not tell James, so my joy might have lasted a little longer? She was struck by a horrible thought. What if he did inform him, but he chose to leave despite the news? The doubt gnawed at her. Now I must stay in this house alone. I shall go mad!

She maintained control of her emotions however, and managed to remark calmly, "Count Cesi, you are truly a generous host in so many ways. The mountains must be beautiful, and I can only imagine the views of the lake."

"Dearest Signora Pruitt, I would not be a good host if I did not offer you a new delight, also. I have a chalet in the mountains, rough in its accommodations, but nonetheless in a lovely setting. I offer it to you while your husband is occupied in pursuit of the stag."

Charlotte breathed a sigh of relief. She would take this opportunity to pray to God for forgiveness and weep until she had no more tears. Death, the count had said, was her state. She would use this time to cleanse her body and soul and be reborn a better wife. She was determined to put this episode behind her and be strong. James was gone, though the thought crossed her mind to beg the count to contact him before he left Italy. She began to see herself as a fool. What made her think his profession of love was true? If James truly wished to be with her, why did he not face Audley? How many women before her had been so used and then come to their senses in the light of day?

"Count Cesi, you are too kind. I gratefully accept your offer and shall use this time for reflection and prayer."

"Egads, Charlotte, certainly there must be more pleasurable pursuits. I will tell you, I took great enjoyment from our journey to Rome, and I shall do the same for this hunting foray. Do not be so dour, m'dear. It does not suit you. It comes from spending too much time in Rosthwaite as a child. So, it is settled. We leave in two days' time and shall be gone for ten days. Such tears in your eyes when I came home. Can you survive without old Audley, m'love?"

"I shall endeavour to do my best," Charlotte responded weakly.

The next days passed slowly. She wandered the grounds of the villa with terrible arguments raging in her head. In one moment, Charlotte daydreamed of the time she had spent with James, longing to hear his voice, but in the next instant, she was calling herself a fool and vowing to never think of him again.

She tried to approach the count twice to beg him to get a note to James, but the first time she lost courage, and the second, Audley entered unexpectedly.

The night before they were to go, Charlotte requested Betsy pack a few items for her, including her needlework and several books. Count Cesi and Audley agreed that they would escort Charlotte to the chalet where she would stay for the duration of their hunting trip. She declined to take Betsy or any other servants with her, wishing to be left alone with her thoughts. Surprisingly, Audley did not argue the point with her.

The hunting party consisted of Count Cesi, Audley, five noblemen from the surrounding area, and a number of servants. Early in the morning they gathered in the stable courtyard and mounted their horses. As they began their ascent into the mountains, the sun was just rising over the lake.

Charlotte found herself wishing she could share the moment with James. She shook her head to clear it. Biting her lip, she looked up the path, and attempted to concentrate on the scenery. The vegetation around the lake gave way to evergreens. Soon, a forest of tall trees enclosed them. They stopped for a meal of cheese, bread, and wine, then set off again, going ever upward.

By late afternoon, they had reached the chalet, which sat in a clearing surrounded by aged oak trees, splendid chestnut trees, and tall pines. In the valley far below, the lake began to take on the colours of evening. Some distance from the chalet sat another smaller house. It was the gamekeeper's cottage. The stables were directly behind it. An elderly man lived in the cottage and watched over the count's lands. The travellers dismounted and entered the chalet, finding he had dinner waiting for them.

Inside the chalet, there was a large room. One wall was filled with a handsome stone fireplace for cooking and heat. There were steep log steps that led to an upper area, big enough for a bed, wardrobe and night table. The beams were carved with the likenesses of small mountain animals.

Charlotte was charmed by the place and looked forward to being alone there.

That night, Audley and Charlotte were given the upstairs bed, while the count and his companions had beds prepared for them on the ground floor. Audley had made no advances to Charlotte since his return, but now he was in an amorous mood. As they lay in bed, he began to grope at Charlotte's body. She recoiled at the touch of his cold hands.

"Charlotte, do not move away. I need you," he whispered.

She fought back tears, thankful that it was dark, so he could not see her face. "Forgive me, Audley. Your sudden approach surprised me, and your hands are cold." She attempted to sound friendly.

"Charlotte, turn over on your side and get that blasted night dress out of my way. My God, I have been away a fortnight. I have missed you, wife," he whispered.

His insistence annoyed her, especially because she was sure the men below would be able to hear their interchange. She rolled over onto her side and dutifully lifted her dress. He pushed her over onto her stomach and spread her legs with speed. He poked about to find his target. Pushing hard and fast, he entered her. Charlotte felt as if she had been stabbed with a knife. She shrieked and buried her face in her pillow. A painful fire burned inside her. Audley proceeded to push, rock, and moan.

Done quickly, he pulled out and rolled off her. Within minutes, he was snoring. Dear God, Charlotte questioned silently, am I damned to this life of pain? I have known paradise and now I am cast out. I shall pray for forgiveness, but in Your mercy do not let me suffer this forever. Her pillow was wet with tears. Her bedding was wet from him. She rose and found her way in the darkness to the wash basin to cleanse herself. Crawling back into bed after covering the wet area, she turned her pillow over and lay on her back. The darkness held ghosts shimmering pale before her eyes. She stared, trying to make out what they were, but they had no certain form. They were like wisps of smoke.

Finally, she fell asleep and began to dream. She walked through a rough-hewn stone corridor that ran into an underground cavern. She was searching for someone. People milled about in drab clothing. Their faces were the same hue as the rocks around them. A tall man stood in front of her, his back to her. He wore a black waistcoat and breeches. She reached out and touched his shoulder. He turned. It was James. He gazed at her kindly, but with no recognition in his eyes.

"James," she said in her dream, "it's me, Charlotte. I have been searching for you."

He smiled but did not respond.

"James," she pleaded, "I am well known to you. Please, do you remember me?" She became more agitated as he looked at her blankly. He was farther away now. She was losing him. His face and body were transforming. It was no longer him. "James!" she screamed. She stood, holding out her arms to him. "James do not abandon me! James!"

She awoke as something hot hit her face. Audley was peering at her, holding a candle close. Another drop of hot wax landed on her cheek.

"Ouch!" she cried and covered her face where the wax had fallen.

"Charlotte, are you ill? You were moaning and crying. Your thrashing about woke me up. I could not understand a damned bit of what you were mumbling.

"James… Audley. I am sorry I woke you. It must have been something I ate or perhaps the thin mountain air. Please, forgive me. Go back to your slumbers."

He peered at her questioningly. "James? You know, I do believe that was what you were saying. James was the name of that fellow at the villa, was it not? What ever happened to him? I had forgotten all about him."

"He was a pleasant enough man, but he left almost directly after you and Count Cesi had gone to Rome. He had some pressing business, I believe. You might ask the count. Sleep now, dear husband. You will be leaving in a few hours." She thought to herself, dear God, now I have added lying to my list of sins. I am lost.

"See if it might be possible, Charlotte, that you not pull the blankets off of me."

"I shall attempt to curb my restlessness. Forgive my disturbing you, Audley. Goodnight, husband."

"Goodnight, Charlotte." Audley placed the candle on the table and blew out the flame. He rolled on to his side and began to snore.

Charlotte lay trapped. She could not rise for fear of waking Audley and the others. Sleep was out of the question. What would Audley suspect if he heard James's name a second time? She lay paralyzed, her mind playing James's transformation again and again. The nightmare image finally evaporated as the first light of dawn began to make the interior of the chalet visible.

When Audley woke and dressed noisily, Charlotte feigned sleep. He kissed her gently on the head. "I am departing, wife. I pray you rest. Your nerves are overwrought."

Charlotte managed a hoarse whisper. "Adieu, Audley. May your hunting be successful."

As Audley came down the steps, he was greeted with hearty hellos and, Charlotte imagined, a few knowing winks from his companions. The group ate breakfast and was soon on its way.

Charlotte, for her part, pushed Audley's pillow off onto the floor and moved to the centre of the bed. She listened to the voices of the hunting party until they faded into the distance. Bird song replaced human voices, and she was thankful to be alone. The chalet would fill with afternoon sunlight before she stirred again.

She rose and dressed. Eating little, she opened the door to the outside. The scent of pine was overpowering. Looking up through the branches of the ancient oaks and tall pines, she saw blue sky. Beautiful as it was, she felt numb to her surroundings. After walking a little, she returned to the chalet and found that the caretaker had prepared a simple dinner for her. She picked at the food, but her restlessness drove her back outside, where she decided to follow one of the paths into the forest.

Flowers were everywhere. She gathered some, finding their colours and scents comforting, yet she could not prevent her mind from wandering to thoughts of James. Her body ached, and her steps became heavy. She sat down on a log, throwing her bouquet to the ground. What am I to do? I will not live another day like this. I cannot!

She stood up, drawn to a break in the trees. Coming closer, she saw a panorama of the lake below. I am damned as an adulteress and a liar. Yet I would do it all again. I am a fool.

Tears blurred her vision. Suddenly, she broke into a run

and, determined to destroy herself, she jumped over the edge. Too late, she saw the wide ledge some ten feet below the edge of the precipice. She hit it and cried out as her leg twisted beneath her. Off balance, she toppled backward, her head hitting the rock wall. Stunned, she lay there immobile. One clear thought materialized above the pain; God must surely be laughing at me, for I am an idiot.

She attempted to sit up. The back of her head was stinging. She looked up to the spot where she jumped from. It was not too far above to make a climb impossible. There were some outcroppings of rock and exposed roots that she might grab onto to pull herself up. A pain shot through her head. She was afraid to touch the wound for fear that it was bleeding. She managed to get on her hands and knees, but she made the mistake of lowering her head. She vomited.

Wiping her mouth on her dress, she struggled to her feet. She took care to favour the leg she had wrenched, supporting herself by leaning against the rock wall. Slowly, she began to climb.

Her head throbbed, and she was having difficulty seeing. It was as if someone painted a picture of the cliff and then ripped it into a hundred pieces. She tried desperately to keep those pieces together, to find her way. Finally, grasping a tree root, she pulled herself to the top. She rested on her stomach, covered in dirt and sweat. God no longer laughed. He was gone, having better places to spend His time. She was alone, blind, and reeking of vomit.

"Charlotte! Oh my God, what happened?" She felt her body being gently turned over and face caressed. She could not speak. The pain in her head made it impossible. She managed to open her eyes, and in one small corner of her vision she saw James.

"I fell," she whispered. "Forgive me."

"Quiet, my dearest. Do not trouble yourself to speak."

She tried hard to focus on him but even the small corner shattered. A million small lights played in front of her, then darkness.

Charlotte awoke with a terrible headache, but her vision had returned. She found herself in bed in the chalet. James lay next to her, asleep on top of the bed coverings. How she loved him! His arm on the far side was stretched up and across his forehead. His lips parted just a little, and a lock of his golden hair strayed down his cheek and rested by his mouth. She wished to kiss him, but when she attempted to move, pain stabbed at her body from her head to her legs. She moaned. James stirred but did not wake.

Perhaps I am dead, she mused to herself. God has granted my wish to be with James, except I shall be eternally in pain and never able to move again. With that thought, she fell back to sleep, hoping that tomorrow might be better.

In the morning, she found herself alone. Her head still ached but nothing compared to the previous day. Sitting up slowly, she placed her feet on the floor. Her leg was stiff and sore, but she was able to stand. Feeling faint, she sat back on the bed. The door below opened. She heard someone enter but was unable to see who it was. Charlotte wanted to call out but dared not, fearing it was the caretaker, or worse, Audley. She stood and made her way slowly to the top of the steps. There she stopped, not sure that she could get down without help. As she peered over the edge, James emerged from the back of the chalet. He carried a bouquet of flowers to the table.

He kept his back to her. "As you slept this morning, I

walked to the cliff. It is solid rock, and nowhere did I see evidence of the ground giving way."

"James," she said, "I feared I would never see you again."

He turned, looking up at her. He was not smiling. "Is that the reason you jumped, Charlotte?"

"Yes, it is." They stared at each other. He moved from the stairs and sat at the table.

His voice was distant and cold. "I could take you back to the cliff. The second time might be more successful."

His words shocked Charlotte. With difficulty, she retreated into a dark corner of the loft and sank to her knees. The next moment brought James flying up the stairs. He ran to her and lifted her to her feet.

"Never attempt such a selfish, dreadful act again. You are my life! What possessed you to do this?"

She looked at his red, sweating face. Veins stood out on his forehead. "Release your hold, sir."

He eased his grip. His face relaxed. She pulled her arms free. "You have no idea what I have endured since you departed. No idea of the humiliation and pain of performing my wifely duties, while every minute it was you I desired and loved. I yearned for your touch, not his, and in those moments what I feared most was that I would never again see you. That fear became truth. I knew you were lost to me." She stopped and gazed at his face. "Bereft of you, I wanted to die."

He put his arms around her. "I pledge to you that I shall always be near. Please, live. Live for our future together. I promise you that time will come."

Their first argument over, James helped Charlotte down the steps. When they finished breakfast, he invited her outside. "Are you fit enough to take the air? Our progress will be slow, I assure you."

Charlotte agreed. Walking outside with James at her side, she thanked God for the ledge. After a few minutes, she needed to rest, so they sat down on a fallen log. James appeared preoccupied.

They sat in silence, then he spoke. "Charlotte, do you recall when you and your mother paid me a visit on the Isle of Man?"

"I shall never forget it."

"What cause did Mrs. Chamier give you for my retreat to Man?"

"As I remember it, she said you suffered a most terrible shock during the campaign in Portugal."

"She said nothing else?"

"Only that there was a rift between you and your father, which Lady Bosworth hoped to mend."

"I was twenty-five when I went to the Colonies. I found the battles and skirmishes I took part in invigorating. Several months later, I was decorated for attempting to protect Wolfe at the Battle of Quebec."

Charlotte took James's hand and smiled. "It was just after that I saw you in Bath, James. You were the hero of the town. I saw you walking down the street in Hotwells and fell in love with you on the spot."

"Would that I had stayed in England, Charlotte, but duty bound me to fight in France. Then, General Burgoyne brought me to Portugal. My first battle there was against the Spanish forces that held the town of Vila Velha de Rodao. It was five days of fierce fighting. Then, on the sixth day we met no resistance. Exhausted, we entered the town unopposed and began searching from house to house.

Corpses lay everywhere. Rats fed freely on whatever they chose. The putrid smell that surrounded us defies description."

Charlotte, still holding James's hand, squeezed it gently.

He turned his head towards her, smiling slightly, before resuming his story. "My commanding officer was a rogue who had risen by cleverness and force of will through the ranks. On this occasion, I walked by his side as he called out in Portuguese, 'Come forward. Surrender. You will not be harmed. Come forward and we will feed you.' "

James paused, gathering strength to continue. "A small lad of five or six emerged from under a stairwell. He was barefoot, dirty, and dressed in rags. His eyes were open wide, pleading for any kindness we might show him. Before a word could escape my mouth, my superior drew his sword and slit the boy open. He fell at our feet, covering our boots with his warm blood. His murderer laughed.

"I was stunned. I turned and sought refuge in the first open door. The main floor was empty. I sat before the cold hearth for several minutes, trying to settle my stomach. My attention was drawn to a soft noise from upstairs. I climbed the steps and found a bedroom door ajar. I entered and saw a young woman laying on a narrow bed with a blanket covering her to her neck. She was beautiful in death. Then, I saw something move on her chest. Thinking it must be a rat, I drew my dagger. I pulled back the blanket ready to stab her attacker. It was an infant." James stopped, fighting back tears.

Charlotte touched his arm.

"A baby nursing at its dead mother's breast. Charlotte, I did not know what to do. I stared at this little one, flourishing with death all around it. I... covered it again and left it to die with its mother."

He wept, holding his face in his hands. Charlotte put her arms around him. He welcomed her touch.

At last, he continued. "I could not bring it out of that house. There was no one left to care for it, and my superior would have skewered it, leaving it to rot in the cold. We left that day. I prayed to God to let the child die peacefully.

"Two days later, we were overrun in a small valley just before dawn. We were sleeping, exhausted from lack of food and exposure to the cold. We were slow to rise when the first gunfire was heard. My friends and I struggled to get up, load our weapons and draw our swords. The enemy swarmed down upon us. I was struck a blow to the head and fell. When I came to, I could not move. At first, I thought perhaps I was paralyzed. In a panic, I thrashed about wildly. When I stopped, I realized I was covered by the bodies of my friends, now cold and stiff."

Charlotte shuddered.

James looked at her. "Forgive me. I am frightening you."

"Please, do not stop," Charlotte replied softly. "I want to hear it. I want to understand."

"My only thought was for survival, Charlotte, to escape somehow from the nightmare. I worked to push the bodies aside. They were heavy and bloated. My dearest friend, Anthony Burton, lay across my chest. When I managed to move him, I saw a gaping hole where his left eye had been. I crawled to the top of the pile of bodies. They were all slashed, gouged, dismembered. Across the field, arms and legs were reaching for the sky. Far down the valley, I saw scavengers, children and adults, picking over the bodies. Crawling towards the woods, I used the corpses to shield my retreat.

"When I finally reached the underbrush near the trees, I rested. I heard a noise ahead of me. I thought it was a scavenger, but I soon realized someone was moaning. One person is alive! Thank God, I rejoiced. One friend has survived, at least one. With as much strength as I could muster, I inched forward towards the sound." He stopped.

"Who was it, James?" Charlotte asked.

"My commanding officer," he replied, rage filling his face. "He was shot in the back. He heard my approach, and thinking me a scavenger, he raised his head and cried out, 'Please, take what you want. Don't kill me. I'll show you where the good pickings are. Help me. Help me stand. I'll show you the rich buggers.' Then his head dropped, and he began to moan. I crawled around to where he could see my face. I waited for his eyes to open. He cried out, 'Clarke, you!' I did not respond. Thinking of the boy's blood on my boots, I moved beyond him further into the woods. 'You can't leave me here, Clarke. I'm an Englishman!'

" 'Rot in Hell, Hawkes,' " I told him. I never looked back. "When I returned to England, I suffered for some time with melancholia. I was unable to conduct myself as I should in polite society. However, when you came to visit me on the Isle of Man, your innocence and beauty made me wish to be sane again. Thank you, Charlotte, for that gift."

They sat listening to the wind rush up the mountains through the tops of the trees. A gust hit them. Everything was still. James looked at her. "Please, let me die before you, Charlotte. Please, stay alive and light my world. I shall go mad, otherwise."

Charlotte held him in her arms.

He put his head on her breast, and she kissed the top of his head. They rose and walked to a secluded waterfall some distance from the path. The water cascaded down from the rocks above and created a large clear pool.

The afternoon had grown hot. James took off his clothes and dove into the water. Charlotte chose a dry rock by the edge and sat down, leaning back against the tree behind her. The pool was deep. James stayed underwater for a long time, then burst forth, gasping for air. He went under again.

Charlotte watched his white body glide just under the surface. Overcome with exhaustion, she fell asleep listening to the hum of the bees. Charlotte's slumber was disturbed by cold water dripping on her forehead. She opened her eyes and found James holding himself partly out of the water with one arm while he used his free hand to drop water on her. He grinned.

"How are you feeling?" he asked.

"Much better, thank you."

"Did you know these are volcanic mountains?" he asked, still smiling mischievously.

"No, I did not, James."

"Please address me as Jemmy, would you?"

"I shall, if you wish, but first you must tell me why you are smiling so broadly, James."

"I have a cure for your aches and pains, madam," he told her as he got out and shook the water off his body. He dried himself as best he could, dressed, and sat down beside Charlotte. "May I kiss you?" he asked.

"Please do, Jemmy."

It was a gentle kiss. He stood up. "Please come with me."

He led her up along the side of the waterfall. They followed the stream for many minutes until a clearing appeared ahead of them. Off to one side, there were three pools close together. Steam rose from their surfaces. There was soft grass and moss covering the floor of the clearing. James carefully undressed Charlotte. She offered no resistance. Her loose-fitting garments dropped away easily. He kissed her on the lips, then ran his tongue down her neck, biting her gently. She laughed.

His tongue continued down between her breasts and to her navel. He was on his knees now and his tongue explored between her legs. Her knees were weak, so she held onto his shoulders. He stopped, instructing her to lie down. She did so, and the soft grass felt like a silken pillow beneath her. He undressed and lay down beside her, caressing her and asking nothing in return.

Finally, her body trembled in the waves of an orgasm. Pulling him gently to her, she guided him to enter her body. She felt as if the centre of her being opened to receive him. A voice within her called out, share this place with me always. You are truly my husband, now and forever.

Afterwards they rested in each other's arms until the oncoming dusk made them realize the lateness of the hour. They slipped into the hot water of the pools and rolled over and over each other, barely touching. Getting out at last, they hurried back, not wishing to risk getting lost in the dark. As they reached the chalet, the first stars appeared, and the bats raced noiselessly over their heads.

That night brought a discussion of the future. They reaffirmed that Emma would be the intermediary for their correspondence, assuming she agreed. James needed to see to Count Cesi's business in Constantinople but would try and return to England in five months. Charlotte suggested that they might rendezvous at Whitestone in the north. She would find some excuse to travel there for a period of time, and James might stay with her there. He agreed and, taking her hand, kissed her fingers. She thought briefly of asking him when he had found out about the count's plan to take Audley on the hunting trip. He began to kiss her neck, and the thought seemed of no consequence.

They spent the next several days visiting their clearing and exploring the mountain. The dreaded day of Audley's return arrived. Charlotte felt numb and clung to James like a child. It was afternoon, a grey rain fell, and fog was settling over the chalet. James made ready to go.

"Please, Jemmy, make love to me one more time," she asked. He kissed her with more force than he had before. His tongue crowded her mouth. They pushed against each other, beginning to move clothes out of the way. Suddenly, they heard horses' hooves and the sound of men's voices.

"Oh, my God! They are back?" Charlotte whispered.

The lovers rushed out the front door as the horses and riders came into the stable yard behind the chalet. In the forest not far from the chalet, protected by the fog, they made love standing up. Awkwardly, James threw Charlotte's skirts over her head and approached her from behind. She braced herself against a tree and tried not to soil the front of her gown. The danger of the moment intensified their climax, and they stifled their cries. After, they stood with their arms around each other.

"I will love you always," she said, knowing there was no time for tears.

"And I love you, Charlotte. Do not doubt it."

She turned and walked toward the chalet, her steps

heavy.

James went in the opposite direction to where his horse was tethered. It had been agreed she would say she had been out walking, giving James time to slip away into the forest.

Charlotte reached the chalet door and opened it.

CHAPTER FIVE

Entering the chalet, Charlotte told herself to be on guard. It was a dangerous new world. She needed to be careful of what she said and did. If she wanted to keep her hope of a future with James alive, she would need to think through her actions. She saw the men sitting with their feet up, drinking and talking. Audley greeted her affectionately. He told her about their adventures, and the others joined in, adding details. Only the count was quiet as he watched her.

A bit later, she expressed her fatigue, said her goodnights, and ascended the steps. When she lit the candle at the bedside, she saw James had left his Irish whistle on her pillow. Glancing over her shoulder to be sure Audley hadn't followed her, she quickly tucked it away in the bag she'd packed for the journey the following morning.

They left the mountain the next morning and reached the villa at dusk. Audley's plan was to leave for Venice in two days' time and from there they would sail for England. On the day before they were to leave Bellagio, the count invited Charlotte to walk in the gardens with him. She looked to Audley for permission. He smiled and replied, "Please, take your time. I have some business to attend to and will join you in a bit."

Count Cesi and Charlotte walked outside. They discussed the weather, and she thanked him for his generosity and hospitality. When they were a distance from the villa, the count stopped and looked at Charlotte. "My dear Signora Pruitt, I have helped James because he loves you with a great passion. He is my dear friend, a brother to me. He saved my life when I thought all was lost. But have a care. He is subject to fits of madness. Please think carefully about your future together. I love James and would not speak ill of him. However, I fear he will die a young man and may take you with him, dear lady. I would be remiss if I did not warn you."

Charlotte was speechless. Her confusion made it impossible to articulate her thoughts. In that instant, she wished to defend James, run from the count's words, but also hear more of what he had to say. Finally, she replied, "I have chosen my path, and it will be with James Clarke for however long God may grant us."

"Then treat your husband kindly. He is a good man and speaks highly of you. I hope we will meet again, signora." He paused, smiled, and said, "And perhaps when James is no longer your amour you will cast an eye towards me." He raised an eyebrow and cocked his head to one side.

Charlotte laughed. "You are certainly unlike any man I have met before, dear Count. Please, let us return to the villa. I do not want Audley to grow anxious."

"Ah, Signora Pruitt, there is only one more vista I would have you see before you leave. Come, it is overlooking the lake." He motioned for her to follow. They walked past statues of lithesome maidens and winged cherubs. She stopped briefly to examine one which intrigued her. An old man with a beard was holding fast to a struggling cherub with one hand while with the other he was cutting the little fellow's wings. The Count, realizing Charlotte had lagged behind, turned to see what interested her. "It is 'Love Clipping Cupid's Wings'. Wonderful, is it not? But please, let us go."

They came to a series of steps leading to the lake. At the bottom hidden from the house, there was a bench on which to sit and admire the island villa in the distance. "It is beautiful, dear Count, but I should be returning to Audley." Charlotte was beginning to feel uncomfortable being alone with this man.

"Sit for a moment, signora. I will not stay. Reflect on what I have said as you look upon your island paradise. *Buonanotte,* dear Mrs. Pruitt. I shall see you in the morning before your departure." Charlotte turned to speak to him, but he had disappeared. It was a warm night. It would most likely be a cold and wet spring in England, but here, a beautiful summer's eve was settling over her enchanted isle. She felt lips on her neck and whirled around with her fist raised. How dare the count take advantage, she thought. James caught her arm before it hit his face.

"Well done! You could have knocked me down," he whispered.

"Jemmy, you came. You should not have. It is far too dangerous. Oh, but you came." She stood, and he caught her up in his arms. They kissed. Charlotte took a step back. "The Count called you a lunatic. Did you know that is what he thinks of you?"

"He is my friend, Lottie, but he adores you. I suppose he is not far off the mark. However, I am a loyal lunatic. I will see you in five months. I must go. I saw your husband looking for you." He kissed her again and disappeared.

"Ah, Charlotte, there you are. Such a beautiful evening, eh?" Audley remarked as he came down the steps. "Is all in order for our journey tomorrow, m'dear?" He stopped close to her but made no attempt to reach out.

"Yes, Audley, all is in order."

"Well, what would I do without you to keep my life in order, eh? You are a marvel, Charlotte, truly." He took a deep breath and exhaled noisily. After looking at the island, he remarked, "Unfortunate that I did not get over there. You did, did you not? Was it pretty? Certainly appears so from here. Not much to do, I suppose. Did you try your hand at fishing?"

"No, Audley, I did not fish."

"What did you do then, m'dear?"

"I ran naked through the gardens, husband."

"Charlotte! I believe it is past time we return to England. You are beginning to sound Venetian. Too much wine and sunshine, I suppose." He laughed. "Although, if the truth be told, I rather enjoyed it myself." Haltingly, he asked, "Did you... did you truly run naked, Charlotte?"

"Audley, no! I read poetry and took long naps. I am very rested."

"Excellent. Now it is time to retire for the evening," he announced and marched off in the direction of the villa. Charlotte followed, stopping briefly to peer into the shadows. No one was there.

Charlotte and Audley left early the next morning. As their coach climbed up and out of the valley, Charlotte tried to hide her sadness by feigning sleep. Audley watched the passing landscape and hummed to himself. When they reached Venice, they were greeted by Countess Cittidini, who was sitting on her balcony doing intricate needlework.

She answered all of Charlotte's questions regarding the masquerade. When at last Audley retired to take care of his business affairs, Countess Cittidini turned the discussion in another direction. "You have fallen in love. Your cheeks have a redness about them, and you walk with the confidence of a woman who knows how to give and to receive love. Is he Venetian?"

"No, Countess, an Englishman."

"Ah, well done. Speaking the same language may help fend off misunderstandings. Though in my experience, not being able to use words enables one to arrive more quickly at what one wants." She winked at Charlotte as Audley entered the room. He thanked the countess for her gracious hospitality, then informed Charlotte that they would be sailing the next day.

Charlotte generally travelled well on the sea, her journey to the Isle of Man being an exception. When they left Venice, she was enjoying the movement of the swells beneath her. However, by the second week of the voyage, she began to be ill every morning and afternoon. These bouts came with such regularity that she now believed she was with child. She prayed to God that it was James's child. How could it be otherwise? But how would she ever know, and if it was too obvious a resemblance, would Audley suspect that he was a cuckold? She recalled her attempted suicide. What if her impetuous behaviour had caused harm to the child? All her anxiety caused her to feel more ill. She took to her bed as the sea heaved and rolled.

Audley entered the cabin fresh from his morning walk of the deck. Charlotte held tightly to a bowl, certain she would vomit with the next wave. "My dear Charlotte, you are white as a sheet. This is not like you at all."

"Husband, it is not seasickness."

"What else could it be but that?"

"I believe I am with child." She closed her eyes as the nausea swept over her.

"This is a blessing, Charlotte, a magnificent blessing!" Audley exclaimed, clearly elated. He kissed the top of his wife's head.

Charlotte prayed he would always think so.

The last few days of the voyage were calmer, though Charlotte continued to feel ill. She was relieved and happy to reach London, their house, and her beloved garden. It had been a month since she'd seen James. She prayed all was going well for him and hoped that she might have received some word of his whereabouts. Visiting Emma, she told her in strictest confidence most of what had happened in Bellagio.

Emma was delighted that her friend was so happy, but she warned, "Charlotte, you must be careful. What if Audley were to find out?"

"He will not, Emma. I promise. But will you be my confidante in this affair? James will send his letters to you, and perhaps, if we need a place to meet, might we use your house?"

"Charlotte, I am shocked at this wanton behaviour," Emma teased. "Rest assured I shall help you in whatever way I can."

Six weeks passed, and Charlotte received no word from James. London became dry and dusty. It was the hottest summer in memory. Late one afternoon, as Charlotte sat in her garden working on her needlepoint, Audley appeared, perspiring and red-faced.

Charlotte rose and went to him, concerned at his

appearance. "What troubles you so, husband?"

"Today, Charlotte, I discovered my supposed friend, Charles Hamill, is attempting to steal away my custom at court. If he succeeds, I stand to lose a great deal of money. I am appalled at his deceit. I have always been fair in my dealings with him. I even lent him money once when his business was faltering, and he returns my good will by stabbing me in the back. I will not endure such foul treatment." Audley shook with anger as he spoke.

"Audley, could there be some possible explanation? Perhaps your informant is mistaken."

"Charlotte, I have it on good authority that he has betrayed me. There is no doubt about it. It is his betrayal that wounds me. I will not endure it!" he cried, striking his fist on the table. His anger terrified Charlotte. She could only imagine what he might do if he should ever discover her secrets.

The next day Charlotte paid a visit to Emma. As she entered the drawing room Emma hurried to her and pressed a letter in her hand. "You have been waiting for this, I believe, dear friend."

"Oh, Emma!" Charlotte's face flushed as she opened the letter with trembling hands.

Dearest, dearest Lottie,

How I wish you were here with me. I have been bereft since last I beheld you in the garden. My travels have taken me far, going first by horseback from Bellagio to Brindisi where I boarded a ship and sailed to Athens. What a marvellous city of ruins. Someday, if God allows, I shall take you on a journey there. Next, I sailed to Constantinople. It was here I met with several Turks and did the count's business without incident.

I have only now arrived back in Bellagio. Tonight, I rest on our island. I am in the garden. All the flowers are in bloom. It is a profusion of reds, pinks, and yellows. Close your eyes, my angel, and imagine. Imagine my lips on your lips.

I shall be here for another month, then Count Cesi and I will journey to Paris. I must attend to some personal matters there, after which I shall leave for London. I hope to see England by the beginning of October. If it is still your desire to see me, would you arrange a meeting place? Perhaps Lady Emma would help secure a safe haven. I shall speak with her as soon as I arrive. And what of Whitestone? I long to spend weeks with you, not just stolen hours.

I pray I still have your affections. My life is with you. Dear God, how I yearn to see you.

Yours forever,
James

Charlotte closed her eyes and imagined the feel of his fingers touching her face. Her left hand ran over her stomach, which had begun to swell ever so slightly. Oh Jemmy, she wondered, how ardent will your love be now? She had written three letters to him, which she hoped he received at Bellagio. She did not tell him about the child, however. She wished him to see the baby and know it was his. Now he would see her first, the child not yet revealed. What would he think?

As for Whitestone in the north, she had broached the subject of a visit to Cumberland on two occasions with Audley. The first time was on the boat as they sailed home, and the second was only yesterday. Both times, she met with resistance. His last words on the subject were, "Charlotte, you have a preoccupation with that damned place. It is wet, cold, and barren as far as I understand. I think this pregnancy has made you a bit mad. If you must go there, make your arrangements, but I shall not accompany you." He left the room complaining of her attachment for such a godforsaken country.

Charlotte was ecstatic. She wrote directly to Mrs. Mungris, the housekeeper at Whitestone, to let her know that she might be visiting in the near future. Now that she received the letter from James, her thoughts were racing as to when she might go north.

Slowly, her thoughts returned to the present, and she became aware that Emma was watching her. "Dearest Emma, forgive me, the contents of this letter sent my thoughts flying."

"You are forgiven. Come sit beside me," Emma said, motioning for Charlotte to sit next to her on the settee. Charlotte obeyed and told her friend what James had written and how she planned to travel to Whitestone. "Please, Charlotte, be very careful. I shall do my best to alert you if your husband decides to join you. Please, do not take too many risks. I understand that you adore James, but you have the baby to think of and your standing in Society. Taking a lover quietly can be done, but you are too ardent. It is dangerous. Your feelings will not be easily hidden. You must understand that James may not be the most constant of lovers."

"Not constant! What do you mean, Emma? What is it that you know and have not told me?"

"Surely, Charlotte, you cannot forget how he was on the Isle of Man. He is unpredictable, and I do not know that a madness such as his is ever banished."

"But if you could have seen how he was at Bellagio. I am sure that he is recovered." Charlotte spoke with conviction, and yet Emma's words made her recall James's outburst at the chalet and his sullenness on the island.

"There is more. I have reason to believe, Charlotte, though it comes by way of rumour, that James married a woman in France after his transfer there. She still may live. I have not heard anything to the contrary."

"No! No!" Charlotte responded vehemently.

"Charlotte, he is going to France. He wrote that in the letter."

"But he is with Count Cesi."

"So he says, dear friend. Please, I only ask that you be cautious in this affair," Emma pleaded.

Charlotte sprang to her feet, desperate to be out of the room. She could not see for tears blinded her. She ran from the house, sobbing and out of breath. Emma rushed after her, calling her name. When she caught up, Charlotte gasped and dropped to her knees as pain shot through her abdomen. She lay crumpled in a ball, writhing on the grass. Emma called for the servants and tried to soothe Charlotte's distress.

Charlotte began crawling away. "Emma, he is my life! He is my life! It cannot be true. It is a lie!" She cried out again and held her stomach. "My baby, oh my God, my baby! Help me, Emma." With that, the pain overwhelmed her, and she fainted.

A haze of fog swirled in front of Charlotte's eyes. As it began to clear, she found herself lying on her mother's bed, a baby crying next to her. She looked at it closely. Its mouth was huge, and two small teeth showed in its gums. She could do nothing to quiet it. The baby began to shrink until all that was left were two bloody spots on the bed coverings. Charlotte ran to her father for help but when he turned it was not her father, but James. He peered at her with dead eyes. She reached out to him, but he did not respond. She tried to speak but found she had no voice.

Slowly, Charlotte came to consciousness. She was in her bedroom. The curtains were drawn, but sunlight came in around the edges. She moved her head to the side and found Audley sitting by the bed. He was asleep with his head on his chest. Charlotte's pain had been replaced by a tremendous fatigue that made it difficult to move or speak. With great effort, she put her hand on her stomach. Dear God, she prayed, please, be with my baby. Do not take it from me. I know I am a terrible sinner, but I love this child. Please, help me. Please, forgive me. Amen. And though she knew her sin was great, her next thought was for James. What if it was true? If there was another woman, what would she do?

A few hours later, the doctor visited and commanded her to stay in bed. She must not move for the next four weeks, he said, or she would surely lose the baby. Audley was attentive and affectionate. Every day, he brought her sweets and read to her. He encouraged her to be brave and follow the doctor's directions. He dried her tears and kissed her gently on the forehead. She began to see Audley in a new way and looked forward to his coming home to be with her. Time passed, and the baby grew inside her. She was thrilled by the first flutters of movement and attempted to describe them to her husband. He listened attentively.

After four weeks of rest, she was allowed to rise and move about with caution. Emma came to visit.

She was subdued, and after tea she said, "Dear Charlotte, I am so truly sorry about your condition. I would never have said a word had I known how it would cause you to suffer. Please, forgive me." She began to cry softly and put her pocket handkerchief to her eyes.

Charlotte went to Emma and put her arm around her. She reassured her friend that she was much stronger now. She shared with Emma about the movements of the baby and how Audley was attentive to her needs. When she finished, Emma smiled and looked away.

Turning back, she took Charlotte's hand. "I have another letter for you. It arrived two weeks ago, but I hesitated to bring it. I hope I have not erred again, but I felt it important that you should receive it."

Lightheaded, Charlotte took the letter and tucked it quickly into her sleeve. "Thank you, dear friend. I cannot tell you the countless hours I've spent attempting to read between the lines of his last letter. I must speak with him, Emma. I have decided to carry through with my plan to see him at your house, if you are still amenable to that. My visit to Whitestone is not possible. The doctor told me such a journey could prove fatal to myself and my child."

They finished their visit, and after Emma left, Charlotte walked slowly up the stairs to her room. There was still some time before Audley would come home. She closed the door to the bedroom and walked to the window overlooking her garden. Audley recently had it planted with sixteen new rose trees, pinks and whites, in hopes of lifting her spirits. A voice inside her was urging her to destroy James's letter. Let go of this infatuation, it cried, and live a normal life. You are going to be a mother. You need your strength for that, not this madness for a man you hardly know. She sat down on the edge of the bed and held the letter for several minutes. Finally, she tore it open and read the contents.

Dearest Lottie,

I received your letters, all three at the same time. What joy I feel when I read them! My dearest, your letters bring me so close to you. I fear I am not the writer I should like to be. I think about you every waking moment, but when I sit to put pen to paper, I am a man without the words I need or want to express all I feel. Forgive me.

The Count and I are on our way to Paris. In about two weeks, I should be able to leave for England. I must travel into the countryside to the village of Barbizon. After that, my business shall be finished, and I will fly to your side. I will see you soon, my love.

I shall contact Lady Emma upon my arrival. I had hoped I might hear from you one more time, but I understand how difficult it must be for you.

You are my angel and my salvation.

Until I see you, I am, as always, your servant,
James

Charlotte rested the letter on her lap. She was numb. She read it again and felt nothing. What business had he in Barbizon, she wondered? She could not remember his face, no matter how much she concentrated. How could she see him now? Anger replaced numbness. She would not see him! The baby fluttered inside her and all her rage disappeared. It was his baby, she knew that. James's child.

Suddenly, her lover's sweet face filled her vision. She recalled how his hair smelled, warmed by sunlight in the garden. She felt his touch as he held her in his arms and caressed her body. All her need and desire for him returned, and she longed to see him. What would they do? She needed to talk to him, to understand what had taken place in his past. She wished they could flee to Whitestone, but it was not possible. Life was impossible. She felt like a petulant child and her stomach began to ache. She calmed herself. James would be there in a week's time. She would simply have to wait, she told herself.

A week passed, and on the morning Charlotte hoped would bring his return, the birds were singing outside her window when she woke. She found it difficult to open her eyes. Pushing herself up and out of bed, she walked stiffly to her garden windows and sat down. She felt tired and puffy. Leaning forward, she opened the centre window and the scent of roses wafted in on a warm breeze. He will come to me today, she thought, and what will he find? There was a part of her that hoped he might turn and run away when he saw her in such a state. She realized she had a choice in all this, too. But it would be so much easier if she did not have to be the responsible one. When had she ever been responsible? Her life had always been comfortable. She had been taken care of by her parents and then by Audley. Her life sailed along like a ship, yet she was not the captain.

No, she thought to herself, I have been impetuous and wilful. Those qualities have brought me to this hour in my life. Another voice countered, wait, you were in love. James brought you to life. You shared moments of ecstasy. And now I retch, and my belly swells daily. Where is the joy in that?

COLLEEN KELLY-EIDING

She knew the answer as she touched her rounded belly. The new life there filled her with joy and contentment.

She lifted her nightdress and let the sunlight fall warm upon her middle. The last two weeks, she had grown bigger, and there was no hiding her condition. Her clothes grew tight and her feet no longer fit in her shoes. She stood and let the nightdress fall to the floor. Walking to the mirror, she looked to see the changes. Her hair fell to the middle of her back as always, but it was thicker and redder than before. Her breasts were fuller. They had swollen soon after she discovered she was pregnant. She was proud of their fullness. Her buttocks were still firm, but her hips were getting wider.

She heard Audley's footsteps and quickly put on her nightdress. He knocked, and she bade him enter. They each had their own bedchamber. Audley, being older when they married, had a set routine and enjoyed his privacy. He would read or conduct business late into the night. He rose early as well to write in his journal or review the company's accounting. At first, Charlotte felt excluded but now was thankful to have her own dressing room and a bedchamber that overlooked the garden.

"Good morning, m'dear. I have a surprise for you."

"Pray, tell me before you burst."

"I have planned a week's holiday for us both. We shall be going to visit Aunt Polly." He smiled broadly as he gave her the news.

"Audley, you know how I treasure our visits to your dear Aunt Polly, but I do not know what the doctor may think of my making such a journey. The carriage bounces so dreadfully even though the road to Broadway is much improved of late. And what of your business?" Charlotte

85

asked, trying to hide her panic.

James will be here, she was thinking as she spoke. I must see him. And to spend seven days listening to Audley's hunting stories, playing cards with Aunt Polly, who cheats openly, and being mauled by her five dogs in the bargain, I shall go mad. Charlotte smiled at her husband.

"Oh tosh, m'dear, I took the precaution of speaking with Dr. Rumsey, and he is of the opinion that it will do you a world of good. Besides, Lord Carleton invited me to the hunt." With that, he turned away from her and looked out the window.

Oh, this is brilliant, she thought, I shall be burdened with Aunt Polly while he goes riding with the hounds. She smiled pleasantly. "Dearest," she offered, "please do not refuse Lord Carleton's offer. Lord and Lady Carleton's custom would be invaluable. Your prowess as a rider and hunter are not to be outdone. You must go, I insist, but as for me, I prefer to stay and rest in the comfort of our home."

Audley turned back to her, relief showing on his face. "Charlotte, you are a dear. Aunt Polly will be sadly disappointed, but she will understand, I am quite sure of it. This will afford me the opportunity of accepting the invitation of Lord and Lady Carleton to stay as their guest at Avonside. An excellent idea of yours, dear wife, an excellent idea." He kissed Charlotte on the cheek and left to see to his packing.

Charlotte dressed at her leisure with Betsy's help and went to her garden. The smell of the roses was overpowering. Her nose reacted, and she wished she might scratch the inside of her skull. Despite her discomfort, she chose several buds that were nearly ready to bloom and cut their stems. She noticed a few tiny bugs crawling in and out of sight amongst the petals. Watching them, she wondered how complicated their lives were. Her thoughts were interrupted by Audley, who came to bid her good-bye. They kissed, and he was on his way.

No sooner had he gone than a footman was announced, who presented a note from Emma. She requested Charlotte's presence for tea that afternoon at her house in Grosvenor Square. Charlotte instructed the footman to tell Lady Emma she would be there.

Was this the hour of her reckoning, she wondered? Her stomach churned, and her palms were damp. Knowing she wouldn't be able to walk the distance to Emma's, she called for her sedan chair, hastily throwing the roses aside and leaving the little bugs among the wilting petals.

CHAPTER SIX

As the servants made their way through the crowded streets carrying her chair, Charlotte tried to calm herself. Was he there? She could not breathe. Close your eyes, she told herself. Take a breath. Yet when her eyes closed, she saw James standing before her, staring at her with lifeless eyes. She started. Why am I going to him? Her chair halted. The chairmen rested it on the ground and helped Charlotte down. Emma's door opened, and her friend rushed to greet her.

"Dearest, come in," Emma greeted her and cheerfully offered Charlotte her arm.

Charlotte took it gladly, leaning against her friend, not sure that her legs would support her. No sooner had she stepped in the door than it was closed behind her. Emma disappeared, and Charlotte was grabbed up into James's arms. He carried her into the drawing room, set her down, and hastily closed the door. They kissed; their mouths open wide as if to devour each other, their hands moving over each other's bodies as if to reassure themselves that each other was real. Suddenly, James stopped and looked questioningly at Charlotte, his hand on her swollen abdomen.

"I am with child, James."

"With child?" he echoed her, looking at her belly

"Yes, and it is yours. I am quite certain of it."

"Mine, yes, of course, but could it be Audley's?"

"It could," she responded, her heart sinking as he backed away a small step

"Charlotte, you should have written me." He furrowed his brow and then smiled broadly. "I would have come post haste!" He lifted her up into his arms, kissed her soundly, then gently put her down. "I am a father?! It is mine... ours? Oh, my God, Charlotte..." He sank to his knees and wept.

Charlotte sat on a chair near him. He moved to her and buried his face in her skirts. She stroked his hair. Charlotte was filled with peace in his presence. She felt complete and wished that she would never have to move from this spot. She loved him now and would love him forever.

At last, he looked up at her. His nose was red, and his eyes still held tears. "Charlotte, we must be together. What are we to do?"

Gazing into his face, she knew he was all hers. Here he was, wanting to create a life together, to be with her and be the father of her child. But in one corner of her mind a small doubt festered. "James, I would sacrifice my life to be with you, but I must know..." She stopped. It was too difficult to speak.

"What is it, Charlotte?" he asked quietly.

"Are you married?"

He cast his eyes down and sat quietly for several seconds, then he drew a breath. "No, I am not married, but I was. She died in childbirth, and the babe died with her. I went to Barbizon to place markers on their graves. I'd had to wait a long time to do that, but it is done now, and I pray for their peace. Doing Count Cesi's business in

Constantinople brought me more wealth than I expected. That is the good news." He paused, smiling seductively. "Charlotte, I want to gaze upon your marvellous belly that holds our future. Take me in, my angel, and give me a home." He played with the edge of her skirts as he sat at her feet.

"James?" she cried out, laughing as she stood up. He caught her round the ankle, and holding fast, made his way under her petticoats. "James! Please, not here. Emma has offered us a bedroom. James!" she whispered loudly as he kissed and licked her thigh. She breathed in deeply. "Sir, I am going to sit down, and I do not give a damn what the servants see or hear."

From underneath her skirts a muffled response could be heard. "Please do, madam." So, she sat. A few minutes later she was flushed and panting. Her ecstasy grew as he advanced up her thighs and brought her to fruition. He uncovered his head and inquired, "Did ye miss me, lass?"

"Aye," she gasped. "Aye, that I did, Jemmy."

"Shall we take tea or find the bedchamber?"

"I think, perhaps, tea, sir, if you are so inclined." Charlotte dabbed her perspiring forehead with her pocket handkerchief.

They found Emma in the garden at her needlework. "Becoming reacquainted, are we?" she asked, raising an eyebrow at Charlotte's flushed cheeks.

"Yes, thank you," Charlotte answered as James smiled.

"I shall have tea sent up to the dressing room, my dears. All the servants then will find themselves sent on errands. I, unfortunately, must go for a visit to Lady Bradwell's. She has been taken ill and needs my company. You shall have the house to yourselves. I dare say you will find ways to occupy yourselves." She excused herself and left.

In a brief time, the house was deserted. "Lord, madam, but I am feeling fatigued," James said, stretching. "Do you suppose there might be a place to rest? Shall we search out our room, you and I?" He yawned and rubbed his eyes.

"It is most likely your long journey, sir, that has fatigued you. Come, I know just the place for you to rest your head." She took his hand and led him towards the stairs. Slowly, they ascended, James one step behind Charlotte holding on to her hand. When they reached the top, he stopped, and she turned to him. He let go of her hand and reached out to touch her face. He ran his fingers across her forehead, over her eyes and down her cheek. Gently, he guided her lips to his and kissed her.

"Charlotte, run away with me. We will go back to Italy. We shall have fifteen children. We shall claim Count Cesi's island for our own and call it New Jamestown or Charlottesburg. What do you think?"

"I think you should come with me to our chamber. Please, we will plan our future, but not now, when we have a moment to ourselves. Please, come with me," she pleaded.

"No," he said and sat down at the top of the stairs.

She stood behind him. "Very well, sit if you must." She took off her stomacher and dropped it over his shoulder and into his lap. He started at this unexpected event and turned to stare at her.

"Charlotte, I am astonished at such behaviour!" he said with mock sternness.

"I suppose, then, that I should not do this, either." She said as she took off her robe and skirt. She moved close to the bedchamber Emma had prepared for them, beckoning him to come.

"Most certainly not!" he called out as he rose to follow her.

She reached the door and began to open it. He stopped her. "You know, I have had a damnable time getting my shirt off lately. I wonder if I might impose on you to help?" She nodded, undoing the lace at his chin and beginning to untie it. She kissed each new area of skin that was exposed until the shirt was taken off and fell to the floor. The rest of their clothing came off so quickly that when they next became aware of their surroundings, they were lying naked on the floor five feet from the bed. James made a pillow for Charlotte out of his waistcoat. She lay on her back, and he sat beside her, surveying her changed form.

"Your breasts are magnificent. And the curve of your belly…" He ran his hand gently over it, admiring its round tautness. He bent forward and kissed her navel. "Hello, my little one. I am so pleased that you are there."

Charlotte watched James as he caressed her stomach and spoke to their unborn child. Why, she asked herself, did she hesitate when he asked her to run away? Because she did not wish to consider the future, she thought. She wished only that this moment would last forever.

"James, you have beautiful hands." He smiled but did not divert his attention from his explorations of her body. She watched his hands. They were large, with long fingers. He moved them now up over her stomach and to her breasts. She took one of his hands and began to suck on his fingers. He closed his eyes and smiled.

"Charlotte, come to bed with me."

"The floor is hard," she replied.

"Yes, and I am not as young as I used to be. Are you

able to walk, lass? I could attempt to carry you, but you are not as light as you used to be." With that, he sprang to his feet and jumped onto the bed.

"James Clarke!" Charlotte shouted and jumped on top of him. They wrestled playfully until at last they lay cradled in each other's arms.

The next two days were glorious. Charlotte wrote a note to Mr. Primm, the butler at Bellagio House that she would be staying a few days with Lady Emma, so the lovers were able to hide away for long hours together undisturbed, making love, talking about their pasts and planning their future.

The third day was cold and dark. It seemed as if the sun never really rose. The rain was pounding down when Charlotte rose and left James to sleep undisturbed while she had breakfast with Emma. Afterwards, she returned to see if he was awake, but still he slept. She closed the door and lay down with him. Just as she began to drift off, she felt James sit up. Before she had time to realize what was happening, he grabbed hold of her and began to shake her violently. She pulled away and quickly got off the bed. He stared wildly at her, then jumped up and ran from the room. Stunned, she sat on the bed for a few minutes, trying to regain her composure.

When he did not return, she decided to look for him. There was a cane in the corner of the room. She took it in case she needed to defend herself. He seemed to be nowhere in the house, so she found Emma and told her what had transpired. Together, they searched outside. The last place they looked was the stables on the mews. The horses were agitated, which caused the women to be cautious.

In the half-light, they made out his shape, huddled in the corner of a stall. He was dazed and shivering. They wrapped a blanket around him, and he came without resistance back into the house. Once in bed, he fell asleep for the rest of the daylight hours. On waking, he had no recollection of the day's events. Charlotte and Emma decided they would wait until the next day to question him. That night, Charlotte stayed at Emma's but did not sleep with James. She looked in on him often through the night.

Very early in the morning, she came to his room and found him awake. A candle burned, and his eyes were open.

"What is troubling you, James?"

"I cannot stay, Charlotte."

"Why?"

"I am a threat to you and to the child. Death is very close, and I am afraid that he may knock upon my door and find you."

"James, why now? I do not understand."

James rose from the bed and began to dress. "I dreamed I was walking in a green field. There were stones protruding from the ground. As I drew close to them, I saw they were grave markers. On the first, I read your name and on the next, was the babe's. I must go, Charlotte. I endanger you by staying."

Charlotte's body grew numb as he spoke. "Wait, my love, until the sun rises. Daylight will help us to see clearly. Please, I cannot think. It is madness for you to leave. It was a dream. Do not go."

She ran to him and grabbed at the clothes he was putting on. He stopped and looked at her coldly.

"Do not get in my way," he ordered.

She refused to obey, and a tug of war ensued. James

became more and more agitated. Finally, he lost control and slapped her forcefully across the face. The blow sent her to the floor, her shoulder hitting first with an explosion of pain. When her vision cleared, she realized she was alone.

Managing to get to her feet, she ran to the window just in time to see James riding wildly through the garden. His horse galloped full speed towards the far wall as he beat it with a crop. He will be killed, she thought, but at the last moment, the horse jumped, clearing the wall. James was gone.

Charlotte sat down on the window seat. The room was cold and damp. The first light of morning revealed the disaster that had taken place. Clothes and bedcoverings were strewn everywhere. As she fell, Charlotte had pulled the tablecloth off the washstand, and the bowl and pitcher were smashed. She realized she was bleeding from a gash in her arm. The sleeve of her nightdress was soaked with blood that spilled onto the window seat. Emma was a sound sleeper, but the servants were not. They roused her, and she now rushed into the room.

"Charlotte, my God, what has he done?"

"He is gone, Emma. I have lost him forever. He is quite mad," Charlotte cried as she fell into her friend's arms.

The next few days Emma tried to keep Charlotte's spirits up as she recovered from the shock she had suffered. At last, Audley was to come home, so Charlotte said her good-byes and returned to Bellagio House. It was quiet at her home, and Charlotte enjoyed walking in her garden and listening to the birds sing. After a nap in her room, she ate a light dinner and picked a bouquet of flowers to greet Audley with when he returned home. One of the servants disturbed her to say that a footman had just arrived with a message from Lord Carleton. Charlotte hurried into the hallway where the young man in fine livery handed her a letter. Thanking him, Charlotte retired to the parlour where she sat down and read its contents.

Avonside
Dear Mrs. Pruitt,

I fear this letter brings you ill tidings. Your husband, Mr. Pruitt, has met with an accident. Yesterday, while riding, he attempted to jump the River Avon. He lost his seat. The doctor has determined that his shin is broken. Please, do not be troubled, as he is at present resting comfortably. However, I believe he needs your gentle touch to help in his recovery. Please, come as swiftly as you might, given your delicate condition. I have taken the liberty of sending my coach. It is at your disposal. I pray it will help to make your journey both pleasant and comfortable.

Yours with most sincere regards,
Lord Carleton

Without hesitation, Charlotte prepared to leave and was soon off to Avonside. Despite the protestations of Lord and Lady Carleton, Charlotte insisted that Audley be moved to Aunt Polly's residence. There, they stayed for six weeks. Lord Carleton sent his personal physician daily to look in on Audley. The October rains soaked the countryside making even a walk down the lane impossible. November arrived, chilling them as they hovered around the parlour's hearth, warming only those parts of their bodies that happened to be facing the fire.

Charlotte tried to stay cheerful for Audley's sake. He was terribly embarrassed at having fallen off his horse, so much so that he would barely speak of it. Charlotte suspected he had been touting his riding prowess to the ladies on the hunt before the accident happened, but she did not question him about it. After a few weeks, his sense of humour returned, and he was less morose.

During this time, Charlotte received five letters from Emma, but there was no mention of James. Charlotte prayed that he was safe. At last, in the middle of November, the doctor pronounced Audley fit to travel home. He was walking with the help of a cane and was eager to get back to his business. They thanked Aunt Polly. She cried as they left, though Charlotte suspected she was probably happy to have her house to herself again.

Two days after they arrived home, Charlotte went to visit Emma. After tea, Emma presented Charlotte with a letter. "It is from Elizabeth, James's sister. She and I have been close friends for years. She is a widow and lives in Chagford in Devon, caring for her parents and overseeing the running of the family estate, Kirkmoor, where I spent several summers as a child. Read the letter, Charlotte. It has news of James, but be prepared, it is not happy news." Charlotte opened the letter with trepidation.

Kirkmoor, Devon
My Dearest Emma,

I received your letter inquiring after my brother and must tell you of the strange events that have lately occurred. Three weeks ago, on a particularly cold night, we were awakened by the dogs barking at a commotion in the stable yard. When I reached the yard,

I discovered my brother, James. His appearance was frightful. His clothes were torn and dirty. I believe he had not eaten a decent meal in days. I took him into the house and called for supper. He spoke only a few words, just enough to request he be allowed to stay in a small cottage we have some distance from the house. It is the one that you and I used to think was haunted. Do you remember? I attempted to convince him to stay in the house, in his own room, but he refused. He insisted he needed privacy and only the cottage would do. I agreed. He would not even allow us to tidy it up but moved in straight away. He has allowed no one in it since.

We rarely see him. Food is left outside his door. He takes it in when no one is about and leaves the dishes outside his door when he is done. He has started riding out on horseback before dawn and not returning until after dark. His gaunt, unshaven face frightens me. You are well aware of the times as a child when he heard voices. Remember how angry my mother would get with his insistence that he was surrounded by spirits? She called it nonsense. He drove her mad, staring off into space and occasionally answering the voices as they spoke to him. But now, dear Emma, it is me he drives mad. I cannot reach him. He is an absolute stranger to me. He is trapped in some other world, pursued by terrible forces akin to the Furies. What shall I do?

There was other news in Elizabeth's letter, but Charlotte read and reread the news of James. She thanked God he was alive, even if he was mad. Her mind searched for some way that she and Emma could contrive to make a visit to Devon. Christmas was a month away. She wondered if it was possible to go before the baby arrived. Perhaps, she thought, the sight of their baby growing in her belly would bring him out of his despondency. She asked Emma to write immediately to Elizabeth and suggest an invitation for the two of them. She waited anxiously for the reply, but when it came, it was a resounding no, accompanied by an apology and explanation. The family was so upset by James's behaviour that they could not possibly entertain visitors, even though Emma was a treasured friend of the family. Elizabeth assured Emma that she would keep in close contact and relay any news of James's illness.

Christmas came and went. Charlotte and Audley began to prepare in earnest for the arrival of the baby. The nursery was decorated. Audley designed a beautiful cradle and crib and had them built by a well-known cabinet maker in Westminster. Charlotte employed two seamstresses to make the baby clothes and decorated them with her own needlework. With each stitch, she prayed for a good delivery and a healthy baby. James's illness was never out of her thoughts. She asked God to spare her child the agony its father was experiencing.

In mid-January, there was a brief letter from Elizabeth, saying only that James was no better. Charlotte vowed that when the baby was old enough, invitation or not, they would travel to Devon.

Meanwhile, Charlotte searched for a wet nurse for the baby. She interviewed several prospective women but found none to her liking. She was of a mind to nurse the baby herself, but Audley was shocked by the idea. What well-born lady, he asked her, would entertain such a thought? Charlotte insisted that she would not have some unknown woman take her baby to her breast. The country women she knew in Rosthwaite gave suck to their children, and they lived to be healthier and stronger than any of the sickly city children she had seen. Finally, Audley relented and agreed. Another argument occurred over the choice of a nurse.

Just north of Spital Square, not far from Charlotte and Audley, there was a family of weavers who had been with Charlotte's father for many years, first in Coventry and now in London. The grandfather, Michael Rourke, had been a master weaver of renown. He had two sons. The oldest, Donald, was an excellent master weaver, in his own right. The younger, Patrick, had neither the patience nor the talent of the elder brother but did have a good business sense and knew how to bargain. On moving to London, Donald and his family settled in a house in Fleur de Lis Street. The workshop was on the top floor, as they all were in Spitalfields. The floorboards were of double thickness to keep the sounds of the looms from disturbing the inhabitants below.

Donald Rourke married Jane Young of a Huguenot family in Coventry, and they had seven children. The oldest two, Annie and Betty, had been trained as throwers, spinners, and finally weavers, even though women were not always allowed to do such work. The boys, Luke, Stephen, Ralph, Michael, and Duncan, when old enough, would learn to weave as well. Annie also took care of her brothers a good part of the day to allow their mother to help their father.

When Audley and Charlotte returned from Italy, they were shocked to learn that Annie had met with an accident. Michael, who was two years old, had run out of the house just as a coach raced up the street. Annie rushed to grab her brother and in doing so, tripped and fell. Three fingers of her right hand were crushed under the heavy wheels. Her uncle, Patrick, ran after the coach, but when it finally stopped, the lord who rode in it refused to take any responsibility. Luckily, the crowd who gathered to see the confrontation was able to prevent Patrick from attacking the man. The family despaired. Annie had had a promising future as a weaver, but in an instant, that was gone. Her fingers were amputated. Being young and strong, her hand healed quickly, and she adapted as best she could.

Charlotte looked upon the Rourkes as family friends. She had known them since she was a child in Coventry and had visited their home and workshop in Spitalfields. She watched Annie with her siblings and knew her as a gentle and caring young woman. Despite the loss of her fingers, she had no difficulty in managing the five boys. She was cheerful and full of energy. Taller than Charlotte by a head, she was thin faced with sharp features, but her smile and happy disposition softened their severity.

In Charlotte's search for someone to watch over her infant, she turned to Annie. They met and talked freely on many subjects. Annie offered her advice on childbirth, since she assisted the midwife in the births of four of her younger brothers. When the talk turned to how Annie would care for the baby once it was born, Charlotte was well satisfied with her knowledge. Charlotte proposed the terms of her employment and Annie's family agreed to them, though she knew they would miss her.

The baby came in the last of January. Annie and her mother were both of great help in the birth, for the labour was long and difficult. Charlotte had never experienced such pain. It began suddenly, then intensified in wave after wave. Charlotte felt herself ripped apart as each wave crashed upon her. The baby was breech, coming out feet first. Charlotte thought afterwards how ridiculous she must have appeared sitting on the birthing chair with his little legs dangling from her groin. But at last, he was out and wailing.

Charlotte and Audley agreed that his name would be Jack William Pruitt. Audley beamed when he held his newborn son. He did not notice or care that Jack's head was covered with a fine fuzz of blond hair. He loved that his son had a strong cry and a happy disposition. He was enchanted.

Jack was a marvel to Charlotte. She adored him even in the middle of the night when he demanded to be fed. Charlotte was with him constantly, for she kept him in her room. They both smelled ever so slightly of sour milk. Charlotte loved the smell. She gazed at him and saw his father. Her heart ached to think of her happiness while James continued to suffer. For the first three months after Jack's birth, Charlotte was too busy to consider traveling. Annie was her saviour. When Jack bawled, she knew how to comfort him. When he was colicky, she rocked him in a darkened room until his howling subsided. Her voice was soft and caressing. She sang to him in French and Irish. She aided Charlotte in getting Jack to take her breast. When Charlotte's breasts became engorged, and she cried out in pain, Annie brought her hot compresses and soothed her distress. Even Audley was charmed by Annie's gentle manner.

When spring arrived, and the household had settled into an orderly routine, Charlotte's thoughts turned more and more to Devon. She broached the possibility with Emma of a visit to Kirkmoor. Her friend agreed to write to Elizabeth to see if it might be a possibility. Two weeks after the letter was sent, Emma received a reply which she quickly brought to Charlotte.

Kirkmoor
Dearest Emma,

I am writing to thank you for all the latest news of London. Your details of the Season and all the latest intrigues delight me.

Please do come, I would be so pleased to see you and to meet your friend, Mrs. Pruitt. A baby would be a particularly welcome visitor in our sad house. I beg you to make your arrangements for the journey soon. I would have you here tomorrow, if that were only possible.

My brother continues in his despondency. He rides out on the moor long before dawn. I do not know where he goes. I have attempted on several occasions to have him followed, but the servants are of no use. He loses them in the bracken and heather within a league of the house. I fear we will find him dead at the bottom of some ravine before the year is out. My mother cries and wrings her hands, and my father refuses to speak his name. Perhaps the spring and your visit will lift his melancholy. I pray that it may be so. Please excuse my sad tone, dear friend. I remain with affectionate esteem.

Yours sincerely,
Elizabeth

When Charlotte finished reading the letter, she and Emma made their plans for the journey. Thankfully, when Charlotte broached it with Audley later in the day, he raised no objections. His annual tour of the Continent would take him away for two and a half months, so he saw no reason why Charlotte and Jack should not go visiting, especially when accompanied by so prestigious a personage as Lady

Emma Bosworth.

"Do give my regards to Count Cesi when you see him, husband."

"I shall indeed, Charlotte. A bit different going to Devon rather than Bellagio, eh?" Audley laughed.

"Quite so, Audley," Charlotte responded while thinking to herself, you have no idea how different. Charlotte aided Audley in his preparations. He had several trunks full of clothes and hunting equipment. He would be busy, of that Charlotte was sure.

Audley regretted having to be apart from Jack. He doted on his little son and took pleasure in the time he spent with him. However, business was business, he told Charlotte, and if he was to stay ahead of his French and Italian competitors, he must be attentive to his clientele. As they stood at the door saying their good-byes, Audley took Jack in his arms.

"I am quite certain you shall be talking by the time I arrive back home. You are my bright laddie, eh? You will have tales to tell your father, I will wager." He smiled at his son and stroked his face.

A cold shiver ran down Charlotte's back. She took Jack from Audley, promising, "I shall take good care of him, husband."

Audley kissed her on the cheek and stepped into the coach which would take him to his ship. Emma arrived soon after to finalize their plans. They would leave the following week, taking three days to travel, and would stay for at least two weeks with Elizabeth at Kirkmoor.

"Devon will be beautiful in May and June. Chagford is a charming little village quite close to the manor. I used to spend my summers at Kirkmoor. They were glorious times," Emma mused. "I shall go directly home and write to Elizabeth about when to expect us."

With that, Emma left, and Charlotte spent the remainder of her day playing with Jack and trying to imagine what she would find when she arrived in Devon.

That night, Charlotte dreamed she was in Cumberland with her brother. They climbed to the top of Scafell Pike, a spot higher than they'd ever attempted before. It afforded a magnificent view. Thomas began to fly. He was circling in the air around Charlotte, shouting, "Come with me, Charlotte!" Without hesitation, she lifted off the ground. Euphoria filled her as she hovered. Yet in that moment of triumph, dread overtook her. She fell to the ground and lay weeping for all she had lost.

Charlotte awoke in despair. Immediately, she rose and went to Jack's crib. He was sleeping peacefully. All is well, she told herself, but despite this reassurance, she could not rid herself of her fear. Only after forcing herself to be fully awake was she able to calm down enough to go back to sleep.

CHAPTER SEVEN

Packing for the journey took two days. This was the first time she had travelled with Jack and there seemed to be no end to the items that were absolute necessities for a baby. The day of their departure arrived, and they were off in Emma's coach. They stayed at inns along the way that had been recommended by friends. Everyone was most solicitous to two well-off ladies, a beautiful baby, and the entourage of servants and coachmen. Lady Fortune smiled on them. The weather was fair and the roads dry. They encountered neither footpads, the thieves without horses, nor mounted highwaymen.

On the third day, as they drew close to their destination, a dark shape began to loom on the horizon. "Emma, whatever is that?" Charlotte asked.

"The Dartmoor, my dear. This is the place that Elizabeth mentioned in her letter, where James makes his daily jaunts." Charlotte shuddered to think of James, in his despair, wandering in that dark and lonely place.

As the coach rumbled up to the front entrance of Kirkmoor, Charlotte was charmed by the beauty of the place. Tall oak and elm trees grew close to the side and back of the house, but from the front expanse of lush green lawn one could see that the distant fields were in full bloom. The house was constructed of soft yellow stone that glowed in the afternoon sun. Built in Jacobean times its round towers looked like pepper pots topped with weathervanes. Dutch gables and a cheery white cupola made it a welcoming place, not like the cold, neoclassical estates Charlotte visited with Audley. As they alighted from the coach, Charlotte's attention was caught by the buzz of hummingbirds that flitted by her head.

They were greeted by Elizabeth Calvert. Charlotte was taken aback by how much Elizabeth, though a beautiful woman, resembled her brother, James. It was most pronounced around her eyes. Elizabeth smiled on seeing Charlotte's expression. "I am most pleased to make your acquaintance, Mrs. Pruitt. I take it that Lady Emma did not inform you that James and I are twins."

"No, she did not," Charlotte replied, wrinkling her nose at her friend.

Emma attempted to stifle her laughter. "Oh, but I think I did, when we first talked about Elizabeth some time ago. The look on your face was priceless, Charlotte!"

"Honestly, Emma, will you never grow up!" Elizabeth scolded her playfully.

"I very much doubt it." Emma grew contrite, seeing how she had wounded her friend. "Dearest Charlotte, I truly am most sorry. I should have reminded you. Will you forgive me?"

Charlotte smiled. "Perhaps in the future, but I shall make you suffer first."

"Well done, I accept."

Elizabeth approached Charlotte, who held Jack in her arms. "He is a handsome lad." She smiled at him, then her gaze fixed on Charlotte. "In my brother's lucid moments, he has expressed great admiration and regard for you. I never wrote this in my letters, fearing it might put you in some jeopardy."

"Thank you for your discretion, and for telling me now," Charlotte said, blushing. "Is it possible to see him?"

"He is not here, presently. Please, come in and get settled. We shall have time for tea and a talk." Emma and Elizabeth chatted as they walked into the house and down the main hallway that led past the drawing room and library. Charlotte followed after putting Jack into Annie's keeping. They moved down a passageway to their bedrooms and dressing rooms.

Elizabeth told Charlotte that her parents were spending the summer in Bath. Lady Clarke's health was failing, and it was hoped that the medicinal properties of the water might improve her condition. Their father was healthy of body, but his mind had taken to wandering of late. Elizabeth was fearful of what might happen to him if their mother died. Both parents were much affected by their son's madness. Her father, a man who was used to getting his way and seeing his dreams realized, could not fathom how his son, a soldier, a hero, his heir, could be a raving madman. "Simply not possible," was his response to it all.

Elizabeth Calvert lived at Kirkmoor with her three sons. She was a widow. Her husband had been a major in the British Army when he was killed by a Maliseet War Chief in the Colonies. By rights, the estate and family fortune would go to James, but because he had never shown much interest in it, Elizabeth oversaw its care and management.

The rooms appointed for Emma and Charlotte looked out onto the pastureland to the village beyond. The dark shape of the Dartmoor rose on the right. The afternoon was peaceful. Jack was asleep as they walked down the passageway. Annie placed him gently on Charlotte's bed where she watched over him while Charlotte left to join Emma and Elizabeth for tea in the drawing room.

After some polite exchanges, Charlotte asked Elizabeth about her brother. "I believe I wrote to Emma of his daily rides. He leaves at dawn, riding out onto the moor, and does not return until late at night. Attempting to follow him is fruitless. He grew up on the moor and has hiding places to which no one is privy.

"A week ago, I resolved to enter his cottage before he arrived back from one of his rides. My hope was to better understand his madness. On my instructions, a servant forced open the door. Inside I found the walls covered with drawings, pictures of angry, staring eyes, pair after pair of them, the faces twisted in agony. Some drawings were on papers that lay strewn on the table. The most disturbing showed a gnarled tree that had faces emerging out the end of every branch. Each face appeared to be struggling in vain to break free. They were wounded and bloodied, missing eyes, ears, teeth. Lost souls, they seemed to be crying out for God's mercy. The words *'Suscipe'*, *'miserere nobis'*, 'hear our prayer', 'be merciful to us', were written among the faces. Dear Lord in heaven, I thought I must pray for my brother's deliverance day and night. At that instant, he was in the doorway, giving me no time to escape. His boots and clothes were filthy with mud. He smelled of the bogs. I put my hand to my mouth to keep from gagging. His shirt was torn, and when he turned to close the door, I saw his back was a mass of bloody welts."

Elizabeth paused. She looked from Emma to Charlotte

109

and back again. "Forgive me, I have had no one to speak to about this. My parents refuse to talk of it, and I attempt to hide it from the boys, though they are not unaware. I have said too much already."

"No, please continue," Charlotte encouraged. "I would hear it all, if you are able."

"Please, go on, dear friend," Emma said softly.

"On seeing his back, I could not help but cry out. He turned to me. He stood, uttering not a word. I will never forget the look of contempt on his face. 'James, allow me to comfort you,' I said.

" 'Sister, I want no comfort,' was his reply.

"I could not bear how he looked at me, so I attempted to divert his gaze. 'What are those drawings? Who are these people? Why do they suffer so?' I asked him."

"He continued to stare at me as one distracted but answered, 'Friends, dead but not at peace. They visit me in an unending procession, asking me why I live, and they do not. They fill this place day and night, crowding in around me. Sometimes, I can barely breathe, they are so thick. Leave, sister. I have work to do.' He walked past me and began to draw."

"I left and ran to the house. I have not seen him since. I hear his horse when he leaves and when he returns. Otherwise, he is a phantom."

As Elizabeth finished, the light in the room was fading and they sat in semi-darkness. Charlotte saw so clearly all that had been described, while at the same time remembering her terror when James had become violent at Emma's. Despite both of these incidents, she felt the need to reach out to him.

"I must see him," Charlotte stated firmly.

"Tomorrow. If he returns," Elizabeth replied. "You shall try at least."

The next morning, Jack woke early, just after the first cock's crow. Annie brought him to Charlotte. He nursed hungrily for several minutes. Satisfied at last, he fell asleep, cradled in her arms. As he slept, Charlotte buried her face in his curls and was overcome with sadness, remembering having done the same with James. She longed to be with him but dreaded in what state she would find him. She left Jack under Annie's watchful eye, sleeping snugly in her bed. With help from Betsy, her lady's maid, she dressed and went to the parlour where she found Elizabeth already up. Charlotte saw at once that Elizabeth was agitated.

"Mrs. Calvert, what is it?"

"My brother did not return last night. I have sent two servants to search for him, but I doubt they will meet with success."

Charlotte wished to join the hunt but knew this was impossible. Not knowing the area, she would only become lost herself. Then, they would have to search for two missing people. She ate little and spent the day waiting for some word. There was none. The mood at supper was subdued, and all present went to bed praying James would reappear in the morning.

He did not. For five days the search continued. No one found any trace of him or of his horse. Charlotte prayed that he would return, but as the afternoon of the fifth day wore on, she began to pray that his soul had found peace. A storm from the west was building all day. Later in the afternoon, the sky turned green and lightning could be seen in the distance. Charlotte and Emma listened as it approached, with the thunder growing ever louder. The house shook as the lightning cracked overhead, and a bolt nearly hit the house. Charlotte held Jack, who screamed with eyes shut tight, as each successive peal of thunder exploded. Thankfully, the storm moved on, but the nerves of all in the house were set on edge.

Jeremy, Elizabeth's oldest boy, ran into the parlour where Charlotte and Emma were waiting out the storm. He was soaked to the skin and dripping water as he shouted, "Uncle Jem is back! His horse is in the stable yard!" He bolted out of the room in search of his mother. Charlotte ran after him holding Jack to her bosom. Emma followed. They found Elizabeth with the housekeeper and cook in the kitchen.

"Mama," Jeremy said excitedly, "I am sure Uncle Jem has returned. Lady Jane is in the stable yard!"

Elizabeth closed her eyes, saying, "Thanks be to God for answering our prayers." She looked at her son. "Jeremy, see to it that John tends to Lady Jane. Mrs. Pruitt and I must speak before we visit your uncle."

Jeremy rushed from the kitchen.

"May Lady Emma take Jack to his nurse?" Elizabeth asked. Charlotte nodded, and Emma took Jack and left to find Annie. Guiding Charlotte out into the hallway, away from the housekeeper and cook, Elizabeth asked, "Mrs. Pruitt, what is your desire? Would you have me accompany you?"

"No, I shall go alone. However, I think it wise if perhaps you and some of the servants be close, in the event I might require aid. I pray that I shall not, but I have felt James's wrath once and do not choose to suffer it again."

Going first to her room, Charlotte found two objects that she hoped might remind James of better times.

Leaving the house, she saw that Elizabeth and several servants were near the cottage. The sky was beginning to clear. The late afternoon sun reflected in the puddles of the muddy yard. Charlotte moved carefully over the slippery surface. When she reached the cottage, she found the door slightly ajar. Peering in through the dim light, she saw eyes drawn on the walls just as Elizabeth had described them. Yet now they were made even more ghastly by vertical red streaks that slashed through them. Charlotte entered slowly, not wishing to startle James or to be taken by surprise herself. On the rough-hewn table in front of her was a single candle, which she lit, enabling her to see into the gathering dark. The room appeared empty at first, until she realized that a narrow pallet in the far corner was occupied. James did not stir as she approached. He wore no shirt. His back was to her. She saw scars and scabs on his back, where he had beaten himself, but they were joined by new, bloody wounds. Aghast, she wondered who could have done this to him.

His once beautiful hair was filthy and matted. Twigs and leaves were encrusted in it. The closer she got to him, the stronger and more terrible the smell became.

"James," she whispered. He did not move. "Jemmy, it is Charlotte," she said a little louder. He stirred, turning his head slowly in her direction.

"Charlotte?"

She started and gasped. Bloody scratches lay in rows down his dirty cheeks. He attempted to focus on her face.

"Charlotte! Oh, dear God," he muttered, dazed, and turned back to the wall, curling up into a ball. She sat down beside him, putting the candle on the floor, and touched his shoulder. She covered her mouth and nose with her other hand to keep from retching. They stayed that way for several minutes. Charlotte concentrated on the candle's flame to try to keep her wits about her.

Finally, he began to speak in a hoarse whisper. "Lottie, I have our baby, but I could not keep it alive. I tried, Lottie, but it does not move. I am so sorry." He began to weep.

Charlotte, unable to make sense of what he said, urged him to turn to her. It was then that she saw the filthy bundle he was holding close. She froze, terrified at what it might contain. As his sobs slowed and quieted, she spoke softly to him.

"Jem, let me see the baby. Let me hold the child, please."

He looked at her, his eyes red and wet. The tears made tracks through the dirt and blood. He did not say a word as he obediently handed her the bundle.

It was a piece of dark grey wool covering something heavy and stiff. Charlotte tried to keep her mounting horror under control, but the putrid smell made it almost impossible. She pulled back the blanket and saw the body of an infant boy. Large, black spots covered its blue-white skin. Maggots teemed in its nostrils and crawled between its small fingers. Charlotte stood up.

"Jemmy, I will take the baby. You must rest. Do not move," she commanded. Charlotte moved slowly and deliberately towards the door and closed it behind her. Once outside, she fainted, falling into the mud. When she regained consciousness, she was back in the house. Elizabeth and Emma were calling her name and wiping her face with a warm cloth. She attempted to sit up, but feeling lightheaded, she lay back down.

"Rest, Charlotte," Emma urged.

"We have found a place for the child. God rest its soul. I shall take care of it. I promise," Elizabeth said.

"What will you do?" Charlotte asked, unable to hold back tears.

"I shall send for Squire Burney, the justice of the peace, in the morning, to see if he has any news of a missing infant. Please, do not worry."

"I must get back to James. I must let him know that the baby is being cared for."

"Jack needs you before you go again. The little fellow is hungry, I daresay," Emma suggested.

"Oh, Emma, of course. Please, will you call for Annie?"

"I shall fetch her myself, my dear."

After Emma left, Charlotte related all that had happened. "I must tend to his wounds tonight, Mrs. Calvert. He is a pitiful sight."

"Please, address me as Elizabeth, won't you?" Elizabeth asked, taking Charlotte's hand.

"Oh, yes, and you must call me Charlotte."

"I shall." Elizabeth smiled and let go of Charlotte's hand. "I will have the servants ready to bring you whatever you might need, Charlotte."

Sitting up slowly, Charlotte untied the ribbons on the front of her robe and removed her stomacher. Emma returned with Annie and Jack. He is so alive, so beautiful, Charlotte thought, as she placed him on her lap and gave him her breast. He sucked noisily. She felt her milk let down all the way through her back. He grasped her skin and held on tight.

A little later, the moon lit her way as she went again to the cottage. Resolved to bathe James, she brought with her a pan of warm water, wash rags, salve and bandages. She was followed by servants, who carried a tub and pails of water. They waited outside the cottage as Charlotte entered. Perhaps tomorrow, she thought, she would even attempt to cut his hair. He was asleep on his pallet. She sat on the floor beside him and stroked his face.

Opening his eyes, he smiled at her.

"I would like to wash your face. May I?" she asked quietly.

"Please, do." He closed his eyes. She moved the cloth gently over his face, taking care with the deep scratches. He did not flinch, but rather seemed to enjoy the warmth of the water and her touch. When she finished, she dabbed on the salve. His gaunt face glistened in the candlelight.

"James, I would like to bathe you. We will go very slowly. If you desire me to stop, you must tell me." He gave a slight nod. She went to the door and indicated that the servants should bring in the tub. Setting it down, they filled it with alternating buckets of hot and cold water. One of them placed a clean shirt, breeches, and stockings on the table. When they had gone, Charlotte helped James to stand and take off his filthy, grey pants. His body seemed so small as he stood naked before her.

She took his hand. "Will you come now?"

He looked at her blankly and did not answer.

"I cannot force you, James."

"Where is the infant?"

"I have found a safe place for him. He will be taken care of. You needn't worry."

He seemed satisfied with her answer and walked to the tub. He stepped in and sat down. Charlotte carefully washed his back, trying to loosen the encrusted dirt without dislodging the scabs. After soaking for a time, he became cleaner and Charlotte decided to take the next step.

"James, I would like to give you a haircut. Your hair needs to be very short or we will never get it untangled. Will you allow me to do that?" she asked.

"How short?"

"I may need to shave your head."

"Shave my head?" he repeated, as if trying to comprehend her meaning.

"You have vermin and filth in your hair. I want it to be clean."

"You will be careful with the razor?"

"I shall," she answered, but wondered if she was asking too much.

"You have my permission."

Charlotte went to the door and requested that the servants bring her a pair of scissors, a razor, and a strop. James got out of the tub, and Charlotte dried him off. She wrapped a blanket around his waist and asked him to sit on the chair. Carefully, she applied salve to his wounds. He winced several times but did not cry out.

There was a knock at the door. Upon answering it, Charlotte received what she had asked for from one of the servants. Returning to James, she began to cut his hair as short as she was able. Her skin crawled to see what was living in his hair. However, he soon sat shorn of his locks. "I want you to come and kneel at the tub for a moment, so I may wash your head and lather it for the shave."

He stood up and let the blanket fall. Walking to the tub he knelt and let her apply the soap. She scrubbed and rinsed his head. She repeated the process and worked up a lather, so she could shave his scalp. This done, she requested he sit on the blanket, and she began to shave. She worked

117

quickly. He sat very still. The last time she dipped the razor in the water, he moved and grabbed her wrist. She held fast to the razor and did not struggle.

"Where is the baby? Where is our son, Charlotte?" He pulled her down to him. Their faces were close together. She did not look at him, watching the razor instead.

"That child is not our son," she answered, not daring to move.

James did not respond. She could feel his breath on her neck.

She continued, "Our child is alive. You will see him. He is here... in the house." She felt his grip ease slightly. "You must let go of my wrist, Jem. You shall see Jack tomorrow after you sleep. I will show him to you in the morning. You will see your son. I promise."

He let go of her.

"I am tired," he said.

She helped him dress in the clean clothes. He sat quietly on the chair as she changed his bedding. "Are you hungry?" she asked.

"No, just fatigued." He crawled onto the pallet.

She covered him, and he curled up as before, his back to her. "Thank you, Lottie," he whispered.

"You are most welcome," she responded as she blew out the candle. On the table, she placed his Irish whistle and the white shell he had given her on the Isle of Man. As she crossed the yard, she looked at the fields. They were glowing in the moonlight. Her body ached, and she felt heavier with each step.

Inside the house, she drank a cup of tea and related the evening's events to Elizabeth and Emma. When she climbed into her bed, the moon was just beginning to shine through her window. She did not sleep well. The dread that had invaded her sleep before was back. She laid awake with her mind racing, until slumber at last overtook her. A few hours later, she woke abruptly and decided to sit up. The room was flooded with moonlight. Long shadows from the windows ran over the bed. A curtain fluttered in the early morning breeze. Gazing at it in confusion, she realized she had not left the window open. Holding her breath, she became aware of another presence in the room. Her gaze was drawn to the corner where Jack's crib rested. A dark shadow stood next to it.

"Charlotte, I wanted to be here with the two of you. Forgive me. It was not my intent to frighten you," James said quietly.

"Jem, come over here, please," she asked. All she could think of was that she wanted him to move away from Jack.

"I will not hurt him. I needed to see him alive, breathing."

"Please, James come over here to me," she repeated as she began to get out of bed.

"Charlotte, I am sorry." James made a sudden move towards the window. In the confusion of Charlotte going one way and he another in the half light, they collided. James grabbed at her to stop her fall. She broke away terrified but stopped herself when she saw he did not pursue her.

"Charlotte, what have I done? What am I doing? Help me. Please, help me," he pleaded as he dropped to his knees.

She stood, trying to catch her breath. She moved to sit next to him on the floor. Reaching out, she put her arms around his shoulders. He returned her embrace, and they held each other silently. Jack stirred and began to fuss. Charlotte stood and took James's hand, leading him to the crib. She lifted Jack up and introduced him to his father. James watched him and shook his head in disbelief.

"Oh, my dear, dear Charlotte, he is beautiful."

"Come over to the bed," she suggested, and they walked over together. She sat down and indicated that he should do the same. Jack was hungry, so she loosened her night dress and began to nurse him. James sat enthralled, watching mother and child. Afterwards, Charlotte lay Jack between them. They watched as he played with his feet and cooed softly.

"Stay with us, James, please."

"Thank you, Lottie. I shall." He moved to lie back on the bed. Charlotte moved Jack next to him and laid down on the other side. They all fell asleep, not waking until the sun was well up. Charlotte heard James rise and go to the door.

"James," she called as she sat up.

He stopped. "Yes?"

"When you are stronger, I pray you will tell me all that has happened to you since I saw you last."

"I shall, all that I can remember. I promise," he answered. He walked out the door.

After breakfast, Charlotte and Annie sat on the front lawn and played with Jack. It was a beautiful sunny day. Charlotte inhaled the aroma of the warm, moist earth mixed with the fragrances of the fields and flowers. She saw James emerge from his cottage. His sleeves were rolled up and he was wiping his hands on a towel. He waved for Charlotte to join him.

"Come see what I have been working at," he called out

to her.

She gave Jack into Annie's keeping and walked to the cottage. James beckoned her to enter. She saw immediately that the drawings were gone. He had scrubbed and whitewashed the walls. The rest of the interior was clean as well. He had swept and mopped the slate floor and cleared the beams and ceilings of cobwebs. On the table, Charlotte saw his Irish whistle and the shell.

"I played a bit of music this morning. It lifted my spirits on the spot. You were most thoughtful to leave it for me." He walked outside and came back in with another chair. "Please, sit down. I would speak with you now, if it is a good time to do so."

Charlotte agreed and sat down. He moved his chair close to hers.

"I have always loved the moor. When I was small, I would wander out on to it and spend all day exploring. There is one small glen for which I have a particular fondness. A stream runs through it, cooling it even on the hottest of days. I was eleven when I first felt the presence of others there."

"Others?" Charlotte asked, feeling uneasy.

"I had made of circle of stones and a small altar, a Christian one, with a cross. I do not remember why. I sat in the circle and became increasingly aware of other beings. I could not see them, but I could feel them there. Their presence filled me with a sense of peace. They did not speak, they simply were all around me. Later, I told Elizabeth about the experience, and she told our mother. I was strictly forbidden to mention it again. I never did, but the spirits continued to be with me, nonetheless. I believe they protected me in Portugal, in the massacre. Yet they could not help me when the ghosts began their visits." He stopped and sat staring into the air in front of him.

"James," Charlotte called to him softly. He did not stir. "James, perhaps you should not talk about it yet. Please, I do not want to lose you again."

He shook his head and blinked his eyes several times. "Charlotte, forgive me. I shall be fine. I am sorry. What was I saying?"

She reached out and touched his hand. "You were speaking about Portugal."

"And the ghosts," he said, putting her hand to his cheek. He touched her fingertips to his lips then placed her hand back in her lap. "The ghosts had voices. They told me I caused the death of my friends, that I was responsible for my wife's death. I grew weaker and weaker as the voices grew more powerful. They first came to me when I was in Constantinople for Count Cesi. First in my dreams, but then they spoke to me when I was awake. When I visited you at Emma's, their voices became unbearably loud. Someday, you must tell me how I behaved. I have only a faint recollection of it and the days of confusion that followed.

"Somehow, I arrived back at Kirkmoor. Perhaps the protecting spirits were able to guide my steps. I do not know. Once here, I stepped over into the world of ghosts. The only time I felt sane was after I took a whip to my back."

"James, I do not believe the fresh bloody wounds on your back were self-inflicted. They are too deep and too numerous. Who did this to you?"

He did not seem to hear her question but stood up and began to pace. "I took to wandering the moor. Every morning, the voices drove me out of bed. I rushed from them, trying to outride their fury but I never could. I would finally stop when I saw Lady Jane could take no more. But then, wherever I looked, I saw the faces of my dead friends, some in the rocks, some in the trees."

James stopped, and turned to Charlotte. "Everywhere they seemed to be moving, trying to get to me. That's how I came to beat myself. I flayed my back until I lay spent, and the voices ceased for a while. Raising my head from the ground, I saw the faces had also disappeared. I knew then what they wanted. So, every day when they began, I would rush to that godforsaken moor and repeat my penance. For several weeks, this punishment sufficed, but at length, they would not be appeased. Even after the worst beating I could inflict, they whispered on. I realized I must kill myself to be rid of them."

"Oh, James," Charlotte moaned, tears filling her eyes.

"No, Charlotte," James said as he crossed to her and sat down in his chair. He leaned in towards her. "I did not fear dying, and I did not want to live tormented any longer."

"What happened? What stopped you?"

"An old pedlar appeared. I was in too much misery to question how he came to be in so isolated a place. He saw me. He saw my bloody back and came to my aid, making a fire and fixing food for me. We began to talk, and I spoke to him of the war. My anguish poured forth; how I had loved Marie and how she died, how my comrades had fallen upon me, how I could not save anyone I loved, but instead caused their deaths. I wept in this old man's arms. He was kind and gentle to me. When I finished, he embraced me. Like a priest, he asked me if there were any other torments unconfessed. I told him about you and of my love for you.

He smiled when I described how I had pursued and won you. At last, with his urging, I confessed that you carried my child, and that I had run away in fear of doing harm to both of you.

" 'Go home,' " he told me. " 'The ghosts will trouble you no more. I am sure of it. Our heavenly father is not so cruel to let you suffer more. You have done penance enough. Go to your bed and let your slumber be sweet.' He helped me to mount Lady Jane, and I rode to the cottage."

"Did you ever see him again?"

James's voice trembled as he replied, "Only once."

"What is it, Jem? What happened?"

"I believe he was the one who gave me the dead infant."

"What?" Charlotte said in disbelief.

"I am so ashamed." He bowed his head and wept bitterly. Charlotte took him in her arms. He grasped her around the waist, pushing his face into her stomach.

"James, do not talk about it. It does not matter. You are safe now," she whispered, trying to comfort him. After his sobbing quieted, he sat up and wiped his tear-stained cheeks.

"I would like you to know all that I am able to remember, though pieces of it are more like a nightmare than recollections." He took her hands and brought them to his forehead. He rested his head on her hands, closing his eyes to collect his thoughts.

She kissed his shaved head. "Tell me all of it and know that you are safe. I am here with you." James looked at her, as if trying to reassure himself that she was indeed real and not an apparition.

"After the old man was so good to me, the voices did stop for a fortnight. I still went to the moor. Spring came, and the days were longer. I felt hope at last. The hell I suffered was at an end. I was sure of it. One morning, I visited the little glen I told you of. The morning was bright. I watched the stream in the glen as it tumbled along. I was content at last. Caught up in my reverie, I was unaware that I was being watched."

"By whom?"

"A man of my age, I believe. I never saw his face. It was masked. He was of middling height but powerfully built. He approached me from behind. By the time I realized what was happening, he had a knife to my throat. My first thought was that he was a footpad and meant to rob me. He was not. He whispered in my ear, 'You look like a man ready to die.' But I was not, Charlotte. For the first time in months, I wanted to live.

"So, I fought him with all my strength. I was not as sound as I had been before my time on the moors, and he got the better of me. He bound my hands and feet, tying the rope around my neck so that if I stretched my legs, I would choke myself. He produced a whip and beat me all about my body and face. I screamed for mercy, but he would not stop. At last, I lost consciousness. When I awoke, it was dark. I was still tethered like an animal. Each lash wound burned. I had a terrible thirst. I tried to loosen my bonds but to no avail. I lay there with my face in the mire and prayed to God to let me die rather than suffer more persecution.

"God turned a deaf ear. The stranger returned before first light. He kicked me to turn me over and poured what I thought was water on my face. I was so parched that I tried desperately to drink. Yet when I managed to get some in my mouth, I gagged and spat it out. He laughed and asked if I did not find horse piss to my liking. He left me alone, and I could hear him stomping about in the brush. He came back and began to strike me repeatedly with a stout stick. I was powerless. He beat me at will, and when I could scream no more, he went away.

"It was then that the old man appeared. He took the ropes off me and gave me water to drink. He tried to clean my wounds. I was dazed. I could not think. He kept asking, 'Who did this to you?' I could give him no satisfactory answer. I slept, but when I awoke it was night again. The old man sat silhouetted against the fire.

"When he saw that I was awake, he came to me and fell upon his knees. 'Forgive me the terrible news I must tell you. Mrs. Pruitt is dead, but the babe is here. I have your son.' He produced the poor, piteous bundle you took from me. Before I could question him, he helped me stand and told me. 'You must go. I am afraid of what will happen to us if that evil wretch who beat you returns.' He again helped me mount Lady Jane, who was already saddled and bridled.

"Once I was settled in the saddle, he handed me the infant and urged me to ride quickly away. I dug my heels into Lady Jane's sides and set off at a gallop. My back and legs were raw. It was excruciating to ride. I did not get far before the pain overwhelmed me, and I fell from the horse.

"I lay there in the mud. The baby rolled out of the blanket, but I did not move. My first and only thought was that I had killed it. Finally, I wrapped it back up and sat there cradling it, rocking back and forth. Suddenly, my torturer appeared. I scrambled to my feet and tried to run from him, all the while clinging to the infant. He overtook me, pushing me down to the ground. He held me down and clawed at my face. I felt the flesh tear and the warm blood drip down my cheeks. He stared into my eyes. His face was covered, and only his eyes were revealed. My face was inches from his. He spat out the words, 'I am going to kill the child. I will kill it, and you will watch me devour it, piece by piece.'

"I fought him, Charlotte. I held onto the child and threw him off me. He was on his knees. I kicked him in the head. He fell. I got on Lady Jane and rode as if the hounds of hell were after me. All the time I knew the baby was dead, but I could not let it go. I rode into the storm, and it seemed as though the whole world had gone mad, so much did the thunder and lightning overcome my senses. Thank God for Lady Jane. She brought me safely home.

"The rest you are privy to, except that when I came into the cottage and saw the eyes, they had become my eyes. I slashed my hands and tried to wash the drawings off with my blood." He stopped and peered at his hands. "I have been mad, Charlotte, but I am no longer. I will find both of these men and make them pay for what they have done. I will do that."

The intensity of hatred that shone in his eyes frightened Charlotte, but the thought that there were such monsters nearby terrified her more.

The sound of horses' hooves was heard outside. James went to the door and looked out. Turning back to Charlotte, he asked, "It is Squire Burney and another man I do not recognize. Are they here about the infant?"

"I should think so. Elizabeth sent word to him this morning."

"Charlotte, I cannot stay. No one will believe what happened to me. I do not know where the child came from, but if it was alive, and they kidnapped it, I will be the one accused of its murder."

He grabbed his coat and crossed to the back door of the cottage.

"I shall hide in the glen. My sister knows where it is. Ask her to keep this counsel close," he said bitterly. As he slipped out the door, he turned back to Charlotte. "I will have to leave the country. Come to me tonight. We will talk about what must be done."

Charlotte was in a panic. She was losing him again and had no words that could keep him near. Following him outside, she put her arms around his waist and kissed him.

"Go, my dearest. I will see you tonight," she whispered.

He turned and ran down a gully and was lost from sight among the undergrowth and trees.

Going back inside the cottage, Charlotte went to the window where she watched Elizabeth talking to the two men in the yard. One was a small, thin, older man, slightly stooped. The other was small, too, but younger and with a broad back. After a few minutes, Charlotte crossed towards Annie who had continued to sit with Jack on the lawn. Before she reached them, however, Elizabeth called for her to join her conversation with the two men.

"Squire Burney, may I present my dear friend from London, Mrs. Pruitt. Mrs. Pruitt, Squire Burney, our justice of the peace."

"How do you do, sir?" Charlotte inquired politely, trying to remain calm.

"Honoured to make your acquaintance, madame. I trust your stay is pleasant."

"Most pleasant, Mr. Burney. Thank you."

"And may I present Mr. Binckes," Elizabeth offered.

Charlotte turned her attention to the younger man.

"How do you do, sir?"

"Well enough, mum," Mr. Binckes responded in a deep, unfriendly rumble.

"Mr. Binckes is the Sheriff of Exeter." Elizabeth paused long enough for Charlotte to nod her head in acknowledgment. Elizabeth continued. "I was just telling the gentlemen that my brother had found and brought in a poor, unfortunate babe only last night. He was most distraught in finding its poor body on the moor. He went out again very early this morning to see if he could find any trace of what had brought it to such a terrible end. I am certain he will answer any questions you might have when he returns.

"Lady Elizabeth," the squire began with a deferential tone, "I have been a friend of your family for many years and would not impugn you brother's good name. However, he has been ill these past months, and his illness has perhaps taken a more violent turn. I would suggest to you that when he returns, you place a close watch on him and convey him directly to my house."

"Squire, James is no murderer of children," Elizabeth returned hotly.

The sheriff, whose lips had thinned to a white line, now spoke. "Madam, your brother had best be at the squire's before this hour of the day tomorrow, or we cannot be held accountable for what consequences he may suffer. The villages on the moor have tolerated his strange behaviour to this point because of your family's rank, but should the child prove to be the one missing from Okehampton, I would not be surprised if your brother might meet with a terrible accident. Good day to ye both." He mounted quickly and motioned for the squire to follow suit.

Squire Burney took Elizabeth's hand. "Please, Lady Elizabeth, have James come to me before I am powerless to help." He mounted his horse with help from a servant. The two men were quickly on their way.

Charlotte accompanied Elizabeth into the house, and they sat in the parlour. Elizabeth, who had maintained her composure in front of the sheriff and the squire, now sat slumped on the settee.

"The baby, if it is the same one, was the youngest child of an innkeeper from Okehampton, a market town, just to the north of the moor. The mother left the little one with her older children Monday last, in the afternoon. The baby disappeared, taken from its basket without a sound."

Charlotte moved to sit next to Elizabeth. She told her James's story. Elizabeth listened, growing more horrified by the moment at her brother's ordeal. In the end, she agreed with James's assessment of the situation. People would undoubtedly believe him the murderer. Some might even believe him possessed by the devil. When she heard James had chosen the glen as his hiding place, she was pleased and agreed to lead Charlotte there later that night.

Before the appointed time, Elizabeth brought Charlotte some of her eldest son's clothes. The women had decided to dress in men's clothing in order to ride more easily and safely on the moor. They left after midnight, riding in the direction James had gone earlier in the day. After crossing a small stream and making their way through the copses, Elizabeth stopped to listen. The moon was nearly full. All was quiet, even the crickets were silent.

They cut across the open moor land, trotting up and over a long rise. Elizabeth stopped to look back. They soon passed a circle of standing stones that cast long shadows in the moonlight and rode on until they slowed to enter a rocky stream bed. Thick bushes and brambles grew over the stream. They dismounted, leading their horses through the water. Thorns snagged their clothes and scratched their hands. The horses balked, but the two women held tight to the reins.

At last, the brambles gave way to a clearing surrounded by tall trees. The glen was beautiful in the moonlight. Soft shadows fell across the ground. A thick carpet of moss silenced their footsteps. Charlotte half expected to see faeries. Her eyes were drawn to a large outcropping of rock at the far end of the clearing.

James emerged from a small cave, greeting them in a whisper. "You saw no one, sister?"

"No one, James," she replied and embraced him. They held each other for a long moment. As they let go, he stepped back to survey their attire. "Excellent costumes. I would never have known what fair ladies are hidden here."

Charlotte looked at him. He was confident and relaxed even in this place and these circumstances. She wanted to believe he was recovered from his madness.

He took her hand and gazed into her eyes. "Forgive me all this, Charlotte."

"You are forgiven," she answered. They held each other, and he kissed her hair. She looked up into his face. They kissed again, and she put her head on his chest. "What shall we do, Jemmy? Where can we go?"

"I have pondered that question all day. I must leave tonight for the coast. From there I hope to make my way to the west of Ireland. I have an excellent friend outside of Galway, in Connemara. I believe he will hide me until I can make plans for the future. I must find the men who killed the child so that I may clear my name and restore my family's honour. You, my dearest, must go back to London as soon as possible. Those men know about you and Jack. You must do all you can to protect yourselves."

"Jem, I want to come with you," she said, holding fast to him. "I cannot be without you. I could not bear the thought of never seeing you again."

"Lottie, I must travel quickly. Think of the scandal if I was captured and we were together. I would be powerless to protect you and Jack. Please, go and wait for me to contact you. We will be together again, my angel. I promise." He finished speaking and held her tightly against him.

Elizabeth, who was standing a few feet away holding the horses' reins, came close to them, saying, "Go and be together for the little time we have left. I shall keep watch." James kissed his sister on the cheek and led Charlotte into the little cave that was his hiding place. There was only enough room for the two of them to crawl in a few feet.

They sat holding each other until he lay down on his blanket and pulled her to him. They kissed. She pulled him on top of her, wanting to feel his weight pressing into her body. Putting her arms gently around his back, she pushed her hips into his, and he responded. They kissed again. He bit her neck. She involuntarily arched her back.

"Dear God, I love you, Lottie. I shall forever, but I have to go."

"Please think of me and of Jack."

"You will be in my thoughts constantly."

They lay there, staring up into the black rock overhead. Charlotte shivered, imagining herself in a tomb.

"We must leave," James whispered. They crawled out,

and he helped her stand. Elizabeth and Charlotte mounted their horses, then James took hold of Charlotte's hand. "As soon as I can, I will get word to you. I pledge to you, and Elizabeth is my witness, I will be your husband and Jack's lawful father someday."

"May God protect you, Jemmy," Charlotte said, squeezing his hand hard before letting go. She and Elizabeth rode out of the glen and made their way back to Kirkmoor.

Once back, Charlotte fell into a fitful sleep. In her dreams, she saw a woman with long, black hair, dancing on a mountain top. Men surrounded her in a circle as her skirts flew higher and higher. Charlotte could feel their desire mounting. They grew mad to possess her. Her eyes burned into their souls. She sang, "Come dance with me. I will hold you forever, never set you free."

CHAPTER EIGHT

The journey back to London was miserable. It began to rain as soon as the coach left Chagford and did not stop for the week it took them to return to the city. At last, they came to Charlotte's house where she and Emma said their good-byes. It was already late in the evening, and at last, the household settled down for the night. Sometime later, Charlotte was up nursing Jack.

When he was finished, Annie settled him back in his crib at Charlotte's bedside and left to go to her room. Charlotte fell into a deep sleep and never heard the stranger enter. In her sleep, she began to hear a whisper that she could not decipher at first, but it became clearer as she awakened.

The voice cooed, "Mrs. Pruitt, do not make a sound." Now she was awake and terrified. The voice was very close. The man's face was next to hers. She could feel its heat. "Mrs. Pruitt, I will slit your son's throat if you utter a word. Do you understand? You may answer me."

"I understand," she managed to whisper. She could not see his face. There was light coming from behind him where he had lit a candle and left it by Jack's crib.

"Good," he said.

He took her hands and tied them together. He pulled

her arms over her head and attached the rope to the head of the bed. She tried to breathe. She bit her lip until she tasted blood to keep from screaming. He threw the bedcovers off of her and sat about halfway down on the bed. He began to lift up her nightdress, then stopped with his hand just above her left knee.

"Tell your lover that I thank him for all the details of your trysts. The island in particular made me want to fuck you, Lottie." He laughed softly. "Now, Mrs. Pruitt, I don't want to give you another bastard. One's enough, eh? He looks like his father. Blond curls and blue eyes. Don't Mr. Pruitt see it? But you are a handsome tart, so he turns a blind eye. Is that it?"

"What is it that you want?" Charlotte asked, rage building inside her.

"Did I give you permission to speak, mawk?"

"No."

"Then you'd best ask nicely, or little Jackie won't see the mornin' light."

"May I speak, sir?"

"Oh, aye that's the way. Yes, Mistress Mawk, you may address me."

"Please, I have money, jewels, and silver plate. Take what you want."

"I will take, but I won't leave you unsatisfied, not a lusty wench like you. You know what I did, bein' such a thoughtful bloke?"

"No," Charlotte whispered, terrified.

"Well, I went into your garden shed this afternoon. I am very familiar with your house and grounds. Know every hiding place. I found a pitchfork. Big thick handle on a pitchfork. I cut the handle off, Mistress Mawk. I have it right here." He took the stick from under his coat. He slid it under her nightdress, then ran it from her neck down her chest and belly to between her legs. She tried to close her legs, but he held them apart. He left the stick and came close to her face. "We will enjoy this, Lottie. But no sound or little Jackie is dead. Here, bite on this." He put a piece of leather between her teeth.

Charlotte was trembling, and tears were running out of her eyes. He did not hesitate, even seeing her suffering. Charlotte felt him move back down the bed. He pulled her legs apart and after tying them spread eagle to the bedposts, he savagely stabbed her with the stick.

She bit down on the leather strap and closed her eyes. I cannot scream. I cannot scream. He stabbed her a second time and a third. Opening her eyes, she watched her tethered hands dance above her head as if they belonged to someone else. She was swimming in a sea of white-hot pain. I cannot scream. I cannot scream. Satisfied, he pulled the stick out and placed it on her chest. He was breathing hard and fast.

"Well done, Mistress Mawk. Much better than your weak-kneed lover. He screamed. But then, I wanted to hear those screams. I should have killed him, but it is not over yet. I must go now. But I'll not be far away. Stay close to little Jacko. You wouldn't want another dead brat to explain, would you?" Untying her hands but leaving her legs bound, he brought his face close to hers and said, "You'd best clean yourself up. Got all wet and hot for me, eh?" He walked to the door. "Goodnight to you, until I come again." She heard his footsteps on the stairs, and the door close as he left the house.

Charlotte lay still, her breathing fast and shallow. She

wanted desperately to go to Jack, but the pain kept her from rising. Reaching her hand down, she touched the bed. It was wet. She pulled her hand back up to her face and held it up to the faint light. Her fingers appeared black. Her thoughts were foggy from the pain. After a moment of staring at her fingers, she recognized they were covered with blood.

Blood? Who was bleeding? Swallowing hard, she tried to clear her head. Her fingers. Her blood. Finally, she realized she was the one bleeding and she needed to stop the blood. That's right. Moving slowly, she pulled the bell cord hanging near the head of the bed.

Annie, roused after a few rings, came in sleepily, "Mrs. Pruitt? She asked.

"Annie, I am bleeding. Help me."

The girl brought the lit candle by the crib to Charlotte's bed. "Oh, my dear Lord! What happened?" she asked as she untied Charlotte's ankles. "Should I send for a doctor?"

"No, just water. Help me wash off. Please change the bed," Charlotte said as if she were in charge, while every second she could feel herself growing colder. "Help me!" she cried and began to vomit. Annie ran from the room calling for help.

Charlotte did not know where she was. She was trying to run but could not. Every move brought pain shooting through her groin and into her chest. He was holding her and would not let go. He was on top of her, and she could not break free. She was alone in her garden, but in the next moment, a man was trying to climb over the wall. Charlotte was in a panic. She could not move, could not call out. He was coming.

She screamed. She looked for Jack to protect him, but

he was nowhere to be found. From very far away, she heard her name. She could see a light. Emma's face was there. Emma was there. The nightmare was over. Charlotte was in her own room. Her body ached, and her head was on fire.

"Charlotte, it's me, Emma. You are safe now. He is gone."

"I hurt, Emma," Charlotte managed to say.

"I know, dear. You were attacked. He is gone. You are safe."

"Jack?" Charlotte asked, trying to see the crib.

"Little Jack is resting peacefully. Annie is watching over him. He is in the parlour. You have been asleep for nearly twelve hours."

Charlotte closed her eyes. She was very tired.

"Charlotte, I should send for the constable. He asked me to summon him when you awoke. He would like to speak with you."

"No!" Charlotte responded in a panic. "Emma, he… that man, will kill Jack if I speak of what he did. He was the man who beat James. He knows my secrets. Oh my God, Emma, he is truly the devil, and I am powerless."

Emma took Charlotte's hand, trying to calm her. She called for soup and toast to be brought to Charlotte. When the food arrived, she watched over Charlotte as she tried to eat.

Four days passed before Charlotte's terror began to subside. She insisted that Annie move into her bed chamber. Charlotte wanted Jack to be watched day and night. The doors and windows were reinforced with extra locks. The servants stood guard in the house and in the garden. Emma stayed, as well. She had a calming effect on

Charlotte's nerves. Yet Charlotte still awoke screaming when she did manage to fall asleep. Shadows terrified her as she moved about the house.

At length, Charlotte spoke with the constable, but she could tell him little. He asked discreet questions about the crime and was duly horrified at the violence of the attack. He assured her that he and his men would do all in their power to protect her and her son. Charlotte lived with the fear that her attacker would reappear.

Charlotte wrote to Elizabeth as soon as she felt able, describing in brief and general terms what had happened. She asked, if possible, to warn James of the danger of this madman.

In the midst of her despair and confusion, Charlotte received a letter from Audley. He told her of the delightful time he was enjoying in Venice. Countess Cittidini, who sent Charlotte her regards, had introduced Audley to her niece, Countess Crespi. Audley went on for three pages describing his adventures with the young countess. He sounded quite smitten, and Charlotte suspected that Audley had taken her as his mistress. Audley was not without charm. Charlotte was aware of that fact. He'd been an ardent suitor when they courted, and she'd enjoyed his company at the time.

Feeling abandoned and stupid in the bargain, Charlotte sat down on her bed and wept. Her lover was in hiding, her husband was enjoying the charms of an exotic, young woman in an intoxicating city, and she was sitting locked in a barricaded house, jumping at every shadow that crossed her line of vision.

The day was hot, the house suffocating. What could she do? Where could she go to feel safe? A plan slowly emerged in her feverish brain. The next day, with utmost secrecy, she arranged passage on a ship from London to Whitehaven, a port city in the northwest of England. After this, she wrote a note to her childhood friend, Hannah Moreland who lived in Whitehaven. Charlotte asked if she and a friend might stay briefly with Hannah and her husband.

Charlotte had met Hannah the summer Charlotte turned ten. She was staying at Whitestone, her grandfather's home in Rosthwaite. Hannah's family, the Foxes, owned an estate on the fells overlooking Thirlmere. Charlotte, her brother, and their mother often were invited to stay at Creighton House for two or three days at a time. Hannah later married a gentleman of means, with large shipping interests, and they settled in a house by the harbour in Whitehaven.

The next letter written was to Mary Mungris, Whitestone's housekeeper, to inform her that Charlotte and her son, Jack, as well as her friend, Lady Emma Bosworth, would be arriving soon and would be staying for at least two months.

In a short while, she received Hannah's enthusiastic reply. Hannah wrote that she and her husband, Mr. Moreland, would be delighted if Charlotte, her son, and her friend would come for a visit. Charlotte prayed that her attacker would not discover her plans. At the very least, she would have a good vantage point at Whitestone, perched as it was on a hill overlooking Rosthwaite and the middle valley of Borrowdale. Besides, any strangers would be immediately noted by the local residents, unlike London, where newcomers were common.

The day before they were to leave, she gathered the staff to give last minute directions on the running of the house. Except for Lazarus Primm, the butler, whom Charlotte had told she was going north, all the servants believed she was off to join Mr. Pruitt in Venice. Even Annie, Jack's nurse, and Betsy, Charlotte's maid, who would be journeying with her, thought they were going to Italy. Charlotte purposely let a few of them overhear her talking to Emma about her concern that Audley had taken a mistress and her subsequent desire to be near him.

When Charlotte invited Emma on the journey, she immediately accepted, saying it would be a great adventure. Emma so enjoyed the deception that she talked at length to Charlotte about her love for Venice, Milan, and Bellagio. Just after Charlotte had spoken to the servants, she and Emma were waiting to have tea in the parlour.

As one of the maids brought it in, Emma declared loudly, "I adore the Grand Canal, especially on those delightful summer evenings when there is no chill in the air. Perhaps, I shall take a lover." She laughed and fanned herself. "Just thinking of it makes me quite warm. Do you think Count Cesi is in the market for a bride?" she asked Charlotte.

"You ought to broach it with him, dear," Charlotte replied.

After the maid left, Emma asked, "Was I too eager in my play acting?"

"No." Charlotte smiled at her affectionately.

"I simply wish to set the stage," Emma said as she picked though the fruit the maid had brought. Most probably I shall fall in love with a simple, Cumberland shepherd. Then, I shall renounce London society and its wicked ways and take up a quiet, pastoral existence." She bit hungrily into a pear.

Charlotte laughed. "You will create Arcadia, no doubt." Her tone became earnest. "Thank you, Emma, for being such a dear friend."

"I live vicariously through you, Charlotte. However, of late, I am afraid you have exhausted me."

Charlotte and Emma spent the rest of the day planning for their time in Whitestone. Emma at last excused herself and left, promising to meet Charlotte the following day at the ship.

That evening, Charlotte wrote Audley, explaining that the summer was unbearably hot and dusty in Spitalfields. "I long to see the green fells surrounding Whitestone and since, dear husband, you are occupied in business matters, I am certain you would not begrudge me time spent in Borrowdale…"

The letter finished, she spoke with Mr. Primm, the butler, asking him to send along any correspondence from her husband as quickly as possible. She asked him to send it by way of Mrs. Hannah Moreland in Whitehaven. She thanked Mr. Primm for his dedicated service. He had been with her family since she was a small child and had come to Audley's when she was married.

Before he left, he paused, and asked, "Madam, if I may speak freely?"

"Certainly, Mr. Primm, what is it?"

"I wish you to know how sorry I am for your suffering. The safety of all in the house is my responsibility, and I was derelict in my duty."

"Thank you, Mr. Primm, but truly your apology is unnecessary. A cunning madman like that would have found a way in no matter what precautions were taken." Charlotte shuddered. She hoped they would escape without incident.

"Goodnight, Mrs. Pruitt. I pray your journey may be a pleasant one." With that, he excused himself.

CHAPTER NINE

Charlotte's slumber was undisturbed for the first time in many days. She awoke rested and excited about the day's events. The household was bustling. Jack was readied with Annie's help. The coach was packed with everyone's belongings. Charlotte's toilette was complete, and her hair dressed. Finally, Charlotte, Jack, Annie, Betsy, and the footmen were all assembled. Betsy and the footmen rode on top of the coach, while Annie, Jack, and Charlotte were handed into it. In Wapping, they met Emma and her servants, and everyone boarded the ship. Charlotte allowed time for all to get settled, then she gathered them together to tell them the change of plans. Though some of the group seemed bewildered when they heard that the shire of Cumberland in the north of England and not Venice was their destination, they were soon buzzing with excitement as the ship set sail.

The journey lasted six days, with a stop in Bristol and a delay in Liverpool because foul weather kept them in port. Charlotte made sure that no new passengers were taken on board in either of the stops. She was pleased with her decision to travel by ship, rather than by coach, where she would have had to be constantly on her guard. At last, they were in sight of Whitehaven, one of the key ports on the west coast. Charlotte's heart began to lighten.

On docking, they dispatched a note to Hannah Moreland, and shortly a coach was at the harbour to carry them to her house. As Charlotte alighted from the coach, she was met by Hannah and her husband. Lady Emma and Mr. Moreland were introduced to each other, and a great fuss was made over Jack. Hannah, a tall woman with black hair and blue eyes, stood a full eight inches over Mr. Moreland, whose wig was of the old style, with grey curls falling over his shoulders. Hannah welcomed them warmly. Once they were settled in their rooms and had changed out of their traveling attire, she showed them the garden, which was in full bloom. After that, they toured the stables. The Moreland's horses were the fastest in Cumberland, Hannah told them proudly.

Charlotte and Emma were introduced to the Moreland's five sons. They were healthy lads, ranging in age from six to thirteen. As young boys will, they paused just long enough to bow to the guests politely before rushing off to their various pursuits. At dinner, Charlotte invited Hannah to come for a visit to Whitestone. She gladly accepted. Mr. Moreland declared that two of their eldest sons would accompany their mother. Hannah told Charlotte and Emma that Creighton House, Hannah's ancestral home, had burned to the ground.

"Just last year, lightning struck during a fierce storm. It burned with such speed and intensity that the servants had no opportunity to save it. Only the chimney of the great hall remains standing. Makes my heart break when I see what is left tucked into the little valley, so alone. I shall ride over there when we are on our visit. Will you join me, Charlotte?"

"Of course I shall, and Emma, too, I suspect."

"I would be delighted. As you describe it, Mrs. Moreland, it sounds most poetical."

Charlotte and Emma stayed at Whitehaven for a week, during which time, Hannah prepared for the next leg of their journey. The morning they departed in the Moreland's coach, the fog was grey and thick. The roads to Keswick were badly rutted, but the coach and the accompanying horse cart managed the trip without overturning. At Keswick, they stayed the night with a family friend of the Moreland's, whom Charlotte believed must have had second thoughts when they saw Hannah, her two boys, Emma, Charlotte, Jack, and all the servants descending from coach and cart. However, they were hospitable and arranged for horses to Rosthwaite.

The next morning, they passed through the Jaws of Borrowdale with its high, rocky crags, and Charlotte's spirits lifted as they entered the middle valley. The green fellsides looked to her like the backs of giant sleeping beasts.

"There is Whitestone!" she called out excitedly to Emma. The grey stone statesman's house with its rounded chimneys and many gables stood perched high above the jumble of white cottages that made up the small village of Rosthwaite. They followed the rutted lane as it turned eastward across the valley floor, crossing the stone bridge over Stonethwaite Beck. There they began the steep ascent up the fellside. Even before the horses reached the crushed white stone in front of the house, Mrs. Mungris threw open the red front door and started down to meet them.

Charlotte jumped from her horse and ran up the hill to greet her. They embraced each other joyfully and exchanged hellos as the rest of the party caught up with them.

At the end of three weeks, Mr. Moreland and the rest of the children joined them at Whitestone for three days. They brought no letter from Audley, nor any word about James. The house was full of life, even though Mrs. Mungris kept shooing the boys outside. Several people of importance from the area, including Rector Lindsay and Squire Ellis, the justice of the peace and their wives, were invited to dinner. The rug was rolled up, Mr. Moreland got out his fiddle, and dancing began. Despite her worries, Charlotte delighted in the mirth and high energy of the evening, a far cry from some of the stuffy routs she had attended in London.

The following day, the Morelands packed up and made ready to return home. Charlotte extracted from Hannah a promise to visit again soon. Charlotte watched them as they made their way down the fellside, finally disappearing on the road north. Charlotte returned to the house. Jack was napping, and Emma was at her needlework. The house seemed deserted.

Charlotte moved into the parlour and sat in a chair near a window, watching drops of rain make their paths on the windowpane as a storm moved across the valley. After a few moments, Emma entered and sat next to her.

She made a pretence of doing her needlework as she wondered out loud, "Perhaps, I should pay a visit to Kirkmoor and see if Elizabeth might have any idea as to James's whereabouts."

"Emma, you are a devoted friend indeed. Let us wait a fortnight, and if we hear no news from Elizabeth, I shall consider your offer."

Eight days later, one of the Moreland's footman arrived, bringing a bundle of letters. Charlotte took them excitedly. Three were from Audley, all sent from Venice. One was from Elizabeth in Devon. This one she tore open first.

Dearest Charlotte,

I was horrified to read of your travail at the hands of that madman. I pray to God you are safely out of harm's way. Please, protect yourself and dear Jack.

We have a visitor at Kirkmoor. He arrived yesterday from Ireland, of all places. He is an acquaintance of our mutual friend. He told me that all are keeping well across the sea. All illness seems to have been cured, which is good news, indeed. It is my hope that future plans may be made known to us soon. I promise I will write if I receive any news or correspondence that might of interest to you.

Adieu, most dear friend.

With sincerest regards and affection,
Elizabeth

Charlotte wished for more, but to know that James was well gave her great joy. Audley's first two letters were filled with news of his adventures with Countess Crespi and his good fortune in business dealings. The third letter brought an abrupt change in tone.

Venice
Wife,

I have just learned the most disturbing news from a source I believe to be reliable. He tells me of liaisons between you and James Clarke that began during our stay in Bellagio and continued for more than a year. You may have thought me a great fool, but I am one no longer. A discreet affair is not improper, but your wanton behaviour is reprehensible. I am determined to divorce you, strumpet, if it takes half my fortune to do so. The issue of your lust will be disinherited and shamed for the bastard he so assuredly is. Pack yourself up and get thee back to London.

You are undone.
A.P.

Charlotte was stunned. The letter, by its date, was written three weeks earlier. Surely, Audley set sail soon after composing it. She wondered if he might already be in Spitalfields with his mistress by his side?

"Emma," Charlotte managed to say, "Audley knows it all." She handed Emma the letter. Her friend read it and reread it.

"Who is this informant, do you suppose?" Emma asked.

"I do not know. But I shall admit to no wrongdoing. I am resolved to play this game on my own terms, if I am able. I will not go to London as he demands. I shall stay here until I hear from James. If Audley wants me, he can come and get me."

Each morning, Charlotte awoke dreading a new letter

from Audley. Her despair drove her to take long rides. Sometimes, she was accompanied by Emma, who warned her about the foolhardiness of riding alone and unprotected. She began carrying a dagger with her.

After a particularly fitful night's sleep, Charlotte rose early and told Mrs. Mungris that she intended to ride to the ruins of Creighton House. Soon, Charlotte was astride her horse as it trotted up Brund Fell, then down through the tiny hamlet of Watendlath and up again across the fells toward the ruins. The morning was growing late when she reached the crest of the hill that overlooked the remains of the house. At a slow pace, she began to make her way down the overgrown pack horse trail.

The foundation of Creighton House and the lonely grey stone chimney and hearth stood against the background of tall trees adorned in golden yellow and deep red autumn foliage. The fog of the morning was gone, and the sun warmed the valley. She trotted her horse over to the chimney. Undoing her hair, she shook her head. Her auburn tresses blended with the autumn colours and felt soft on her face.

The whinny of a horse in the distance snapped her to attention. Remembering Emma's warning, she guided her horse behind the hearth and chimney and dismounted. She drew her dagger. The horseman drew closer, she peeked out to see him coming down the hill. Was he looking for her or was he simply a rider who happened to be going her direction? There were highwaymen about, but generally they held to more travelled routes. Who could it be?

Dear God, Charlotte prayed, please, do not let it be that madman from London. She prayed he would ride on. He stopped and dismounted. She could hear him now, his steps drawing closer to where she hid. Her heart was racing. She drew a breath and lunged out at him with her dagger raised. His horse bolted in one direction, hers in another. The man grabbed her arm before she could stab him. Then, their eyes met.

CHAPTER TEN

"Jem!" Charlotte exclaimed, taking a step back in disbelief. She could not hold her tears back. "Oh, my God, I thought you were…"

"Lottie," James said. "Thank God you are safe." He took her in his arms, and they kissed. Hardly able to comprehend that they were together at last, they held on to each other in a tight embrace.

At last, seeking a comfortable spot, James found a patch of soft grass and sat with his back against the chimney. He invited Charlotte into his arms. He told her of his adventures getting to Rosthwaite. As soon as he received the news from his Irish friend of the attack on her and her flight north, he was determined to come to her. He was able to find passage on a ship leaving Galway bound for Whitehaven. From there he came without difficulty, riding most of the night since the moon was full and the sky clear. When he arrived at Whitestone, Emma directed him towards Creighton House.

James hesitated, looking at Charlotte, he asked about the attack. She shuddered but recounted what had happened. "Charlotte, forgive me. I have brought this on you. I betrayed our secrets. I will find this man, somehow. I will destroy him."

"We have more immediate concerns, James," Charlotte said, and she told him the arrival of Audley's letters, she confessed she was frightened by his knowledge of their affair, and his threat to divorce her and ruin Jack. She rested her head against James's chest and felt the steady beat of his heart.

He stroked her auburn hair. "Lottie, I do not want you and Jack to suffer public ridicule and ostracism. Perhaps I could see Pruitt and work out a settlement of some kind. If I could offer him more money than he could hope to win in a com crit case, he might let you go without attempting to secure a divorce from Parliament. We could go to France, or perhaps the Colonies. All I want is to live in peace with you and with Jack."

Frightened at the prospect of such a meeting, Charlotte clung to James, saying, "It is too dangerous an undertaking. What if Audley brought the authorities with him? You would be arrested. Please, we can go without a lawful separation. I do not give a fig what is said about me. I am yours. I have been since Bellagio. I have income from my grandfather's estate. Audley cannot take it from me. Let me make arrangements, and we will leave for France directly."

James gathered Charlotte in his arms and rocked her. He did not say whether he agreed with her or not. It did not matter in this moment. He was here. But the shadow of the madman was there with them even in the bright sunlight.

When James moved to touch in a way that had delighted her before, she could not breathe. She was not ready to make love. Her body held the terror and the pain of the rape. She panicked and pushed him away. He understood, and patiently, he reached out to her. They held each other surrounded by the yellows and reds of the autumn hills and ruins of the once great house.

They had a great celebration the following week. Musicians were hired, and Charlotte invited friends from Rosthwaite, Watendlath, Grange, and Keswick. Everyone danced, ate, and drank until late into the night. People fell asleep all over the house and in the barn. When they awoke in the late morning, Mrs. Mungris fed them all a hearty breakfast and sent them home to rest.

In the afternoon, Emma approached Charlotte and told her that she wished to return to London before the first snowfall. She proposed to visit Hannah Moreland and her family for a few days while she made arrangements for her passage home.

"I shall miss you terribly, Emma," Charlotte said, "but given the possibility that James and I may soon have to flee, it may be for the best."

As they were finishing their conversation, James entered the room. There was a commotion outside the front of the house. Mrs. Mungris came bustling into the parlour with the news that a rider from Keswick had arrived with a letter for Charlotte marked "urgent". Charlotte greeted the man and took the letter. She sent him to the kitchen to refresh himself before riding back to Keswick, as she tore open the letter.

Bellagio House, London
Mrs. Pruitt,

I pray I will not have to call you by that name for much longer, for you are odious to me, and I would be done with any connection to you.

I have not written in some time, as I have been compiling my divorce suit. I will go before Doctor's Commons in two months whether you are here or not. After I gain my judicial separation, I plan to seek a Parliamentary divorce. You may offer your side if you wish, but I have no doubt that with the evidence I have of your carnal knowledge of James Clarke that the decision against you will be swift.

I have decided I shall claim the bastard as my own. You will never see Jack again. I will raise him to hate you for the ungrateful fool and harlot that you are. You have made me the joke of London society, ridiculed by my friends and associates and hounded by the press. I will ruin you and that lunatic you have taken into your bed. Be assured, I will do all that I say I will.

If you have any response, you had best send it quickly.

A. Pruitt

When Charlotte finished reading, her hand dropped, and the letter fell to the floor. She sat staring into space. James picked up the letter, read it, and passed it to Emma. As Emma read it, James sat and put his arm around Charlotte. When Emma was done, Charlotte found her voice. "Jem, we must leave immediately for France. I will never surrender Jack to that man. Never! I do not know who feeds the flame of Audley's hatred, perhaps it is his mistress, but if he knew you were here, I cannot imagine what he would do."

James took her hands in his. "Charlotte, I cannot in good conscience run away. Audley Pruitt has every right to feel such animosity. If the tables were turned, I might take the same tone. I must go to him, Lottie."

Appalled, Charlotte began to speak, but James held up

his hand, stopping her. "Please allow me to finish. If I can offer him some monetary settlement, he might reconsider his drastic course of action. Perhaps he would agree to a separation. I will not allow him to keep Jack. He is my son, and I will claim him as such, but I do not want your reputation ruined. Your only sin is that you love me. I must find a way to settle this."

"James," Emma interjected, "you still have a price on your head. All Audley has to do is to have you arrested. Is your need for an honourable settlement so great that you would risk imprisonment?"

"I fear it is, Emma. My life has been spent making wrong decisions and hurting those I love the most. But Charlotte is no wanton woman, and I am no scoundrel. Our love has a right to exist."

"Please," Charlotte pleaded, "please, do not do this, Jem."

"I must, Charlotte."

She could not dissuade him. He spent the next two days trying to decide his course of action. Finally, he hit upon a plan. He would make contact with Audley through an intermediary. The man he thought of first was John Fuller, a close friend of his from Devon. John, an ex-Quaker, was a man of principle and high moral standing. He would ask John to go to Audley as his representative and propose a meeting at an inn in Oxford. They would decide on a time and specific place. John and another of James's friends would watch the inn and environs to make certain Audley did not arrive with authorities in tow. Once this was assured, John would meet Audley and transport him to another meeting place, where James would be waiting.

James had made a good sum of money in Turkey. He

hoped to offer Audley enough to make him consider foregoing the divorce proceedings and thus avoid public exposure of Charlotte. Charlotte held out little hope for the plan. Audley's pride had been wounded; he would not be easy to deal with.

Setting his plan into action, James wrote to John Fuller and waited for his friend's response. In the meantime, Emma made ready to go to Whitehaven. The morning she left, Charlotte and Emma embraced tearfully. Emma promised Charlotte that she would send her all the news of London.

The first snow fell two days after she left. Charlotte awoke early that morning and watched it coming down swiftly and silently outside the bedroom window. James was asleep next to her. She looked at him and her heart ached. His hair fell across his face and down his neck. She moved a strand and kissed him on the cheek. He did not stir. She tried to imagine that they had been living peacefully at Whitestone for several years. Would she ever see that time, she wondered? She prayed to God to allow them to be together without danger.

Later, they took a walk in the new-fallen snow. James carried Jack, who was bundled up against the cold wind. They walked up the path above the house, big flakes falling around them. As they gazed out over the valley to Honister Pass in the west, the snow stopped, and the clouds parted to let a ray of sunlight shine down on Eagle Crag. Sheltering Jack with their bodies, they hugged and kissed. For a brief instant, they were a family.

A few days later, despite the heavy snow, a rider arrived with a letter from John Fuller. In it, he agreed to carry out James's plan and reported that he had set it into motion.

Audley had already agreed to meet in Oxford on the appointed date and time with the proviso that he could be accompanied by one friend.

"Perhaps," John wrote, "Mr. Pruitt thinks he may be in need of a second."

James smiled, but Charlotte shuddered to think of a duel. John Fuller's note continued, saying that Pruitt was interested in discussing a monetary settlement, but that if that settlement could not be reached, he would pay to have James hunted down and brought to justice for his crimes. James sent his reply to John Fuller in London. He agreed to allow Audley to bring an associate. He explained to Charlotte that he and John would meet at a mutual friend's house outside Birmingham and from there ride together to Oxford.

Desperate at the thought of James riding into such a dangerous situation, Charlotte tried once more to persuade him to leave the country. James refused to consider it. "Pruitt will have us hunted down, Charlotte. He is determined to steal Jack, ruin you, and have me hanged. I must try to dissuade him if we are to have any hope of a life together."

The night before James was to leave, Charlotte asked Annie to take Jack into her bedroom so that she and James would not be disturbed. A fire in the fireplace took the chill from Charlotte's bedroom as she and James undressed each other and crawled into bed.

"This is my heart's desire, Jem. To be with you and to love you. Why does it seem so impossible?" Charlotte asked as he held her in his arms.

"I do not know, Lottie," he answered softly.

Not wishing to sink into melancholy, Charlotte tried to

lighten her tone, fighting the panic that welled up at the thought of what she was about to ask. "Make love to me, Jemmy. Please, I want you to. Our Jackie needs a little sister or brother." She ran her hand over his chest and down between his legs, her heart beating wildly. He smiled gently and kissed her on the nose.

"I think you may be right, lass," he replied, "but are you sure? I don't want to frighten you."

She nodded and he began to nip lightly at her neck. She sighed, relaxing into him, then giggled as he licked her ear. He was ever so patient and paused each time they reached an area that caused her distress. He murmured softly and caressed her gently until she relaxed and felt safe again. Her moment of climax was made sweeter by his tenderness. Settling into his embrace, she stared sleepily into the fire as it burned down to glowing embers. She felt loved and protected, and soon, she was sleeping peacefully.

The morning sunlight, brilliant from the snow's reflection, streamed into the bedroom window and woke Charlotte. James was already up and dressed. Charlotte rose reluctantly and joined him for breakfast. He told her he hoped to ride to Manchester the first day and to arrive in Birmingham the second day, but with the heavy snow, it could take longer. John Fuller would meet him at an inn called the White Oxen. From there they would venture to Oxford and carry out the plan. If John saw that Audley brought only one friend, he would bring him to James. If there were any complications, Charlotte would be apprised as soon as possible. James made ready to leave, and his horse was brought around to the front of the house.

"Please, be careful, dearest," Charlotte whispered as they embraced.

"I shall, Lottie. In a week, you will be a free woman, I promise." James held Jack in his arms and hugged him. "Be good, Jackie," he said, his voice catching in his throat.

The morning was crisp and clear as James mounted his horse. He rode up the pack horse trail towards Watendlath. Charlotte watched as he disappeared over the crest of the hill. As each day passed, Charlotte's prayers for James's safety became more fervent. After a fortnight, with still no word, she was sure that the plans had gone seriously awry. Mid-morning of the fifteenth day, Mrs. Mungris came huffing and puffing into the parlour to tell Charlotte that a rider had just been sighted, starting the ascent up the hill from the village.

Charlotte grabbed her cloak and ran outside to see if it was James. She slipped and slid partway down the path then stopped, her heart going into her throat. It was a stranger. A man of middling height and weight, his dark hair pulled back in a queue. He wore a brown cloak and a brown tricorn hat. As he came closer, he nodded to her, his serious expression softened by his large brown eyes. He stopped his horse, dismounted, and introduced himself as John Fuller.

Charlotte could not contain herself. "Mr. Fuller, pray tell me what has happened."

"I shall, Mrs. Pruitt, but it is news best told inside out of the cold, if you please."

"Of course, forgive me. Please, come inside."

Mr. Fuller gave his horse to the stable boy. Charlotte led him in through the warm kitchen and into the parlour. They sat opposite each other by the hearth. Charlotte asked Mrs. Mungris, who had joined them, to have the cook prepare a meal for Mr. Fuller. As she left, Fuller stood up and moved closer to the fire to warm his cold hands.

He turned to Charlotte, saying, "Mrs. Pruitt, forgive me for being the bearer of ill tidings. I will come right to the point."

"Oh, dear God!" Charlotte exclaimed. "What's happened?"

"James walked into a trap. One that was set to catch your husband, as well."

"What do you mean, sir?"

"James is accused of murdering your husband."

Charlotte felt faint. The room began to spin. Mr. Fuller rushed to Charlotte's side. He called for Mrs. Mungris who came quickly from the kitchen. "Forgive me, Mrs. Mungris. I fear my news was too much for Mrs. Pruitt to bear.

"There, there, dear," Mrs. Mungris whispered to Charlotte. "Take a deep breath. Lean against me. Give me your hand." Charlotte obeyed her commands and felt comfort in the older woman's presence.

Mr. Fuller sat down and waited.

At last, Charlotte felt ready to go on. She thanked Mrs. Mungris for her care and asked if she might bring them tea.

"Forgive me, Mr. Fuller," Charlotte apologized. "Please tell me what happened."

"James and I met in Birmingham at the White Oxen as planned and rode from there to Oxford. I went to the inn where your husband agreed to meet me. However, when I arrived, the innkeeper presented me with a letter from Mr. Pruitt. Opening it, I read that because of pressing business matters Pruitt found himself unable to travel to Oxford. He suggested that if I wanted to choose an inn closer to the city, he would agree to meet me there."

"London!" Charlotte exclaimed. "But you both must

have known that that was not safe."

"James and I discoursed at length on this change. I counselled him against going, but he had such a desire to speak to your husband in hope of freeing you, that he was willing to take his chances. At the same time, he thought he would be able to secure a meeting place that would have the least possible risk involved."

"Forgive my outburst, Mr. Fuller, but I am sure that James acquainted you with our history. From the beginning of these dealings with my husband, I felt the greatest foreboding of disaster, and now it has come to pass. But, please, tell me the rest. You say my husband did not know of the trap? How is that possible?"

"Allow me, if you will, to tell the whole story, otherwise I do not know if bits and pieces will make sense."

"Of course, pray continue, sir."

Mrs. Mungris brought in the tea and Charlotte poured it for Mr. Fuller and herself.

"James and I rode to Hampstead. The Spaniard's Inn lies on the great Northern Road, hard by the toll house and not far from Lord Mansfield's estate of Kenwood. James reckoned that this would afford him the best escape route if he needed one. I sent a note with a messenger to Pruitt saying I would meet him at the Friar's inn in Golders Green on the following afternoon. I did not say, of course, that if I was satisfied that he had not brought the authorities then I would lead him to the Spaniard's Inn and to James. When Pruitt arrived the next day, he was accompanied by a lady and by a man who introduced himself as Jonas McHugh."

"Was the lady's name Countess Crespi?" Charlotte interjected.

"I believe that was her name. Pruitt was not happy

when I asked him and his party to follow me to another inn. The day was wet and cold. At last, he agreed, and got back into his coach, and I led them to Spaniard's Inn. When we arrived, I asked for a private room upstairs where we might dine. Mr. Pruitt and I met alone, and he was quite civil, giving me to understand how wronged he felt. I told him it was James Clarke's hope that he might consider a settlement of some kind. He said he was not opposed to hearing what the offer was. I asked him to wait a moment as there was another person who would discuss with him the terms of the settlement. I left and got James, telling him what had transpired. We came back to the room where Mr. Pruitt waited. He was very surprised to see James. I left them alone and waited outside. Pruitt soon began to raise his voice. James's tone remained calm from what I could hear. I know the sum he offered was a goodly amount, but it must not have been enough to satisfy Mr. Pruitt, because I suddenly heard him challenge James to a duel."

"Audley challenged James to a duel?" Charlotte asked incredulously.

"Pruitt shouted that he wanted satisfaction directly. 'You have sullied my marriage bed, turned my once good wife into a wanton bawd, and sired a bastard who I foolishly took into my heart as my own. I am not a man to be mocked, sir.' "

Charlotte was shocked to realize the pain she had caused Audley. "What happened next, Mr. Fuller?"

"James agreed to the duel but asked Mr. Pruitt to wait one hour. He asked him to reconsider the offer and to speak with him one more time before duelling. Mr. Pruitt reluctantly agreed. James came out, and we retired to our rooms and waited. He did not fear a duel, but he kept upbraiding himself for not being able to come to an agreement with Pruitt. Just before the end of the hour, James received a note saying that Pruitt was willing to discuss terms again. James was very happy. 'I believe I can convince him,' he told me and left to meet with him.

"I have tried to reconstruct what happened next, Mrs. Pruitt. After no more than five minutes, I heard someone shouting from down the hall, 'Murder! Get the constable!' There was a great commotion, and I ran to see what was happening. When I arrived at the meeting room, I saw three men holding James down, and to my horror, not five feet from James, Mr. Pruitt lay dead of a knife wound to his neck."

Again, Charlotte could not breathe. She blinked her eyes several times, her heart racing.

"Mrs. Pruitt, I am sorry," John Fuller said, seeing the colour drain from her face. "I am too blunt. Do you require assistance? Shall I call for Mrs. Mungris?"

Charlotte sat looking at the fire. She poured herself more tea. At last, her composure regained, she asked John to continue.

"I would hear the whole story, Mr. Fuller."

He waited for the colour to return to her cheeks. Satisfied she would not faint, he went on. "I could not believe my eyes. James's hands and shirt front were covered in blood. Large welts were rising on his face where he had been beaten into submission. He stopped struggling when he saw me. 'John, I am innocent. Please, tell Charlotte.' These words spoken, the constable and the justice of the peace entered. Surveying the carnage, the pustice instructed James should be taken to the Hampstead gaol, and from there, in the morning, to Newgate Prison."

"Were you able to see James after that?"

"No, for no sooner was he in Newgate but the gaolers found out about the baby's murder in Devon. This news, added to Mr. Pruitt's murder, caused them to chain him up, and no one is allowed to speak with him for the present. I discovered all this when I went to Newgate the following morning. A mob was gathered outside, threatening to hang James on the spot. I contacted a mutual friend of James and mine, Allen Peters, who promised to see James as soon as possible to get him money or 'rhino', as they call money in cant, which he will need to survive in prison."

"Cant?" Charlotte asked.

"The language of the streets."

Charlotte nodded.

"I left London then and came straight here."

"Mr. Fuller, what shall I do? I must travel to London immediately. There are arrangements to be made for my husband's funeral. I cannot believe he has come to this horrible end. I must find a barrister for James."

Charlotte paused. "Who could possibly have murdered Audley?"

"On my journey here, I went over that afternoon many times. I believe it was Jonas McHugh, the man who accompanied your husband. Though what reasons he had, I do not know."

"What was his appearance? Is it possible to describe him?"

"Mrs. Pruitt, I would be hard pressed to tell you what his face looked like, for truly I paid little heed to it. I do know with certainty that he and James are of a similar height, about six feet. He is heavier built than James. By no means is he fat, just well-muscled. He wore his hair long, not in a queue, which I thought odd.

"When I entered the room just after the murder occurred, I do not recall seeing McHugh. I did attempt to speak with Countess Crespi. She was an acquaintance of your late husband."

"You need not be delicate, sir. I am aware that she was my husband's mistress."

"She entered the room just after the justice of the peace. On seeing Mr. Pruitt's body, she fainted. I assisted the innkeeper in getting her back to her room. I went to speak with her a short time later, but she had left the inn."

Charlotte called for Mrs. Mungris and asked her to see to John Fuller's needs. After he was settled, she spent the rest of the day arranging a wet nurse for Jack. Mrs. Mungris found a woman from the village who was in good health. She had a baby Jack's age and she produced more than enough milk for both children. Annie, with Mrs. Mungris's guidance, would take care of Jack while Charlotte was in London.

A day after John Fuller's arrival, Charlotte received a letter from Harold Wooten, Audley's solicitor. It informed her of Audley's untimely death at the hands of a violent man. Fortunately, it was cold, Mr. Wooten wrote, so Audley's body would be kept on ice until Charlotte returned from the north. Lastly, the will would be read, and details of Audley's business would need to be seen to when she returned to London and was settled in Bellagio House.

The next morning saw John Fuller, Charlotte, Betsy, her maid, and two footmen riding to Keswick, where the women waited at the Boar's Head Inn for the southbound coach. The men rode ahead. John Fuller carried a message to Emma asking if Charlotte might be a guest at her house, at least initially, on her entry into London. Charlotte was certain there would be a great maelstrom of rumour, and she hoped at least in the beginning to be able to get her affairs arranged with some anonymity. Her greatest desire was to see James. She had no idea what obstacles might be in her path. She knew solicitors through Audley's business dealings. Perhaps one of them could advise her in finding a good barrister.

Charlotte realized that she need not have worried about Emma's welcome when she arrived in London. Her friend embraced her warmly, saying, "Charlotte, when I read in Town and Country that 'Mr. P of Spitalfields has been savagely set upon by Sir J of Devon, the reported friend of Mrs. P…,' I was aghast. You cannot imagine the number of ladies who came to call the next few days, inquiring discreetly, and some not so discreetly, if I knew any more information that I might share with them on this report. After Mr. Fuller brought your letter, I have waited anxiously for your arrival. You should be aware, my dear, that you are being sung about in the streets. I have it on good report from one of my servants. The tune is an old one, but the lyrics are new. The title being, 'Charlotte Bird'. It is all about a dove with a snowy white breast and her lover, a rather savage falcon. Quite a ditty."

Charlotte shook her head. "I must contact Mr. Wooten, my solicitor, at once to arrange Audley's funeral."

"Of course, as soon as you have composed a note to him, I shall send it off. I think you should know that Countess Crespi is a resident in your house."

"Oh, Emma, no, she cannot be that brazen!"

"It is only a rumour, but I would suggest before you go to Bellagio House that you ask Mr. Wooten to make certain she is not there."

"I shall indeed. Emma, have you heard any news of James?"

"Not a word."

Charlotte looked down at her hands, fighting the tears that threatened to fall. Dear God, she prayed silently, please protect my dear Jemmy.

CHAPTER ELEVEN

The next morning, as Charlotte awaited Mr. Wooten's arrival, John Fuller called with news of James. Charlotte invited him into the drawing room after they exchanged greetings. She sat down on the settee. He sat opposite her on a chair.

"James has his own chamber, albeit small," he began. "He does not want for food or clothes, Mrs. Pruitt. My friends and I have given a good deal of 'rhino' to the gaolers, who for the right price, will turn a blind eye to whatever you wish to bring to their wards, excepting files, of course."

"How are his spirits, sir?" Charlotte asked.

"Passable, madam, given the circumstances."

"Is it possible for me to see him, do you think?"

"It is. However, I would advise against it."

"Why?"

"There are two reasons. One, you have your reputation to think of, Mrs. Pruitt."

Here, Charlotte jumped in. "My good name is quite sullied, Mr. Fuller. Though I do not care to give the gossip mongers more to delight in, it is true. Perhaps, I might go in disguise of some kind." She eyed John's simple dress. "I might be a Quaker, or would that counterfeit greatly offend you?"

John could not resist a smile. "I would take no offense, madam. I, myself, have kept this manner of dress, though I am no longer a Quaker. However, I would have you schooled in their ways, if you choose that disguise. There is another reason I would ask you to reconsider visiting Newgate, however.

"And that is?"

"James told me he does not want you to come."

Charlotte felt as if she had been hit in the stomach. "And what is his reasoning?"

"He gave none, but it is a dreadful place to behold, and I think he would spare you that."

"I will see him. I pray you will prepare him for my visit. If I had wanted to avoid unpleasantness, I would have stayed in Rosthwaite."

At that moment, Mr. Wooten, Charlotte's solicitor, was announced, and John Fuller took his leave, saying that he would return later that day, with Charlotte's permission, so that they might talk about the Quaker customs. Charlotte suggested he come at tea later in the afternoon, an invitation he gladly accepted before bidding her good-bye.

Mr. Harold Wooten was shown into Emma's drawing room where Charlotte greeted him. Mr. Wooten, a round man with red cheeks, was civil, but not overly friendly as he had been in times past. Charlotte asked him to assist her with the funeral arrangements. He nodded his agreement and assured her he would help in any way he could.

He cleared his throat and said, "Mrs. Pruitt, I made inquiries as you requested about Countess Crespi, who was, as you know, an acquaintance of your late husband."

"Yes, and what did you discover, sir?"

Mr. Wooten cleared his throat. "Well, she is still in residence at your home in Spitalfields, and I understand that, though grief stricken, she has been doing quite a bit of entertaining in the last few days."

Charlotte sat up straighter in her chair. "Mr. Wooten, I would ask you to remove this woman from my house as soon as possible."

"Yes, Mrs. Pruitt, I shall make arrangements forthwith. I shall return in the morning, with your permission, and advise you as to the progress of events." He stood up, making ready to take his leave.

"Before you go, sir, there are two more matters I have for you."

Mr. Wooten stood awkwardly, looking unsure whether he should remain standing or sit again. After a moment, still standing, he replied. "Yes, madam."

"I wish you to postpone James Clarke's trial, so that it will not be heard at the next scheduled sessions at the Old Bailey."

Without blinking, he responded, "That will cost a goodly amount, Mrs. Pruitt."

"Money, sir, is not a problem. Please, see how it is best done and tell me the sum that it will cost. I also wish to meet with James Clarke."

Mr. Wooten's complexion paled, and he sat down. "Mrs. Pruitt," he spluttered, "I would most highly advise against such a course of action. The mob is calling for James Clarke's blood for the murder of the babe in Devon, and London society wants to see him hang as quickly as possible for your husband's brutal slaying. To openly associate with him would put yourself and your son in jeopardy."

Charlotte listened, and answered curtly, "Thank you,

Mr. Wooten, I shall consider your counsel, but I want you to understand that James Clarke is an innocent man. We simply need time to prove it. Now, good day to you, sir."

For the next several hours, whenever Charlotte closed her eyes, she saw James swinging from the gallows. She determined she must save him from that fate, whatever the cost or risk. Charlotte retired to her room until it was time for tea. When she arrived at the parlour, she found John Fuller and Emma already talking about life in London. Charlotte greeted them both and was soon asking questions about Quaker life, which John was happy to answer. Charlotte noted that Emma seemed pleased to have this gentleman's company.

The next day brought the news that James's case would not be heard at the upcoming sessions. Mr. Wooten had done the job that Charlotte requested. She sent the amount required to his office. Now they would have five weeks until the next round of trials. She planned to ask Wooten to see what influence he might have with the witnesses and jurors. She hoped they might be persuaded to reconsider what they witnessed at Spaniard's Inn and to recant their depositions. The jurors, perhaps, could be swayed to James's side if the price was right. Late in the day, Charlotte received a second message from Mr. Wooten saying that Countess Crespi would vacate Bellagio House on the morrow.

Charlotte reinstated herself in Bellagio House as soon as the countess was gone. The servants gave no hint that life in the house had been in upheaval. Mr. Primm did approach Charlotte to give his and the staff's condolences for Mr. Pruitt's "untimely passing". She thanked him and asked him to do a tour of the house with her. Mr. Primm showed her the new china and silver plate in the dining room, the new carpets in the parlour, an assortment of ladies' silver shoe buckles, jewelled mirrors, and ornate snuff boxes in Audley's dressing room, and the new, very large bed that Audley had purchased for his bedroom. His mistress's taste ran to the rococo, Charlotte noted as she surveyed the ornate bed posts. Charlotte asked Mr. Primm to remove the bed and replace it with the old one.

Audley's funeral was arranged and took place at Christ Church, Spitalfields, where he had had a pew for years. Many of his business associates attended. They all offered Charlotte their heartfelt condolences. She could not help noticing that there was an inordinate amount of whispering, and a good many glances in her direction.

The next day, Charlotte met with Audley's solicitor for the reading of the will. Audley's fortune, business holdings, and houses would pass to Jack as his heir. Since he was a minor, she would oversee it all until he came of age. Charlotte was bequeathed a yearly income of two thousand pounds. Countess Crespi was not mentioned. How fortunate that Audley had not gotten around to changing his will, Charlotte thought.

On returning home, she sent a note to Mr. George Sharp, the man entrusted to oversee Pruitt and Byrd, Ltd., when Audley was out of the country. Charlotte asked that Mr. Sharp call on her so that they might discuss the future of the business and his place in it. Sharp's name, Charlotte thought, described both his physical features and his quick mind.

On meeting with her, Mr. Sharp agreed to stay on and advise her on the running of the company. "I have one more request at present, Mr. Sharp, that I would like you to fulfil."

"What might that be, Mrs. Pruitt?"

"To raise the amounts paid to our weavers for their work."

"I would caution against that course of action, Mrs. Pruitt. The other silk merchants will be most unhappy with it, and Pruitt and Byrd will have to raise prices in order to make up the difference."

"Nevertheless, I wish it done. Our weavers work hard and deserve better than we give them at present." Mr. Sharp left, agreeing to fulfil Charlotte's request.

The rest of the day, she attempted to clean out Audley's armoire and chest of drawers, but it became too painful a process and she stopped. During the last six months, she'd had no feelings for Audley except anger turned to hatred when he threatened to take Jack, but now as she faced the reality of this death, she wept. It was her fault, she told herself, that he had met this terrible end.

The thought of Jonas McHugh crossed her mind. Who was he? Why had he done this? Suddenly, her mind jumped to the stranger who raped her. How could she have forgotten? Suddenly, she felt alone and afraid. She needed protection. She did not tarry. That day, she sought out and hired three guards to watch the house and accompany her when she went abroad in the town.

When John Fuller came to call early the next day, he was met at the door by a guard dressed as a footman. With Charlotte's permission, he was ushered into the parlour. They spoke briefly of the funeral.

"Mrs. Pruitt, would you care to accompany me today to Newgate prison?" John asked. "I believe the disguise I have brought will protect your identity. I have paid the gaolers to give us some time alone with James. He already has been visited by several wealthy and curious men and women who would have it known that they have associated with him in his fallen state." Charlotte accepted his invitation, but before she could retire to her dressing room to put on the Quaker attire he had brought her, John added, "James is immovable in not wanting you to see him, but I think it is important that you do visit him."

Concerned, Charlotte asked, "Why, what is it?"

"He has fallen into a most deep melancholy, Mrs. Pruitt. Even though he has candles, he chooses to sit in the dark. He has stopped eating. Though these things have only begun to occur in the last two days, they portend ill."

"I shall be ready quickly."

Charlotte left the room and had Betsy, her maid, help her prepare. Brushing her hair into a simple bun, Betsy pinned it into place. She helped Charlotte dress and made sure all the rouge was wiped from her face. When Charlotte joined John, he complemented her on the transformation and presented her with a hooded, brown, woollen cloak.

"I would suggest you keep your face covered until we reach James's cell."

"I shall."

"And take this posy, too. Put it in front of your nose to ward off the prison fever and help with the stink."

Charlotte took the little bunch of flowers and thanked him. She shuddered, imagining this new world she was about to enter.

The coach bumped along over the cobbled streets. When they were near their destination John cleared his throat. "James is being badly persecuted by the gaolers who feel justified in beating him for the baby's murder. Each time I visit him, he has some new injury. I hope in saying this that you may be able to prepare yourself for his appearance and his melancholic state."

Charlotte nodded her head. "Thank you for the warning, sir."

They took Charlotte's coach to St. Sepulchre-without-Newgate church, and from there they walked the last hundred yards to the forbidding entrance to Newgate prison. John gave Charlotte a steadying hand down the slippery stone steps. They entered the dank entry way, where John spoke with a tall, obese man who appeared to be in charge. The man's right eye drooped, and he face was badly pockmarked. Charlotte pulled her cloak more closely around her.

The fat man called to a short, withered gaoler, then turned to John Fuller. "E'll take ye." He let them pass. Charlotte stayed close to John as they started down the first of many dark, stone corridors they would traverse to reach James.

The stench was horrific, and Charlotte put the posy to her nose. Urine, excrement, rotting straw and filthy bodies all combined into an indescribably rank odour. The posy was no match for it. In the third passageway, screams and moans met Charlotte's ears. As they moved along, hands emerged from little windows in the cell doors and tried to touch her cape and hood. She fought her rising panic by looking straight ahead. She noticed John was praying softly as they walked.

They followed the old, withered man through a heavy wooden door and entered yet another corridor. Here, defiant curses were spat at them. Charlotte could hear chains being dragged across the stone floor. When she let her eyes stray to the side, she saw leering eyes and tongues being run over toothless gums. As they crossed a small courtyard, John told Charlotte that they were crossing from the ordinary prison to the press yard, a place reserved for those who could afford it. She found little difference between the two.

Finally, they climbed three flights of winding stairs and came to the door of a small tower chamber. The gaoler turned the key and opened the door. Charlotte was hit with a cold draft of air and a rank odour filled her nose. The room was lit from the outside by a small slit in the wall.

" 'Alf an 'our," the withered gaoler croaked at John, who pressed some coins into the man's open hand. "An 'our then. I'll be back." He turned and made his way down the steps, counting his money as he went.

"James?" John called as he stepped into the darkness. "I have brought you a visitor."

"Who?" The question came from one of the corners.

"It's me, James," Charlotte said as she stepped into the cell.

"Charlotte?"

"Yes," she answered.

"You should not have come. John, I told you not to bring her here." James said in a low growl.

"I insisted Mr. Fuller bring me."

"I am dead to you, Charlotte. Do you understand?" His voice was cold.

Charlotte walked toward him, trying to make out his form. John lit a candle, and she stopped. He sat on a stone bench with his knees pulled up to his chest. His wrists were shackled together, as were his ankles. His face, what she could see of it, was gaunt and pale.

"I will not abandon you, James," Charlotte said.

"They will hang me," he said, turning his face to her. She gasped. The left side of his face was reddish purple with bruises. One of his eyes was blackened and swollen nearly shut.

"You are innocent," she responded emphatically, unable to draw her gaze away from his swollen eye.

"Yes, I am, but the man who killed your husband has made certain that all evidence points to me."

"Who is he, James?" Charlotte asked.

"Edward Hawkes, my commanding officer in Portugal. The one I left to die because of his brutality to that boy."

"Edward Hawkes and Jonas McHugh are the same person? James, I do not understand," Charlotte whispered, unable to comprehend.

"He wants revenge. He is a madman," James answered.

Charlotte sat down on the bench next to James. She put her arms around him and stroked his hair. Wanting to give them some privacy, John Fuller stepped from the cell, pulling the door closed. James was shivering.

Charlotte noticed his arms were cold. She took off her cloak and wrapped it around him. He rested his head on her breast and began to weep. She held him, closing her eyes.

When his tears ceased, she spoke. "Tell me what happened, Jem."

"John told you some of it."

"Yes, but he did not say what you encountered when you came the second time into the room to meet with Audley."

James took her hand and sat up. "Charlotte, I went to that meeting, hopeful that your husband had had a change of heart. The room was long and narrow, lit by three candles on a table at the far end. Pruitt was standing by the table. He beckoned me to come to him. There was an alcove in the wall about two thirds of the way down. I did not know it was there. I followed his directions and approached him. Pruitt said that he had reconsidered my offer and felt he had been too hasty. I said I would ask only that he retract what he had said about you. He became choleric. By this time, I was standing close to him.

"For an instant, his eyes moved to something over my shoulder and behind me. He called out, 'No! We agreed, no violence.' I began to turn but was pushed forward into Audley at the same moment a knife slashed down through his neck and throat. Soaked in blood, I caught him as he fell, but I was off balance and went to my knees. I felt a knife at my throat. A voice close to my ear said, 'So Jem, it's me who get to leave you to die this time.' I knew it was Hawkes. He made insulting remarks about you and me. He slashed my ear and kicked me in the head. I fell onto Audley's body. Hawkes ran to the door crying, 'murder!'

"He escaped by a door hidden in the opposite wall. I attempted to follow him, but several men entered and wrestled me to the ground. John came next, followed by Countess Crespi. John tried to calm everyone down, but the justice of the peace and the constable, who had been dining at the inn, were ushered in and I was bound and transported to the local gaol and then to Newgate.

"Jem," Charlotte said, "perhaps if I talk to Countess Crespi, she might know where Hawkes is. If I can find him…"

This caused a violent reaction in James. He jumped up, and despite his manacles, grabbed Charlotte, pulling her to her feet. "No!" he hissed. "Hawkes is a monster. He will destroy you! Charlotte, he was the man who violated you and tortured me on the moor. He must be. How else would he have known our secrets? When he had the knife at my throat, after he killed Audley, he called you Mistress Mawk and described what he had done to you." Shocked, Charlotte stared at James. "I have spent my time in prison thinking of what I must do to protect you and Jack. I have no hope of proving my innocence. If I am dead, Hawkes will have no reason to harm you. You will be safe."

"Jem, do not say that! Your case will not be heard for five weeks. My solicitor is talking to witnesses and jurors. We will win your freedom. You must not give up hope."

John Fuller knocked on the door. "The gaoler is returning."

"Jem, I will write to you. John will bring you my letters. You must promise me you will not sink into a melancholy state. I will come again." They held on to each other for a moment, then James broke away. "Please, Charlotte, I stink of this prison."

She moved to him and kissed him. "And I do not care." She smiled.

"I love you, Lottie."

"And I love you, James. Do not forget that."

They moved apart as John opened the door. The withered gaoler stood beside him, still fingering the coins. James moved to give Charlotte her cloak, but she refused it, indicating for him to keep it. Leaving the cell, she heard the sound of James's manacles and leg irons as he moved back to the stone bench.

The gaoler, looking at Charlotte after he locked the cell door, cooed suggestively, "Oh, you're sure to go to 'eaven for your good works, Mistress Quaker. But what's the use o' that since old Jemmy there will burn in 'ell for what 'e's done."

Shocked, Charlotte bit her tongue, not wanting to seem other than the Quaker lady she was pretending to be.

Walking back to the coach, Charlotte neither felt nor heard anything around her. She concentrated on James, wanting to hold onto the sound of his voice and the image of his face. The mist outside had turned to a cold, hard rain. She sat trembling as they rode back to her house. When they arrived, she thanked John for all his assistance.

"Do not lose heart," he told her, "I will take your letters when you are ready to send them."

"Mr. Fuller, I would give you money to see that James lacks for nothing. Whatever clothing, candles, books, or food he needs, please, make certain he is provided with them."

"I shall, Mrs. Pruitt. I promise."

"Please, if you would, address me as Charlotte," she asked him.

"I would be most honoured to, Charlotte, if you will return the favour and call me John."

"I shall, John, thank you. And thank you for all your assistance," she said, smiling despite her melancholy.

After John left, Charlotte summoned Mr. Wooten to her at Bellagio House. He was in the process, he told her, of meeting with the witnesses to Audley's murder. He was also beginning to visit with jurymen to see if there was any hope of keeping the bill from the grand jury in Guildhall. As he made ready to leave, Charlotte asked him to see what information he might find about Edward Hawkes. He promised to do his best.

It was odd, Charlotte thought to herself after Mr. Wooten left, to be in London and to be so isolated. True, she saw Emma frequently, and through her was kept abreast of the news of the town, but otherwise, she travelled abroad little and was certainly not invited anywhere. Her thoughts turned to Jack. It seemed so long since she had seen him. Was it only two weeks? She missed him terribly. As she sat in her bedroom, looking out at her barren garden in the cold rain, she began to cry. She would miss Jack's first Christmas and most probably his first birthday. She felt fatigued and cold. Getting up, she moved toward her bed, and as she did, her eye caught Jack's cradle. Audley had been so proud of it. He invested so much time in its planning and supervising its building.

"Dear Audley," she whispered, "please forgive me."

Please, dear Lord, she began to pray, please be with Jack and with me. Please, save James and let us be together. Please, forgive me for the part I played in Audley's death. Please, forgive all my sins, dear God. The light was fading outside. The rain pelted the windows. She wrapped herself in her blankets and tried to keep warm.

Sometime later, she was awakened by Betsy, her maid. Charlotte heard her voice from what seemed a long distance away, saying, "Mrs. Pruitt, you were moaning. Oh, dear Lord, you're burnin' up. I'll get Mr. Primm. Don't move now."

The chills made Charlotte's body shake. She held the blankets closer, but she was perspiring so profusely that the covering became wet, and she grew cold. Mr. Primm told her afterward that she had been sick for five days. Her only recollection was of light and dark. She would open her eyes and there was light in the room, the next time she came to consciousness it was dark. She lost all track of time.

Mr. Wooten came to call while she was ill. After that,

he checked in daily with Mr. Primm and when Charlotte was feeling better, he was her first visitor. He was much kinder towards her, seeing how pale she was and that she could not stand without assistance. They talked briefly about the current news of London, and he asked her to sign some papers regarding Audley's business ventures.

The discussion turned to the search for Edward Hawkes. Mr. Wooten brought Charlotte the news that the official records reported that Hawkes died in Portugal in the service of his King. How convenient for Hawkes, thought Charlotte. It has made it so much easier for him to assume whatever identity he desires. But we will find you, Edward Hawkes, Charlotte vowed silently, wherever you may be.

Wooten had spoken with all seven of the people who had made depositions in Audley's murder case. Five were willing, for the right price, to cast doubt on what they had witnessed. Unfortunately, two were intransigent. One was a clergyman from Leeds, Reverend Walter Coates, who had been traveling through on his way to a new post in Guilford, when he stopped at the Spaniard's Inn. He was the first person to enter the room that night, directly after the murder. When Mr. Wooten spoke with him, he said he never witnessed such a brutal crime before and would never think of recanting his testimony.

The other witness, who had just come forward, was Audley's mistress, Countess Isabella Crespi. Mr. Wooten tried to set up an appointment to see her, but she refused, which did not surprise Charlotte, since they had evicted her from Bellagio House. It was imperative, Charlotte realized, that she speak with the countess. She saw the error in alienating this woman.

"Mr. Wooten, I appreciate all your work in these matters. I shall try myself to see the countess. She is, I think, our link to Edward Hawkes, although she knows him as Jonas McHugh."

Mr. Wooten finished his report, saying that he would be meeting with three jurymen next week and would report directly to Charlotte with any news. He promised he would not give up on Reverend Coates, then he took his leave.

The rest of the day, Charlotte spent thinking of how to approach the countess. The woman had taken up fashionable residence in the West End and was presently, from Emma's accounts, invited to dine with the lords and ladies of London. Charlotte knew that she was not a wealthy woman, for her aunt, Countess Cittidini, had told Charlotte that her niece's late husband lost much of his wife's fortune through gambling. Charlotte suspected that Countess Crespi, herself, had been gambling on winning Audley's fortune before he died.

Suddenly, Charlotte thought of all the beautiful items Audley had bought to furnish Bellagio House for his mistress. Perhaps, Charlotte thought, she could entice the countess to visit her. She would say that as a friend of Countess Crespi's aunt, she wished to make amends for the hasty eviction. She would invite the countess to take whatever mementos she might want from the house. Perhaps Charlotte might even offer her the rococo bed. She sat down and wrote a carefully worded letter to the countess.

Bellagio House, Spitalfields
Dear Countess Crespi,

I fear the most unfortunate of circumstances have set us at odds. As I count your aunt, Countess Cittidini, among my cherished friends, I hope I may make amends for my rash ill treatment of you so recently. Please accept my invitation to join me at Bellagio House Wednesday next, at 1:00 in the afternoon. There are many beautiful items I know my late husband would have wanted you to have. It is my hope that you will come so I may present them to you.

Yours most faithfully,
Charlotte Pruitt

Charlotte sent a footman off directly after finishing the letter, afraid that she might turn coward if she did not proceed immediately with her plan. To her surprise, she received a reply back by the same messenger.

To Mrs. Pruitt,

I accept.

Yours,
Countess Isabella Crespi

Going to her escritoire, Charlotte penned an invitation to Emma, who answered almost as quickly as the countess. Emma was eager to be involved and helped Charlotte with everything from planning the menu, to the seating arrangement in the drawing room, to what items Charlotte would first offer the countess. They decided to bring the rococo bed out of storage. Mr. Primm and several of the stronger servants hauled it, sweating and panting, back up the stairs and placed it in Audley's bedroom.

The day of the meeting dawned crisp and bright. The storm that had dropped continuous cold rain for eight days blew on to other places, and the birds rejoiced in the sunny wet garden. Emma arrived early. She and Charlotte arranged all the smaller items that Charlotte was sure Audley bought for the countess, at one end of the drawing room.

At one o'clock in the afternoon, an elegant landau arrived at the front door, and out stepped Countess Crespi. Emma and Charlotte watched from Audley's bedroom window. She was tall, several inches taller than Charlotte and big boned. She had a lovely face and masses of blonde curls that sat atop a foot of pads and hair pieces. In her arms she held a King Charles Cavalier Spaniel. Mr. Primm ushered her into the house, and Emma and Charlotte quickly came down to receive her in the drawing room.

The ladies made their introductions as the countess's little dog barked. They sat down to open negotiations before refreshment was served. Emma did much of the talking initially. The countess sat very straight and answered Emma's inquires with a clipped yes or no.

After a moment of uncomfortable silence, Charlotte spoke. "Dear Countess, I realize this is an extremely awkward situation for you as, you must understand, it is for me. I know from the letters my late husband wrote to me that you brought him much happiness and that your company was a consolation to him during our estrangement."

The countess watched Charlotte as she spoke, and when she took a breath, the countess interjected, petting her spaniel rather more vigorously than necessary. "I am here, Signora Pruitt, because my aunt would wish it. I had great affection for Audley Pruitt and would have been his wife had not your lover murdered him."

Charlotte, at that moment, wished to murder her, but she held her tongue and smiled with some difficulty. "Dear Countess Crespi, I will attribute your breach of etiquette to a different cultural sensibility, but I will tell you straight out that James Clarke did not murder Audley Pruitt."

"*Oddio!*" the countess responded heatedly. "I went into that room. I saw Clarke drenched in Audley's blood. I saw the wound torn in Audley's neck. I saw with my own eyes these horrors!"

"Countess, Audley was murdered by Jonas McHugh, the man Audley called his friend. The man who accompanied you to Spaniard's Inn."

"That is impossible!" the countess retorted. "The man you speak of is a kind and gentle man. He could not possibly have done such an act. He and Audley were inseparable. I assumed they had known each other for many years."

"I never knew Audley to mention this man," Charlotte said emphatically, which seemed to give the countess pause. "I certainly never met him. He was with Audley in Venice?"

"*Si*, they had just come back from a hunting trip in the north when my aunt introduced me to Audley. Jonas McHugh was with him."

"Had they been with Count Cesi?" Charlotte asked.

"No, I believe the count was out of the country, but he offered them the use of his horses and dogs for hunting. They stayed several nights in his chalet in the mountains."

"Countess Crespi, where is McHugh now? Do you

know?"

"He is gone to Paris, I believe. He came here to the house to say good-bye. He was melancholy at the loss of his friend. He wept openly. Business, he said, called him away."

Charlotte shuddered, imagining Hawkes in her house again. She prayed he had gone to France and not travelled north instead. She felt an urgent need to get word of warning to Annie and Mrs. Mungris. They needed to be vigilant and wary of strangers. She continued her inquiry.

"Did McHugh speak to you of his past or from where he hailed? I must find him, Countess Crespi."

"He was a quiet man," the countess said, "very reserved in my company. The only occasion we had to speak, just the two of us, was when we were waiting for Audley to come down to dinner. We were both partaking in a glass of champagne. I was anxious that Audley might not find my company pleasing, but Mr. McHugh was complimentary and eased my fears. He told me he knew Audley cared for me and that he would do his best to see that Audley and I were together. This delighted me, and I impulsively attempted to embrace him to show my appreciation. He almost fell down trying to elude my touch. It was most embarrassing. I apologized for my boldness, and he assured me it was only his shyness that caused him to move away in such haste. Audley appeared, and we spoke no more about it. However, after that, Audley's interest in me increased." The countess looked at Charlotte. "Did you love your husband, Mrs. Pruitt?"

"I did, Countess. I cared for him. When I realized that Audley and I would separate, I wished only for his happiness, and I am certain with you, he would have found it."

"And you love James Clarke?"

"Yes, and will spend my life with him, God willing."

"I had knowledge of you Mrs. Pruitt, from my aunt, who is most fond of you, and from Audley, who, when we were first introduced spoke highly of you. However, a few weeks later, that good opinion changed most abruptly. When he called on me one morning, he was like a different man. He was filled with rage. He told me you betrayed him. I do not think it was that you had taken a lover that so inflamed his jealousy, but rather the passionate abandon of your affair. He felt a fool, and when he discovered his beloved son was a bastard, it was too much. That was when he came to me as a lover. He was most ardent, almost Venetian in his seduction. I welcomed his advances. I am a widow. My husband gambled away my dowry and family fortune and died. Audley promised to give me a new life."

The countess's mouth tightened, and she began to cry. Her spaniel looked concerned. Charlotte reached out and took the countess's hand in hers. Countess Crespi moved closer to Charlotte and wept on her shoulder. Emma caught Charlotte's eye. Her expression showed she was as touched by this unexpected display of sentiment as Charlotte was.

Charlotte called for the servants to bring in coffee and cake. The three women adjourned to the table for the anticipated refreshments. Charlotte guided the discussion to more light-hearted subjects. When the food and drink was brought in, Charlotte served her guests. The countess poured a little saucer of cream for her dog, who lapped at it daintily. The countess regaled them with the latest scandals of Venice. Emma and she talked of the people they knew in common, from the Lennox sisters to Fanny

Burney. When they finished eating, Charlotte proposed that
the countess choose which items she might wish to take
away with her. Countess Crespi obliged, viewing the china,
silver plate, and linens assembled in the drawing room, as
well as shoe buckles, snuff boxes, and jewellery. Charlotte
urged her to take it all.

Then, she broached the subject of the rococo bed. "I
could not possibly take it," the countess responded. "It is
an exquisite piece of furniture, but it belongs in his
bedroom."

"Please, dear Countess Crespi, you must accept it. I
know he purchased it with you in mind. Please, I wish you
to have it," Charlotte insisted.

"Thank you, Mrs. Pruitt. It was to be a wedding present,
though he bought it prematurely, to be sure." The countess
paused, then, weighing her words carefully, she spoke. "I
understand your love for Signor Clarke. Venetians
appreciate passion, perhaps more than the English, I think.
Do you agree?"

Charlotte, remembering the island and the summer
nights, responded, "Yes, I do. Countess, please, if you will,
address me as Charlotte."

"I shall, my dear Charlotte, and you must call me
Isabella. What a strange day, eh? I did not expect to be
pleased by your company, but I am. I have been so alone in
London. However, I am not prepared to return to Venice.
Not yet."

The rest of the afternoon, the three women spent
talking of their lives and their upbringings. Charlotte and
Emma found Isabella delightful company. They lost track
of the hours. As the room began to grow dark, the servants
entered and lit candles. Charlotte offered the countess

dinner, but she declined. She told them that she had an invitation to visit Richmond House that evening. She promised, however, to see Charlotte and Emma again. As she made ready to go, Charlotte asked her one more question.

"Isabella, how would you describe Jonas McHugh?"

"Signor McHugh is a tall man with long blond hair. Broadly built. His eyes are blue. He is attractive in his way, though I never saw him with a female companion. He was so serious and seemed interested only in business. Yet when we spoke, he was kind to me. I find it difficult to imagine he could have hurt Audley."

"I believe he is a consummate actor, Isabella, better even than our acclaimed Mr. Garrick," Charlotte said.

Before Isabella and her spaniel were handed up into the landau, she bid good-bye to Emma. Turning to Charlotte she said, "It has been a most delightful afternoon. I realize we have more to speak about, but I must go. *Arrivederci.*"

During the following week, Charlotte received three invitations from people who before would not have deigned to have her in their houses. She knew it was the countess's doing. Emma, who had come to call, teased that Charlotte was becoming a celebrity and would soon have no time for her old acquaintances. A servant entering the parlour announced that Mr. John Fuller had just arrived. Charlotte noted that Emma appeared quite delighted by this news. John entered and greeted them both. He presented Charlotte with a letter from James. While she read it, John and Emma spoke quietly.

Newgate
Dearest Lottie,

I have just been taken to a better cell. There is a small desk and a stool so that I may write or read whenever I desire. I can see the street from my small slit of a window. The gaoler allotted me three candles, so when it is dark so early on these winter afternoons, I may find some comfort in my chamber. Thank you, dear Lottie, for making these joys possible. As my thoughts wander, I ofttimes find myself imagining I am with you in Rosthwaite.

But there is little peace. The gaolers continue to hound me. I do my best to hold my tongue and endure their beatings. The worst is to hear St. Sepulchre's bell tolling. There are so many people here that are without hope. I think sometimes I shall go mad, knowing the bell's ringing means more hangings. From my window, I can view the processions starting their journeys to the gallows at Tyburn. I see the people in the carts, sitting on their pine coffins. This is a grim place.

I pray that someday I shall be free again to be with you and with Jackie.

Your obedient and loving servant,
Jem

Charlotte quickly wiped away her tears, tried to take a deep breath, and closed her eyes. The room, she noticed, had become very quiet. Opening her eyes, she saw John and Emma looking at her, concern on their faces. "Forgive me," she said.

John spoke, "Perhaps, Lady Emma, you would accompany me on a walk to Spital Square, so as to allow

192

Charlotte a brief time alone. When we return, Charlotte, I could take a response to James if you wish."

Charlotte smiled. "That would please me greatly, John. Thank you." She turned to Emma. "Do you mind a walk, dear friend?"

"Not a bit. An excellent idea," Emma replied, smiling at John. After they left, Charlotte sat at her writing desk and began to compose a note.

Bellagio House, Spitalfields
Dearest Jem,

I thank God that we may write to each other. I have just read your letter, and I feel as if you were here with me. Do not despair. Block out the sound of the bell. Think only that we will be together.

There are two witnesses that stand in the way of our winning your freedom. One, the Countess Crespi, Audley's mistress, will recant her deposition, I believe. The other, a clergyman from Guilford, is determined to testify against you. However, Mr. Wooten, my solicitor, may be able to convince him otherwise.

I am spending much of my time attending to Audley's business with the help of Mr. Sharp. The scandal seems to have made Pruitt and Byrd more popular than ever. Several new clients of wealth and rank have written us just this week. At the same time, I am being invited back into Society, both through my business dealings and through Countess Crespi's influence. People are curious, I suppose. I am sure the ordinary qualities of my person disappoint them greatly.

I miss you, dearest. I, too, try to imagine us back in Rosthwaite, unburdened by the problems that now beset us. We shall be there again, I promise you.

Until tomorrow, when I shall write again.

Yours with most sincere affection,
Lottie

John and Emma returned from their walk. Emma's pleasure at being with John was apparent to Charlotte, who was glad to see her friend so happy. John promised to take the letter to James. Charlotte gave him money to help in his dealing with the gaolers and thanked him for being such a loyal friend.

After he left, Emma told Charlotte all he had said on their walk. He related that he and James were childhood friends from Devon. "It is a wonder that I never met him at Kirkmoor. John left there and accompanied his father to Pennsylvania to help with the family's new estate. He and James met again when James came with General Campbell to protect the Colonies against the French. James had at this time told John of Hawkes's illegal trafficking in guns and whiskey with the Iroquois. James threatened to expose Hawkes, but the rogue transferred to another command before James could prove any wrongdoing. It was later, when James went to Portugal, that he again encountered Hawkes."

"Emma, I believe I shall ask John to speak to Reverend Coates in Guilford. Perhaps, he can convince him that James is not a murderer."

"An excellent idea, Charlotte. His simple dress and plain speaking give him an air of respectability and honesty that Mr. Wooten, as a solicitor, does not have."

A several days passed. Charlotte and James wrote to each other daily. He wrote that when his spirits fell, her words kept him from sliding into unrelenting melancholy. Yet her anxiety grew as each day John reported new incidents of the gaolers' cruelty. How long, she wondered, would James endure their words and blows? Mr. Wooten was unsuccessful in keeping the jurymen from bringing the bill to Guildhall. The case was to be heard in one week. John convinced Reverend Coates that there was at least a possibility that James was innocent. Charlotte prayed that this doubt of culpability might be passed on to the jury and judges.

Three days before the sessions were scheduled, Elizabeth, James's sister arrived from Chagford. She'd had trouble getting away, she told Charlotte. Her mother, Lady Clarke, was gravely ill, and Elizabeth had been attending her day and night. Her father did not believe his son murdered the baby, but when James was arrested for Audley's killing, he became despondent. He spent hours, Elizabeth related, sitting and refusing to speak.

"But, Charlotte, I must tell you that just before I began my journey here, I heard the most distressing news."

"What was it, Elizabeth?" Charlotte asked.

The Sheriff of Exeter is coming, or perhaps has come already to London. He has sworn that if James does not hang at Tyburn, he will take him back to Devon for trial."

Charlotte felt at her wits' end. She could not imagine what this news would do to James's flagging spirits. "I must go tomorrow and see him, Elizabeth. He needs to know this turn of events."

At that very moment, James was being dragged and kicked up three flights of stairs to a small, round room known as the Castle. Unable to control his rage at one particularly cruel gaoler who beat him nearly senseless, he feigned death. Bending over him, the man dropped his guard. James threw the chain of his shackles around the man's neck and began to strangle him. He would have killed him, had not one of the other gaolers come in and knocked James unconscious. As he lay on the floor of the Castle, they locked his leg irons into the floor next to the cold fireplace. With a final kick to his stomach, the gaolers left him in darkness, the stone floor his bed.

Despite his pain, a smile played across his lips. This was the room he prayed they would bring him to. This was the place from which Jack Sheppard had made his famous escape. James remembered every detail of the story he had heard as a boy. He began to work his hands out of the cuffs, as he had been practicing for the last fortnight. He listened for the gaolers, ready to put the cuffs back on if need be. A file was what he needed now, for the leg irons. He fell asleep, dreaming of walking free on the moor.

In the morning, he woke to the half-light of the cell, his body stiff and aching. When a gaoler came, he requested that he be allowed to write one last letter. The gaoler agreed, smiling nastily.

"One last to your Quaker lady, eh, Jem?"

James finished the note just as John Fuller was ushered into the Castle. After checking that James was not mortally injured, John laughed. "I had to pay dearly for an audience with you today. Your fame is growing hourly. There is an actress and Whig ready to come up to have tea with you when I am done."

"John, I have one last note for Charlotte. Please, take it to her on leaving here. I would have her read it directly."

"I shall, James."

"Tuck it away in your boot. I want no one else to see it

but her." John agreed and left for Bellagio House.

After reading James's note, Charlotte lost no time in finding a file. She sewed the file into the stomacher of her Quaker dress, then finished readying herself. She had to stand very straight to keep the point from piercing her breast.

The withered gaoler leered at her as he led her to the Castle. "Mistress, will you visit me after your lover has hung from the triple tree? Old as I am, I can still make a young wench squeal if she opens her legs to me."

Disgusted, Charlotte wished she had come accompanied by John. She looked straight ahead while feeling the man's breath on her as they walked. When the door was unlocked to the Castle, she ran to James's side. The old man stood and peered at them.

"Please leave us," Charlotte implored. "I have paid your price." The gaoler held out his crippled hand. She took some coins from her pocket and crossing to him, placed them in his palm. He caught hold of her wrist. James, infuriated, tried to get to him but was held back by his shackles.

The old man pulled Charlotte painfully down to her knees, the file cutting into her, as he whispered in her ear. "I've a long tongue to lick your thighs, Mistress Quaker. Remember me in your prayers. Jem'll be dead a week Sunday. Oh, what a brave man he is, killin' little ones. If t'were me doin' the sentencin', I'd have him disembowelled." The gaoler pushed Charlotte to the floor, slammed the door and locked it.

Charlotte moved to James and kissed him. She quickly undid the ribbons holding her stomacher, ripped out the stitches and took out the file.

"My saviour," James whispered and kissed her. Removing a loose stone in the floor, he put the file in and covered it up.

"Jem, Elizabeth arrived last night. She told me the most terrible news. The Sheriff of Exeter is in London and swears if you are found not guilty of Audley's murder, he will arrest you and take you back for trial in Devon.

"Then it is settled, Charlotte, my only hope is escape. I am praying that I remember all the details of Jack Sheppard's escape from this room."

"James, Pruitt and Byrd Ltd. have a large shipment of silks leaving for France in four days from Wapping. We have a warehouse where the High Street meets the Old Stairs. I will leave a key by the bottom of the door behind one of the loose bricks on the right side. Hide there until the night before the ship leaves. I will arrange a meeting with the ship's captain, a tradition Audley began years ago. He used to take two rooms at the Owl's Inn. They are upstairs at the end of the hall. Come to me there after the captain departs. I will find a way to smuggle you on board. At the first opportunity in France, you can escape and be away."

"I will go to Venice," James said, his eyes bright at the prospect of freedom. I am certain Countess Cittidini will aid me in my search for Hawkes. Charlotte, when I have left for France, you must tell John what has transpired. Ask him to join me in Bellagio at Count Cesi's villa in a month's time."

"Jem, will you make your escape tonight?"

"I think it best. Every gaoler who comes in here threatens to beat me senseless. With a broken arm or leg, escape would be impossible. If Benedict, the one I attacked,

198

recovers sufficiently, he will want to extract his pound of flesh, I am sure. Lottie, you must stay at your house all evening. Soldiers will be dispatched to search for me. Give them no reason to suspect you. I will find clothes and food myself. I will meet you at the inn, as you suggest."

"I shall fetch the key and go directly to the warehouse," Charlotte whispered. Not a minute later, a gaoler was at the door.

"Yer time is finished. You'll have to watch him in the bail dock and swingin' from Tyburn tree now, mistress," the man smirked.

It took all of Charlotte's will power to step around the man without replying.

Chapter Twelve

James waited until the sun set, then quickly removed the cuffs and began to loosen the leg irons with the file. Once freed, he grabbed his blanket and went to the fireplace, climbing up the chimney to the room above. He felt his way through the darkness to the door. Finding the bolt box, which he pried open with the file, he entered the next room. In it, he found a stairway that led up one more flight to another locked door. He listened for voices, but there were none. Throwing himself against the door, it opened. All was blackness. Again, he moved carefully along the wall until he felt a ladder. He prayed it would lead to the roof. He began to climb until he was stopped by a trapdoor.

With a burst of strength, he lifted the door and found himself on the top of Newgate. James crawled to the ledge and looked down on the roofs of houses next to the prison. Securing one end of his blanket to an iron post, he lowered himself down until he was able to jump ten feet to the nearest roof. He thanked God that the roof held him. Ripping his clothes to make himself look like a beggar, he was off to Wapping.

Charlotte, after leaving the prison, changed her clothes and went to Wapping. She made a great show of inspecting Pruitt and Byrd, Ltd.'s warehouse as the company's watchman looked on. She noted several bales of silk as special orders for clients in France. As she exited the warehouse, she stopped to look at loose bricks by the door.

"We must get these repaired," she said to the man as she slipped the key in behind one of the bricks.

Later that evening at Bellagio House, Charlotte was at a game of cards with Elizabeth, Emma, and John when a loud knock was heard at the front door. Mr. Primm entered the parlour followed by several soldiers. Their leader, a young lieutenant, informed Charlotte that the house was to be searched.

"For what reason?" she demanded.

"James Clarke has escaped from Newgate Prison, and we have reason to believe that you, madam, might be harbouring him," the lieutenant said.

"I most certainly am not. I have been entertaining my friends all evening. You may look from top to bottom, but you will find no fugitive here."

"Very well, Mrs. Pruitt, we shall conduct our search."

The young man went back into the hallway and Charlotte could hear him deploying his men to different parts of the house. When Charlotte turned back to her guests all three were eyeing her suspiciously.

"I know nothing of this," she said innocently.

A few minutes later, the lieutenant, satisfied that James was not there, took his men and left Bellagio House. However, he posted two soldiers outside for the night. Charlotte prayed they would be gone when she went to Wapping. She did not want to risk being followed.

As Emma and John made ready to leave, Emma took Charlotte aside. "You must be careful, my dear. This is not a game. The authorities will hang you without a second thought."

"Emma, I am not involved in this, I swear to you. Please, you need not worry. I just thank God that he has escaped. We must pray for his safety."

Before going out the door, John said, "If I may help in any way, I am at your service. Please, tell James that if you see him, not that you will, mind you."

Emma looked from John to Charlotte and shook her head.

"Thank you, dear friend," Charlotte replied.

After Emma and John departed, Charlotte and Elizabeth had a cup of tea and sat by the fireside. "Unless there is some reason for me to stay, I should return to Kirkmoor tomorrow, Charlotte. Mama, as I told you, is not well. I fear for her health," Elizabeth said, looking into her teacup.

"It would be best for you to go home. I am so sorry, Elizabeth, that you have to bear this burden by yourself. I pray Jem will escape the country. If he sends word to me, I will write you directly."

"Thank you, Charlotte. I will be off in the morning, then. What will you plan to do now?"

"I have some business to attend to with Pruitt and Byrd while I am in London. After that, I shall return to Rosthwaite. I have been away from Jack far too long."

After Elizabeth said goodnight and retired, Charlotte wished she could go after her and tell her what was truly taking place. Charlotte knew, however, that any of her servants overhearing such news would not hesitate, for the right price, to betray her to the soldiers posted outside.

In the morning, Charlotte sent a note requesting Mr. Sharp to visit Bellagio House as soon as possible. He came to her within the hour.

"Mrs. Pruitt," he said on entering the parlour, "I am glad to see you looking so well. I heard the news of James Clarke's escape, and when I saw the soldiers outside, I could only imagine what a state you must be in."

"Thank you for your concern, Mr. Sharp. It has been a most trying night, to be sure. However, I am determined to carry on as if all were well. To that point, I would ask you to arrange a meeting between Captain Philips and myself for two days hence. I want to check the shipment lists and wish him a good voyage. Perhaps, you could see to the private rooms at the Owl's Inn that my husband often used."

"I shall do it at once, Mrs. Pruitt. I know just the ones."

Two days later, as Charlotte's meeting with Captain Philips at the Owl's Inn drew to a close, she informed him that a few more bales of silk would be brought on board just before the ship sailed the following morning. "They are last minute orders that have only just been finished. Immediately upon your arrival in France, they should be delivered to our warehouse with the ones I have already labelled. I will arrange for their delivery from there. Please, forgive this last-minute change. You know how demanding the Parisian aristocrats can be."

"Oh, aye, Mrs. Pruitt, I have seen them strutting like peacocks and ordering everyone about. I shall do my best to see to these orders personally." Captain Philips stood up from the table.

"Thank you, Captain," Charlotte said, extending her

hand. "I realize how busy you must be. I shall keep you no longer."

Captain Philips kissed her hand and bowed. "Good evening, madam. Do you have someone to see you home?"

"I have decided to stay the night at the inn and watch the ship sail in the morning, much better than braving the London streets at night."

"Excellent idea, Mrs. Pruitt. Goodnight, then."

"Goodnight, Captain Philips."

After he left, Charlotte sat at the table listening to the sounds coming from the inn below. She looked around the low-ceilinged room. A door led into a bedroom that was dark except for firelight. She had seen no one follow her to the inn. Thankfully, the soldiers watching her house were gone by the evening of the next day after James's escape.

There was a knock at her door, and a serving girl, who was giggling and blushing, came in to clear away what was left of the supper that Charlotte and Captain Philips had consumed. Charlotte looked at her.

The girl, attempting to apologize for her behaviour, commented as she backed out of the room, her hands full of dishes, "Forgive me, mum. There's a Scots gentleman in the hall, what's makin' me laugh."

Through the open door, the unseen man in the hallway said to the girl, "Ach now lassie, what are ya tellin' the fine lady?" Charlotte heard the girl tittering as she went down towards the kitchen.

In the next instant, the Scotsman stepped into her room. Charlotte gasped. Standing before her was a dark-haired man with a small moustache. He was dressed all in black velvet with the exception of the fine lace at his chin. His tricorn hat was black and trimmed with lace around its brim. His black boots met his breeches at the knee.

"Do I haf the pleasure of addressin' Mrs. Charlotte Pruitt?" the man asked.

"You do, sir."

"Then, madam, the reports of your beauty do nae do you justice."

"How so, sir?" Charlotte asked.

"You are more beautiful than three days ago, when I thought you the most beautiful woman in the world."

"You might wish to close the door, sir."

"Should I, madam?"

"Yes, do."

"You would haf me stay?" the gentleman asked.

"Yes, forever if I could make it so."

"I am afeared it will only be the night."

"Then, we should not tarry with idle chatter, sir."

He closed the door but did not move to her. "What would you have me do?" he asked.

"I might ask for a kiss," she said.

"Would you be sincere?"

"Perhaps you should attempt the kiss," she suggested.

"But what would your lover think?"

"I have no other lover, sir."

"Not even that fair-haired rogue?"

"No, only you, sir. That is, if I find your kisses pleasing."

"You would be rid of that handsome James Clarke?"

"To take you to my bed, I would." She smiled coquettishly.

"I do not know if I care for this game," he said frowning.

"Then take off your wig, Jemmy, and kiss me."

"How long did you know my identity?"

"From the instant I saw that girl blush. You are a rogue, and I would have you naked," she said with a laugh.

James crossed to Charlotte, pulled her to standing, and kissed her. Letting her go, he took off his wig and moustache. She shook her head and laughed as he quickly stripped off his coat, waistcoat, and shirt.

"The boots are a damned nuisance," he muttered.

She had him sit and pulled them off, taking off his stockings as well. His breeches were all that remained. She made him stand as she undid them and let them fall. She went down and took him into her mouth, and he groaned in delight. When he was aroused, she stood up and began to take off her clothes. He watched, aching to make love to her. When she stood naked before him, their bodies touched. They kissed. He bit her neck, making her jump and laugh. He picked her up, and sitting on the chair, he positioned her on top of him. She rocked and sighed. Together, their ecstasy built to climax.

Later, he carried her to the bed, where they held and stroked each other. She, feeling the strength of his arms while she rested her head on his chest. He, touching the curve of her neck and softness of the skin on her belly. They made love again and rested afterwards, he still inside her.

Finally, separating from her, he told her the details of his escape and how he had acquired his Scotsman's costume.

"I stole it from a brothel. As I walked over roofs and passed windows, one was open, and a gentleman and lady were involved in their pleasure making, so seeing that the man and I were of a similar size, I lifted his clothes, his wig, and his boots, leaving my beggarly attire for him. I would have enjoyed seeing him exit the brothel, but I did not have the luxury of time. That is the story of the Scotsman."

Charlotte ran her fingers over his face, tracing lines at the corners of his eyes. She loved these lines when he smiled. He played with her hair, giving himself an auburn moustache. They laughed and kissed until they fell asleep in each other's arms.

It was still dark when Charlotte was awakened by the sound of movement in the room. Blearily, she looked up and saw James dressing to the light of a single candle.

"I must go back to the warehouse. When will you come?"

"In about two hours. Please be aware the warehouse watchman will be there. Are you able to roll yourself up in the cloth that is closest to the door?" He nodded his head. "You must leave me some small sign as to which bale you are in. I will have you loaded last, so you may get out while the ship is under sail. Be sure to be back in the bale when the ship docks. You will be unloaded first and left in the warehouse. Once alone, you can be off. I have brought you money for your journey. You must promise to write me as soon as you are able.

"I promise, Lottie, and I shall use the name Iacomus in case anyone is intercepting the letters. You will never be out of my thoughts."

"Nor you out of mine, Jem. I love you, Iacomus." She gave him a leather pouch containing the money.

"I love you, Lottie." He smiled and kissed her. Then, he slipped out of the room and down the hall.

After eating a small breakfast in her room, she walked to the warehouse, accompanied by her coachman and two footmen. She was glad of their protection, since the dockside was peopled by unsavoury characters. On entering the warehouse, she checked the special shipment and found James's handkerchief, just the tip showing, tucked in one large bale of silk. Her heart was racing as she saw the watchman coming from the back of the warehouse.

"Everything appears to be in order," she said to him as he came to greet her. Turning to the footmen, she ordered, "Please, go and inform Captain Philips that these are ready to be loaded."

The men ran off quickly, bringing back several sailors to carry the bales of silk on board ship. Charlotte walked beside James's roll, hoping he was able to breathe. She mentioned again to the captain, after greeting him, that this part of the shipment should be left apart so they could be easily unloaded.

"It shall be done, Mrs. Pruitt," he reassured her.

"Thank you, Captain Philips," she said, then retired back to the inn.

Gazing out the window, she watched the ship cast off and move down the Thames. "Good-bye, my dearest," she whispered. "May God be with you."

CHAPTER THIRTEEN

Two days after the silk ship sailed, Charlotte received a letter from Hannah Moreland. Annie and Mrs. Mungris had brought Jack to Whitehaven to celebrate his first birthday. He had taken sick with the ague. All three women were watching over him. Hannah assured Charlotte that his fever would be gone soon.

Despite what Hannah had written, Charlotte was thrown into a panic. She felt pangs of guilt for being so taken up with James that she had not thought about her son's well-being. She knew many children died daily, so how could she have imagined that he would be safe? She feared doctors and their potions. Children were routinely poisoned by their medicines. Charlotte prayed that Hannah would know how best to take care of Jack. After all, she was raising six children of her own and was much wiser than herself, of that Charlotte was sure. Still, her mind raced with dire possibilities. She packed and made preparations to depart for Whitehaven.

She asked both Emma and John to call on her and told them of her plans to go north. They promised to look after Bellagio House. When Emma excused herself to freshen up before leaving, Charlotte took the occasion to give John a letter explaining James's escape and his request that John join him in a month's time at Count Cesi's villa to search for Hawkes.

John read it quickly. He smiled as he put the letter in his pocket.

"Rest assured, I will be there." Charlotte thanked him just as Emma returned.

After they left, Charlotte wrote to Mr. Wooten asking that he and Mr. Sharp forward all business matters to Whitestone. In the future, Charlotte thought as she finished the note, Whitehaven, the largest port next to London and Liverpool, might be the place to base her business in the north.

Charlotte retired early, hoping to leave at first light on a northern-bound coach. She assumed that Annie would stay with the Morelands until she heard from her. As Charlotte got ready for bed, she cursed herself for having left Jack at Whitestone. She was so sure at the time that it was for the best, now she prayed that God would keep him safe.

The journey took six days. The rains made the roads quagmires, and several times, the travellers had to disembark to allow the driver and postilions to right the coach before it sank in the mud. The cold penetrated Charlotte's wool cloak and petticoats. She felt frozen for most of the trip and miserable with worry about Jack. At last on the sixth day, Charlotte arrived at Hannah's house by hackney from the coaching inn. Hannah and Mr. Moreland were still awake, and they greeted Charlotte with warm embraces. "Jack, is Jack here?' Charlotte asked anxiously.

Hannah, seeing the panic in her friend's face, replied soothingly, "Yes, dearest. He is here and quite recovered.

He is asleep, upstairs in the nursery. Let's get you settled—
"

"Hannah, please, I must see him now," Charlotte insisted and started up the stairs without waiting for her friend.

"Of course, Charlotte," Hannah agreed following after her. "Let me show you the way."

Charlotte stepped aside and let Hannah lead her to the nursery. With the door quietly opened, Charlotte crept into the bedroom. There he was, her son, sleeping peacefully. He coughed, one small cough, then rolled over. Her eyes filled with tears. She sank to her knees beside him and prayed softly, dear God, thank you, thank you. Charlotte reached out her hand to touch his face. Her breasts hurt. She had been away from him for nearly two months and thought her milk had dried up, but suddenly the front of her dress was wet. She began to laugh and cry at the same time.

She and Hannah went back down the stairs and Charlotte told her friend the news of James's imprisonment and escape. Hannah listened, her mouth agape in astonishment. When Charlotte finished, Hannah insisted that she stay with them.

"My dear, after such an adventure, you need to rest and be looked after. I will not hear of you going to Rosthwaite for at least a week. You must spend Christmas with us."

Charlotte gratefully accepted her invitation. The Moreland's acquaintances were most gracious. Nearly every night, the house was full of people talking about politics, dancing to music, playing cards, eating, and drinking. Jack was delighted and entertained by all the activities.

During the time that Charlotte had been in London,

Jack had learned to walk. Now Charlotte had Annie bundle him up each day, and the three of them went for long walks through the town. Jack loved holding onto their hands and having them lift him up into the air. They would swing him up, and he would throw back his head, letting out squeals of laughter.

When the week was over, Charlotte, Jack, and Annie bid good-bye to the Morelands, thanking them for their hospitality. She made Hannah promise that she and the boys would come to Whitestone soon.

In the middle of February, Charlotte received a letter from John in Venice, saying that, "our mutual friend, Iacomus, sends his regards to you and Jack. He wants you to know he arrived safely in France and has recently made his way to Venice. He hopes this finds you and your son in good health."

Charlotte wrote to John the next day with the happy news of Jack's learning to walk. She asked John to pass on her highest regards to their mutual friend and to "tell him I pray for his continued good health".

Six weeks passed quickly and soon the end of March brought spring to Rosthwaite. The bracken was still red on the fellsides, but here and there patches of bright yellow daffodils could be seen proclaiming the end of winter. Charlotte knew with certainty that she was pregnant but spoke of it to no one in the house. So many things were changing, Charlotte thought. Just yesterday, she had received a letter from Emma with the wonderful and not unexpected news that she and John Fuller were to be married. They had set the date for the end of September.

John had gone to Italy to help in the search for Hawkes, but Emma wrote, "He has promised me he will return with time to spare. You and Jackie must come, as well. Please, tell me you will be there."

And now, Jack had said his first word, "dada". The activity in the parlour stopped as all eyes turned to him. He repeated it as Charlotte, Annie, and Mrs. Mungris gathered around him. He looked surprised by the sudden attention. They encouraged him to say it again. He did, then turned and toddled off to see what cook was doing in the kitchen. By the end of April Jack added "mama" and "che", for cheese, to his vocabulary.

The last of the raw wool from the summer's shearing was prepared and woven into bolts of cloth. All done by farmers and their wives on hand looms in their houses. Many dozens of pairs of woollen stockings were knitted as well by the families. All the finished products were logged and collected by Ned Duddon, Whitestone's steward. Charlotte now planned a trip to Kendall to meet the wool buyers.

A letter from John in Rome arrived much to Charlotte's delight. The news was that they had tracked Hawkes to Rome. Their mutual friend sent his regards and told her he was trying to keep up his spirits but that he missed seeing her beautiful face and bright eyes. She wrote immediately back to them, sending the letter to the countess in Venice. Jack's first word, she wrote, was "dada". How she wished she might be there to see the delight on James's face. She hinted at her pregnancy saying, "The 'Scotsman' may have created a joyful gift for us, but it is still early." She finished the letter with the news of their going to Kendal.

The day arrived for the trek. Ned Duddon, with the help of two farmhands, loaded the packhorses with the heavy bales of wool and stockings. Each one weighed almost seventeen stone. Using a rope called a wanty, he secured them onto the horses after the bales were fastened into sheets of cloth with skewers.

Charlotte, with Jack and Annie, made ready to go. Kendal, "the auld grey town" as it was called, would be a bustling centre of activity, and Charlotte looked forward to the adventure. With Ned in the lead and the farmhands behind, urging on the packhorses, they travelled past Creighton House, Leath's Water, and over the Dunmail Raise to Grasmere. Night was coming quickly, and the light mist that had been with them all day turned to rain. Charlotte and the others found refuge at the local inn, while Ned and his two helpers stayed outside, alternately taking turns watching over the wool and sleeping.

The next day, they arrived at Kendall and had difficulty finding rooms. The town was full of buyers and sellers. At last, weary and hungry, they found shelter at the Fleece Inn. Charlotte, with Ned's help, found a buyer for the wool. With money in hand, she took Jack to a toymaker's shop. He wanted every toy, but finally settled on a small wooden bear on wheels that he could pull along. He tried it out, walking unsteadily down the street. On their way back to the inn they encountered a group of boys. By their ragged clothes and dirty faces, Charlotte suspected they were cast out apprentices. She scooped Jack up into her arms after several gathered around him to admire his toy.

For three rainy, cold days, Annie and Jack stayed at the inn and were entertained by the innkeeper's children while Charlotte and Ned shopped for much needed supplies. The journey back was dry and uneventful.

Ten days after the purchase of the toy, Charlotte began to feel feverish and slept a good part of the day. She awoke shivering with chills. She thought of her last bout of fever when she was in London and hoped this would pass more quickly. She became sick to her stomach. Mrs. Mungris helped her into her nightdress, and she slept a bit more. During the night, she was awakened by Jack screaming. She tried to get out of bed but could not. Her head was whirling and every joint ached.

Annie checked on her and assured her that Jack was being taken care of. He had a fever, as well. By morning, Jack was feeling better. Charlotte's illness persisted several more days. She remembered little of it. She did not know, until after she recovered, that she had lost the baby. Mrs. Mungris told her that in her fever and delirium she had bled profusely. Charlotte felt empty and exhausted. She held onto Jack and rocked him. When he went away, she cried. She wanted to die.

A week passed, and she began to get her strength back. On one warm spring day, she picked an armful of wildflowers and walked slowly down the hill, through the village and to the churchyard where her grandfather was buried. Placing the flowers on his grave, she asked him to watch over the little soul she had lost.

"A little life I will never get to watch grow, Grandfather. Hold it to your breast and let it know that it was loved."

Later that day as she sat outside the house, watching the clouds' shadows move over the fells, a man came from the village bringing a letter for Annie. After reading it, Annie tearfully told Charlotte the news that her father, Donald Rourke, the master weaver, had died suddenly. He had been complaining, her mother wrote, of feeling tired. He had a particularly complicated pattern he was working on and needed to finish quickly. He told Jane, his wife, to go to bed without him. She awoke in the middle of the night and realizing her husband was still up, went to the workshop. She found him dead on the floor. No one had heard him fall, because there was a double thickness of floorboards to muffle the sound of the looms.

Charlotte insisted that Annie go to London to be with her family. She asked Annie to give her mother a letter in which Charlotte offered her condolences and assured Jane that business would continue between them as it always had. Her brother-in-law, Patrick Rourke, could act as Jane's go-between, Charlotte suggested, arranging orders and collecting monies owed. That would satisfy the legal and customary regulations and still allow Jane to run the family business. The next morning Annie left for London.

As the showers of May made the fells greener still, Charlotte received news from John. Enclosed in his letter was note from Iacomus.

We are back in Venice, having followed Hawkes's trail all the way to Naples, where he seemed to disappear. We believe he boarded a ship, but which one we could not discover. My dearest friend, is there any more word of the Scotsman's gift?

Charlotte found it impossible to answer at first, but on seeing Jackie play with the new lambs and delight in the sheep shearing, her sadness lessened. She wrote to John and enclosed a brief note to Iacomus.

My treasured friend, the Scotsman's gift came to nothing and left me with a melancholy heart. Jackie has lightened my spirits, though, with his joyous love of the lambs. We miss you so.

Mid-July brought two more letters of note. One was from Mr. Sharp, who wrote with news of Annie. She wished Charlotte to know that she was teaching her brothers how to throw and weave so that they could help their mother. Her uncle, Patrick, was proving difficult to deal with, being more interested in politics than in helping Jane Rourke carry on the family business.

John wrote as well enclosing a note from Iacomus saying,

I am so very sorry to hear of the loss of the baby. I wish with all my heart that I could hold and comfort you. Know that I love you and Jack, and we will be together again. We are meeting with Count Cesi's agents to see what they may know. We have heard a rumour of an Englishman in Greece that fits Hawkes's description.

Charlotte stared at the words and shook her head.

In the beginning of August, Charlotte received a letter from Elizabeth Calvert, James's sister in Devon. She wrote that Lady Louisa Clarke, James's and her mother, was dying after a long illness. It was just a matter of days. Elizabeth feared her father was not far behind. Charlotte immediately wrote back, saying that she would bring Jack and come to Kirkmoor to help in whatever way she could. She was feeling stronger and thought it imperative she be there to aid Elizabeth.

She then wrote a letter to Count Cesi.

Contact Iacomus, if possible, and tell him his parents are ailing, but I am going to help his sister in whatever way I may. He does not need to worry or think of coming home.

Lastly, she wrote Mr. Sharp to inform Annie that they were traveling from Whitestone to Devon, so that when she was ready, she might join them there.

Charlotte, with Jack in tow, left the next day for Kirkmoor. Betsy, her maid, had become Jack's nurse until Annie returned to the position. Charlotte's head ached from the jostling of the coach, but she refused to be deterred. She made a promise to Elizabeth that she would be there, and so she would. Jack was as good as could be expected, being confined for six days in a small space.

They arrived at Kirkmoor in the last hours of Lady Louisa's life. She was frail and small in her great bed, surrounded by bottles of medicine. Her doctor hovered over her. She had not recognized anyone for at least ten days. Elizabeth, Charlotte noted, looked as if she had slept little for weeks.

Sir Rufus Clarke, Lady Louisa's husband and Elizabeth's and James's father, wandered about the house, blowing his nose and cracking his riding crop against his left leg.

After Elizabeth took Charlotte to see Lady Louisa, she introduced her to her father. He stopped and looked at Charlotte. He appeared to be trying to sort out how she fit into the chaos of his life. It was too much for him. He smiled weakly and went back to pacing and hitting his leg.

Sometime later, he came up to Charlotte and taking her hand, he said, "I love her, you know. She gave me eight children. Six of them died. But the twins survived. Elizabeth is a dutiful child, always has been. But it is Jem I love, the stupid son of a bitch. He should have been stronger. I was strong. What the hell is wrong with that boy?" He dropped her hand, hit his leg and strode off.

Charlotte stood speechless, staring after him.

Elizabeth called to Charlotte from upstairs. The urgency in her voice made Charlotte run to the top of the stairs and into Lady Louisa's chamber. The woman was sitting bolt upright in bed. Her eyes were wide open, staring at something unseen just beyond the foot of the bed. She stretched out her arms, a look of longing on her face, and collapsed backwards onto the bed.

Elizabeth grabbed her limp body and cradled it, sobbing. She closed her mother's eyes and rocked her gently.

Charlotte went into the hallway and sat down on a chair. She prayed to God to receive Lady Louisa's soul.

A few minutes passed, and Charlotte went downstairs to the kitchen where she found the doctor eating and flirting with the scullery maid. Charlotte informed him that Lady Louisa had passed on and that his services would no longer be needed. He blinked his bulbous eyes and went back to devouring the roast beef and eyeing the maid.

Charlotte found Sir Rufus standing in the stable yard. When she walked up to him, he took her proffered hand. "She is dead. I just felt her pass over me," he said looking into the air.

"I am sorry," Charlotte said.

"I am not afraid of dying, you know. I rather look forward to it. More, now that she is there. Will you accompany me to her room?" he asked.

"Of course."

As they walked, he asked her, "Who are you, again?"

"A friend of James and Elizabeth," Charlotte answered.

"Is James here?" he asked hopefully.

"No."

"Oh, I did not think I saw him."

Once in Lady Louisa's bedroom, the old man wandered up to the bed, where Elizabeth had arranged her mother's body. He peered down at his dead wife, while Elizabeth sat some distance off, crying.

"Well, that is done," he said. "Do not imagine, Louisa, that you have escaped me." He began to crawl onto the bed.

"Papa, please!" Elizabeth shouted. "No! Leave her in peace."

Sir Rufus stopped. Looking like a small boy who just got caught doing something naughty, he got off the bed. Standing up straight, he looked at Elizabeth and said, "Do not reprimand me, woman. I am still your father." With that, he walked out of the room and down the stairs.

Charlotte went to her room and wrote a letter to Iacomus. She told him all she had seen since arriving. Urging him to carry on his search for Hawkes, she assured him that she and Elizabeth were capable of running the estate. She told him briefly about his father's erratic behaviour and that it made her uncomfortable. She quickly added that she and Jack would be fine and not to worry. She enclosed the letter in a note to Count Cesi asking him to forward it to Iacomus. She sent off one of the footmen to take the letter for posting.

Later that day, she helped Elizabeth prepare Louisa's body for entombment. As they worked, Charlotte recalled that James had spoken little of his mother. He had said she was distant, finding it easier to have someone else tend to the children. His father, on the other hand, had doted on his older brother, Charles. James always knew his father favoured his brother, but he tagged along on their hunting and fishing forays in hopes of some acknowledgement.

James's brother was killed at sixteen. He was riding through the neighbouring estate owned by the Earl of Chagford, William Warrender. The earl's son, Thomas, was Charles's closest friend. The two had been daring each other to jump stone walls. Charles's horse failed to clear the last wall of the challenge. The boy was thrown into the wall and died instantly of a broken neck. Sir Rufus had been heartbroken. In the years that followed, he told everyone how much he loved James. However, rather than giving Jem the affection the boy needed, Sir Rufus became obsessed with making him into a hardened soldier.

Thomas Warrender, two years older than Charles and six years older than James, was blamed by James's father for Charles's death. He was never allowed at Kirkmoor again. At the funeral, Sir Rufus and the old earl had a loud and bitter argument that left the families estranged. More recently, James told Charlotte, Thomas Warrender had inherited his father's estate, wealth, and title. He spent most of his time in London now, where he sought to gain power in Court.

Elizabeth sent for the vicar, who came quickly, and the funeral service was reviewed. After he left, Charlotte urged Elizabeth to rest, which she agreed to do. Charlotte took care of the running of the household and kept an eye on Sir Rufus. He sat in the drawing room most of the time, staring at his hands. Behind him, Charlotte noticed, hung his portrait painted by Reynolds. In the painting, a much younger Sir Rufus stood regally looking out at the viewer. Behind him, the house and Dartmoor appeared small in comparison. However, in life, it had become reversed, and now he was the one who was dwarfed.

At the end of the second day, with Elizabeth still in bed,

and her boys, Jeremy, Robert, and Benjamin playing quietly outside, Charlotte went into the drawing room to see if Sir Rufus needed food or drink. He'd had little of either since his wife died. When Charlotte addressed him, he looked up from his hands, and she saw a resemblance to James.

"I am in a bit of a fog, m'dear," he said.

"You should eat, Sir Rufus," she suggested.

"No." He paused and looked at her. "I told him, you know. I told him; you must respect your horse. Jem understands that, but Charles is a hothead... was a hothead." He stopped and blinked his eyes several times.

"Sir," Charlotte said softly, "I believe you should eat and go lie down." Charlotte prayed he would cooperate.

"Louisa, what shall we do?" He addressed Charlotte, but it was not her he was seeing.

"You must rest. All of this has been a shock, sir. Come. I will help you to your room," Charlotte offered, trying to get him to stand.

He reached out and pulled her down onto his lap, resting his head on her bosom. "Louisa, please, do not ever leave me. I would die without you."

Charlotte stroked his head, feeling uncomfortable. Finally disengaging, she stood up. "Thank you. Now, you must get up and go to your room." She did not know what else to say. She desperately wanted help.

"Why do you move away from me? Why do you do that? You have always behaved that way." Becoming agitated, he stood up. "You do not care! You are unmoved that our son is dead!"

"No, I am not. I assure you," Charlotte responded, trying to move towards the door. "But we have James and Elizabeth. We must give them our love."

"Dammit, madam, James is a strange boy. I do not pretend to understand him, and Elizabeth is a girl. She is your domain, when you deign to pay attention to her," he said, raising his voice.

"Please, do not address me in such a harsh manner, sir. There will be time for this talk after you have slept."

"No!" he shouted and rushed at her, grabbing her arm. "We will talk of it now!" He raised his hand and struck Charlotte hard across the face. Pain shot through her cheek and mouth. She felt hot blood run from her nose.

"Unhand me, you crazy fool!" she screamed.

Elizabeth ran in, followed by the butler and housekeeper. "Father, stop!" she shouted. She moved between them and shielded Charlotte from further blows. Mrs. Rich, the housekeeper, helped Charlotte out of the room and sat her down in a chair. Using her apron to catch the blood that dripped down Charlotte's front, she tried to help clean Charlotte's face.

The shouting continued in the drawing room, followed by silence. Charlotte sat back in the chair and closed her eyes. Her head swam as the pain radiated from the spot where she had been hit. She sat dazed and confused.

After several minutes, Elizabeth and Mr. Taggert, the butler, brought out a subdued Sir Rufus. They led him off in the direction of his room. He did not look at Charlotte as he passed. Mrs. Rich walked with Charlotte to her room where she helped her change clothes and wash her face. Charlotte laid down, and the housekeeper put cold compresses on her face.

Mrs. Rich smiled at her. "I used to help Lady Louisa in just the same way, Mrs. Pruitt. Sir Rufus has always been quick to anger."

The pain subsided, and Charlotte fell asleep. Sometime later, she was awakened by Elizabeth who sat down on the bed next to her.

"I am so sorry, Charlotte," she said, taking her friend's hand. "Father always strikes with his fists when he is angry or confused. My mother bore the brunt of it, although James and I have felt his wrath, too." She looked at Charlotte's face. "Do you believe your nose is broken?" she asked.

"It is extremely painful. It may well be," Charlotte managed to answer. "It hurts to talk."

Elizabeth shook her head. "I am afraid of what will happen at the funeral, but I will try to be prepared for however my father may act." She held Charlotte's hand tighter. "I wish with all my heart that Jem could be here."

"So do I," Charlotte agreed.

"You have written to him?"

"I sent a letter to Count Cesi that I hope he will be able to forward to Jem. I told him of your mother's passing and your father's health. I urged him not to come. We cannot risk his being arrested."

"I agree. I pray he does not return. But he may, you know," she said looking out the window to the moor.

CHAPTER FOURTEEN

On the day of the funeral, it rained. It began as a cold mist and fog in the morning, but by midday as they began the procession, the rain pelted down. At the mausoleum, there was a brief break in the weather, allowing them to hear the vicar's words as he sent Lady Louisa to her eternal rest. Sir Rufus was quiet and sombre as he hung on Elizabeth's arm. Her three sons walked behind, eyes on the ground. Charlotte wisely left Jack at the house in Betsy's care. The coffin was placed in its tomb in the mausoleum, and the mourners began to file away, mumbling their condolences.

Elizabeth thanked them, but her father never looked up. As the last people began to walk back to the house, Sir Rufus raised his head and quietly asked his daughter to allow him a few minutes alone with his wife. Elizabeth looked at him to assess his mood and gave her permission. She motioned for the boys and Charlotte to leave, and she followed them. As they passed the vault, Charlotte heard the old man sobbing inside, then all was quiet. Puzzled, she stopped and looked at Elizabeth, who shook her head sadly, but stopped as well.

After several minutes, Elizabeth called, "Father, we should be getting back to the house now."

There was no response.

"Father!" she called again. "Answer me, please."

When there was still no response, she disappeared back into the mausoleum and in an instant called for Charlotte to join her.

On entering, Charlotte saw Elizabeth standing facing her mother's tomb. Sir Rufus had pushed the heavy lid open enough that he could curl up on top of the coffin. He lay there, eyes open, humming softly.

"Father, we need to go now. Please, come down out of there," Elizabeth said, trying not to let her voice falter.

"She needed to breathe, Lizzie. Louisa could not breathe with the damned stone lid on," he said.

"Come with me, Papa. Mama is safe now. That is her resting place."

He blinked his eyes several times and sat up. Peering at the coffin, he said, "Louisa, forgive me. Are you warm enough? Damn rain. It is cold. I am cold. Lizzie," he scolded, "your mother must be cold as ice." He shot Elizabeth an accusing glance.

"I will see to her needs, Papa," she answered firmly. Awkwardly, he climbed down. His black coat, breeches, and stockings were covered in dust.

When they arrived back at the house, people were eating and drinking. The lively conversations fell quiet as Sir Rufus passed through but picked up again as he went upstairs to lie down. Elizabeth introduced Charlotte to several people, saying that she was a friend of the family, down from London. If any knew of her connection to James, they did not indicate it in their behaviour toward her. However, some did look questioningly at her nose and the bruises that had appeared under her eyes.

About an hour after they had been back at the house, a

large coach arrived and halted at the front entrance. Elizabeth, peeking outside to see who it was, became agitated. She left the room hurriedly and Charlotte followed.

In the main hallway, one of the footmen was just opening the door. A tall, handsome, brown-haired man entered. Where James was fair, this man was dark. His large brown eyes and thick black brows gave him an intense expression. His aquiline nose and high cheekbones bespoke an aristocratic heritage. Charlotte had difficulty not staring at him. Elizabeth rushed to him and he took her hand and kissed it. It was apparent that they had more than a passing acquaintance. Charlotte could not help overhearing their words.

Elizabeth spoke first, drawing her hand away. "Thomas, you should not have come. Father's behaviour is unpredictable. If he finds you here, there may be violence."

"Elizabeth, I had to see you. I heard the news in London of your mother's death. I wanted to be with you. It is you I am concerned with. How are you, my dearest?" His gaze did not leave her face.

Charlotte felt awkward but feared that moving would draw more attention to her presence, so she stayed rooted to the spot.

The gentleman saw her, and Elizabeth, seeing him look over her shoulder, turned also. "Charlotte, forgive my ill manners. May I present my dear friend Mrs. Pruitt, Lord Chagford. Lord Chagford, Mrs. Pruitt."

Extending her hand, Charlotte stepped towards the couple. "I am most pleased to make your acquaintance, Lord Chagford."

"As I am yours, madam." When he smiled at her,

Charlotte was charmed. She was also thankful he did not inquire after her bruises.

Wait until I speak with Elizabeth alone, she thought. How could she have kept her feelings for this man from me? Other people now came into the entrance hall and, seeing Lord Chagford insisted that he join them in the drawing room.

As they followed Thomas into the room, Elizabeth confided to Charlotte how she and Thomas had become reacquainted recently after years of their families being estranged. They began to meet without her parents' knowledge. She developed a strong affection for him, and knowing he shared her sentiment, hoped they would have a future together. Charlotte embraced her friend and wished her all the happiness in the world.

"He is quite fond of the boys. I have sworn them to secrecy, making them promise to never utter a word of our meetings to their grandparents. The boys tease me mercilessly about it."

As they stood in the drawing room, everyone gathered around Thomas to hear the latest news from London. Suddenly, the door burst open, and in strode Sir Rufus. He held a cane raised over his head.

"Where is he?" the old man cried out. "The murderer!" He spied Thomas. "How dare you come into my house!" He headed straight for Thomas, the crowd scattering to get out of his way.

Elizabeth shouted, "Father, no!"

As Sir Rufus closed in on him, Thomas, the taller and stronger of the two, was able to grab the cane before it came down on his head. They stood, the weapon in mid-air, Thomas keeping it from falling and Sir Rufus still pushing it down. The old man glared at him.

Thomas said as calmly as possible, "Sir, I am aware you have a strong antipathy for me. I only wished to offer my respects and condolences. I shall be going."

He guided the tip of the cane to the floor and turned his back on his attacker. As he passed Elizabeth on his way out, their eyes met briefly but they did not speak. Neither of them wanted to give her father cause for another outburst.

When he had gone, the butler and Mrs. Rich approached Sir Rufus, one on each side, and helped him back to his room.

After the guests said their good-byes, Elizabeth and Charlotte retired to the former's dressing room for a cup of tea. Elizabeth told Charlotte that she was unsure about how to proceed with her relationship with Thomas. Charlotte urged her to visit Thomas in the morning. With the servants' aid, Charlotte said, she would be able to watch over Sir Rufus.

Elizabeth thanked her and agreed she would take the opportunity to go. During the next three weeks, with Charlotte's help, Elizabeth was able to slip away to the Warrender estate quite often.

Sir Rufus calmed down and seemed to come to his senses. He played cheerfully with Jack, though Charlotte stayed near.

On one particularly warm day in the beginning of September, Charlotte gave Jack to Annie, who had arrived from London the day before. She asked her to put him down for his nap while she walked outside. She noticed Sir Rufus standing by the abandoned cottage where James had stayed.

The old man motioned her to come to him. "He is here, you know," he whispered to her as she got close.

"Good afternoon, Sir Rufus," Charlotte responded, not wishing to be drawn into his world.

"You do not know, eh? He has not shown himself to you. Clever boy, he is wise not to."

"Sir, it is time for your afternoon rest. Please, come into the house," Charlotte urged.

"You women are always trying to feed me or get me to lie down. Why is that? Tell me, why that is?" he demanded.

"Please, do not speak so harshly to me, sir," Charlotte said, beginning to lose patience. "Come in or not. As you wish." She began walking back towards the main house.

"Charles is here," he called after her.

Charlotte stopped, exasperated. "What?!"

"Well, perhaps it is me and not you he is here to see," he said and started off towards the moor.

Charlotte could not resist. She followed him. "When did you see him?" Charlotte asked. "Where was he? Please, sir, stop and tell me."

He turned to Charlotte. "Oh, so now you will talk to the old man, eh? Well, I have nothing more to say to you, young lady, except keep your silly eyes open."

With that, he turned and hurried down the path. Charlotte watched him go, wondering who or what he had seen. Was it a ghost or was it a person? It was late afternoon, Sir Rufus walked to the west. He reached the top of a small rise and stood silhouetted against the setting sun. His form appeared like a shadow puppet, as he talked and gesticulated to the air. Charlotte felt alone and afraid. She wanted to go gather up Jack and leave this place. Madness seemed to haunt the premises. If only James could be here with her now. Perhaps he could help her understand his father, and perhaps she would not be so terrified at night when she heard footsteps and whispering in the hallway. She tried to pretend it was only the wind and the creaking of the house, but she knew better. Yet James was not here, and he must not risk coming.

Charlotte decided to speak with Elizabeth to find out how much longer she was needed at Kirkmoor.

When Charlotte came into the house, Elizabeth had just arrived back from seeing Thomas. She greeted Charlotte in the entry way, pulled her into the drawing room, and shut the door behind them. Elizabeth smiled broadly and hugged Charlotte.

"I have decided to marry Thomas, no matter how Father feels about the match. I am determined to find some happiness in my life. I do not care if it means being called a wanton woman and a faithless child. Thomas will take the boys and myself even if we are penniless, which, if Father disinherits us, we will be. I am determined," she announced triumphantly.

Charlotte was exceedingly happy on Elizabeth's behalf, but felt as if a weight had descended upon her shoulders. Where, she wondered, did her duty lie now in terms of caring for Sir Rufus?

"Elizabeth, I am elated for you. You and Thomas deserve every happiness. Have you decided upon a date for the wedding?" Charlotte asked as she sat on the settee.

"The sooner the better, as far as I am concerned. Thomas would like the ceremony to take place in about three weeks. Do you think we are mad?" Elizabeth said as she sat down next to Charlotte.

"Not at all. However, you do need to be prepared for

what your father may do when you tell him the news. You may find yourself with no roof over your head quite quickly. I do not begin to suppose how this may affect his sanity. I do not mention this to dissuade you, Elizabeth, only to have you consider what the consequences of your decision may be.

"I must ask you, for my peace of mind, how you see Jack and myself in this. I have great affection for you, Elizabeth, as if you were my own sister. I desire you to have every happiness. I do, truly. However, if you are estranged from your father, I would think it my responsibility to care for him, and frankly, he frightens me greatly." Charlotte stopped, feeling she had said far too much.

Elizabeth grew serious as she listened. She dropped Charlotte's hand and rose to her feet. "Charlotte, I have acted hastily, I fear. I want so much to be with Thomas and away from Father that I have not considered you in all this. Father is James's and my responsibility. I would not ask you to take care of him, nor would my brother. That old man has ruled our lives for so long. He must fend for himself now. Charlotte, I must escape this house. It is suffocating me. Forgive me," she whispered as she sat down in a chair across from Charlotte on the settee. Her fists were clenched, and her eyes closed.

Charlotte went to her and sat at her feet. "Elizabeth, we will arrive at a satisfactory solution. There must be something we can do to allow you to begin a new life and provide for your father's care. Perhaps, Jack and I can take a house in the village and check on him every day. We could at least attempt it for a short period of time, until we see that he will be fine alone. All the servants know him and will see to his needs. You have shown me how to manage the estate, and with the steward's help, it should continue running well without incident. I will do everything in my power to help, but I do not want to be alone with him. I do not." Charlotte looked at Elizabeth, who in return reached out and stroked her friend's hair.

"You are a sweet woman, Charlotte. I understand better every day why Jemmy loves you so dearly. Thank you for understanding. Let's have some supper, and we'll talk more about how to proceed."

"Elizabeth, there is one comment your father made this afternoon that was most disquieting," Charlotte said and proceeded to tell Elizabeth how her father had sworn that he had seen Charles. "I am sure it was imagined, but I feel uneasy since Jem has still not been able to locate Edward Hawkes."

"I will ask some of the younger, stronger servants to keep watch over the house the next few nights, in case someone is out there, wanting to get in," Elizabeth said.

A day later, Charlotte received a letter from Emma. She wrote that all the plans for her wedding were in readiness. She and John would have the ceremony in the church she'd attended since childhood, St. Martin-in-the-Fields. John promised to be back from Italy one week before the September 30 date that had been set. He was having his wedding suit made by a Venetian tailor who Countess Cittidini had suggested. It promised to be very elegant.

Charlotte had given Emma some suggestions for her bridal dress, in terms of style and material, and Emma had taken these to heart. She reported that the dress was the finest work her dressmaker had ever done. Emma was pleased as well that the long summer evenings allowed her time to do much of the embroidery work herself. She finished the letter expressing how much she wished Charlotte was there to share her joy and excitement.

As Charlotte read the letter, she longed to be in London. The Season was just beginning, with its balls and parties. Everyone would be in the newest fashions, rested from the summer's relaxation and talking about the latest news and scandals.

Charlotte chided herself for never being comfortable in London Society. When she was in the midst of it, she wished only for the peace of the country. Yet now, in the country, she woke every day filled with trepidation. The feeling would not leave her. She felt as if invisible hands were closing around her throat. Perhaps it was only her fear of Sir Rufus's erratic behaviour, or was it, as she sometimes felt, a malevolent force that emanated from the very ground?

Answering Emma's letter immediately, Charlotte wrote that she and Jack would be going up to London a week hence. Charlotte expressed her loving friendship and thanked Emma for standing with her through all that had happened.

Here, Charlotte stopped. She began to weep. All the fear, fatigue, and desire to see James came pouring out of her. She put her head in her arms as they rested on the desk and cried for several minutes. When she lifted her head, the first sight she saw out the window was Annie and Sir Rufus ambling after Jack. Her son was running as fast as his little legs would carry him and laughing with abandon. She could not help but smile. After watching the three of them, she was able to finish her letter to Emma.

Elizabeth was going to attend the wedding, as well. Thankfully, she decided to postpone telling her father about her plans for the future until after Emma and John's nuptials. Thomas, she said, was also hoping to travel to London. Elizabeth was excited about the possibility of seeing him without the need for secrecy. Whenever she spoke of him, she beamed like a young girl. Charlotte looked forward with anticipation to their union, although she dreaded Sir Rufus's reaction.

Sir Rufus had been in good spirits of late, but he talked to himself a good deal. Charlotte was quite sure he was discussing urgent matters with an invisible Charles. He was animated and intense in his gestures and speech, which was evident even from a distance. He had not, however, mentioned his son since he had told her of his arrival.

There had been no news of James in over six weeks. Charlotte prayed nightly that all was going well. She hoped he would send a letter along with John. She missed him and would lie in her bed at night imagining his body next to hers as she tried to recall his smell and the feel of his hair. She wanted to hear him play the penny whistle and see him carry Jack on his shoulders. She remembered the warm, intoxicating Italian nights and hoped that he was not being tempted away from her by some beautiful seductress. Imagining such a scenario only plunged her deeper into melancholy. Charlotte would shake her head and sit up in bed. No, she said to herself, I will not allow these images to ruin my sleep.

Charlotte concentrated on Jack instead, and he was always foremost in her thoughts. He was already a year and a half old. He moved on sure legs and loved to run. He and his grandfather played daily. Each morning, if it was not raining, one of the kitchen maids would bring Sir Rufus stale bread. He and "Jackie Boyo", as he called his grandson, would go out on the front lawn. Here, they tore the bread into little bits, and dancing about, would throw the pieces to the waiting birds. Flocks of starlings, sparrows, and finches whirled, darted, and fought each other for the crumbs. Sir Rufus would wrap his arms around Jack as they watched the birds gather.

A moment after the birds alighted to eat, he would release Jack, who would run full tilt into the flocks. The terrified birds rose all at once and for a moment Jack would be lost in a swirl of feathers. The two of them would let go with gales of laughter. Grandfather and grandson doubled over red-faced. Finally, Jack, having caught his breath, would jump into his grandfather's waiting arms. Charlotte feared that Jack would be pecked, but he never was, and it gave Sir Rufus such joy, she did not stop the game.

However, there were other times during the day when Jack would approach his grandfather and there was little or no reaction from the old man, his mind having wandered off into another time.

At those times, Charlotte warned Annie to be ready to snatch Jack up and protect him from any angry outbursts, but none came. At night, Charlotte would hear Sir Rufus moaning. The sound would grow in intensity, punctuated by loud laughter or shrieks. Charlotte would gather Jack up from his bed and bring him to hers.

Sometimes, in the morning, she would find Annie curled up at the foot of Charlotte's bed. The poor girl would look up apologetically and rush to get Jack up and fed. Charlotte did not scold her, because she shared her fear.

Elizabeth and Charlotte supervised the packing for London and were soon ready to depart. September was still dry and warm. They hoped that their trip would be fast and smooth. It took two coaches to accommodate themselves, servants, and trunks. Mr. Kyd, the steward, Mr. Taggert, the butler, and Mrs. Rich, the housekeeper, all promised to watch over Sir Rufus. The old man grew more and more sullen as the time of departure neared. He asked that Jack be allowed to stay at Kirkmoor, but Charlotte gently refused his request.

Elizabeth's younger sons, Robert and Benjamin, also said they would keep an eye on their grandfather. They were upset because Jeremy, their older brother was accompanying their mother to the city. Elizabeth told them to be patient. Jeremy was the eldest, and it was time for him to go to Christ Church College Oxford, their father's school. She would see to it that arrangements were made on this visit.

Their journey went well, and they arrived in London four days before Emma's and John's wedding. Charlotte had written to Mr. Primm, so he had Bellagio House readied for their arrival. Elizabeth and Jeremy rode off to visit family friends, with whom he would stay until the school term began. She planned to return later and stay with Charlotte through the wedding.

After settling in, Charlotte sent word to Emma inviting her to breakfast at Bellagio House the following morning.

It was late afternoon, and Charlotte's garden was full of the golds and reds of autumn. The warm, wet summer had produced a glorious fall, and Charlotte breathed deeply, taking in the scents of the earth.

Jack ran ahead of her. He fell down laughing and rolling in the leaves. His curls were long and golden. When he got up, his hair was full of leaves. Charlotte picked him up and hugged him. He threw his arms around her neck and hugged her back.

He took her face in his small hand and looking at her very seriously, said, "Mama! Mama!" She carried him to a bench and sat down. He allowed her to gently pull the leaves from his hair. The sun was warm, and he soon began to nod off. He rested his head on her chest and fell asleep. She held him, rocking gently and humming his favourite lullaby.

A short time later, the clouds began to gather and a cool breeze to blow. She carried Jack into the house and asked Annie to watch over him in the parlour as he napped.

The next morning, Charlotte rose early and prepared for Emma's arrival. She cut some of the last roses of the season, arranging them in a vase and putting it on the table. The sun streamed in the parlour window and the roses seemed to catch fire in the sunlight. Charlotte felt light-hearted for the first time in months.

At ten o'clock, Emma descended from her coach at Charlotte's door. Her smile told Charlotte everything about the joy in her heart. Emma embraced her friend.

"My dear, sweet Charlotte. Thank you, thank you for all your counsel. You must come back later to the house with me and see my dress."

Elizabeth joined them, and she and Emma greeted each other. Smiling, Emma produced a letter and handed it to Charlotte. "John brought this note directly from James for you. We have been very good and not taken a peek."

Charlotte was thrilled and asked the ladies to excuse her while she read the letter in private. They both nodded. Rushing out into the garden, she sat down amidst the roses and tore open the letter.

Venice
My dearest Charlotte,

I am sitting on my balcony overlooking the Grand Canal. Countess Cittidini tells me it is the same room in which you stayed when you visited her. I am imagining that you are here with me and that you have just stepped out of the room. Any moment, you will reappear, and we will never again have to be parted. Sadly, the truth overtakes me, and I know that you are far away.

I hope you and Jack are in the best of health. I pray daily that God will permit me to come home soon and safely. I miss you, my dearest. You are in my thoughts all my waking hours. When you read this, I will have been gone nearly four months. How my Jackie must be growing! Does he still remember me, do you think? I pray he does and that he will forgive me for being away for so long a time.

I am sailing tomorrow for Greece. John can tell you the details of our journey and our search for Hawkes. Countess Cittidini has provided me with invaluable information about Hawkes's friendship with Audley. She has been making enquiries of anyone here who associated with them. Hawkes pretended to be an English art impresario. He even had forged letters of introduction from the Duke of Richmond. He contacted a local art dealer, an Irishman, by the name of Eugenio Swinny, who sells to all the English in Venice. Through Swinny, he must have traced Audley's whereabouts. The contact established, Hawkes began to play his role of Iago to Audley's Othello.

Neither Countess Cittidini nor the count suspected Hawkes. He was quiet, charming company and appeared to be well connected. Count Cesi recently questioned his servants and found out that Hawkes spent a good deal of money discovering the details *of our secrets, which he then told Audley. I despair to think of what I, myself, confessed to Hawkes. He returned to Venice after murdering Audley. He feigned shock and grief at the loss of his friend. His demonstrations of sadness so moved Countess Cittidini that she insisted he remain with her. After a few days of playing the grateful guest, he disappeared with several of her family's art treasures. His art expertise allowed him to choose his booty wisely. The countess was enraged and had him tracked down as far as Piraeus.*

I struggle to act honourably, Charlotte. I have tried to be the son and soldier my father wanted. I work to be the husband you deserve and the father Jack needs. Forces in my life pull me from these chosen paths. Forgive me, my dearest, for rambling, but I do not know how soon again I will be able to send a letter home.

The sky is an azure blue, Lottie. I pray the seas will stay calm for my journey. Please, convey to Emma my wish for her happiness and good fortune in her marriage to John. Thank her for allowing John to attend me in Italy. His help has been invaluable. I do not want to end this note, Lottie. I feel as if you are sitting here with me and if I stop you will vanish. I long to hear your sweet voice and to see Jackie laugh. I will be with you soon to kiss your ankles and whatever else you might allow.

Until then, I am your faithful and loving admirer.

With sincere regard and affection,
Jem

Charlotte finished the letter and sat with her eyes closed, imagining James near her. Where was he now? In a place she had no knowledge of, she thought. She wanted him home, not at the mercy of strangers, not in a place where any second, he could encounter the one man in the world who wanted him dead. How would he ever get Hawkes to admit to any wrongdoing? Charlotte could see no happy ending to this, and she became angry with James's being so far away. The instant her anger emerged, it became like an ugly stain that she wanted to expunge but did not know how to remove.

I love you, Jemmy, she said to the air, desperately afraid that her anger would hurt him and keep him from ever coming home. All her joy at receiving the letter took wing, like the birds Jack loved to chase, leaving only a cold emptiness.

"I love you, Jemmy," she cried. "Please, come home to me." Please, God, she prayed, bring him home to me.

CHAPTER FIFTEEN

Charlotte collected herself and went in to her friends who were playing with Jack. On hearing his laughter, Charlotte let go of her melancholy thoughts. They ate breakfast and took a walk in the garden.

Finally, Emma could contain herself no longer and she insisted they return to her house to see her bridal dress. Charlotte turned Jack over to Annie, and the three ladies were driven to Grosvenor Square.

Once there, Emma led them to her dressing room and carefully took the robe and skirts out of her wardrobe. The plain cream-coloured satin that made up the robe was of the finest quality and much in fashion. The Holland lace Charlotte had suggested was delicate and finely made. It was used for the three ruffles on the sleeves as well as covering the stomacher and providing the ruching on the hem of the open robe. Emma's embroidery was beautifully done and adorned the robe's edges, the stomacher, and the front of the skirt. Both Elizabeth and Charlotte praised her work.

"Emma, you will be a most beautiful bride," Charlotte said, and Elizabeth agreed.

That night, it was planned that they would all go to the Theatre Royal at Drury Lane to see Barry perform King

Lear. In particular, the ladies wished to see the beautiful Mrs. Barry do Cordelia. John would join them at the theatre. Charlotte was eager to talk to him about his time with James in Venice and Bellagio.

Charlotte tucked Jack in that night and kissed his forehead before going downstairs. She waited in the parlour. When Elizabeth made her entrance, she was the picture of grace. Being in London and away from her father, she was at ease and moved with a serenity Charlotte had not observed at Kirkmoor. There, Elizabeth always seemed to be running to finish some task or dodging her father's verbal abuse or physical blows. Now, she was able to move at her leisure, and she was truly beautiful.

Elizabeth's mood was coloured by melancholy, however, for she missed Thomas and was not sure if he would be able to join her. He had come to London early that morning but was immediately called upon to help with urgent matters of state at Westminster. She had received a heartfelt note from him attesting to his love and his disappointment at not being at her side. Charlotte had to admit she felt a hint of jealousy for all of Elizabeth's happiness. It was not fair, she knew, given all that Elizabeth had suffered, but nonetheless, there it was.

Hush, she told herself, but could not suppress the thought, why should she be happy when I am miserable? Why should her lover be here while mine chooses to be far away? That is what Jem is doing. He does not want to be here with me. He is enjoying himself. I know he is. Azure skies, indeed? I get rainy London, and he gets glorious sunsets on the Aegean. She put her hands to her ears and shook her head. She wanted to flee her self-pitying thoughts, but she was trapped. Elizabeth noticed Charlotte was distracted and asked her if she was feeling ill. Charlotte laughed and said it was just the excitement of the day. Elizabeth asked no further questions, and they were off to the theatre.

The Theatre Royal at Drury Lane had always been Charlotte's favourite theatre. As a young girl after her family moved to London, going there was the most exciting outing of her young life. She was sure the actors were illusions created solely for her enjoyment. Charlotte was in awe of the players. As Elizabeth and she walked into the theatre, her childhood feelings of enchantment returned. Elizabeth described for Charlotte her delight in seeing Philip De Loutherbourg's scenic paintings for several of Garrick's productions. As she finished her story, they were ushered into Emma's box. Emma and John were there already. The friends greeted each other warmly.

Charlotte realized that her fan was missing and thought perhaps she had dropped it just outside in the hallway. Excusing herself, she went in search of it. Everyone was rushing to get to their seats. Charlotte, walking with her head down, searched the floor. Just as she spotted the errant fan and knelt to reach for it a man's hand snatched it up. Surprised, she stood up quickly and came face to face with the mischievous smile of Thomas Warrender.

"Madame is this yours by any chance?" he asked.

"Yes, Lord Chagford, it is. May I have it, please?" Charlotte asked smiling back at him.

"Only if you come closer," he replied.

"Sir?"

"Come closer," he directed.

She followed his instruction, although it made her a bit uneasy. Her heart was pounding as he held her in his gaze.

When she was quite near him, he looked in her eyes.

"You are a beautiful woman, Charlotte Pruitt," he said in a whisper, "especially without the bruises on your face."

"Thank you, Lord Chagford," she responded as formally as she could. "May I have my fan?" she asked, taking a step back from him.

"Yes, you may, Mrs. Pruitt." He raised an eyebrow as he smiled and handed her the fan. "Where is Lady Bosworth's box?" he asked casually, as if nothing had just passed between them.

"This way, sir," Charlotte said leading the way.

Elizabeth was excited to see Thomas. They embraced warmly, after which Emma and he greeted one another. She introduced him to John Fuller. He shook John's hand and wished the couple good fortune in their married life. He put his arm around Elizabeth and told of their plans to wed.

Charlotte watched it all, feeling as if she was watching actors upon the stage. Had she imagined what just happened in the hall? How could he address her in such a way and then play the happy lover to Elizabeth? Charlotte wondered if her jealous heart and miserable soul were playing tricks on her eyes and ears. After they all sat down, Elizabeth turned to Charlotte and again asked if she was feeling ill. Charlotte smiled the best she could and said it was simply the excitement of being in the playhouse.

"Please, pay me no mind, dear friend. I am quite well," Charlotte reassured her, but she had grave misgivings about Elizabeth's future happiness.

At the interval, as they were all chatting, John took Charlotte aside and began to tell her about his time in Italy. She put her finger to her lips. He stopped, understanding this was not the place to talk about James.

"I long to hear all about your travels, but the interval is too short to do your stories justice."

She looked over her shoulder to the others. Thomas caught her eye and moved towards them.

"Mrs. Pruitt," Thomas said, his tone the epitome of politeness. "Please, accept my invitation to come and stay with Elizabeth and me when we are married. I know how it would please my wife-to-be to have your company at Scorhill Hall."

On overhearing his invitation, Elizabeth was overjoyed. "Oh, Charlotte, you must. We would be so pleased to have you. You said you have no desire to stay at Kirkmoor. Scorhill Hall is beautiful. Please, say you will!" she implored her friend.

"Your invitation is most thoughtful and timely, Lord Chagford," Charlotte replied. "I have to attend to my late husband's business affairs while in London, but I would be delighted to come to Scorhill when I am back in Devon."

Thomas looked pleased. "It is settled then," he said.

Charlotte rode home by herself. Emma had invited everyone to her house after the theatre, but Charlotte felt the need to be alone. She was exceedingly uneasy about her encounter with Thomas and his "innocent" invitation to Scorhill Hall. Charlotte knew she had promised Elizabeth that she would help with her father's care, but now she wished to be very far away from Chagford and Thomas Warrender. The night was damp, and fog settled over the city. The coach crawled along the street. Figures drifted in and out of the mist. A man and woman, inebriated, swayed as they walked. He grabbed at her breasts and, laughing, she pushed him off of her. They disappeared back into the gloom.

A lone man stepped suddenly into the street. Charlotte started, thinking he was coming towards the coach door, but instead, he crossed furtively behind the coach. Charlotte felt alone and unprotected.

By the time she reached Bellagio House, she was determined to go to James, wherever he might be. Jack and she required his presence and protection. The question was how to find him. Charlotte was too tired now to think about it, but in the morning, she told herself she would plan the journey.

Upon waking, she saw the rain pouring outside her window. It had knocked the autumn leaves from the trees and sent Charlotte's rose petals hurtling to the ground. The garden looked sad and bare, where just yesterday, it had been an explosion of colour.

Annie and Jack were playing in the nursery as Charlotte ate a quiet breakfast. She pondered how she might find James. Elizabeth slept late. Charlotte dreaded having to tell her that instead of coming to Scorhill Hall, she was planning now to go to the Continent.

She heard her friend come down the stairs. Elizabeth was singing merrily to herself. She entered the room and greeted Charlotte affectionately.

"Charlotte, my dear sister, for truly that is what you are to me, I have never been so happy. We had such a lovely visit at Emma's. I wish you had felt better, so you could have joined us. Did you know, Emma knew Thomas when we were children? We all played together when she came to visit. Oh, we had such a time talking about our adventures."

"I am so happy for you, Elizabeth. You and Thomas made a handsome couple at the theatre last night."

Charlotte knew she was not hiding her melancholy

humour from her friend.

"I wish Jem could come home, Charlotte. I know you do, too. Please, try not to be so sad. It is a time for weddings and new beginnings," Elizabeth said brightly.

Charlotte could not find it in her heart to tell Elizabeth that she planned to leave the country. Instead, they spent the rest of the day getting last minute fittings on their dresses. There was only one more day before the wedding. Tomorrow would be spent with the hairdressers and helping Emma in whatever way they could.

Thomas called on Elizabeth briefly in the afternoon on his way to see the King. Charlotte took her leave of Elizabeth before he entered and went to her room. After he left, the ladies had a quiet dinner until Jack came running into the room, followed by Annie. He crawled into Elizabeth's arms and snuggled against her.

As she looked fondly down at him, Charlotte saw James in her profile. Elizabeth looked up and saw the expression on Charlotte's face.

"What is it?" she asked.

"Forgive me. You reminded me so much of Jem. I miss him and am fearful he will not come back."

"Charlotte, he will come home," Elizabeth answered in a tone too cheerful for Charlotte at that moment.

"He has chosen to follow that madman, Elizabeth. I do not know where he is or what might be happening to him. Surely, you realize the seriousness of his course of action," Charlotte said angrily.

Elizabeth put Jack down gently, and he ran from the room, pursued by Annie. She looked at Charlotte sternly, saying, "I do understand the seriousness, dear sister. I am afraid for my brother, but what else can he do? He is banished from our home and from England unless he can prove Edward Hawkes exists and is the murderer of both that child and your husband."

The next words out of Charlotte's mouth were ones she regretted immediately. "If only you had not alerted the Justice of the peace about the baby." Charlotte stopped, shocked at her own candour.

Elizabeth sat, staring at her. She stood up. "I did what I was honour-bound to do. It was my responsibility. What would you have done? Bury the poor child behind the stables? Would you have denied its parents some peace of mind and it a Christian burial?"

"I do not know! But I want James here, not ten thousand miles away!"

"Stop pitying yourself, Charlotte. We all have crosses to bear. Do not begrudge others their happiness. I lost my husband, the man I adored, in a war fought for what? I have run the manor for years because my father wanted James to be a soldier. I have born my father's insults and ingratitude. I have raised my sons as best I could, alone. I have suffered, and I have worked. Now, I will enjoy my happiness with Thomas Warrender. Goodnight, Charlotte. I believe I am done with this discussion."

"Elizabeth, please, I..." Charlotte's words trailed off. Elizabeth was already going up the stairs to her room.

Well, I did a good job with that, Charlotte said to herself. Dear God, where did that come from? Charlotte sat with her head in her hands. How could I have been so stupid, so ill mannered? What could have possessed me? She went to her room and to her escritoire to write Elizabeth a note of apology. She asked Elizabeth if she could find it in her heart to forgive her and that she was

truly sorry for all she had said. Slipping the note under
Elizabeth's door, she prayed that her friend would read it
that night.

Sometime later, as Charlotte tossed and turned in her
bed, there came a soft knocking on her door. Elizabeth
crept in with a candle.

"Charlotte, are you awake?" she asked.

"Oh, yes, Elizabeth," Charlotte responded groggily.
"Thank you for coming. Can you forgive me?"

Elizabeth sat down next to Charlotte. "I am sorry, as
well. I know these last two years have been difficult for
you." She hesitated. "Please, let us be friends again. I need
your sisterly love so very much."

"And I need your love and affection, as well. Thank you
for being so understanding, Elizabeth. Thank you." They
smiled shyly at each other. Charlotte took her friend's hand
and Elizabeth moved closer and hugged her.

They talked for another hour, laughing at childhood
stories and at their own children's follies. When at last they
were both falling asleep, Elizabeth got up to go. Charlotte
could not bear her leaving.

"Please, stay, Elizabeth." Charlotte moved over in the
bed and offered her a place.

Elizabeth hesitated, but then crawled in next to her
friend. They said goodnight and Charlotte blew out the
candle. At first, Elizabeth turned her back to Charlotte.
Both women wanted to be together, but the first few
moments were awkward.

Finally, in the darkness, Elizabeth turned to Charlotte
and put her arm around her friend's shoulder. Charlotte
moved in close until their bodies touched. They caressed
each other. Comforted, they fell asleep in each other's arms.

The next morning brought unexpected excitement. Charlotte received a letter from James, written just two weeks before. It was delivered to her by one of the count's own messengers who had been in Greece with James. James wrote that he was in Athens visiting a friend of Count Cesi. This gentleman, Pericles Rellas by name, had a shipping business that served Turkey, Egypt, and the Greek Isles. He was aware of an Englishman who fit Hawkes's description. He was a pirate, according to Rellas, who hijacked small, rich ships and smuggled stolen goods into Cairo and Constantinople. This Englishman had a reputation for being ruthless and crueller than most of his kind. He was said to hide himself and his crew on the south coast of Crete, which was riddled with caves and hidden inlets.

James had passage on one of Rellas's ships bound for Chania on Crete. He promised he would go only to see if these rumours had any validity. He finished his letter with admonitions of love for both Charlotte and Jack.

"I wish to face the future a free man, Charlotte, able to protect you and Jack. I love you, my sweet angel. Please, keep loving thoughts of me in your heart."

As she finished reading, Charlotte prayed for his safe return and pledged to purge her heart of melancholy. She would put her mind to whatever needed to be done at present, but she was still determined to go to him as soon as possible.

As they breakfasted alone, Charlotte shared with Elizabeth the news in James's note. When the hairdresser arrived and began arranging their hair in the latest fashion, they talked excitedly about all that their friend, Iacomus must be seeing and experiencing in his travels. They were soon caught up in watching their hair grow to dizzying heights with the addition of pad and sets of extra hair. When they were satisfied, the hairdresser applied large amounts of pomatum to hold the hair in place. The hairdresser promised to be at Lady Emma's the following morning to powder their hair and do the final decorations with ribbons and flowers.

Emma invited them to spend the night at her house, so they could all proceed to the church together in the late morning. John would be coming from his lodgings with his contingent of the wedding party to meet them there. They were like young girls that night. They giggled and chatted late into the evening.

Charlotte was the first up in the morning and in her undergarments as Emma's maid helped her with her corset. The hairdresser arrived and began to dress Charlotte's hair with rose-coloured ribbons. Emma's hair was powdered and dressed with cream-coloured ribbons and pearls. As the time drew nearer for them to leave, they helped Emma put on her petticoats, skirt, and robe. She was radiantly beautiful as she paraded for them in her dressing room. Elizabeth and Charlotte applauded her movements and praised her beauty. Emma was pleased with all the attention.

When they arrived at St. Martin-in-the-Fields, it was filled with autumn flowers. Their perfumes were light and pleasing to the nose. Each row end of the pews was festooned with cream-coloured ribbons, and there was a special carpet laid down for the bride to walk upon. Music by Handel played, and everyone talked in whispers of anticipation. John had put aside his simpler way of dressing for this occasion.

Charlotte thought he looked quite handsome in his Venetian suit of velvet and satin. His waistcoat and jacket were beautifully embroidered with golden and silver flowers. His heels were of the higher Italian fashion and had large, gold buckles. He wore no wig, but his hair was carefully powdered. Together, he and Emma were a magnificent pair.

Elizabeth and Charlotte cried as the couple said their vows. When they were pronounced man and wife, the ladies could barely restrain themselves from shouting out in joy.

Afterwards, they all adjourned to Emma's for an elegant reception. The guests were in a festive mood and seemed ready to welcome Charlotte into their midst. This reprieve came, she assumed, because she was Emma's matron of honour. Also, many of those invited were friends of Countess Crespi and mentioned her in passing to Charlotte.

Charlotte carefully avoided contact with Thomas Warrender, except to exchange greetings at the church. However, towards the end of the party Charlotte found herself alone in one of the hallways leading to the garden when Thomas suddenly appeared.

"Mrs. Pruitt, are you avoiding me?" he asked, blocking her way.

"Forgive me if I have given you that impression, Lord Chagford," Charlotte said, taking a step backwards. "I have been so extremely busy helping Emma today. Please, excuse me."

He took a step to the side and let her pass without incident. However, he followed behind her. "I must ask you to forgive me, Mrs. Pruitt, if I have acted inappropriately," he offered. "I fear I overstepped my bounds when I expressed admiration for your beauty. Please, I would be heartbroken if I drove you away. Your friendship means so much to both Elizabeth and to me. Please, say you will forgive me," he said, looking contrite. His words halted Charlotte's escape. She was charmed. Perhaps, she thought, I have been too harsh in my judgement.

"Thank you, Lord Chagford. I am touched by your words. Let us start afresh," she said, much relieved.

"Nothing would please me more, but you must agree to address me as Thomas."

"I shall, Thomas."

When they returned to the guests in the drawing room, he was swept up into a political discussion, and Charlotte sought out Elizabeth to see how she was faring. Charlotte was pondering when the best time to tell her friend of her plans to join James. She found Elizabeth engaged in a lively conversation about the American colonies and decided not to bother her.

Emma and John planned to go next morning for a five month visit to France and Italy. Their ship was to sail with the morning tide, so the party ended after dessert was served.

Charlotte and Elizabeth were the last to go. Emma embraced Charlotte, saying, "You must promise to stay out of mischief while I am away."

"I will, my dear friend," Charlotte agreed.

As the coach drew away from the front door, Charlotte saw John reach out for Emma to kiss her. It was a delightful picture, and one Charlotte was determined to hold in her mind's eye until she saw her friends again.

Elizabeth, Thomas, and Charlotte spent the next two

and a half weeks fulfilling all the social obligations they had made at Emma and John's wedding. Charlotte delayed her plans to go to the Continent.

Late one night after a party at Holland House, a messenger arrived from Devon. He carried a letter addressed to Elizabeth, written by Mr. Kyd, Kirkmoor's steward. Charlotte, Thomas, and Elizabeth sat in the parlour at Bellagio House. As Elizabeth read the letter silently, her expression changed from concern to horror as her eyes moved down the page. When she finished, she covered her mouth with her hand and stared at the floor. Thomas crossed and knelt at her feet. Elizabeth looked at him, her eyes welling up with tears.

"Elizabeth, dearest, what is it?" Charlotte asked. Unable to answer her, she handed the letter to Charlotte. Thomas comforted Elizabeth as Charlotte began to read. It was written in an unsteady hand.

Kirkmoor, Devon
Dear Mistress Elizabeth,

I have most sad tidings. On Wednesday last, Sir Rufus slipped out of the house. We were unaware that he had gone, me being taken up with the birth of a colt to Lady Jane, and Mrs. Rich and Mr. Taggert both busy with their duties. Later in the day, after we had been searching for him, he was brought home by a Mr. Rhodes, who told us that Sir Rufus and he had been wagering on the horses at Frampton Strand. The master, sure of his horse, bet a very large amount. His horse came in last. Not having the money in pounds, Sir Rufus is insisting that Mr. Rhodes must take three quarters of the estate including the manor house. We tried to stop him, but he

signed a note, and barred himself in his room. Mr. Rhodes has
given you until the end of the month to vacate the house.

When we tried to speak with Sir Rufus, he loaded his
blunderbuss and shot a hole through the door. No one was injured,
thank the Lord. He fell to ranting and crying. He seems to have
fallen asleep now, though no one dares to go near his door. We sent
for the doctor in hopes he may give him a sleeping draught when
he wakes.

I am sorry to be the bearer of such sad news, Mistress
Elizabeth, but we need you to come home. Forgive me for not better
watching your father. I fear I am responsible in all this.

Your faithful servant,
William Kyd

The three sat in silence. Charlotte's mind was racing.
What was she to do, she wondered? The moor, the damned
moor, was dragging her back. I cannot get away, she
thought. She stopped, realizing how selfish she was being.
I must think of Elizabeth and how I may help her. That is
my duty now.

"Elizabeth, I propose we go at once to Kirkmoor. We
must find out the exact terms of this agreement. Is the
property entailed?"

"No, so my father may do with it as he wishes. There is
no protection for James or me. The damned fool has given
it all away. Thomas, Charlotte, I do not comprehend how
this happened."

"Dearest," Thomas whispered, "I will help in any way
I am able. Go back and gather up your father and the boys.
Come to Scorhill Hall. Mr. Rhodes will no doubt be

insistent on payment. Do not let him humiliate your father any further. We must determine what is left to the family. I will work it out with Rhodes." Thomas's face brightened, and he knelt before Elizabeth. "Consent to marry me tomorrow before you leave London. Let nothing come between us. Go back to Devon as my wife, Lady Chagford. Please, do me that honour. I will arrange it with the archbishop."

Elizabeth gazed at him fondly. "You are a dear, impetuous man, and I shall never be able to refuse you anything. See him, Charlotte? In the middle of chaos, he has made me smile."

"If you will allow me, Elizabeth, I shall write a note to Mr. Kyd informing him that we will be arriving in the next few days," Charlotte suggested. "I will have all our belongings packed in the meanwhile, except for what you will need for the wedding. If you will excuse me now, I shall retire and let you have some time alone. I will see you in the morning. Goodnight." As Charlotte left the room, Thomas followed her, stopping her in the hall.

"Charlotte, thank you for being such a devoted friend to Elizabeth. I again extend the invitation for you to stay at Scorhill Hall. You and Jack would be most welcome, and I know your presence would make Elizabeth very happy," he said with a charming smile.

Then, his expression became serious. "You do realize that it is James's fortune that Sir Rufus has lost. There is some land left, it appears, but it will be a shock for James when he learns the news. Goodnight." He left without waiting for a response.

After giving instructions to Mr. Primm about the packing and the maintenance of Bellagio House while she was absent, Charlotte went to her room. She kept thinking of Thomas's words. The loss of the land would be a bitter blow to James. Yet, she thought, perhaps it is a blessing. If the remaining land were sold, perhaps Sir Rufus would consent to giving James a portion of the money from the sale. Then, he would never have to return to England. If, in the end, he was not able to clear his name, he would have the means to start a new life in France. Charlotte realized, though, that with Sir Rufus as mad as he was, it would be impossible to broach that subject with him. She woke several times during the night as her mind raced with what she would write to James.

By mid-morning, Thomas had spoken with the archbishop and received his permission to wed. The rector at Thomas's church came rapidly when he was summoned by the earl. It was a simple ceremony. The vows were made, and the bride kissed. Thomas thanked the rector and gave him a sizeable donation for the church as well as his fee.

Jeremy, Elizabeth's son, came from his friend's house and was told of all that had happened. It was decided that he would stay at his new father's house in Portman Square until he went to Christ Church College. He did not rejoice at this turn of events, but after some arguing with his mother, he agreed to the plans.

Thomas promised to join them at Scorhill Hall in a few days' time. He sent word along with Elizabeth, instructing the household staff to welcome the new Lady Chagford and her retinue. It was decided they would take Charlotte's coach as well as one of Thomas's so that Charlotte would have transportation back to London when the time came for her return.

Anxious about what condition her father was in,

Elizabeth found it difficult to rejoice in her newly wedded state. She sat silently for much of the journey. The rest of the time, she and Charlotte tried to plan what they would do when they arrived.

For her part, Charlotte decided she would accept Thomas's invitation, for a short while at least. She resolved to postpone writing a letter to James until she had an opportunity to speak with Sir Rufus.

CHAPTER SIXTEEN

Upon arriving at Scorhill Hall, Elizabeth spoke with Mr. Hamm, the butler, who quickly called the staff into action. Elizabeth, Charlotte, Jack, and Annie were shown their rooms and settled in comfortably. Elizabeth and Charlotte determined that they must go directly to Kirkmoor and gather up Sir Rufus and Elizabeth's sons. Elizabeth also hoped to learn from Mr. Kyd, the steward, exactly what had been agreed to with Rhodes.

The day clouded over and became grey. As they rode in the coach, they passed the Clarke family mausoleum that now most likely belonged to Mr. Rhodes. Tears welled up in Elizabeth's eyes.

"Charlotte, our family is ruined. I may not even visit my mother's resting place without asking permission from a stranger. I have known of other families to whom this happened, but I never imagined that in one wager we would be brought so low. My father is a sick, old man whom I despise. He was not always so. When I was a girl, I worshipped him. He was handsome and intelligent. My mother worshipped him, too, else she would never have put up with his anger. He could be so loving and witty. He would entertain us for hours on cold and rainy days. His favourite amusement was puppet shows. We still have a collection somewhere in the house that he and Mama made. I must take them, if Mr. Rhodes will allow it." She stopped, trying desperately to control her tears. "It is pointless to cry about what is gone, is it not? I am so thankful for Thomas. God has granted me my fondest wish, threefold; a husband, a lover, and a father for the boys. It was a wish I imagined was so far beyond me that I had all but given up hope. Thomas is a passionate man, Charlotte," she admitted, blushing. "I am most thankful that he has come into my life."

The house came into view with the moor looming up behind it. "What will become of our tenants? Charlotte, some have been with our family for generations. And what of the servants and Mr. Kyd? I must help them however I can!" Elizabeth declared.

The coach halted at the front entrance and Mr. Kyd emerged from the house, followed by Mrs. Rich and Mr. Taggert. Mr. Kyd came right to the point after the ladies were handed down from the coach.

"Mistress Elizabeth, Sir Rufus is upstairs. He's barely eaten in a week. He wanders the halls calling out for your mother, God rest her soul. It is a terrible sight. Mr. Rhodes told us he means to take over the house at the month's end. I thank God you have come so quickly, mistress, and you too, Mrs. Pruitt. The doctor told us to put Sir Rufus to bed. He tried bleeding him, but as soon as the leeches were in place, the master ripped them off and threw them at the doctor and those of us assembled. For all his illness, he still has fight in him."

Elizabeth thanked him for his news and motioned for them all to follow her. She gave directions to the staff about packing the house. "I have decided we will take all that is moveable. If Mr. Rhodes wishes to fight us, he can come to Scorhill and ask for it back, item by item. I will give him a battle if that is what he is after. Tell the grooms to take the horses to the Earl of Chagford's stables, and all the tack, as well. Leave the hounds. He shall have the house and the dogs, but nothing more."

With these orders, everyone went to work. Mrs. Rich had one of the maids bring Elizabeth and Charlotte tea and biscuits before they ventured upstairs to Sir Rufus. The friends sat quietly and looked around the parlour. It was the most intimate spot in the house. A crackling fire warmed the room while the rain pelted the windows and ran down the glass. Those windows looked out on the front expanse of lawn and to the copse beyond.

The door suddenly flew open and Sir Rufus strode in dressed in his night shirt. "Lizzie," he said, "you must come see." He grabbed Elizabeth by the hand and pulled her up from her chair and into the hallway.

Trying not to upset him, Elizabeth asked, "Father, how are you feeling?"

"Fit as a fiddle," he answered as he pulled her up the stairs. Looking back at Charlotte, who followed them, he called, "Hurry up, girl, this concerns you, too." He tugged a reluctant Elizabeth into his room. Charlotte trailed a few feet after them. Once she was in, he closed the door. "See," he said, pointing to an empty wall.

"See what, sir?" Charlotte asked.

He looked disoriented. "Well, just a moment ago, Jem was here. Where did he go? Did we pass him in the hall?" he asked, looking from Charlotte to Elizabeth. He sat down hard in a chair, as all the life seemed to drain from his body. "He *was* here," he murmured.

Together, the women got Sir Rufus dressed. He talked no more about James. The old man came willingly to the coach as the rain continued to pour down. Neither Elizabeth nor Charlotte said one word about their destination. The three of them sat, cold and silent, as the coach pulled away from the house.

Finally, Elizabeth's father spoke. "Well, at least I will not have to die in that house. I have always had a great fear of dying there, ever since I was a child and my three younger brothers all succumbed to consumption. Then Mama and Father were eaten up by the place. God, I hate that house. And your dear, sweet mother dying there." He paused and smiled. "So where are we off to Lizzie?"

"Scorhill Hall," she said matter of factly, waiting for an explosion. None came.

"Ah, you and Thomas, eh? Well, just yesterday, Charley told me, yet again, that Tom was a good boy. No, he called him a man. 'Thomas is a good man,' he said. 'Lizzie could do worse,' he said. Would you like my blessing? Well, you have it, if you want it, but who would want the blessing of a crazy old man?" He stopped speaking and looked out the window.

They were just passing the family mausoleum when Sir Rufus pounded on the ceiling of the coach with his cane, commanding the coachman to halt. He was out the door and headed up the hill to the mausoleum before the women could stop him. Elizabeth told the coachman to wait. She and Charlotte chased behind him in the pouring rain. Charlotte nearly lost her shoes in the mud outside the building. When she got inside, she found Sir Rufus lighting candles with a tinder pistol and telling Elizabeth to be quiet as she tried to urge him back to the coach.

"There is someone here that wants to see you," he said, laughing mischievously and looking at Charlotte. "He said he would be here waiting for us."

His words sent a chill down Charlotte's soaked back until she saw who emerged from the shadows. "Jemmy!" she cried and ran to him.

Sir Rufus turned to Elizabeth, saying, "I told you he was back." Elizabeth stood with her mouth agape.

James grabbed Charlotte up in his arms and kissed her. She held on to him and would not let go, feeling safe and complete for the first time in months. Finally, she loosened her grip but still did not let go. Charlotte looked up into the face she loved so much. He gazed back at her and they began to laugh.

"Oh, Jemmy, should I believe my eyes that you are here?" Charlotte whispered.

"I am, my love. I am. Before I boarded the boat for Crete, I was overcome with a feeling that I needed to come back home. Lottie, I could not stay away from you another instant. You are truly the most beautiful and enchanting woman in the world. I missed you more that I can possibly express." Charlotte smiled, thrilled by his words.

Elizabeth interrupted their reverie. "What of Edward Hawkes, dear brother?"

"When I left, Count Cesi's men were planning to follow his trail to Crete, where it is rumoured he hides his pirate gold. The Venetians are excellent hunters and are eager to catch Hawkes."

"Jemmy," Charlotte said, motioning towards Elizabeth, "I should like to introduce you to Lady Chagford."

"Lizzie's finally got herself a husband," Sir Rufus giggled.

"Congratulations, sister!" James exclaimed. "You are deserving of a good husband. I wish you every happiness". He walked to her and they embraced. Stepping back from Elizabeth, James spoke. "I fear I have come too late to save our house and lands." An uncomfortable silence fell as Elizabeth looked at their father.

It was decided that James would not be safe at Scorhill Hall, since he was a wanted man. They agreed that the mausoleum was a good rendezvous point, and that he should stay in the glen where Charlotte had bid him good-bye when he left for Ireland. It would be a cold, wet existence, but better than him being discovered and put in the gaol. Saying good-bye after such a quick hello was difficult. Yet knowing he was close by would sustain her joy, Charlotte thought. She promised that if the weather was clear the next day, she would bring Jack to the glen.

"He has grown so much," Charlotte told James.

A look of sadness came over his face. "We must settle down and be a family, Charlotte. I want to be with my son as he grows."

"He is a bright little fellow, Jem. Fond of his granddad, he is. I have kept an eye on him," Sir Rufus said. "Come on now, we need to go. Don't want to draw attention to this place. Got to think of the right battle plan." He turned and walked outside. Elizabeth said her good-bye and joined her father. Charlotte and James held each other.

"I cannot go, Jemmy. I will stay here with you, at least for a little while," Charlotte declared. She did not wait for his answer but followed Elizabeth and told her that she'd decided to walk back to Kirkmoor and help supervise the servants. She requested that Elizabeth send the coach for her later in the day.

Elizabeth smiled and embraced Charlotte. "The coach will call before dinner and bring you back to Scorhill Hall."

Walking back into the mausoleum, Charlotte felt wet and chilled, but when she saw James, she forgot any discomfort she felt. He had spread his bedroll out onto the stone floor and was placing candles in a circle around it. Standing, watching him, she realized again how deeply she loved him.

"May I help?" Charlotte asked.

"No, come sit," he said, motioning to the makeshift bed.

Charlotte followed his instructions and sat, smiling contentedly. He produced a round loaf of bread, a large chunk of cheese, a jar of butter, and a bottle of claret from a cloth bag. He sat down beside her.

"Whose larder did you rob?" she asked in admiration of the meal before her.

"I know Kirkmoor's kitchen very well. There are several ways to steal in and out without detection. I have done it since I was a lad. The wine, however, I brought from Italy. It is a gift from the count. He asked me to drink it only with you. Please, forgive a poor man's table. I have no glasses, but I do have a corkscrew." He opened the bottle and handed it to her.

"To your safe return to me!" As she drank, a warm fire went down her throat and her body relaxed. She gave the bottle to James.

"To you, Lottie, and to Jackie. I thank God we are all together again, and I pray that these moments we share may multiply." He turned the bottle up and took a long drink. Finishing, he said, "*Quant'è buono. Grazie mille*, Count Cesi!" He put the bottle down and took Charlotte in his arms. She

had her hair pulled back in a braid, which was pinned up
the back of her head in the country fashion. After James
kissed her, he undid her hair and let it fall. He took her locks
into his hands and gently brushed them against his face.

"Oh, Charlotte, I have missed your smell," he sighed.
"Your hair is so silken, your skin so soft. I love you, my
dearest. I will love you forever."

It was her turn, and she loosened his hair. It had grown
long again over his months of absence. Charlotte ran her
fingers through it and pulled it forward over his shoulders.
Its golden hues caught the candlelight. It had become
blonder in the Italian sun, just as his skin had become
darker. Some small creature scurried from one dark corner
to another. Charlotte's attention was drawn to the tombs
nearby.

"Does it feel odd to be surrounded by your ancestors?"
she asked.

"No, I rather think they must be enjoying themselves.
I cannot imagine my mother disapproves," he replied with
a humorous tone.

"Why do you say it like that?"

"My brother told me, not long before his accident, that
mother had had an affair with the earl," he answered.

"Thomas's father?"

"The very one. This was one of their trysting places.
When I was planning where I would hide, the story came
back to me. My mother was a beautiful woman. I think her
love affair was one of the ways she got her revenge on my
father for his violence."

He was looking towards where his mother's tomb was.
He turned his attention again to Charlotte. "Your clothes
are wet. We must dry you off and warm you up." He began

to help her off with her jacket and her outer clothes. It was damp and cold. They could make no fire, so when Charlotte was undressed, he wrapped her in his blanket. As she sat, he took off his coat, his boots and stockings, his shirt, breeches and the rest. He stood naked in the candlelight, and Charlotte desired him more than she ever had before.

"Jemmy, come to me. Warm yourself," she whispered.

He sat down on the makeshift bed. She sat on top of him and covered them both with the heavy blanket. She touched his lips with hers, exploring his full lower lip with her tongue. She felt warm shivers run down her back. They drank more wine and slowly explored each other's bodies. She kissed his strong, smooth shoulders and bit at his neck.

Soon, he slipped inside her and she closed around him. It was a moment of exquisite pleasure for them both. They rocked together, gently at first. However, their passion building, they moved more rapidly. Their moans echoed off the stone walls. When the moment came for Charlotte, she cried out. Never had she experienced such a release. James laid her down tenderly, and they began to move again. The blanket fell away, and Charlotte delighted in watching and feeling James's body as it moved with hers. He gasped and drove himself deep into her. Afterward, he lay carefully on top of her, so they could stay as one. Charlotte thanked God for her lover's return. He kissed her softly, then slipping out, he lay beside her, pulling the blanket over them.

There was so much to say that Charlotte chose to say nothing. She wanted to hold on to their time. Everything else was past or future. This was their present moment. They fell asleep briefly. When they awoke, they ate and finished the claret. Time was passing, and Charlotte knew she needed to go.

Once dressed, she looked outside and saw that the rain had ceased, and the clouds were parting. The soft, diffuse light made the surrounding hills a pale, shimmering green. It was late afternoon, and she would have to walk some distance to get back to Kirkmoor. James held her, and they kissed one more time.

"You are God's gift to me, my beloved. Please, stay safely hidden," Charlotte whispered.

"I promise, I shall. Please, bring Jack when the weather permits it. I miss him, Charlotte. I will stay here until just before dawn and then ride to the glen. I love you." He kissed her and disappeared into the darkness of the mausoleum.

Charlotte walked back to the house, trying not to get stuck in the mud. There were a few times when she was not sure if she could finish her walk, because of the claret she had consumed and the relaxed state of her body. She giggled and smiled, glad that she met no one on her way back.

At Kirkmoor, she found all the servants hurriedly packing. The coach arrived about an hour later and she rode to Scorhill Hall. It was all she could do not to stop the coach again at the mausoleum, but she kept quiet and arrived back without incident. Dinner was served in a grand style. Afterwards, Elizabeth and she retired to the drawing room to discuss the day's events and to plan what must happen next.

Elizabeth told Charlotte that when they returned earlier in the afternoon, her father settled into his rooms comfortably and no more was said about her marriage to Thomas. Her boys, Robert and Benjamin, went off to explore their new surroundings and came back every now and again to report their findings. Elizabeth reminded Charlotte that Thomas promised to deal with Mr. Rhodes. Hopefully, they would hear from her husband in the next few days as to which part of the estate Mr. Rhodes felt he was entitled. Perhaps the family mausoleum would be saved after all.

The rain poured down for the next three days, which made it impossible to go to the glen. Charlotte prayed that James was able to stay dry. Perhaps, she thought, he is staying in the mausoleum, which would afford more protection from the weather. Stopping there on the pretext of taking flowers to Lady Louisa's tomb, Charlotte found no trace of him. She left a note, *"With all my love, to my sweet angel,"* next to the bouquet. Charlotte knew he would understand they were from her. Anyone else finding them, would, hopefully, assume they were for the dead and not the living.

On the fourth day, the sun shone and the road between the estates began to dry out a little. Jack was eager to be outside and ran to the door when his grandfather offered to take him on a walk. They had spent the last three days with Annie running up and down the long gallery and playing hide and seek upstairs and down. Sir Rufus slept later than usual and awakened complaining of a headache, but now he seemed in good spirits.

They were out for only a short time when Charlotte heard them return. Sir Rufus was coughing and having trouble catching his breath. Charlotte rang for a servant, who came quickly, and she told the girl to fetch Elizabeth. She helped Sir Rufus sit down and got him a glass of water. His face was red, and he was having difficulty breathing.

Elizabeth rushed in and knelt at her father's feet. He looked at her, patting her hand, trying to indicate that he would be all right.

"Just tried to run a bit too much, Lizzie, Charlotte. Nothing to worry about. Go tend to Jackie. He got his feet wet out there. It is a bog. I am fine. My God, women, can't an old man cough or pass wind without the whole world coming running?" He got up and walked slowly out of the room in search of Jack.

"Elizabeth, I do not think your father is well. I believe I should get word to Jem. Is it possible to ride to the glen?" Charlotte asked, determined she would see James.

"I shall call for the horses to be saddled. I want to see him, as well. Should we take Jack, do you think?"

"I would like to. Jem asked to see him. If the weather begins to change, we will turn back," Charlotte said. They made ready to go, taking extra clothes and blankets in case they were needed.

The kitchen packed a large meal for them, and Elizabeth asked for a few extra items, saying for any ears that might be listening that she had wanted to give Mr. Taggert and Mrs. Rich something extra for all their hard work packing up the house. Elizabeth instructed Mr. Hamm, the butler, to watch her father until she returned. Annie dressed Jack in so many layers he could hardly move. Charlotte helped him shed a few, which she stored in with the other extra items they were bringing. They mounted their horses, and Annie handed Jack up to Charlotte. His coming along would slow their pace, but Charlotte hoped it might look like a pleasant outing, in the event anyone was watching them.

Jack loved to ride. As they started out, he was laughing

and pointing at the horses and sheep in the pasture. Charlotte imagined him as a young man riding out among the moors. She kissed his head and held him tighter, praying that he would have a long and healthy life. They headed west across the moor, careful to avoid the bogs, made all the more treacherous by the heavy rains.

Halfway into their journey, they passed the actual Scorhill. Charlotte told Jack it was a fairy ring, for there was something magical about the ring of standing stones. Who, Charlotte wondered, had carried and set them there? Did their spirits still dance in the circle, invisible to mortals? Charlotte remembered how strange they looked the night Elizabeth and she had ridden to see James before he fled to Ireland.

After Scorhill, they began to go northwest towards Yes Tor and High Willhays. Elizabeth had told Charlotte that when she and James were younger, Charles would bring them to the Tor, and they would spend hours on clear days looking over all Dartmoor.

"My brothers imagined themselves ancient high kings, and I chose to be a powerful sorceress. We would often end up in arguments about who ruled whom."

Armed with the knowledge of the geography of the moor, Charlotte felt more at ease as they rode this time. She told Jack to keep an eye out for the wild ponies.

"Perhaps we can convince your papa to catch you one. Would you like that, Jackie?"

The wind picked up, but the day was still clear. Jack turned his head into Charlotte's chest to keep his eyes from watering. Elizabeth led them this time to an easier entrance to the glen, where they did not have to brave the bramble and the gorse bushes. They dismounted, and Jack began running towards the stream. Charlotte ran after him, afraid of the water, which was high and traveling fast. After Charlotte got hold of Jack's hand, she guided him back to the clearing.

Elizabeth tended to the horses and checked to see if James was in the small cave. He wasn't.

"I wonder where he could be," Charlotte murmured when Elizabeth returned without him.

"If I know my brother," Elizabeth replied, frowning a little, "he's off trying to get some answers. Never mind that he's an escaped prisoner with everyone out looking for him."

"So, we wait?" Charlotte asked, trying to keep her worried thoughts in check.

"We wait," Elizabeth replied.

The women put down two blankets, laid out their meal, and ate. Jack was hungry after the ride. By early afternoon, the wind had blown away the clouds and the sunlight turned the remaining leaves on the trees a bright gold. Jack fell asleep, and Charlotte soon joined him on the blanket. The ground under their bodies was soft with moss and fallen leaves. They rested peacefully.

Elizabeth decided to take a walk and disappeared from sight. It was very quiet. One lone bird sang Charlotte a song, the rest of his fellows having already begun their journey south. Charlotte closed her eyes. She was just falling asleep when she felt something tickle her forehead. She was too sleepy to open her eyes and brushed it away without a thought. Again, something lit on her face. She opened her eyes and became instantly alert. A man in filthy clothes stood over her. He had his cloak pulled over his head. A long, thin stick dangled from his hand. He reached out to touch her again. Charlotte's first thought was to protect Jack, but before she could react, the stranger threw back his head covering and knelt down. It was James.

"Forgive me, Charlotte. You both looked so peaceful, I could not resist."

Charlotte was still trying to catch her breath and calm down when James remarked, "Look how he's grown, Lottie. He is a handsome boy." He lay down beside his son and watched him sleep. "It is your father, Jack. Do you remember me? The fates have not been kind to us. Would that I had never had to flee. Nothing is more important to me than the two of you."

"Where have you been this morning?" Charlotte asked.

"I decided to take a chance and see what I might discover about Mr. Rhodes. I have spent the last four days talking with villagers from Dawlish, Teignmouth, and Newton Abbot. The most I have garnered is that he is newly come to these parts. Made his fortune, so he has told everyone, in shipbuilding. He came with the intention of settling in the west country."

"Jemmy, no one suspected who you were, did they?" Charlotte asked.

"No, with the enclosures being enforced, there are people from all over England who pass through this area looking for work. No one suspects one more wanderer. I would not take such a chance in Chagford or Okehampton, though, I assure you." He smiled and moved closer to her. He had blackened his teeth and his clothes smelled of horse manure.

"I love you, Jem, but forgive me if I do not kiss or embrace you." She could not help moving away from him.

"For you, dearest, I will bathe." He grinned.

Crawling into the cave, he came out with fresh clothes, which he dropped next to Charlotte, and a blanket to wrap himself in after his bath. He followed the stream until he came to a deep pool. She knew the water was frigid, but he plunged in without complaint. He emerged, his body glistening in the as the sun filtered through the trees. He washed his dirty clothes and left them to dry on some bushes. Returning to Charlotte wrapped in the blanket, he sat down next to her.

"Jack's asleep, would you like to join me in this blanket? I am freshly washed. My teeth are clean. I even used my tongue scraper." Charlotte could not help giggling in delight. However, she declined his offer.

"Elizabeth could come back any moment. I do not want to give her a shock."

"It will not take long. You are more beautiful than ever. I am halfway to heaven already despite the cold water." He extended his hand trying to reach under her dress.

"James Clarke, stop that at once!" She laughed and crawled away, but he caught her ankle and started to pull her back.

Jack woke, and seeing a strange man, began to cry. Charlotte took him in her arms, attempting to soothe him.

"You do not want to share your mama? I do not blame you, lad," James said as he rose and dressed quickly.

When he sat down again, Jack stopped crying and watched him. James began to play peek-a-boo behind Charlotte's back and soon Jack was up and chasing after his father. In the end, James had the boy so thoroughly charmed that Jack allowed himself to be picked up. He laughed with abandon as he was hoisted up in the air and brought down to earth again. In all the gaiety of their reunion, Charlotte had forgotten about Sir Rufus. Jack's laughter reminded her of the joy he had playing with his grandfather.

"Jemmy, I need to speak with you," Charlotte said with urgency.

James, holding Jack suspended in mid-air, gently brought him down. "Papa's home, Jackie. I love you," he whispered as he sat Jack on the blanket. He tried to hold the squirming child for a minute, but this proved impossible, so he let go. Jack went off exploring, but James kept him in view.

Charlotte sat next to James. "Forgive me for startling you," she apologized, "but I suddenly remembered an important reason for our coming here. Your father's health is failing. Only this morning, he had a terrible coughing fit. He made light of it, but we were all frightened by its severity. I need to have a better way of communicating with you, in case he suddenly becomes very ill, heaven forbid."

They sat in silence for a minute or two, then James spoke. "Charlotte, I know Scorhill Hall has some secret passages and hidden rooms. I remember exploring them as a child when we were still allowed to play with Thomas. Both Mother and Father took us for visits there, though more often than not, it was Mother. When I think of it now, I understand her haste in getting us off to play on our own. She and the earl would disappear together and we, thinking nothing of it, would search out secret hiding places. Perhaps, between Elizabeth and her sons, they could ferret them out again."

"Are you thinking you might hide at Scorhill Hall now?" Charlotte asked.

"Yes, for a little while. It would be drier than here. And

I could come to you at night."

"That is an appealing proposition," Charlotte replied. "Ravished by the ghost of the manor. There must certainly be enough of them floating around there. What's one more?"

Jack, who had not strayed far, came back and pulled on James's collar until he pulled his father over. James grabbed his son and held him upside down. Turning him upright, he held Jack fast. He kissed his face over and over. Jack giggled and squirmed.

Elizabeth returned, and they acquainted her with their plan. She thought having James closer was a good idea, although she was fearful that he might be discovered. James assured her that he would be careful. It was agreed that, weather permitting, he would slip in the house that night through one of Charlotte's bedroom windows. The room was on the ground floor, and she would leave candles burning in both her windows.

Elizabeth promised to speak with her sons to see what secret places they had discovered as well. She recollected a few spots herself. Between them all, she was sure they would find a safe place for James to hide. In case of any problems, James would leave clothing and food in the cave. James and Charlotte embraced, holding Jack between them. He looked up into both their faces and smiled happily. Charlotte closed her eyes and prayed to God to let them be together as a family. They all kissed and said good-bye.

CHAPTER SEVENTEEN

The weather was turning colder as Elizabeth and Charlotte rode with Jack back across the moor. At one point when they stopped to rest, Charlotte asked Elizabeth if she thought James would be safe traveling the moors with the bogs at night.

Her reply was simply, "Let us pray that it stays clear."

It did not stay clear. Clouds scudded across the sky after dinner. A cold, hard rain began to pour down. The wind howled as it moved across the moor. It smashed into the house with great force and blew in at every nook and cranny.

Sir Rufus, they learned, had been in bed the entire day. When they arrived home, he had briefly risen and had a small bowl of soup for dinner. "It is this house," he said. "There are memories here that will not die until I do." Having said that, he walked slowly back to his bedroom. Charlotte took Jack to visit him and say goodnight. The old man was in bed and bid them sit beside him. He held Charlotte by the wrist. "Charley will not enter this house. I have lost him again."

"Sir, please calm yourself. You need to sleep," Charlotte urged.

"Forgive me, Charlotte. I have been obstreperous. With

old age, my manners are appalling. I cannot control myself, not that I ever could. You have been kind to me. If I were thirty years younger, I would chase you myself." He paused. "I am being unmannerly again. Do you know what else is difficult to control? Reality. Charles is real for me. I know you think me crazy, but he was with me at Kirkmoor. I do not blame him for not coming here. This is where I found them. I had my suspicions, and I came here and found them together."

"Who?" Charlotte asked, suspecting he meant his wife and the earl."

"Charley," he said, softly.

"Charley?" Charlotte repeated, not sure where he was going.

"Charley, on his knees, naked, in front of that bastard, Thomas."

"Oh, my God," Charlotte gasped.

"Oh, Thomas was naked too. The two of them. But Charles Clarke on his knees..." Sir Rufus struggled to sit up.

"Please, calm yourself. You do not have to..."

He did not hear her and continued, "I had a crop in my hand. I rushed at them, hitting whoever came in reach. 'No son of mine!' I screamed at them. 'No son of mine.' They grabbed their clothes and ran. They were on their horses before I could stop them. I would have killed them both, but God took care of that. He did. My Charley. How I loved that boy! I would have forgiven him anything. I would. What a fool I was!"

Charlotte felt sick and disoriented. Jack began to fuss. "Sir Rufus," she said quietly, "I will return. We can speak more, if you wish." He did not reply. He sat staring into space. Charlotte carried Jack to his room. When she came back, Sir Rufus was sleeping sitting up. She covered him as best she could, and he opened his eyes.

"Louisa, I know what you have been doing." His voice was filled with rage. Charlotte tried to move out of his reach, but he shifted too quickly. Grabbing her wrists, he threw her on the bed and held her down while he tried to straddle her. "You had his bastard. Thought I wouldn't find out? You whore! Well, you can have me in you now. Bitch! Strumpet!"

Charlotte struggled to throw him off and screamed for Elizabeth. Thankfully, some of the servants heard her and came running into the room. They pulled him away, and he slumped to the ground. Elizabeth came in, having been roused out of bed. She knelt down to check on her father who looked up at her. "Lizzie, I have been bad." he said.

"Yes, you have, Father." She moved to check on Charlotte.

"Charlotte, how are you?"

"Terrified, but I will recover."

"Charlotte, forgive me," Sir Rufus called from the floor where he sat.

"Goodnight, sir," Charlotte said as she and Elizabeth walked out of the room.

"Lock your doors, daughters. You never know what prowls the halls," the old man warned.

Closing the door to her father's room, Elizabeth turned to her. "What in the world happened? What provoked him?" Charlotte held her tongue about the tryst between Charles and Thomas. She told Elizabeth only that Sir Rufus had been upset about her older brother.

"We talked about the past," Charlotte related, "and Jack

began to fuss, so I left. When I returned, he mistook me for Lady Louisa. It was apparently an incident between your mother and a man that inflamed your father's jealousy."

"What did he say?"

"He spoke about a bastard. Perhaps he was referring to her lover being a bastard," Charlotte hedged.

"I am sure my mother did have lovers. But who, I do not know. It was not a subject we children ever discussed, and certainly Mother or Father never told me." She rolled her eyes. "I do not begin to know the secrets of my family, and tonight I am not interested in learning any. I have talked to Robert and Benjamin, however, and I have located a good spot for Jem to hide. Come. Follow me."

Charlotte was relieved not to have to talk anymore about Elizabeth's father. She only wanted to be with James, but what to tell him about his brother, she did not know. For now, she prayed he would get to the house safely, and they would be able to keep him hidden for as long as needed.

Elizabeth stopped in front of the door to Charlotte's room. They entered it, lit the candles, and placed them in the windows. Elizabeth bade Charlotte sit on the bed. She crossed to the far wall and stopped just beside the washstand. Charlotte watched as she ran her hand along the panelling.

Suddenly, at shoulder level, one small panel slid open, revealing a door handle. Elizabeth turned it, and the wall moved open. It was a door. Small, to be sure, but large enough for them to fit through one at a time. Behind it, a chamber was hidden with room for a cot and chair. It needed to be dusted and cobwebs cleared from the ceiling, but it would do for a hiding place for James, Charlotte

FAVOURED BY FORTUNE

thought.

The best feature was that there was a passageway that led directly outside. The exterior door was concealed by vines, Elizabeth explained. They began to clean the little room. Not having access to a bed, they piled blankets on the floor to make a soft resting place. Tomorrow, they would search out a bed, a chair, and perhaps a small rug. Charlotte longed to have James in her room, but this hiding place would be the next best thing for them. After working for about an hour, the room was ready for occupation. Now, Charlotte thought, if only the storm passes, and he arrives at my windows without being seen, all will be well.

It was late by the time they finished, and they both were weary from the long day. Charlotte unlatched one of the windows and hoped it would not blow open if the wind began to howl.

"I am going to lie down and hope he comes soon," she told Elizabeth as she moved to the bed.

"If you don't mind, I shall sit next to you on the bed and wait. I am wide awake now and would rather spend my time here than fretting alone in my room," Elizabeth said.

"Please, join me." No sooner had Charlotte laid her head on the pillow and closed her eyes than she fell fast asleep.

A short while later, a soft noise woke her. She opened her eyes and saw James's face.

"I've caught you napping twice in one day, woman. Are you not getting enough rest? And sleeping with my sister no less. I have no objection, but what would her husband say?" he teased.

Charlotte grabbed him around the neck and kissed him. "Thank God you are here. It was a terrible storm. Did you

282

have any trouble?" she asked.

"None, except for getting caught in the middle of a downpour which turned the ground I was standing on into a bog. I found myself sinking and had to run for what I hoped was high ground. I need to change my clothes. Did you find a place for me to stay?" he asked.

Charlotte showed him the trick of opening the hidden door, and they entered his room.

"Very cosy," he whispered. "So now will you make love to me? We will not wake Lizzie. She sleeps like a log. Always has."

"Let me help you off with those wet clothes," Charlotte offered. "It is one of the benefits of living in a wet climate. Better to be naked and dry than dressed and wet."

They made love quietly in the tiny room. The wavering of the candle's flame made their shadows dance on the walls. After lying together for some time, Charlotte kissed James goodnight and went to check on Elizabeth. She was still asleep. Charlotte covered her, slipped onto her side of the bed and fell asleep.

Charlotte's dreams were filled with naked men. James, Thomas, and Charles were all running, dancing and wrestling. They moved with abandon and joy, when suddenly Thomas pushed Charles down and stepped on his neck. James attempted to pull him off, but he would not move. Thomas appeared to be made of stone and Charles gasped for air. Horrified, Charlotte tried to cry out, but her mouth seemed full of cotton.

Finally, she woke herself. She was sweating, and her heart was pounding. Thankfully, the sun was up, and her feelings of dread evaporated as she looked out her window. She noticed that Elizabeth had already risen. Charlotte wanted to find her and tell her that James had made it through the storm. Just as she got out of bed, there was a knock on her door.

"Come in."

Elizabeth entered. She was beaming. "A messenger came early this morning. Thomas will be home today. He has communicated with Mr. Rhodes and says he will tell us all when he arrives. He also asked me to go on a wedding trip, for a few days at least. Oh, Charlotte, would you watch Father and the boys for me while we are gone? I would be indebted to you."

"It would be my pleasure to help," Charlotte said. "You and Thomas deserve time together."

As Charlotte spoke, she kept having flashes of Charles and Thomas together. She tried to clear her mind and put it down to the ranting of an old man. "I have good news, also. James is here. He came last night after we had both fallen asleep."

"He is here, now?" Elizabeth asked.

"Yes, come." Charlotte opened the secret door, and they peeked in. He was sleeping, so she closed the door quietly. "Let us eat here, or do you think that would draw undo attention?" Charlotte said.

"It is a grand idea. I may ask for double portions. I am feeling particularly hungry this morning."

"An excellent thought, Lady Chagford."

When breakfast came, Charlotte entered the secret room and kissed James as he slept. He stirred and turned towards her, rubbing his eyes and stretching his arms over his head.

"What a pleasurable experience to behold your fair face in the morning."

"Elizabeth is here, and we await your presence at breakfast, Sir James," Charlotte teased and tickled him. He tried to stifle his laughter. He grabbed for her arms, but she was too quick. She stood up just out of reach and blew him a kiss. He feigned exhaustion and lay back down on his makeshift bed. "Do not let your breakfast grow cold," Charlotte warned and went into her room.

When he was dressed, he joined them. Elizabeth greeted him warmly. After they talked about his journey over the moor and Sir Rufus's behaviour of the night before, she told him that Thomas would be returning today.

"I think I should tell him you are here. It is his house, and I know he will want to help," she said, looking to James for agreement.

"I would rather wait, Lizzie. If I were to be captured, I would not want you or Thomas implicated in any way. I think it wise, at least initially, to let it be a secret known only to ourselves." He stopped, looking to see how she was reacting to his idea.

She bristled. "You and father always treat me like a child. It is infuriating! I do not want to start out my marriage having secrets from Thomas. I have had enough of everybody's secrets, thank you very much!"

They sat staring at each other. "If we are to have no secrets, Elizabeth," James said, trying to hold his temper, "I will tell you this; I do not trust Thomas Warrender. It is my neck in the noose if I am caught, so if you feel obliged to tell him, I shall leave at the first opportunity."

"So, does the high king or the sorceress win today?" Charlotte said, trying to bring humour to the highly charged moment. They both turned and looked at her.

"I beg your pardon?" James asked.

285

"Elizabeth told me that you used to play a game when you were on Yes Tor. The two high kings and the sorceress, do you remember? Did you not say you always ended up in an argument?" Charlotte asked Elizabeth.

"Yes, but I failed to say that my brother's pig-headedness was usually the cause of our disagreement," she replied testily.

"Please, Elizabeth, James, arguing will serve no purpose. We need to think of your father and James's safety," Charlotte pleaded.

"Charlotte, I am tired of bearing the responsibility of caring for our family while my brother does nothing but get into trouble. And now I am supposed to keep secrets from Thomas because James says so. Well, I will not do it, brother. Say whatever you need to say to Father and get out of my house and my life!" she said loudly. Rising, she walked out of the room, slamming the door behind her.

Charlotte rose to follow, but James stopped her. "I think she will be back in a bit. She needs to rant and rave and call me names. It has been like this since we were very small. She is right, you know, I do not amount to much. She is the steady one. Even now, here I am running around the countryside in disguise and living in a cave like an animal. My life is of little use to anyone."

"That's not true. I love you. Jack loves you. We both need you. I was not alive until I met you, Jemmy. You bring me such joy, please do not see yourself like this. It is simply not true. We are a family. Whatever the past has been, it does not matter. It is gone, and we have to go forward from here." He sat in his chair, looking at Charlotte, not saying a word. She went to him. "Do you believe me?"

"Yes," he admitted. "I adore you, Lottie. You are the

centre of my existence. When I first fell in love with you, all I saw was your beauty. Now I am overwhelmed by your strength. I thank God you are in my life."

Charlotte pulled her chair close to his. "James, there is something that your father told me last night. I did not tell Elizabeth. It is too awful. However, I think you should know." He looked at her questioningly. "It's about Charles and is very difficult to say."

"Tell me, please."

"Your father said he came here to Scorhill and found Charles and Thomas together. They had no clothes on. Charles was... kneeling in front of Thomas." Charlotte stopped. James had taken a deep breath, his jaw was set, and he stared straight ahead. "Your father confronted them, and they ran, escaping on horseback. You know the rest. Your father blames himself. At Kirkmoor, he was visited daily by Charles's ghost, but he said your brother's spirit will not come into this house." Charlotte reached out her hand to comfort James. There were tears in his eyes.

"I loved Charley, Charlotte. He was everything I am not. He was gifted in so many ways. He was brilliant. Even at sixteen, he could manage the estate. Father would go over the books with him, and he would find errors that had been overlooked by both Father and Mr. Kyd. He rode, he hunted, he was charming and kind. All my parents' friends who had daughters had their eye on him as a future son-in-law. The tenants loved him because he was fair but also sympathetic to their problems. I adored him. Followed him around like a puppy. Most of the time, he was a good friend to me. He would stand up for me when Father became violent."

James paused, his eyes moved back and forth as a

thought came to him. "Those few weeks before my brother's death were difficult for me. Charles and I had been close until Thomas came back from the Grand Tour. Suddenly, Charles did not want to be with me. I felt hurt and angry. I never understood why I was being shunned. I admired Thomas. When Charles was killed and my father refused to let me see Thomas, I hated my father. All the warmth and joy were taken from my life. I felt as though I had been sent to wander the moor, alone and bereft.

"I need to see Father. I doubt he will be so forthcoming with me, but I need to be with him. We must plan what we will do. He may tell everyone I am here, and even if he does not, Elizabeth will tell Thomas, I imagine. Who knows what the great earl will do?"

Stopping him from rising, Charlotte told him about the incident involving Thomas at the Theatre Royal at Drury Lane and his later apology.

"I do not know what he is thinking, and I fear for Elizabeth in all of this," Charlotte said, shivering.

"This gives us more reason to be wary of him," James replied, drawing near to Charlotte. "I will say my good-bye to Father and ride tonight to Taunton. You must order your coach in the morning and leave mid-day. We will meet at the Squirrel's Inn at Taunton, and I will ride the rest of the way to London with you. I think I should sail from London as soon as possible. We will stop in Paris and enlist John's and Emma's help. From there, we will go to Bellagio. I am praying that the Count's men had luck in apprehending Hawkes. There is no question that my father's wager must be honoured, but I fear the rest of the land and our family's title may be forfeit if Father dies, and I am still an outlaw. I must clear my name, Charlotte, or else

I am powerless to help Elizabeth or Father if they should need me."

There was a knock on the door. James went into his chamber to hide. Charlotte took a deep breath, walked to her door, and opened it. Before her stood a sombre-faced Elizabeth.

"I have come back, as I always do, to apologize. May I come in?"

"Of course. Please do. Let us sit. You have a right to want your voice heard. Jem and I do not want to put you in an untenable position. However, he does not want Thomas to know he is here."

Elizabeth opened her mouth to speak.

"Please, let me finish," Charlotte said.

Elizabeth looked at the floor.

"He will leave tonight after he speaks to your father. Jack and I will go tomorrow. I will write and let you know of our plans when they are finalized."

Elizabeth continued to stare at the floor. Charlotte sat down in a chair next to her. Not looking up, Elizabeth began to speak. "I love you, Charlotte. Your presence in my life means so much to me. You are my friend and have helped me through so much. Please, do not hate me. I do not want to drive you away, but I owe my loyalty to Thomas now. My future lies with him. I will do my best to take care of Father, I promise." She reached out and took Charlotte's hand and touched the back of it to her cheek. Looking up, Charlotte saw James standing behind his sister. Charlotte was not sure how long he had been there.

He put his hand on Elizabeth's shoulder, saying, "Forgive me, Lizzie, for not being the brother I should be. You held our family together, and I never appreciated your sacrifice."

She touched his hand. "Thank you," she replied. She did not turn to him, however. "When do you want to speak to Father?"

"Soon. Before Thomas comes, I think. Did he say what time he expected to arrive?" James asked.

"In the late afternoon, before dinner," Elizabeth said. "I will bring Father here now, if he is awake. I cannot guarantee how he will react to your leaving." She stood up, her back to James. As she turned and met his gaze, she stopped and stood still. James reached out to touch her, but she held up her hand and shook her head. He began to speak, to tell her that he loved her.

"No, I cannot hear this. I have loved you too much. I have grieved for you too many times, Jem. I will not let you into my heart. Not now. It is too painful. I will get Father." With that, she turned and left the room.

He sat down and waited. Charlotte took his hand and sat beside him. He looked at her with sadness in his eyes, but he did not speak. In a few minutes, Elizabeth was back. She ushered her father into the room. He was in his nightshirt, robe, and slippers. He looked at her resentfully and clutched at papers he held in his arms. He moved to get away from Elizabeth. Shuffling, stoop-shouldered, he reached a chair and sat down. He was breathing heavily. James sat down next to him.

"Father, I have come to see you."

Sir Rufus looked up perplexed, not sure who this stranger was. Then, his face relaxed. "Jem, it's you."

"Yes, Father," James responded. "How are you?"

"I have been writing. Up all night. I have it all here. I wanted you..." He looked at Elizabeth then back to James.

"YOU to know all of it!"

He shoved the papers at James, who attempted to put them in some order. After he arranged the bundle, he studied the first page briefly. He handed the papers to Charlotte. Their eyes met, but Charlotte could not tell what he was thinking. She looked at the writing. It was impossible to read. Page after page, it seemed, of unintelligible scratches.

"I will read it, Father," James said, "after we have had our visit." His father appeared satisfied. He began to cough violently, loud, dry, racking coughs. He doubled over in pain. James tried to hold him steady. The fit passed, and Sir Rufus caught his breath. He rested against his son.

"It's my chest. I am frightened, Jem."

"I'm here, Papa. Just rest," James comforted him.

"I'm afraid to close my eyes. I see terrible sights when I do. Snakes, sometimes worms, crawling in and out of my hands. Bursting out of my legs. Itching, horrible itching, all over, and now the damnable cough. I gag, and worms come crawling out of my throat. I cannot stop them, Jem." He held his throat and tried to swallow. "Jem get me my blunderbuss. Get me a goddamn gun! I hurt, Jem. I don't want to choke to death. Please, help me," he pleaded.

Elizabeth came and knelt down at her father's feet. She felt his forehead. "Papa, please, you are burning up. Please, do not do this. Calm yourself," she urged.

With all the strength he could muster, he pushed her hand aside. "Go, get away. You'd keep me alive. Jem understands. I do not want to be an old, drooling fool. An idiot, shitting my pants. Let me die." He turned his face to James. "Help me, Jem." He grabbed onto James's shirt. But just as quickly, he pulled away. "I hated your mother. Beat her. She loved me, but I went away. Went away. When I came back, she hated me. I broke her arm. She went away. Never came back. She was there, but she never came back." The old man slipped off the chair and fell to the floor before they could stop him. He kept talking and crying, but none of them could understand his words. James sat on the floor and cradled his father in his arms. His father looked up at him. "I have wet myself, son." Tears ran down his cheeks.

"I will bathe you, Father," James responded. He looked to Charlotte. "I need water and a cloth. Would you fetch them for me, please?"

Elizabeth, who had retreated to a corner after her father's rebuke, said that she would get towels. She left the room, and Charlotte locked the door behind her. As she retrieved the water and washcloths, she watched James. He ran his fingers through his father's hair, trying to brush it out of the old man's eyes. He kissed his forehead. Sir Rufus's eyes were closed, but he smiled at the kiss.

He looked up at James, saying barely audibly, "I am not afraid to die, son."

"I know, Papa, but you are not going to die. Not yet, you are too bull-headed. Anyway, I spent my life running from you, and now that I am here, I will not let you leave without a fight." James took a deep breath.

"Jemmy, I know I loved Charley too much and you not enough. I am sorry, son."

"It is all in the past. It does not matter," James said, but he could not look at his father. He felt his father's eyes upon him. "If it helps, I do forgive you. So does Charley."

"I hope you are correct. I will find out soon enough," his father responded. He coughed, and James tried to hold him. Sir Rufus fought for breath, his face turning red. Charlotte brought the water over to them. James took the cloth and wiped his father's face.

There was a knock at the door. "I have the towels and a clean nightshirt," Elizabeth called softly through the door. Charlotte unlocked it, and Elizabeth entered, giving James the bundle. The women moved off to the far side of the room. Lifting his father, James carried him to Charlotte's bed. Sir Rufus appeared so small in his son's arms, hardly bigger than a child. James lay him down and began to undress him. In a moment, he lay naked. His arms and legs were thin. The skin on his chest was white and smooth. James washed him with great care, as if he were bathing a baby. His father offered no resistance. After he dried him, James dressed his father in the clean nightshirt. He combed his father's silver hair. The old gentleman seemed quite content as he fell asleep. James and the ladies sat in the chairs at the foot of the bed. Charlotte held James's hand.

"Elizabeth, you must give me one night's stay in the house without telling Thomas. I will go tomorrow. I just want to see Father through the night."

She did not respond at first, then, she nodded her head. "I need to see that everything is in order for Thomas's arrival. Charlotte, summon me if you need me." She rose to leave, and James stood also.

As she passed him, he held out this hand to her. She looked at him and let herself be taken into his embrace. They held each other. Her head buried in his chest, and his cheek resting on the top of her head.

"All of this," she began, "hurts so much. Mother's death was horrible, Jemmy, but this, this is too painful. I am losing him, and I am afraid I am losing you. I don't know what to do. Please, forgive me."

"I love you, Elizabeth. I will stay up with Father tonight. With the fever and the cough, I do not know how long..." James could not finish.

Elizabeth let go of her brother. "I am glad you're here," she said, trying to smile. "I will return in a little while."

James and Charlotte sat in silence. He looked out the windows at the November sky. "I think he might die tonight, Charlotte." He stood up and walked into her dressing room. She followed him, and he turned to her. "I feel angry and powerless. I have spent my life hating that old man, and now that he is dying, I am desperate to keep him alive. I love him."

"What can I do, James?" Charlotte asked, wanting to ease his pain.

"I don't know. I need to be alone. Please, watch him, and call me if he awakens. I am sorry, Charlotte." James left the room to go to his chamber.

Charlotte felt abandoned, alone, and then angry with herself. She looked out the windows and realized that the day was already beginning to grow dark. She did not look forward to what this night might hold.

CHAPTER EIGHTEEN

Charlotte sat alone in the darkness, remembering her own father's death. The damp and cold of that day came back to her. He had tried to bathe himself but could not. Instead, after disrobing, he vomited on the floor. She'd found him standing naked and befuddled, trying to locate a rag. After helping him clean and dress himself, she'd put him to bed and wiped the floor. He'd fallen asleep, snoring loudly. Her mother's door was closed. She had taken to her bed. The house was quiet.

Charlotte had decided to walk to clear her mind. However, instead of going towards the beauty and safety of Bethnal Green, as she usually did, she'd chosen a different way. The streets twisted and turned, and the weaver's tall houses seemed to close in overhead. Hopelessly lost, she'd begun to feel as if she was spiralling down into Dante's hell. The need to return home had become overwhelming, and she'd felt a rising panic in the unfamiliar surroundings. A group of dirty children had started to follow her, the older ones pushing the younger into her and nearly knocking her over.

Just as she'd turned to scold them, a short man, well dressed, stepped out of one of the weaver's houses. He was not unfamiliar to her. His name was John Wilkes. To some, he was a reformer and a politician. To Audley and Charlotte's father, he was an outlaw whose radical ideas incited riots. Wilkes spoke out against the King in his paper, The North Briton, and had had to flee to Paris. He only recently had returned home, and it was rumoured he might be arrested. Charlotte found his ideas exciting, although she heard his "Essay on Woman" was too risqué to be tolerated.

The crowd of children had dispersed when he came to her side. He'd told her he had been in a weaver's workshop on the top floor, and looking down, saw that she was in need of help. Wilkes had offered to accompany her home, and Charlotte gladly accepted.

They'd ridden in his modest coach, and she'd told him how she came to be lost. He'd been moved when he heard how ill her father was. His parents recently had died, and he continued to grieve their loss, he'd said. The coach arrived at her parents' house and Charlotte had thanked him for his assistance.

Dorothy Byrd, Charlotte's mother, had sent for the doctor, who had seen Mr. Byrd while Charlotte was out. The doctor had reported that he could find nothing wrong and gave her mother some powder to administer later in the day. Not an hour later, Charlotte's father had passed away in his sleep. The doctor was at a loss for an explanation.

After Mr. Byrd's funeral, which was well attended by other merchants in the silk trade and aristocratic clients, Charlotte's mother and she had taken an extended trip for two and half months to Cumberland. Audley encouraged them to go.

For his part, he had immediately taken up Charlotte's father's end of the business and appointed Ralph Sharp to oversee the ribbon manufacture and lace import.

When the ladies had returned to London, Charlotte's mother was taken ill with a terrible cough and fever. She'd fallen into a deep sleep from which she could not be roused, and three days later, died with Charlotte and Audley at her bedside.

Now with Sir Rufus, Charlotte found herself in the midst of another death watch. Charlotte had mixed emotions about Rufus Clarke. Jack and James loved him; she did not. He had been cruel and abusive to her more than he had been kind. The old man began to stir, and she knocked on the wall to let James know that his father was waking. James emerged, looking haggard. His face was ashen with dark circles under his eyes, and his hair was pulled back haphazardly from his face. His appearance reminded Charlotte of the time she saw him on the Isle of Man.

"Jemmy, please, is there any way I may help you?" Charlotte asked as she crossed to him. He avoided her embrace.

"No, Charlotte. I will be fine. Please, do get Jack, though. Let my father say good-bye to him."

"I will go. But I do not want to be shut out like this, James."

He looked at her, surprised. "I am most sorry. I will endeavour to take your feelings more into consideration. Would you get our son, please?"

Charlotte left the room, angry with her lack of patience, but angrier that James was distancing himself from her. She found Annie sleeping in a chair next to Jack's bed. He, too, was sound asleep and looking peaceful with his thumb in his mouth. Charlotte sat down for a few minutes and tried to clear her head. Then, she rose, kissed Jack, and gently picked him up. Annie awoke and was embarrassed to be caught napping. Charlotte told her to go back to sleep while she took Jack to see his grandfather. Annie gratefully closed her eyes.

Back in her bedroom, she found the old man sitting up in bed. James was helping him drink a glass of water. On seeing his grandson, his face brightened, and he reached out for the little boy. Charlotte came around the bed and gave Jack to James, without a word.

Jack took hold of his father's hair and pulled. James flinched, and Sir Rufus laughed, saying, "That's my man. Take him down, Jackie!" The boy let go of his father's hair and reached out for his grandfather.

"Bampa! Bampa!" he called as he tried to wriggle out of his father's grasp.

Standing back watching them, Charlotte found her anger subsiding. She moved nearer and touched James's back. He looked at her and smiled. Turning back to his father, he helped Jack crawl into Sir Rufus's arms. Jack rested there briefly. Quickly and before they could stop him, he grabbed his grandfather's nose and squeezed.

The old man howled.

Jack screamed.

James picked the boy up and took him away from the bed, trying to comfort him.

Sir Rufus began to cough violently.

Charlotte, standing close to him, felt helpless to stop his painful hacking. When he was able at last to control the coughing spasm, Charlotte noticed that the front of her dress was covered in a spattering of blood and spittle. She helped Sir Rufus rest against his pillows and wiped his chin.

She looked to James, who frowned at her soiled dress. Without a word, Charlotte went to her dressing room to change into a clean robe.

Just as Charlotte came back into the bedroom, there was a knock at the door. It was Elizabeth, but she made it known she was not alone. James handed Jack to Charlotte and disappeared into his hiding place.

Opening the door, Charlotte saw Elizabeth and Thomas. Elizabeth looked tired but happy to be on her husband's arm. Thomas greeted Charlotte with a kiss on the cheek and shook Jack's hand.

Jack stretched out his arms wanting "Tantie E" to hold him. She let go of Thomas and took Jack into her arms. Sir Rufus had closed his eyes after the coughing bout and was resting quietly.

In hushed tones, Charlotte told Elizabeth about his most recent attack. She put Jack down and crossed to her father's bedside. Sitting on the edge of the bed, she felt the old man's forehead.

"Jem?" he asked, as he opened his eyes slightly.

"No, Papa. It's Lizzie," she answered.

"Where is Jem?"

"He's not here, Papa," she responded. She looked to Thomas and shrugged, as if to say, poor man, it is the fever. "Rest, Papa. It is almost dinner. I will bring you some soup and bread."

As Elizabeth ministered to her father's needs. Thomas turned to Jack and Charlotte and inquired if everything in the house was to their liking. Charlotte assured him it was. He asked her to join Elizabeth and him for an informal dinner in the parlour. Charlotte told him she would be there presently, after she had made sure Jack was settled back with Annie.

Thomas looked to Elizabeth, but she was busy. He turned slightly, so his back was to his wife and said softly, "I have missed seeing you, Charlotte."

"And I you, Thomas," Charlotte responded, choosing not to acknowledge that he gazed at her more intently than he should. Just as he was about to add something, Jack ran to Charlotte and began crawling under her skirts.

"Jack!" she exclaimed, trying to move away, but in her attempt not to step on him, she lost her balance and fell into Thomas. He grabbed hold of her arm.

As he righted her, he whispered, "May I join him under there?" Charlotte laughed and moved out of his grasp.

"My son needs to learn the rules of etiquette, I am afraid," Charlotte said. "And I need to find Annie, so I may join you both in the parlour."

Grabbing up Jack, she left the room, her heart beating loudly in her ears and her head swimming. Thomas's advances within earshot of Elizabeth unnerved her.

Jack was wriggling in her arms, but she held him close and kissed his forehead. She let him down, and he ran ahead of her. She guided him into his room where they found Annie up and sorting clothes.

"Annie, please put together traveling clothes for yourself and Jack. Pack the rest of the belongings in the trunks. We will probably be going back to London in the morning." Charlotte bent down and kissed Jack. He responded by hugging her neck, trying to pull her down to the floor.

He laughed and called out, "Mama, Mama!"

She picked him up. "I love you, my Jackie, with all my heart. Mama loves you. Do you hear?" As she looked at her son, she prayed that they would all get away safely. She gave Jack over to Annie's keeping and went to prepare for dinner.

She entered her dressing room from the door in the hallway and looked in on Sir Rufus, who was sleeping soundly. She went to the wall and knocked softly, but there was no reply, so she opened the secret door. The small room was empty. Looking down the passage that led outside, she saw no sign of James. What, she wondered would be his response to Thomas's latest flirtation?

To her, it made their situation all the more dangerous. She would make sure the doors of her dressing room and bedroom were locked tonight. Perhaps, she thought, she was wrong in her assessment, and Thomas was simply playing. She felt sick and uneasy.

Going out of the bedroom, she closed the door and moved quietly about her dressing room. It was good that Sir Rufus was in her bedroom. James could watch over him tonight and, hopefully, be away safely in the early morning hours. Once dressed for dinner, Charlotte left to see Elizabeth and Thomas.

Entering the parlour, she found Thomas regaling Elizabeth with the goings on at Court and in Parliament. He was doing a most unflattering imitation of John Wilkes's recent address to the House of Commons.

Seeing her, Thomas stopped and addressed her most affectionately as "Dear sister." He held her seat as she sat next to Elizabeth, who was smiling.

"Thomas has great difficulty, as you might imagine, with Mr. Wilkes and his following. I am afraid my husband has no sympathy for your weavers."

Charlotte responded pleasantly. "My weavers work

very hard. I have always said they should be better recompensed than they are. Each person is entitled to some human dignity."

"Oh, yes," Thomas said, "I remember the stir you caused after your husband's untimely demise, when you raised the weavers' wages. You were unpopular for more than one reason. Although, when I think of it, a murder and scandal make one the talk of the town, and uneducated interference in the established economic system makes people angry."

"My mother always accused me of being wilful."

"Probably what makes you so damnably attractive," Thomas retorted.

"Thomas!" Elizabeth feigned shock and laughed.

"Attractive to your brother, dear wife," he laughed. "James has always been a bit of a renegade, or at least a misfit." Thomas looked at Charlotte. "Sir Rufus certainly longs for him, does he not? The way he called out to him, you would think he had just seen him."

Elizabeth laughed. "Thomas, my father has been carrying on conversations with Charles for months. It does not seem out of character for him to imagine James is here, as well."

Thomas turned back to look at his wife. There was a moment of silence. Finally, he spoke, his voice sounding sad. "Charles, dear Charles. I miss him." He paused, then continued, his tone lighter. "Please, let us dine. I'm famished."

Charlotte could not help but think of Charles on his knees.

During their dinner, Thomas continued his stories of the latest scandals of the Court. The King had had a brief illness not unlike James's. However, it passed, and everyone was much relieved. The American colonies were a thorn in the King's side. He had dispatched more troops in hopes to take care of the rowdy elements there. In London, the mob had become uncontrollable after a particularly gruesome execution of a mother and her young son. Their crime was stealing half a loaf of bread.

"These people have to learn that they cannot take whatever pleases them," Thomas said, as he reached for a thick slice of roast beef.

After having wine with their meal, they all enjoyed a brandy. Charlotte was becoming light-headed, but Thomas urged her to have one more drink. She acquiesced.

Just before she decided to bid them goodnight, Thomas became quite amorous with Elizabeth.

"My dear friends," Charlotte said, trying to get to her feet without swaying. "I think you should be left alone to enjoy Thomas's homecoming. I will watch over your father in my room, Elizabeth. I don't think we should move him. Please don't worry about him. I will summon you if need be." They thanked her, and Charlotte left, concentrating on walking in a straight line.

On her way to her room, she checked to see if Jack was asleep and found that he was. She kissed his head, and he shifted away from her. Annie was in her bed next to his, fast asleep as well. She had done as Charlotte requested and both of their trunks were packed.

In her dressing room, Charlotte assembled her belongings and put on her nightdress. In the bedroom, Sir Rufus continued to sleep, but his breathing was shallow and rapid. She reached over and felt his forehead. He was hot, so she poured water in her wash bowl and dipped a cloth in it. Wiping his face gently, she took pains not to wake him, afraid the coughing would begin again. Moaning softly at her touch, he continued to sleep.

Sitting on the bed, her back to James's entryway, she did not see him come in. The first she knew of his presence was when he kissed the back of her neck. She nearly knocked him down, she reacted so strongly. He caught her before she toppled over.

"Had a bit to drink at dinner?" he asked in an amused tone.

"Yes, but I am also on my guard for Thomas. His manner this afternoon was very familiar. I do not know what to expect from him, James. He frightens me."

"What did he do that upset you so?" he asked.

"He made remarks to me that he should not have. When he saw Jack attempting to crawl under my skirts, he said he wanted to join him. He said it while Elizabeth was in the room, tending your father. I am sure he would protest that he meant nothing indelicate, but I think differently. At dinner, he was flirtatious and said that I was attractive. When Elizabeth chided him, he said that he meant attractive to you. It is his tone and the fact that he stares at me. He makes my skin crawl, Jemmy. I am afraid of what he may do."

"You are correct to be afraid, Lottie. Thomas takes what he wants. He always has. We must leave tomorrow as we planned. I want you and Jack out of danger. I do not begin to know how to warn Elizabeth. She is too angry with me to give my advice any credence. Perhaps you might suggest she be on her guard, but I doubt that would be received well, either.

"Charlotte, forgive me for stealing up on you. It was

not my intention to put a fright in you. Let me apologize, also, for being a stubborn ass this afternoon," he said. "I do not consider my confusion and grief to be manly attributes. I have great difficulty in letting you see my weakness and in accepting your consolation."

"Thank you, Jemmy. May we begin again?"

"With pleasure," he responded, bowing low. "May I be so forward as to ask for the pleasure of a kiss from your lovely lips, dear lady?"

"Why sir, I am most honoured by your request. Please do," Charlotte said, feeling her body warm to his advance.

As he kissed her gently on the lips, his father whispered hoarsely, "I have never heard such bloody nonsense in my life."

"I am sorry we woke you, Father," James answered, smiling as he crossed to the bed.

"I was dreaming about your mother. She was young, beautiful, like the day I first saw her." He paused and sucked in air. He was having difficulty speaking. "I have written it all down, Jemmy. What I brought with me and there's more in my room, take it. I wrote it for you, to know the truth. Do not tell Elizabeth. She loved your mother. She cares about Thomas. I regret so much."

He stopped again and tried to breathe, causing him to gag and cough. James sat down and held on to him, but his body doubled over with each wracking spasm. When he stopped, James helped him rest against his pillows. This time, it was James's shirt that was stained with blood. Not spatters, but large crimson patches, James looked down and closed his eyes.

When he opened them, he spoke softly. "I will return quickly, Papa. Try to rest. Charlotte is here." He crossed and disappeared into his room.

Charlotte moved to sit at Sir Rufus's bedside. He opened his eyes and attempted to smile at her. "Take care of him, lass. He loves you and Jackie. I wish I had been so fortunate." He was having great difficulty breathing. Finally, after struggling for a moment, his body seemed to relax, and he rested.

Returning, James sat next to Charlotte and put his arms around her. They remained that way for some time. Sir Rufus slept through the night, and his fever appeared to have broken the next morning. Charlotte rested in her dressing room while James stayed at his father's bedside. In the early morning hours, she checked on them and found James sleeping in a chair. When she kissed his cheek, he stirred and opened his eyes.

"Are you still planning to leave this morning?" she asked.

"I should."

"Perhaps we could convince Elizabeth to give us one more day. Although Thomas being here makes me uneasy," Charlotte said.

"Keep a dagger close for protection." James yawned. "I would like to sleep for a short while. I'm so tired. Will you watch Father?"

"I will, dearest. With morning almost here, I feel much safer. I will speak to Elizabeth when she comes. Perhaps she will agree to another day. I shall ask." Charlotte smiled and sat on James's lap. He held her in his arms. "I love you, Jemmy. We will survive all of this."

"I pray we do." He kissed her forehead, and they both stood up.

After he went into his room, Charlotte crossed into her

dressing room. She did her morning toilette and dressed. She sat and wrote a letter to Emma, informing her that she would be in London for a short time. She expressed the hope to meet Emma and John in France.

"Perhaps," Charlotte wrote, "we might spend Christmas together in Paris."

She put her pen down and imagined a merry holiday. It made her smile to think of being with their friends, unencumbered, however briefly, of the fear and sorrow they now suffered.

"A penny for your thoughts?" a voice whispered.

Charlotte jumped. Turning, she found Thomas standing in the doorway to the hall.

"Sir, you startled me. I thought the door was locked."

"I am the lord of the manor, dear lady. I have a key. I see Sir Rufus is sleeping peacefully," he said, pointing to the open door of the bedroom.

Her mind raced. James, she had to protect James. The hair on the back of her neck rose. As Thomas closed and locked the door to the hall, she knew why he was there.

"I missed you, Charlotte." Thomas stepped closer to her.

"Thomas, I fear you have misinterpreted my joy in seeing you. It is only as a sister is glad to see her brother, I assure you." Charlotte tried to keep her voice steady.

"I would never presume it to be anything else. However, my joy, dear sister, is more of the carnal nature. I am sure that is obvious at this point. I am a man who acts on his passions. I think you will not find me wanting once you have had me."

Charlotte stood and backed up towards the open door to the bedroom. "Thomas, how can you want to do this, when you say you love Elizabeth?" He stood in front of the drawer where her dagger rested.

"I do love my wife. You are just too much of a temptation for me. I am a weak soul, who cannot control his sensual side. Forgive me." His tone became more menacing. "Besides, I do believe you want me, though you protest." He advanced towards her.

"I will not have you, Thomas."

"You have no choice in this, dear Charlotte."

"I will not hesitate to tell Elizabeth."

"Oh, I think you will. I know you have said nothing to her yet. Why is that? Could it be because you don't want to break her heart, or is it that you enjoy this little game, this flirtation? But you cannot tease without expecting some reaction, dear Charlotte." He moved quickly with great agility. Charlotte managed to escape his grasp but reached the door just in time for him to meet her there.

"You don't want to wake dear, old Sir Rufus. Let the poor man sleep. I have a tender touch," he said, shutting the door.

He pushed himself on her and held her against the door. Being a head taller than she and of a large frame, Charlotte could not move. He tore at her dress front as she tried to push him away. Her resistance annoyed him. He grabbed both her wrists and held them.

"You are no lady to fight a gentleman so. Thus, I will not treat you as one." He began to grope under her petticoats.

Charlotte pulled her wrists towards her mouth and bit his hand as hard as she could. He yelped and let go. He raised his hand to strike, but in doing so, he stepped back enough that she managed to get the door open. As she was halfway out into the bedroom, he tried to shut the door. It caught her in her middle. She called out in pain and fell. He came after her and was on top of her before she had a chance to rise.

The noise startled Sir Rufus, but he was too weak and disoriented to understand what was transpiring. Thomas sat on Charlotte's back and held her to the floor. He waited for the old man to settle down. He whispered angrily in her ear, "I will take you here in front of him if you make me. Is that what you want? Does that excite you?"

Charlotte shook her head. The searing pain in her side was heightened by his weight. She wanted to scream out for James but was too terrified to make a sound. Let Thomas have his way, she thought. I do not want him to discover James. But then he did something too horrible for her to abide. Grabbing her by the hair, he pulled her to her feet and pushed her towards the foot of the bed. "I shall have my pleasure here, while you do your duty and watch over Father." He pushed her over the bedstead and began to reach under her skirts.

"Please, no," she pleaded, barely able to speak. "Not here. Not in front of him."

"Very well," he said, coldly, "over here."

He grabbed her hair again and wrenching one arm up behind her back, he dragged her towards the corner. "On your knees, slut," he ordered. He pushed her down just beyond the entrance to James's hiding place. Her side was throbbing. She stifled a cry of pain, tears coming to her eyes. She prayed he would not discover James.

In a rage, he undid his breeches with one hand and reached inside. "Take it," he hissed. Before she could move, his body jerked backwards abruptly. He toppled over, clutching at his throat.

"Jem!" Charlotte cried. "Jem!" But to her unbelieving eyes, she saw her saviour was Sir Rufus and not James. He had thrown the belt of his dressing gown around Thomas's neck and dragged him to the ground.

"Not her! You son of a bitch!" he cried. "You filthy, son of a bitch!" The old man was in a fury. He pulled the cord tight. Thomas's tongue thrust out of his mouth as his face turned purple.

However, Thomas, managed to get a hand under the belt, took a gulp of air, and swung his elbow back, hitting the old man in the chest. Sir Rufus fell hard to the ground. Thomas, gasping for air, did not see James rush into the room.

James threw himself on Thomas's back, knocking him down. On top of him in an instant, James grabbed him by the hair and began pounding his head against the floor.

"James, stop! You will kill him," Charlotte called as she cradled Sir Rufus in her arms.

His blind rage abating, James left Thomas unconscious and went to his father. Sir Rufus was pale, beads of perspiration stood on his forehead.

"Thank you," Charlotte said to the old man as she held his hand.

He looked from her to James. He coughed twice and began to choke. James tried to sit him upright. His father held tight to his son's arm. A slow minute passed, and he could not get his breath. Blood began to spill from his mouth.

"Father!" James called out.

The old man's body stiffened, and he collapsed into Charlotte. He was still.

"Father?" James said quietly.

Sir Rufus did not move. James held his father against him. His shirt and hands were covered with his father's blood. Great sobs welled up from deep inside him. He buried his face in his father's chest and wept.

Charlotte cried, also. She took Sir Rufus's hand and kissed it. He had protected her. She silently thanked him.

They were so involved with Sir Rufus that they did not see Thomas regain consciousness.

"You!" he hissed as he rose to his knees.

James let his father's body down and sprang at Thomas who was now on his feet.

Thomas hit him, and he staggered back against the bed. Taking out his dagger, Thomas raised his arms and rushed forward to strike.

James rolled out of his reach.

Righting himself and turning on James again, Thomas smiled nastily as he and James stared at each other. "I will kill you, you arrogant fool, and have her in the bargain." He shot a glance at Charlotte, who sat terrified on the floor, still holding on to Sir Rufus's hand.

That look cost him, for in that second James saw his advantage, grabbed a chair, and swung it full force at Thomas's side. The dagger flew from his hand as he fell to the floor. Grabbing it, James was on top of him and at his throat.

"Jem, no!' Charlotte screamed.

He looked at her horrified expression and, throwing the knife to the side, hit Thomas hard on the jaw with two explosive punches. Thomas's head lolled back, and he went limp.

"Jemmy, you must get away. I am afraid of what

Thomas will do when he regains consciousness. Please, go now."

James crawled on his hands and knees to his father's body. "I have lost him, Charlotte," he said, not hearing her words.

"I'm sorry, Jem." She moved and held on to him as he rocked.

She repeated her plea for him to go. This time he heard her. They held each other, there on the floor, beside his father's body. He brushed a strand of hair out of her face.

"Why did you stop me, Lottie? Warrender deserves to die." His face was full of sorrow. He looked at Thomas then at Charlotte.

"He does, but not by your hand. All hope would be lost to us then."

"Charlotte, did he hurt you?" he asked in a whisper.

"My side only. When I tried to run from him, he hit me with the door. It caught me in the ribs and knocked me down. He would have raped me in front of your father. He is a monster, Jem. Your father saved me."

"I must leave. Meet me at Taunton, at the Squirrel's Inn. You must tell Elizabeth the truth. The man is a scoundrel. She should be made aware of his true nature, whether she chooses to believe it or not."

Thomas stirred.

"I cannot think. Please, Jem, go. I will meet you as soon as I can. I love you. Protect yourself."

"I love you, Charlotte. Get away quickly with Jack," he responded. "Tell Elizabeth what you must. Please, be careful."

In a moment, he was gone.

Without delay, Charlotte rose and rang for the servants.

She tended to Thomas, praying that he would not wake up fully until Elizabeth arrived. When the maid came, Charlotte asked her to summon both her mistress and Mr. Hamm, the butler. The girl ran from the room. Charlotte went back to Sir Rufus's body. She folded his arms on his chest and rested her hand on top of his. She prayed that he was at peace and thanked him once more for his aid.

Elizabeth rushed into the room, followed by the butler and several servants.

"Charlotte, what is it? Is it Papa?" She stopped, dumbfounded, seeing two bodies on the floor. Painfully, Charlotte got up, went to her, and took her hand.

"We have lost your father, Elizabeth. Thomas has been hurt but will recover, I think. He needs your attention," Charlotte said as calmly as she could.

Elizabeth crossed quickly to Thomas, knelt down, and touched his face. He stirred slightly but did not open his eyes. "Oh, my love, who has done this to you?"

To the servants, she commanded, "Carry his lordship to his room. Send for the doctor directly. Have more servants sent up to help with my father's body. Charlotte, please direct them to take him to his room." She exited, going after Thomas.

Sir Rufus's body was removed to his apartment. When they were all gone, Charlotte sat, overwhelmed by feelings of melancholy and loss. Her side ached, and she was having difficulty catching her breath. She told herself she should rise and escape this place as soon as possible. She needed to gather Jack and Annie and make ready for their departure. As she walked towards the door to the hall, Elizabeth came in and shut it. Charlotte could not pass.

"What has been going on in this room?" Elizabeth

demanded, her eyes red from crying.

"I am sorry, Elizabeth," Charlotte said, trying to console her.

"What has happened, Charlotte? Where is my brother?"

"He's gone." She sat down heavily on a chair, unable to stand any longer. The pain was too intense.

"Was it him? Did he attack my husband?" Elizabeth demanded.

"No, it was your father. He attempted to help me."

"I don't understand any of this! Why in heaven's name was Thomas here? Why would my father attack him?"

"Please, Elizabeth, sit with me. You are distraught." Charlotte said offering her a seat.

She refused to sit. Her eyes narrowed as she looked at Charlotte. "It was you. Thomas came to see you. He has hinted to me that your behaviour was less than modest. He was too much of a gentleman to accuse you outright. I knew he was upset and tempted. Last night, the way you carried on with him was disgraceful. Did you think I would not notice? I know your appetites, Charlotte. I loved you as my sister, and this is my repayment."

"Please, Elizabeth, I was not disloyal to our friendship. You misinterpreted my behaviour at dinner. I have never given Thomas cause to expect favours, despite what he may have suggested to you. I spurned his advances. He came here uninvited, and when I refused him, he assaulted me." Charlotte rose to her feet. "Your father stopped him. Your father saved me."

"You are a despicable liar! You wantonly seduced my husband in front of my dying father. You are an abomination. I will never believe otherwise."

"Elizabeth, please do not do this. Thomas is a

dangerous man."

"No, it is you who are dangerous! You ruined my brother's life and brought on my father's death. You'd best pray to God that Thomas recovers, or I will see you hang for murder. Get out of my house, whore!"

Charlotte pushed past Elizabeth, opened the door and fled down the hallway. She roused Annie and Jack. She was able to quickly organize their departure despite the house being in an uproar. There were no fond good-byes. The doctor came rushing into the house as they loaded into Charlotte's coach. She did not see Elizabeth, but one of the servant girls, a friend of Annie's, reported that Lord Chagford had regained consciousness. As their coach pulled away from Scorhill Hall, Charlotte prayed she would never see it again.

CHAPTER NINETEEN

The ride was rough. The roads were badly rutted from the recent storm. Jack crawled into Charlotte's lap, and she held him close to her. His warm little body next to her gave comfort to both of them. He soon fell asleep. She gazed down at his beautiful face, so flawless and innocent. Closing her eyes, she prayed to God to quickly reunite them with James.

The rain began to pour, and their pace slowed to a crawl. They were forced to take refuge in a small inn still some distance from Taunton. The next day brought some small relief in the weather, and they arrive at the Squirrel's Inn by midday.

The innkeeper's wife, Mrs. Hadley, showed them to their rooms and promised to bring food as soon as possible. She praised Jackie's golden curls and pretty face and warned them to be careful on the road because of the highwaymen who just yesterday murdered a gentleman on his way to London.

"What did the gentleman look like?" Charlotte inquired, fearing it might be James.

She responded that he was a portly fellow, from Landsend, who had stayed at the inn on many occasions. Charlotte thanked her for the warning, and Mrs. Hadley went off to her kitchen.

The three of them rested and stayed warm in their rooms. Charlotte spent a good deal of time looking out her windows, which faced the road. After dinner, she gave up hope of James meeting them that evening.

Charlotte slept fitfully; her dreams filled with fearful images. In the morning, she was the first to rise. Jackie lay fast asleep, sucking his thumb, while Annie snored lightly in her bed next to his. The view out the window promised them a clear, dry day.

Charlotte's stomach churned from worry, but she tried to reassure herself that all was well. She decided they should press on towards London and not spend more time at Taunton. Waking Annie, she instructed her to ready Jack for the journey, before she went down to breakfast.

As she waited for her food, she overheard a conversation at an adjacent table between two men and Mrs. Hadley.

"It's about time they catch him," said Mrs. Hadley firmly. "More than a year since the murder of that little one. It's been a terror to anyone with children, let alone babies." The two men nodded agreement.

One added, "Why he's come back is a mystery. We were all certain he was long gone."

Charlotte's side began to ache, and her head grew light. She attempted to stand but had to sit down. Mrs. Hadley, seeing her distress, came quickly, asking if she was ill. Charlotte assured her it would pass. She tried to appear calm as she questioned Mrs. Hadley as to who they were talking about, hinting that she was unfamiliar with the area.

"A baronet's son from over in Chagford. Crazy, they say. He killed a baby about a year ago. Stole it away from its mother and murdered it. She and her husband, Mr. Norton, own an inn at Okehampton. Scared us all so's we could not sleep. The lunatic got away and murdered a man in London. Then, wouldn't ye know, he escaped from prison. Now he's back, they say. Doesn't that figure, bein' one the high and mighty. Well, I hope they'll get him and hang him!"

The two men agreed.

Charlotte excused herself, saying that she was still not feeling well. She couldn't breathe. She staggered back to her room and asked Annie to take Jack and feed him. She warned Annie not to say anything about who they were other than that they were traveling to London. Annie promised to do so and left with Jack.

Laying down on her bed, Charlotte wept bitter tears. Blackness encompassed her. Jem, I must get to Jem. She knew it would not help him to behave like this. Terrified as she was, she told herself to settle down and find out what information she could. She needed to know more, in order to plan what they should do. She dried her eyes and collected her thoughts.

Going back downstairs, she was determined to question the two men. They were still eating. She sat down with Annie and Jack. He crawled into her lap and one of the men, who was exceedingly fat, commented on what a handsome lad Jack was.

"Sirs, where are you journeying from?" Charlotte asked.

"Just come from Okehampton," the fat man replied.

"Oh dear, that was where that unfortunate family lived that Mrs. Hadley just told me about," Charlotte said. "Please tell me more of this murderer. He is still at large?"

"He is indeed," said the other man who had a large, brown birthmark on his forehead. "Why, he was seen comin' down this very road yesterday. Somebody recognized him, I'll wager. There was a tremendous fight, so I heard. He bested ten men. You need be careful, traveling alone as you are. I have heard, and this from a good friend, that he's crazy as they come and strong as an ox. Likes the ladies too, eh?" He winked at his friend.

"It was not ten men, Burt," his friend said disgustedly. "Excuse him, mum. He does not know about it at all. I personally know a soldier, billeted in Exeter, who was in a party out searching for this scalawag. He said they was sent out by the earl. They caught up with him, not a mile from here, but lost him when the fog rolled in," the man said. "There was no fight, I tell you, Burt."

"There was a fight, and there were no soldiers. He's an aristocrat, Frank. Don't be stupid. Why would the earl send soldiers? He's his brother-in-law for God's sake. What sense does that make? There was a fight, take my word for it. The boy's a war hero. He's smart. Anyway, what difference does it make? He'll get off. Who cares about some innkeeper's brat anyways." Burt snorted.

"This rogue was not injured in the fight, then?" Charlotte tried feigning mild interest.

"Nary a scratch. Bested them, all ten! Then rode off into the fog, whooping like a wild man. They tried following him but lost his trail outside Wellington by the river." Burt looked towards his friend. "Do not contradict me, I know this for a fact."

Charlotte turned to Annie and Jack. "It's time for us to be on our way. Good-bye." The two men went back to sorting out the details of what they had heard.

In a short while, they were loaded into the coach. The light mist swirling about them turned into driving rain.

Water began to rise on the road, making for slow progress. The coach driver, fearing the deeply rutted road would become a quagmire, stopped at an inn at the foot of Glastonbury Tor. As Charlotte got out of the coach, she looked up at the tall hill, its top lost in the fog. Buffeted by the wind, Charlotte, Jack, and Annie ran for the inn door.

Inside, they found a friendly innkeeper by the name of Reliance Kirk, who stood by a blazing fire. He settled them in their rooms and invited them to join him downstairs by the hearth, where his daughter would serve them dinner.

Delighted at the thought of food, they took their place at the high-backed bench in the inglenook, where they were soon enjoying hot soup and freshly baked bread. They ate in silence. Jack finished his portion and curled up next to his mother, his head in her lap.

Darkness came quickly outside. Charlotte was deep in thought when the door opened. Six soldiers came in, greeting Reliance Kirk loudly and calling for drink. Peering around the corner of the bench, Charlotte caught sight of the leader, a short, solidly built man with a pug nose so pushed up that the thick hair in his nostrils was clearly visible.

Kirk rushed towards the men with tankards of ale, which he slapped down on their table. The innkeeper inquired after their health as they began to drink. Complaining first about the drenching rain, the pug-nosed soldier proposed a toast to "the murdering blackguard we dispatched to hell today." All six raised their tankards, agreeing loudly, and drank.

"You got him, then?" Kirk asked.

"Oh, aye. After a great bloody chase across half of England. We almost lost him at Cheddar Gorge. Thought he'd gone into the caves, but he bolted, and we followed on his heels over the Mendips all the way to Wookey Hole. Why the mad fool took to the River Axe I'll never know. Churning and raging with rain, it was. He went under, horse and all. Drowned. No way out. The river goes underground. Pulled him down. A dark, watery grave he's got himself to match his deeds. Killed that babe on the moor, slit a man's throat in London, and now only days ago, attacked the Earl of Chagford, nearly murdering him, too. Raving lunatic, and he the earl's kin by marriage."

Charlotte's sight contracted to a pinprick of light. She pulled back into a dark corner of the bench, pressing the back of her head against the wood, pulling Jack close to her.

Annie looked at Charlotte in alarm.

Charlotte tried to take a slow breath. The sound of the soldiers' laughter and the innkeeper's congratulations on their brave exploit filled the room. She wished she might die that instant. Jack shifted his weight and pressed his face into her stomach. She gathered him into her arms and forced herself to rise. Bidding the innkeeper goodnight, she passed the soldiers, daring not to look in their direction.

Waking after another fitful night, Charlotte stretched and looked around at the room. Yesterday's events flooded her thoughts. She closed her eyes, fighting back tears. Rising, she looked out the window and found the rain had passed. The rays of the morning sun shone pink on the top of the Tor.

In hopes of keeping her rising panic at bay, Charlotte decided to climb the hill. Jack and Annie were asleep as she left. Following the path, she hurried forward to begin her ascent towards the remains of St. Michael's Chapel on the top of the Tor.

King Arthur came here to die, it was rumoured, and he and Guinevere were buried in the churchyard in the town. How she wished she could hold James one last time. To at least possess his body would be of some comfort. His disappearance into Wookey Hole left him not dead, not alive.

She climbed higher up the path. The Tor, in ancient times, was thought to hold an entrance to the Otherworld, where the dead passed through on their way to new realms. If only she could find it, she might go in search of him. Yet the hill did not reveal its secret. Instead, the birds sang happily, and the purple heather appeared to glow, so brilliant was its colour in the morning light. She gazed out over the patchwork countryside of the Sedgemoor Plain.

Coming to the top of the Tor, she walked around the outside of St. Michael's tower and looked northeast. Wells Cathedral was visible far in the distance, but she could not see Wookey Hole beyond. Come back to me, James, she thought. Do not be gone. His face filled her vision, calm and handsome. She closed her eyes. His face vanished, and she could not call it back. Disconsolate, she returned to the inn to continue their journey.

A week after her return to London, at letter arrived from Count Cesi. Its information was for James, though it was addressed to Charlotte. She read the startling and welcome news that Edward Hawkes had been captured and was currently the count's prisoner in Venice. His men, the count wrote, had continued to pursue Hawkes after James had gone back to England. Finding him on Ios with only a few of his crew, they dispatched his followers and took him captive.

"A confession will be extracted in no time, my friend.

We shall restore your good name."

Charlotte rejoiced that this devil would never again plague them and, though James was dead, people would now understand that he was neither madman nor murderer.

That afternoon, the light was fading as Charlotte climbed the stairs to her bedroom. Looking out her window, she saw Annie chasing after Jack in the garden. He was laughing and running as fast as he could go.

Charlotte smiled and went to her desk. From a drawer, she took out an enamelled box. Opening it, she found James's Irish whistle and the small white shell he had given her on the Isle of Man. Looking at the little wooden flageolet, she remembered the day on the count's island when James's music had led her to him.

Taking up the shell, she pressed its cool, fragile surface to her cheek. "I will go on, my dearest, but with emptiness in my heart," she whispered. She took a piece of white paper and her quill and began to write.

I love you and shall always love you; though your body has been taken from me, I will hold your memory close. Let there be ghosts, so you may come to me and whisper in my ear that you love me still. I shall never say good-bye.

Folding the paper in half, and half again, she slipped it in the box under the shell and his Irish whistle. She closed the lid, setting it on her night table next to the bed. With deep sorrow in her heart but determination to go on, she descended the stairs to join Annie and Jack in the garden, reaching them just as the last rays of the sun faded.

EPILOGUE

To come upon him in the half-light near the cave's mouth, you might have thought the tall man with barley-coloured hair was dead. His bloodied arm floated in the rising water of the river as it rushed underground. The rest of his body lay unmoving on the dry limestone of the cave floor. He appeared a castaway, with no boots, one stocking gone, the other down around his swollen ankle, his breeches and shirt torn.

In deep sleep, he rolled away from the water and threw his freezing, wet arm over his face. The sudden cold revived him. He opened his sea-grey eyes and attempted to sit upright. Dizziness overcame him, and he lay back down on the rock.

Who was he? Why did he find himself here? He could remember nothing. All he could register were physical sensations; the cold of the water, the roughness of the rock, the dim light to his right. He focused on the sound of the rushing river. He smelled smoke. Alarmed, he turned on his side. There was a fire deep in the cave. He coughed and pain shot through his chest. Suddenly, the water began rising faster, and he crawled toward the fire… away from the light, away from the water, away from the world outside. A primal force drove him now, a need to warm his body.

He pulled himself forward, deeper into the earth.

From the shadows just outside the light of the fire, a dark figure watched his progress and smiled.

COMING SOON

Face
of
Fortune

THE SHADOWS OF ROSTHWAITE
BOOK TWO

by

COLLEEN KELLY-EIDING

ABOUT THE AUTHOR

Colleen Kelly-Eiding is a member of the Screen Actors Guild, American Federation of TV and Radio Artists, and Actors' Equity. Her husband is an actor, as are their two adult daughters. Theatre, acting, and above all, storytelling, are part of her family's DNA.

Colleen was in the first class of women at Kenyon College in Ohio when the school went co-ed. She studied drama and political science at the University of Manchester in England. She received an MFA degree in acting from the University of Minnesota, and has since been an actor, director, casting assistant, 3rd grade teacher, and audiometrist.

Favoured by Fortune has been occupying Colleen's imagination for a quite a long time. After both daughters graduated college and were out on their own, she and husband Paul became empty nesters. The time seemed right for Colleen to bring young Ms. Pruitt, our heroine, to life and let Charlotte tell her story.

During her time in Manchester, Colleen fell in love with the country. When she returned to England to do research for her novel, she was beyond elated. She interviewed a curator at the Victoria and Albert Museum, spent time researching indictment records from the 1760's at the Guild

Hall in London, walked the route that the carts of the condemned travelled from Newgate Prison to the Tyburn Tree. Visiting the tiny village of Rosthwaite, located in the beautiful Borrowdale Valley in the Lake District, where much of the action takes place, helped give context and inspiration to Colleen.

Colleen continues to act for stage and film. She studies sculpting and ceramics. And enjoys traveling to Comic Cons around the world, where her husband is a frequent guest.

Watch for her second book, *Face of Fortune,* set for release in early 2020. It is part of her series, The Shadows of Rosthwaite.